CW00524912

Resurrection

BOOK I OF THE MARTYR SERIES

By MC Hunton

ISBN: 978-1-955479-01-1

DEDICATION

For Mom, who might not have lived to see the final product come to life but never once doubted one day it would.

CONTENTS

ACKNOWLEDGMENTS

To Serena, for being my first raving fan and giving me the confidence to keep writing.

To Scott and Joe, for being the best writing group a no-chill author could ever hope to find.

And to Sam, for everything.

CHAPTER ONE

"DO NOT CROSS."

A mechanical voice called out, louder than it ever had before, as it repeated the warning with robotic regularity. A bright red hand blared across the street. A splattering of dead LEDs left the outstretched fingers pocked and misshapen inside their black box. Dozens of people walked through the intersection anyway, while the red hand continued to flash its incessant, pointless warning. The people of the Williamsburg Street Market ignored it, dragging along antsy children and empty carts as they rushed across the asphalt.

But Darius Jones stopped.

He paused on the far side of the street, and a nervous tickle ran up the back of his neck. People pushed around him, bumping him with their shoulders and grumbling as they sped past. He adjusted his long, brown jacket, patting the empty pockets to distract himself as he looked out, across the northern edge of the market. It stretched for several blocks around and underneath the Williamsburg Street Bridge. Vendors and stalls and busied patrons filled in the roads as far as he could see, and a dreary haze of smog hovered in the air, making the whole scene gray and bleary. High on the bridge above, cars drove by, unaware and unconcerned with the community struggling just beneath them.

Darius ran a hand over his chin, and his calloused fingers caught the stubble there. Green eyes shone out bright against his tanned, olive skin. They narrowed as he stared at the crosswalk light, with that nagging feeling he was missing *something*… but he couldn't put his finger on what it was. A voice spoke up in the back of his head—

"Darius?"

Darius was rattled from his thoughts as a small hand reached up and wrapped around his palm. He looked down to see a dirty little face staring up at him. A young girl's fingers tightened around his, and it melted his reserve.

"Hey Sophie," he said softly, and he tried to shake his tension away. She just watched him with wide, worried eyes, so he squeezed her fingers twice. She relaxed a little and squeezed back twice in return. "You good?" he asked.

She just nodded.

Darius turned to the rest of the kids. A half-dozen of them waited expectantly behind him. They were a mismatched group. One boy, tall and dusky. A girl with short legs and shorter hair. Another, freckled and pale. This one young—that one, younger. But where they were diverse in physical features, they all had something in common. Their clothes hung loose on their skinny bodies. Eyes, sunken into faces stretched a little too thin through malnutrition, watched Darius closely. They smelled earthen, like dirty hands, oily hair, and musk—a testament to living without access to running water… or much of anything else, for that matter. Darius looked them over, and his frown deepened.

"What's wrong?" the oldest child, a dark, slender boy named Aren, asked. His brown eyes were hard and cautious.

"It's nothing," Darius said, and he took a deep breath. He hoped it was nothing. Then he looked down at Aren and slapped a smile back across his face. "Just counting heads and making sure no one wandered off. We've got a lot to do before winter gets here, so let's get started. Who's ready to get to work?"

He was met with a general cheer from the group. Sophie drew closer to Darius's side, clutching his hand more fiercely. Darius held her tight before he turned back toward the flashing red hand, and together, they made their way into the market.

The street market took up large, sprawling swaths of the old, unkempt streets on the Lower East Side. Thousands of voices murmured together, bartering and arguing. The percussion of footsteps and metal coins clanging together in pockets or the exchange between human hands doused them in an incessant, droning hum. Darius turned over his shoulder and called out over the noise.

"Everyone, hold hands," he said to the kids, and the few that weren't already immediately reached out and grabbed the fingers of their nearest neighbor. "What do we do if we get separated?"

"Find a grown-up," a young girl said.

"Just any grown-up?" Darius asked.

"No," Aren said. "A grown-up we know."

Darius nodded. "Good. And if someone you don't know—"

"Darius," one of the other boys moaned, and he rolled his head back. "We *know* already!"

Darius laughed. "All right, Ned, so what do you do?"

"We throw away our manners," Ned said. "If someone we don't know grabs us, we kick and scream and bite and don't care if we're mean."

"That's right," Darius said. "Manners aren't more important than *you*. We have to be really careful, because—"

"Kids are disappearing," Aren finished. There was a solemn note to his voice, and Darius turned to consider him.

"Yes," he said. "So stay sharp, stay close, and keep your

eyes open."

They wound their way through busy streets and alleys tucked between abandoned and decrepit buildings. High columns of smoke blotted out the distant glimmer of towering skyscrapers. It was easy to forget they were still in the city at all. The market and all the neighborhoods beside it were like a dirty smudge on the map—a malignant cancer you ignored until it was too late to stop it from spreading.

But it was spreading. Every year, the market grew as more people, sick, tired, and so, so poor, found their way here.

Stalls crept onto empty stoops. Make-shift tents and shelters coated the roads in coarse, gritty color. People toted in whatever goods they had the means to sell: fruits and vegetables, cured meats, pickled *somethings* floating in briny green jars, jewelry, illicit drugs, clothing, the occasional live animal, blankets, falsified documents, and even artwork.

"All right, Ned," Darius said as he stopped by a baker's stand. He reached out and shook the man's hand above the table before he turned back to the boy and ruffled his hair. "I'll get you tonight."

"Kay," Ned said, and he bounced off and got to work kneading dough on a table behind the counter. Darius smiled after him briefly before he hurried on his way with the remaining five children.

As they continued through the market, they passed all kinds of people—low-income families, unsheltered veterans, street musicians, undocumented immigrants, and the mentally unwell. Mayor Bently called them "The Undesirables," and this was where New York City had abandoned them. They all blended in together, finding refuge in the masses of others just as broken, scared, and alone as they were. They huddled in doorways and underneath awnings. Passed between tables and shops. Pulled items to barter from tattered bags at their sides as they tried to make ends meet in a world that was becoming progressively *more* challenging to survive in.

As Darius and the kids passed through the winding, busy currents, people smiled and waved to greet them. Darius chatted at a few tables, shook hands with the owners of others, and every so often, he dropped off another kid to work. Ned helped the baker in exchange for loaves of hard, stale bread. Lola had nimble fingers, so she wrapped packages of cured meats and brought home a link of sausages at the end of the week. Over the summer, one of the jewelry vendors had asked Darius specifically for Aren's help warding off thieves. The kid had hit puberty, and he'd shot up a couple of inches in the last few months. Now, he stood watch beside the table, his face set and stern as he kept guard and stopped thieves from pocketing long strings of beads. He was one of the only children who was paid in cash—five bucks for the day.

Soon, Sophie was the only child left. The little girl stuck close to Darius's side, her tiny hand wrapped tightly around his. She gazed around at the market in wide-eyed terror, her blonde hair plastered against her dirt-streaked cheeks. Darius looked down at her, smiled, and squeezed her fingers in reassurance.

"You're gonna do *great*," he told her.

She just nodded.

A woman laughed up the street, and Darius looked up to see her flirting with Jalal, the man who owned the fruit stand. This wasn't the first time Darius had seen him so absorbed in a conversation with a pretty woman he didn't notice her kids sneaking around the table, pocketing his apples.

As Darius neared, the children caught sight of him. They quickly thrust their tiny hands into their pockets and scurried away. The younger one knocked the table, and several apples tumbled toward the ground.

Darius caught one of them. The children floundered off and followed their mother down the street. Jalal looked disappointed to see them go. He didn't notice the thick bulges in the kids' jackets.

He didn't notice Darius right away, either. As he crouched there, with the girl's fingers in one hand and the apple in the other, he suddenly realized how *hungry* he was. His stomach rumbled greedily. It would have been easy for him to quickly slip the fruit into his pocket before Jalal turned around.

With a smile in Sophie's direction, Darius stood back up and put the apple back onto the table. Jalal glanced back at last.

"Darius!" he said. "Assalamu Alaikum! My friend, I met the woman of my dreams last night."

"Marriage material?" Darius asked with a smile.

"Oh, yeah."

Darius laughed. He'd heard of three girls in as many months Jalal had sworn he was going to marry. "What's her name?" Darius asked through his grin.

"It's so strange," Jalal started, and he took a deep, whimsical breath. He leaned against his stall with a soft smile on his face. "I was packing up for the evening, and then the street filled with smoke! It was so thick I couldn't breathe. The next thing I know, there are gunshots! Then this… this absolute *goddess* jumps over my stand, grabs my shoulder, and pulls me to the ground!"

Darius's smile all but disappeared, and that nervous tickle ran back up his neck. He watched Jalal with wide, wary eyes. "There were gunshots?"

Jalal dismissed him by waving his hand. "Yeah, yeah. Like I said, this woman pulls me to the ground, and Darius! She was magnificent!" He slipped into a dreamy, almost poetic cadence, which sounded mismatched against his thick, New York accent. "Her hair was dark like a raven's feathers. Her eyes black as the night sky! Her clothing was tight like a second skin. I have never seen a woman *so* beautiful."

"Right," Darius said. He shook his head and pinched the bridge of his nose. "But Jalal, someone had a gun?"

"Oh, yeah," Jalal said. "She did. It was in her hand." At Darius's shocked expression, he continued. "But she didn't use it! She wasn't dangerous! She protected me! 'Jalal,' she said. 'Keep your head down!'" Darius frowned. He would have bet this conversation didn't happen. "She held me down like a… like a… like a *lioness*. So strong. So fierce. I could have died. And then, she was gone. She ran off into the smoke." Jalal heaved a heavy, lovesick sigh. "Keep an eye out for her, eh? I'd love to see her again…"

"All right, man," Darius said with a leery smile, but his head was spinning. This wasn't the first Darius had heard of things like this happening in the market. In the last two weeks alone, there had been at least a dozen weird incidents. Strangers had begun to appear out of the blue, people who clearly didn't belong on the market. The level of violence, which was already higher than Darius was happy with, had increased.

And kidnappings were on the rise. The thought made Darius sick. He squeezed the little girl's hand a little more tightly.

"Anyway," Jalal said, shrugging away his daydreams, and he acknowledged the child for the first time, "is this little Miss Sophie?"

Darius smiled and put his hand around her shoulder. "Yep. It's Sophie's big day. She's starting with Mrs. Miller, learning how to make leather boots."

"Ah," Jalal said, crossing his arms and nodding eagerly. "Perfect time. Supposed to be a bad winter!"

"I know," Darius said. "She's getting paid in one pair of shoes a week. It won't get all the kids boots before the first snow, but it'll help."

"How many you got now?"

"Twelve."

Jalal let out a low, impressed whistle. "I don't know how you do it," he said, "keeping all those kids fed. You're a saint, my friend."

Darius gave him a kind smile. "Thanks, but I'm just doing what I can. Speaking of—can I borrow a bag of oranges? I'll make it right by the end of the day."

Jalal waved his hand dismissively. "Of course. Take whatever you need. But remember," he said, waggling a finger at Darius. "No pork!"

Darius laughed. "And anything else has to be halal, I know, I know!" He turned back to the table and scooped a brown paper bag, filled to the brim with fruit, carefully off the edge. Another pair of mischievous children ducked down and out of sight. Jalal shouted something in Urdu Darius had come to understand was a swear word. As the shopkeeper darted off to protect his merchandise, Darius called a thank you out to him and grabbed Sophie's hand again.

"All right, Soph," he said. "Let's get to Mrs. Miller."

Mrs. Miller's stall was just up the street. She was a kind, but firm, middle-aged woman who had ended up on the market five years ago, when her husband had died from cancer. Their medical bills had left her penniless. Darius had the good fortune to run into her on her first day in the Lower East Side, and he'd played a big part in getting her shop set up and established with the locals. She saw them approach and smiled widely.

"Darius! It's good to see you."

She opened her arms and took Darius in a warm embrace before she pulled back and looked down at Sophie. "And you must be Sophie." She crouched in front of the girl. Mrs. Miller didn't have any children of her own, which Darius had always felt was a shame. She'd have made an excellent mother. "It's good to finally meet you! Darius has told me so much about you. Are you excited about today?"

Sophie gave a soft, dishonest nod as she tucked behind Darius's legs. Mrs. Miller didn't push the subject. She stood up again and looked back to Darius. "We'll start slow."

"Thanks so much," Darius said, but then he leaned in a little and lowered his voice. "Hey, Jalal just told me there was a woman with a *gun* here yesterday?"

Mrs. Miller's smile disappeared. Her stony eyes rolled up with a sigh. "Oh, yes, his *new* girlfriend. I swear, that man falls for any pretty little thing that walks by his stand." She took a huffing breath and shook her head. "What's so pretty about someone terrorizing the market? A gun? For god's sake! If that's all it takes to be *pretty*, I should just strap a rifle to my back!"

"Mrs. Miller," Darius said, raising a hand to stop her before she really got going on her rant about Jalal and his choice in women. "Did you see her?"

"No, thank *god.* I'd gone for the day, but I don't like it. She ain't the only one I heard about who doesn't belong here. Keep an eye out and let me know if you see anything weird, yeah? You're probably the most perceptive person in this whole damn neighborhood…"

"I will," Darius said with a dark nod. Then he took a breath and put a smile on his face again as he turned to Sophie. "All right, Soph. It's time to go. I'll pick you up tonight."

But as Mrs. Miller walked around her stand to get Sophie's materials set up and Darius moved to pull his hand out of Sophie's, the girl's grip tightened. Tears swelled behind her eyelids, and she stared determinedly down at her bare, dirty toes. Darius frowned and crouched in front of her.

"I don't wanna go," she whispered. She was trying hard to keep from crying. Darius could hear it in the way her voice trembled. He heaved a sigh but provided a warm, comforting smile all the same as he grabbed Sophie's shoulder in one firm hand. She was so small her whole collar disappeared behind his palm.

"Hey," he murmured. She slowly raised her eyes to meet his. "I know it's scary, but that's part of life. Sometimes we have to do things that scare us in order to grow. It makes us stronger."

"I don't want to."

"I get it. You know… there are a lot of things that scare me, that *I* don't want to do, but I do them anyway."

Sophie's chin lifted a little bit from her chest, and her eyebrows pinched in over her bright blue eyes. "Really?"

"Really."

"Like what?"

"Like this," he said, squeezing her shoulder. "It scares me to bring you guys out here, but I do it because I know it's good for you. You get to learn how to do some cool stuff you can't learn at home, and when you grow up, you'll be ready to do whatever you want. You could open your own stall, master a trade, maybe even get a job out in the city."

Sophie frowned again and took in a huge sniff. "I don't want to grow up."

Darius laughed. "That's too bad, because you're *going* to grow up, and you're going to make an *awesome* adult. Now, take some deep breaths. I'll be here to get you before the market closes."

Her frown deepened a little, her eyes glistened with new tears, but she gave Darius a big hug, whispered "I love you" into his chest, and quietly allowed herself to be led to Mrs. Miller's stall. After she got Sophie all set up, Mrs. Miller came back to Darius with a soft smile on her dry lips.

"You make a good daddy," she said with a wink. "When are you gonna have a few kids of your own?"

Darius laughed. "Yeah, that's what I need to do—bring *more* kids into this messed up world. Nah, I'm happy taking care of the ones who are already here. I love them. It's more than enough for me."

Mrs. Miller nodded. "You're a good man, Darius Jones. Watch yourself. Sometimes I think you're the only one out there."

Then she went to work to sell her merchandise and teach Sophie how to sew, and Darius sighed. He wasn't sure he believed he was one of the only good ones, but there was a whole lot of bad out on the market.

Especially lately. Something in his gut still felt off, and Darius couldn't shake it. That tiny voice in the back of his head whispered:

Be careful.

So, he made a mental note to pay attention a little more closely. His instincts hadn't let him down before. Taking a deep breath and shifting his bag of oranges, Darius set out into the hot, busy organism of the Williamsburg Bridge Street Market.

A lot had changed in the eight years since Darius had found himself on the street market. It had never been *small*, but now the market took up almost the whole of the area beneath the Williamsburg Bridge, as well as several blocks of the side streets adjoining it. The population in the Lower East Side was burgeoning. As more and more people found themselves homeless and alone, they began to filter here. And, while this place could be dangerous and scary, it was also self-sufficient. The street market didn't need New York, just like New York didn't need the street market.

Darius had changed a lot, too. He'd been an aimless and scared nineteen-year-old just looking for a way to survive.

Now he was widely recognized and respected.

It wasn't because of the goods he sold; he borrowed and bartered for his needs on the market. He didn't have power, or notoriety, or a name that meant anything to people who mattered outside of the Lower East Side. There was only *one* thing about Darius that made him stand out.

He was the man who took in abandoned children.

People loved him for it. When Darius came by to trade his oranges for clothing or dried meats, shopkeepers graciously offered him generous deals. He bartered for everything, from beads to spices to paper money, which was a rarity on the market. Occasionally, he stopped to chat. He shook hands with everyone and hugged the people he'd come to know as friends. They laughed with him, joked with him, and always asked him how the kids were.

Darius didn't always feel like he deserved his reputation, or the accommodations it allowed for him, but he was grateful for it. It made his job easier. The market could be heartless, but somehow, Darius seemed to avoid that part of this world. The people here knew what he was doing, and they wanted him to succeed.

They also needed his help.

"Darius!"

It was almost noon. Darius was laden with merchandise. His heavily pocketed coat was bulging with everything from bottled water to canned beans, and he had a couple of blankets slung over his shoulder. He was trading a string of beads for a bag of rice when he heard someone call his name, and he turned around.

A young woman was waving him over to her tobacco stand with big, desperate gestures. He'd met her on a few occasions but was ashamed to find he'd forgotten her name. Darius turned around and squeezed through the crowd, across the grain of the foot traffic. When he managed to make it to her stand, he saw what she was so worked up over.

A small child curled up under the rickety, wooden table. His skinny body was still and quiet, but silent tears streamed down his hollow, brown cheeks, leaving dark streaks in the dirt caked to his skin. Darius's stomach dropped.

Abandoned children had a specific look about them. It was in their eyes. A potent blend of sadness, fear, and betrayal. It poured out of the boy, thick and lonely. Darius had been doing this for years, but that look broke his heart every single time. There were certain things he just couldn't get used to.

"Thank god I foun'ya." The shopkeeper sighed and wiped the sweat from her brow with the back of her leathery hand. Her croaky voice was heavy and tired. "His dad dropped 'im off this mornin'. Asked if I knew ya. When I said I did, he just left 'im here. Poor thing's been cryin' ever since."

She cleared her throat and crinkled her nose up. Darius saw tears shining at the corners of her eyes. She didn't even ask if he could take the boy because they both knew he would. Darius wasn't in the business of leaving kids behind.

"Did he say anything else?" he asked. He slung the blanket he was carrying off his shoulders and knelt next to the boy. The child withdrew upon himself and let out a scared whimper, like a cornered animal. He was desperately clutching a filthy, gray stuffed rabbit in his bony fingers.

"No," the woman said. "Didn't speak much English."

Darius just nodded before he gently spoke to the child. "Hey, buddy. You hungry?" He reached into his pocket and pulled out a rice cake. As he opened it and held it out, the boy gave it a wary glance, but there was no denying the starved look in his eyes. They eagerly darted between Darius and the food. His crying had stopped. Hunger and the drive to survive overcame his devastation. "Take it."

Darius held the rice cake out further and placed it onto the cracked pavement between him and the child. The boy immediately snatched it up, tore the plastic packaging off, and nibbled at the edge. The whole time, he didn't look away from Darius's face—he just watched him with big, brown eyes.

The woman sighed and shook her head. "I don't think he speaks English, either. 'Least he hasn't for me. Dad looked Mexican."

"Ah, okay." Darius rubbed his temples and thought. Over the years, he'd developed a rudimentary, working knowledge of several languages spoken here at the market. Hopefully, it would be enough to help this kid understand what was happening. He strung together a few words and hoped he got his point across: I'm here to help you. I can take you somewhere safe. You can have more food.

His broken Spanish seemed to do the trick. The little boy's shoulders eased down, and he lifted his head a bit from his food. Then he began to quietly talk in Spanish back, and if Darius wasn't mistaken, he was asking where his papa went.

He had a soft spot for boys abandoned by their fathers.

It hit close to home.

"Voy a… cu… cuidando." Darius hoped that meant "I'll be taking care of you," or something similar. He gestured to himself and then the boy with a comforting smile. The boy's eyes filled with tears again, and Darius said the one phrase he *knew* he always said right.

"No te dejaré."

I won't leave you.

Then the boy nodded. Darius came forward and scooped him up. The child clung to his neck desperately. Rice cake crumbs stuck to his chin and scratched gently against Darius's collar. As he leaned down to grab his blanket again, the woman thanked him.

"I hate seein' kids hurt like this," she told him. "Thank you, Darius."

"Absolutely," Darius said. "I'll take good care of him. I promise."

He made his way back onto the street, holding the frail, small body of the little boy against his chest. What would he have to do to keep that promise? They were hardly making ends meet as it is, but he'd find a way. He always did.

He didn't have any other options.

But now he had other things to attend to—namely, lunch. As Darius continued down the market, the scent of cooked meat caught his attention. His stomach rumbled, deep and angry. He was nearing the food court. Cooking stands sent out alluring aromas, boasting of curries and pastries, cuisine from around the world mixing their unique smells together in the dense, hot air. This sector was always bustling with customers, adding their own sound pollution into the air to accompany the scents beckoning other hungry customers forward.

His stomach clenched upon itself, and Darius touched a hand to the hollow spot beneath his ribcage. Shifting the boy's weight in his arms, he pushed his way in through the human mass gathered outside the food stalls and found the line for his favorite empanada stand. The people around him were hurried and angry, pushing in against each other as they fought to the front. Darius moved with them, part of them, but not engaged—

And suddenly, he was hit with an icy chill. A shiver rushed down Darius's spine, and he looked up.

A man stood at the front of the crowd. He was tall, looming above Darius's six feet by at least two inches, and broad-shouldered. He stood with his back straight, dignified, and far too calm. His tan skin was clear and clean, and he adjusted the sleeves of a purple suit beneath his gunmetal blazer. Darius knew his type. Professional. Successful. He had a warm home, reliable meals, and an income large enough to support dozens more than he used it for.

What the hell was he doing in a place like this?

The man at the front of the line paused. He turned around briefly and searched the crowd. His metallic eyes passed over Darius once and then landed right on him. Darius tensed. The man's eyes were steely, cold, and… *carnal*; he looked unsatisfied and uncivilized. Unpredictable.

Fear bubbled past the hunger and wrapped itself around Darius's throat. He held the boy a little tighter. His small frame pressed up against his chest.

"Oy! Are you gonna order?"

Miguel, the owner of the empanada stand, reached over his table and roughly tapped the man on the shoulder. The man's gray eyes watched Darius for only a moment longer before glancing down at the boy in his arms and then to the crowd beyond them. He must have seen something then, because his eyes suddenly filled with intense fear, for just a second, before going blank again.

Then he turned and looked down at his shoulder, where Miguel's filthy fingers had left an oil spot on his suit jacket. His upper lip curled into a snarl. He looked up and down Miguel before finally speaking.

"I should cut your fingers off." The man's voice was young and deep. It boomed over the crowd with surprising clarity. Darius's skin crawled.

The threat cut like broken glass. The chatter and anger from the nearby crowd slowly boiled down to the closest thing the market ever saw to silence: whispered suspicions.

"Who is that?"

"What's going on?"

"What did he say?"

Miguel frowned and pointed out into the crowd. "Get the fuck off my counter."

The very air around the man seemed to shimmer with power, but Miguel didn't budge. He threw his arms around his chest and pulled his shoulders back as the man continued to stare him down.

At last, though for no apparent reason other than maybe the filth of the market was finally too much for him, the man let out a loud, hollow laugh and said, "You're lucky I have other, more pressing engagements… Next time, you won't be."

With that, he turned around and pushed his way back through the crowd. They made room for him, separating around him like water breaks for stone. As he neared, Darius's heart thumped painfully against his ribs. He pulled back, held the boy's small body against his own as tightly as he could, and tried to blend in with the people around him.

The man walked by without so much as a glance in Darius's direction.

Then he disappeared into the crowd.

CHAPTER TWO

Chatter resumed in the market, quickly returning to its normal, loud chorus as though nothing out of the ordinary had happened. Darius made it to Miguel's counter.

"Ah, Jones," Miguel said, clearing his throat and wiping sweat from his forehead. "Usual?"

Darius agreed, and Miguel took to the back. While his food was being prepared, Darius glanced over his shoulder across the market. The man was gone, but Darius's anxiety wasn't.

"Your order," Miguel said. He plopped the four foil-wrapped empanadas on the counter, and Darius passed the money over the wood. Miguel counted and pocketed it before saying, "See you tomorrow, yeah?" Then he moved to go to the next customer, but, remembering something, he clapped his hands and came back. "Oh! I almost forgot—a couple was looking for you. Uptown folks. Said they wanted to talk about adopting a kid?"

Darius's heart skipped a beat. "Really? That's great! Where are they?"

"I told them to wait at that old Java Hut stand and said I'd send you that way. Dunno if they stuck around, though," he added. "They seemed pretty uncomfortable down here."

Darius nodded and shook Miguel's hand over the stand. "Thanks, man."

"No problem, Jones."

Darius turned around and shoved his way back through the crowd of hungry people. He held the empanadas close to his chest with one hand, under the folds of his coat to stop them from being picked or prodded at. His stomach purred, as though it could tell food was just a few layers of cloth and flesh away.

But before he could eat, he had to deal with the boy. With his other arm, he hoisted the child onto his hip.

"C'mon," he said. "Let's get you fed."

In the middle of the strip was a makeshift plaza where the spaces were left wide open so people could sit down on the ground and eat. A few battered and beaten tables were spread out, but most people huddled in tight groups and ate quickly before heading back into the market for the day. Darius's best friend, Saul, was waiting for him there.

"Damnit, Darius," Saul said a few minutes later as he dug into his half of the empanada. His sister, Eva, was sitting with the boy. They were talking quietly in Spanish, sharing her food, while Saul and Darius watched them. "Can we really take in another kid?"

Darius didn't care for the kids alone. Over the years, he'd collected a group of people who helped him run things. Saul and Eva joined a little over five years ago. He didn't know their whole story. Juniper was the only one whose old life he knew anything about. All Saul and Eva had ever shared was that their stepfather had been abusive, and after a particularly rough evening, Saul had grabbed his little sister and walked out. Part of Darius wondered if Saul had killed the man, but he never asked. For a few years, the two of them made their living the way many unsheltered children did—by stealing.

Every day, Saul and Eva would head out to neighborhoods around Lower Manhattan, working as a team to grab food and other essentials from shops and suppliers. Eva played a distraction card while Saul swiped the goods. It made Darius uncomfortable, but he couldn't deny how much they needed it. He didn't bring in enough supplies to keep them all alive on his own. Saul and Eva had kept them going through several harsh winters.

"We'll manage," Darius said. He looked at Eva. "How's he doing?"

"Eh, okay," Eva said with a small, sad smile. It made her cheeks seem even more hollow. She wrapped her arm around the boy's shoulders and hugged him close to her side. "Scared, confused… You know, the usual."

"What's his name?" Saul asked.

"Alejandro."

"Ah, Alejandro." Saul flashed a big, wide smile. His teeth looked bright white in contrast to his brown skin and scruffy, black stubble. "¡Nombre poderoso! Debes ser muy fuerte, eh?" He laughed and ruffled Alejandro's dirty brown hair. For the first time, the boy's eyes lit up, and a big smile broke across his face.

Darius chuckled. As much as Saul was always saying they shouldn't take on any more kids, Darius knew he'd never be able to say no to another one. They all just wanted to do what they could to help. Which reminded Darius…

"Anyway, I gotta go," he said. "I'm meeting a couple who's looking for a kid."

Saul raised his eyebrows and nodded. He took a big bite of food and said, through a full mouth, "Fingers fucking crossed. We're barely making ends meet as it is."

"I hear ya," Darius said. "I'll be back soon. Eva?" She glanced up to him as he wrapped the uneaten half of his empanada and handed it over along with the two unopened ones. "Do you mind taking Alejandro back to the house and dropping these off for the others?"

Eva smiled. "No problem. Good luck!"

He thanked her and headed to the western rim of the food court, where Miguel said the couple was waiting.

Decades ago, in the 2070s, the Java Hut had been bustling and popular. Then the economy tanked, the Lower East Side had turned into a slum, and it had been abandoned, like so much else in this neighborhood. People at the market used it as a place marker—it sat on the furthest western edge, right on the distinct line where their world blended into the rest of New York City. On the other side of the street, things were clean and modern. On this side, sidewalks were unswept, buildings unpainted, and graffiti colored the brick in bright, vibrant euphemism.

The couple was sitting there, at an old, cast-iron table, waiting for him.

Darius watched from a distance for a few minutes. He did this every time he met with new people wanting to adopt. He looked out for nosy onlookers and police. They weren't common in this neighborhood, but Darius didn't take chances. Cops didn't treat people like him with extra kindness. The last thing he needed was to get arrested—or shot in the back when he walked away.

He always had to be careful. Black market adoption was illegal.

It was also many people's only option. Infertility was on the rise, medical support had become ludicrously expensive, and the foster system had disintegrated into a for-profit sham. As a result, the price of private adoptions had skyrocketed. New York City was in the tragic position of having too many kids without families, too many families without kids, and no honest way to bring them together.

Darius tried to bridge that gap.

This couple seemed genuine. They'd clearly worked hard to fit into the market. Their clothes were oversized and mismatched, their skin natural and make-up free, but it was still clear they didn't belong. Their hair was too clean, their nails too short, and their cheeks too full and healthy.

But they had come alone, and the familiar look of honest

desperation let Darius know they were the real deal. So he approached. The two of them stiffened as Darius walked up to the table and sat at the chair on the other side with a smile.

"I hear you've been looking for me."

The man frowned and leaned forward. "Are you Darius?"

"That's me. How can I help you?"

He knew how he could help them. As trafficking children for illegal adoptions had become more and more prevalent, Darius's name had begun to circulate further and further north. People liked that he was careful. They liked knowing they were adopting true orphans and not kidnapped children from poor families.

And they liked that he worked on donations alone.

Darius didn't demand money in exchange for a child. All he wanted was to know the kids were loved and cared for, so he was selective. There was a badge of pride from the parents he worked with. They had been *chosen.*

And more often than not, they threw money his way, if only to say *thank you.*

"We just want to start our family," the woman blurted out. "We've been trying for so long, wasted so much money… but the doctor doesn't think it will happen." Tears glistened behind her bright, blue eyes. Darius's heart lurched in his chest.

He'd seen that look too many times to count.

Darius reached out across the table and grabbed the woman's hand. She was startled at first, but her fingers relaxed in Darius's palm, and soon, she was squeezing back. "It's okay," Darius said, and he looked between them with a soft smile. "Let's start at the beginning."

They relaxed and opened up. They called themselves Oliver and Grace—fake names, Darius assumed. Most people gave him fake names at first. They talked a little about their lives—about how they got married in their early twenties but waited over ten years to have a family thanks to financial hardship. When the time finally came for them to start trying, they struggled.

Darius listened patiently, but he'd known from the minute "Grace" opened her mouth he was going to give her a child. He'd always had a knack for being able to read someone, and within the first few minutes of meeting prospective new parents, he would know if he trusted them to take in one of his kids. It was like he could read some unspoken, invisible signals—like the very energy they gave off was warm and inviting and full of promise. He knew it when he saw it, and this time, he saw it right away.

"Do you have any preference?" Darius asked. "On age or sex?"

"Not at all," Grace said. Her voice was gentle and calm, and when she spoke to Darius, she looked him straight in the face. Darius appreciated it. So often people shied away, ashamed on Darius's behalf. It was always nice to be seen—really seen—for who he was and what he did. Grace nervously brushed a stray lock of hair behind her ear and looked back to her husband. "What do you think?"

Oliver sighed. He was young, but the stress of life had already given him a streak of gray hair at his temples. The pain in his words jutted out like a barb—frustrated, Darius assumed, that he couldn't provide his wife with the child she so desperately wanted. "I don't care. All I know is this woman would make the world's *best* mother, and I'll do whatever it takes to make that happen." Tears welled up behind Grace's eyes, and Oliver smiled as he reached across the table to grip her hand.

This was a look Darius was familiar with, too. He'd met hundreds of couples over the years, and he'd found one of two things could happen. Either continuous pain and heartbreak drove a wedge between two people, tainting whatever love they'd once had with bitterness and resentment, or it pulled them together. For some, trauma was the final crack. For others, it fortified them and made them stronger.

"So." Oliver cleared his throat and looked back to

Darius. "Can you help us?"

"I just have a few more questions."

The interview was more for show. It was what prospective parents expected. No one believed he could just give them a kid without knowing who they were, so Darius played the part. He asked about their families. He asked about their home. He asked about their medical histories and their passions and how they planned to raise a child. He asked all the same questions he'd learned people *wanted* him to ask over the years—the questions they'd rehearsed the answers to. By now, he knew them by heart.

When he was satisfied Grace and Oliver would feel eased by his effort, he sat back in his chair and smiled. "I think you'd make great parents to any of my kids."

Grace gasped and covered her mouth with trembling fingers. "Really?"

Darius laughed and dug into his pockets. "Really. Here—" He drew out an old wallet. The leather was so worn and weathered down it was almost white. It didn't have any money or credit cards or identification inside. Instead, it was filled with photographs. He slid the wallet over to Oliver and Grace and said, "These are the children I have available right now. Take some time to look through them and see if anyone jumps out at you."

As Grace looked through the photographs, Oliver shook Darius's hand above the table. Then, the two new parents huddled together. As they flipped through the pictures and read the details Darius had written on the backs, silent, happy tears were streaming down Grace's face. Darius stepped away—this was an intimate moment that deserved space and silence—but as he watched her, he couldn't help but give a small, contented smile.

Life was hard. He struggled to feed his family, to keep them clothed, and to help each and every one of them make the most of the cards they had to play. But in the end, this, right here, made it all worth it.

He hadn't had a win like this in a *long* time.

At last, Oliver called him back. Darius rejoined them at the table, and Grace drew one photograph out of the stiff, plastic casing. When she handed it over to him and he looked down into that sweet, darling face, his heart flipped.

"We want her."

Little Lindsay. Darius's favorite.

He wasn't supposed to play favorites, but he couldn't help it. There was something about Lindsay… He had been drawn to her immediately, and in the few months since she'd been in their care, she'd nestled a special place in each of their hearts. Juniper was especially fond of her. It would be hard for her to give her up, but she would if it meant Lindsay could have a better life.

It would also be hard because Lindsay was sick.

"Lindsay is an incredible little girl," Darius said. "I'll need some time to sort everything out."

Grace frowned. Her newfound hope seemed to be fraying at its already fragile edges. "Like what?"

Medication. But Darius didn't say that out loud. "Paperwork," he said instead. "A birth certificate, mostly. I'll need your names—your *real* names—so I can get it all set up."

"You can get us a birth certificate?" Oliver asked.

Darius just provided a coy smile and nod. There wasn't much he couldn't get on the market. "Give me a week, and I should have it all figured out," he said. "Does that work for you?"

"Yes," Grace said, and she nodded eagerly. A fresh wave of tears streamed down her face. "Yes, of course. Thank you so much. Thank you, thank you!"

Darius smiled. "It's no trouble at all."

He talked Oliver and Grace—actually David and Michelle—through the details he'd need to set up all the fake documentation they'd need to make Lindsay officially theirs. They wrote it all down on a scrap of paper and handed it to Darius from across the table. Darius finished the meeting with his standard monologue—about how there were no fees, but he would gladly accept donations to help him with his work. David and Michelle promised to bring something when they met next time. Anything, they told him, to help him after he made their dreams come true.

Then they parted ways, and Darius headed back into the heart of the market. His high spirits were dampened now. He had to get Lindsay some antibiotics, and there was only one place he could go—

Darius's thoughts were suddenly disrupted. The little hairs on the back of his neck stood up again. A cold chill rushed over him, and something caught his eye. A flash of black. It disappeared in the bustling crowd.

What was that?

He pushed his way through the market, but the atmosphere was odd. Tense. People around him walked slowly, glancing over their shoulders at something—back in the direction Darius was trying to go. Then, he saw it—someone dark and pure and definitely out of place.

It was a woman.

She strode through the market. Head high. Stares and whispers followed her. She didn't seem to care. Her long, raven-black hair was tied in a loose ponytail at the base of her skull. Darius frowned. Was this the woman Jalal had told him about? The one with the *gun*?

He had to know. If she had a gun on the market, his kids weren't safe. He followed after her.

She was slender, but not in the way most people were slender here. Lean muscle held tight against her body. Surrounded by people who wore their skin like loose rags on a broken frame, she stuck out. She was too strong, too *healthy*.

And too clean. Her complexion was cool and pale; the pretty, angular features of her face stunningly flawless. The smoke and the grime and the stink of the market didn't cling to her shining white skin or black clothes the way they would have if she lived here. Her tank top and leggings gripped her tight and moved with her in fluid, silent grace. Her forearms were covered in rich black, fingerless gloves.

But while it was her clothing and figure that caught

Darius's attention, they weren't what kept it. It was her eyes. The irises were a chilling and deep shade so dark Darius could think of no other color to call them but black. They seemed almost like a void. Empty and alone.

Darius was filled with sudden and urgent dread.

Then the woman found what she was looking for in the crowd. Her expression shifted from stoic to full of a rage so palpable Darius could almost feel it from across the plaza. Dark brows furrowed. Thin lips went even thinner. She drew two things from a satchel at her side: a small, round item and a pistol.

And she slammed the item into the asphalt.

A heavy hissing sound, then dense, overwhelming fog suddenly filled the food court square. It erupted into suffocating chaos. People ran in every direction. The chatter gave way to panic. Screams and cries exploded around him. Darius forced his way through the crowd, back the way he'd come.

The kids… He had to get the kids.

The further he got from the smoke, the more dispersed the pandemonium became. Darius coughed and rubbed his eyes to try to see through the blurry residue the smoke had left behind. Mrs. Miller was the first stop on his way back. The crowd pushed so closely around him Darius had a hard time pulling himself away. People barreled in, rocking him side to side and almost knocking him to the ground.

Soon he saw the faded sign for Mrs. Miller's shop, but something was wrong. She was crying and frantically searching the crowd, calling out Sophie's name. Darius's heart dropped.

The girl was gone.

CHAPTER THREE

"Did'ya find the girl?"

Darius walked up the steps to the back patio and sighed. The old bar he and the others lived in was located several blocks north of the market, in the old projects of Alphabet City. Like most buildings in this neighborhood, it had been abandoned years ago. The walls were pock-marked and faded, the roof torn and leaky, and most of the windows were loaded up with heavy, thick wood.

But it was home, and Darius felt awful returning to it empty-handed.

Without Sophie.

"No," he said.

Thad sat at the top of the steps, picking grime out from under his yellow fingernails with an old wood screw. He didn't even look up as Darius shrugged off his coat. The old man sighed, and his thick, gray beard moved, just slightly, as he sucked on a wad of chew jammed down under his lip.

"She's a goner," he said. "Probably picked up by some fuckin' pervert."

Darius's stomach knotted up, angry and sick. Thad was probably right. Darius knew it. They all did. Sophie wasn't the first child they'd lost on the market, and she wouldn't be the last.

Sometimes Darius wondered if he'd eventually be as callous and indifferent to those losses as Thad was. He hoped not. If it always felt like a part of his soul was being ripped away, it would keep him all the more motivated to stop it from happening to anyone else. And right now, he was really damn motivated.

Motivated enough to do something crazy.

"We need to talk." He cleared his throat and looked down at Thad. "I made a deal with Max."

Thad frowned and stopped picking at his nails. "You did *what?*"

Darius didn't answer him. He just threw the door open and walked into the kitchen. Thad jumped to his feet as fast as his old, arthritic hips would let him and followed after.

More than anything, Darius wanted to take the time and properly mourn Sophie's loss, and part of him was pissed he didn't get to. Another part of him, though, knew he couldn't lay down and stop every time a child disappeared or died. He had to keep moving forward and find a better way to survive.

If that meant dealing with Max Douglas, it meant dealing with Max Douglas.

"Damnit, boy, hold on."

Thad lumbered after Darius and grabbed him by the shoulder as Darius tossed his jacket over the back of a chair. A few apples tumbled out of one of the pockets and rolled across the floor. Saul leaned down to pick them up. He and his sister were sitting at the table, sorting through the goods they'd gathered for the day. Saul looked between Darius and Thad and frowned.

"What's going on?"

"Darius made a deal with Max!"

The room went silent. Eva paused midway through folding a child-sized t-shirt and watched Darius with wide, shocked eyes. Saul got to his feet, put the apples in a box of fruit on the table, and crossed his arms.

"What the hell for?"

"That's what I wanna know!"

"What else? Prescriptions," Darius said flatly. He collected the fruit box from the table and walked across the room to a trap door in the corner. "I'm going to meet him tomorrow to grab antibiotics for Lindsay."

The other three just stared after him as he pulled the door open. The wood creaked, echoing through the stone cellar below. A wide beam of light fell across the packed dirt floor, and a couple of quiet, hushed voices retreated into the darkness. Darius couldn't help but allow himself a small smile as Thad grumbled a swear word.

"Damnit, Aren!" he growled, and he shoved past Darius and hoisted himself down into the ground. The moist, cool air rushed around him and wafted against Darius's cheeks. *"Get out of here."*

Thad was protective of the cellar. It was the most valuable room in the house because it was where they stored all the items they needed to survive: food, blankets, clothing, firewood, shoes, and first aid supplies… when they had them. They even had a collection of plastic jugs full of water they collected in rain barrels on the roof. Thad had a meticulous system for organizing things, and he *hated* when the kids got down there and messed it up.

Aren's head popped up over the edge of the floor, and he threw Darius and the others a sheepish grin. He was the oldest child they had now—maybe thirteen—and the most daring. After him came Ned, a boy who took himself to be Aren's protege. Darius gave them both a stern look.

"Do you *like* making Thad angry?" he asked.

Aren shrugged. "I mean, kinda."

"C'mon, man. You know better."

"We just wanted to see the tunnel!"

"There is no damn tunnel!" Thad reached out of the cellar, roughly grabbed the box out of Darius's hands, and slammed it down on top of a crate. "Now *keep out!"*

There *was* a tunnel. Several of them. A couple of months

ago, Thad had accidentally stumbled upon some of the old, underground trade routes from the drug prohibition of the 2040s. Thad had started exploring the tunnels, but he'd almost been caught in a cave-in twice. So instead, he'd moved a large bookcase in front of the opening to try to stop the kids from finding it and getting themselves killed. But, as with all things, it turned out to be impossible, and the children were horrible secret keepers.

And Thad was a horrible liar.

"There *is* a tunnel," Ned grumbled as Eva ushered them out of the kitchen and into the main room. The loud, disorganized sound of kids playing and laughing and talking whipped through the double doors. Thad climbed back into the kitchen and glared after the boys until Eva returned. Then he turned on Darius again.

"Now out with it, boy," he said. "What the *hell* did you make a deal with Max for?"

"You made a deal with *Max?*"

Darius sighed and dropped his face into one hand as Juniper walked into the room. Her thin, blonde eyebrows were pinched angrily over her bright, tired eyes. Wispy, orange hair fell out of the clip she kept it in, making her skinny neck look even thinner as she crossed her arms and stared at him.

"Yeah," he said. "We don't have a choice."

"To hell we don't," Saul said. "He's a criminal."

"You're a criminal," Darius pointed out.

"I'm a criminal because I *need* to be," Saul said. "Max is a greedy *pendejo* who only cares about money."

That was true. When the new CEO from Pfizer, the largest pharmaceutical company in the world, had hiked drug prices four years ago, it had devastated the Bridge Street Market and everyone who relied on it to survive. Almost overnight, every single prescription dealer on the market had been forced out of business.

Then Max had swooped in. Rumor had it he worked for Pfizer and smuggled drugs out in order to make a hefty profit—and he did. Max sold his merchandise for prices that would bleed even the lower middle class dry. He didn't have a presence on the market—the shop owners hated him for his greed and heartlessness and refused to let him do business there—but his name circulated every winter as people desperately tried to pool money together to get medications for their sick and dying.

Thousands of people—mostly children—had died after Pfizer's price hikes, and Max was getting rich off their suffering.

Darius hated him for it, and he hated even more that he needed him. Every time he saw the guy, Darius just wanted to punch him in the face. Maybe he would, one of these days, if he ever caught him without his bodyguard.

But he didn't have any other options.

"If I don't do this, Lindsay is going to die," Darius said.

The others went quiet and looked between one another for a moment.

"She's *this* close to having a family," Darius went on, pinching his fingers together for emphasis. "*This* close to getting out of this hellhole, and she's going to *die* if we can't get antibiotics for her. I can't let that happen. I can't lose her. Not like this. So, unless any of *you* have a better idea, I'm doing this."

More silence. Juniper's arms fell quietly to her sides, while Thad's came up around his torso as he furrowed his heavy, bushy brows and considered Darius. Saul and Eva looked at each other and together came to some unspoken agreement. Saul nodded, and Eva heaved a sigh. "What's the deal?"

A weight lifted off Darius's chest. He was prepared to fight this battle alone, but he was glad he didn't have to.

He came back around and leaned against the countertop. "I'm going to help him get his product on the market in exchange for whatever medications we need for ourselves. We'll be able to save thousands of people."

"That's it?" Saul asked. "Why not a cut of the profits?"

"Because I got him to agree to lower his prices," Darius

said. "That's the only way the people on the market will ever be okay with Max peddling his merch. It has to be affordable."

Juniper shook her head. "I can't believe he agreed to that."

"It took a *lot* of convincing."

"Feels like a trap," Thad said. His beard and mustache moved to the form of a frown. "You gotta be careful. That sonnova bitch'll ruin yer name."

Darius sighed and rubbed his eyes with one hand. "Yeah. I know. I'll keep an eye on him."

"There's a reason Max doesn't already have a presence on the market," Eva said. She was pacing, irritated, between the door and the sink, and she counted off the reasons on her fingers: "Nobody trusts him, he only takes *cash* for his merchandise, *and* his prices are so high no one can afford them. Even *if* you get to keep the lower prices, I don't see how you can *avoid* ruining your name if you're selling drugs for him."

"You've worked hard for the place you have there," Juniper said. She walked across the room and came to stand beside Darius, and she gave him a soft, nervous look. "You're able to do a lot of *good* work because of that place. I don't think it's worth the risk."

Darius scoffed and shook his head. "It is. It *has* to be. If we lose Lindsay, she'll be the *fifth* kid this year. I'm not letting that happen."

"He's gonna try to fuck you over," Saul said. He kicked back in one of the chairs around the rickety table. "My bet is he never gives you the drugs you need, but there *is* a way you can guarantee you get them…" His eyes gleamed a little bit, and he winked.

"Just spit it out, *cabrón,*" Eva grumbled. Saul's smile widened.

"Skim 'em off the top," he said with a shrug. "You're gonna have some of the product on you, right? Just pocket a tiny bit every day. Small enough so he won't notice. You can build up some storage over time, and when he backs out—which he *will*—you won't be shit outta luck."

Darius frowned and crossed his arms. He hated the idea of stealing—always had—but he recognized the necessity of it. They'd never survive here without Saul and Eva's work. But stealing from Max wasn't an option.

"Nah, man." He shook his head. "I can't do that."

Saul sighed. "Sometimes you've gotta cut some corners if you want to survive."

"Sure," Darius said. "But not here. Max will notice if the money doesn't match up with the product at the end of the day. At the very least, he'll cut us off. At the worst, he'll get me arrested. Or killed. There *has* to be another way."

The other four shared a look, and Juniper shook her head. "I think you're being idealistic, Darius," she said after a quiet moment. "Working with Max is a mistake."

"It's either that, or we let Lindsay die," he said. "Is that what you want?"

Juniper's mouth dropped open, and a flash of pain crossed her vibrant blue eyes. She crossed her arms and sent Darius a hot look. Her oversized clothes made her look tiny, wrapped up in folds of fabric that totally eclipsed her body. "You know that's not what I want."

Then she stormed out of the room and disappeared. Darius groaned and rubbed his eyes with the tips of his fingers.

"So, you're meeting with Max tomorrow?" Eva asked.

"Yep," Darius said. "I told him I need an advance on a bottle of antibiotics for Lindsay."

"I still think you should be asking for cash," Saul said with a shrug.

"Nah," Eva said. "Darius is right. Drugs are better. Since Cyrus was killed, we haven't been able to stock up on medications."

The four of them all shared a quiet moment of silence. Cyrus Murphy had been a beacon of hope for them. He was one of the first children Darius had taken in, and a little over four months ago, he'd become the first of those raised in the orphanage to go out and get a legitimate job. He'd been working at a nearby convenience store, and thanks to him, they'd been able to afford basic first aid supplies for the first time in years.

But shortly afterward, he'd been caught in a shootout in the streets outside the shop. Darius heard about the incident and rushed to check on him. All he'd found was a street full of cops putting bodies into bags and cleaning blood off the asphalt. Cyrus never came home.

He was probably rotting away in an unmarked grave somewhere, surrounded by other people too poor for a proper burial. Just like all the other kids they'd ever lost.

Darius couldn't lose another.

He excused himself and walked through the double doors and into the living area. Years ago, they'd ripped the bar counter up from the floor to give them more space, and the wood added extra fortification to the windows and doors. The ground was covered in pillows and blankets. A few old toys were strewn around. Kids of all ages, from five to thirteen, sprawled across their makeshift beds, talking and playing. Eleven little, lively bodies.

A little girl raised her head and caught sight of Darius. Her wide smile broke into a grin.

"Darius!"

Suddenly a dozen pairs of eager eyes were on him. Skinny children grinned, their noses wrinkled above mouths full of oversized or missing teeth. A handful of the younger kids leapt to their feet and ran to him, giggling.

"Will you read to me?"

"I'm hungry!"

"I lost a tooth today!"

"Wow," Darius said to the last little girl. She beamed up at him, poking her tongue through a new gap between her front teeth. "That's great! Maybe the tooth fairy will surprise you!"

"I hope I get an apple," the girl said. "Then maybe I'll lose another tooth!"

Darius laughed. "How can you eat an apple if you're missing *two* teeth?" he asked with a teasing grin.

"Darius, is Lindsay getting a new Mom and Dad?"

The last question kind of caught him off guard, and his smile faltered a little bit as he said, "Hopefully! We'll see in a couple of days."

A wave of disappointment and jealousy flooded through the room for a brief moment. The older children, like Aren, who had given up their daydreams of adoption years ago, busied themselves with folding blankets or reading books. The younger ones who were still full of idealistic wonder began talking again.

"Are they nice?"

"Is the mom pretty?"

"Next time, can you find me a family?"

Darius reached out and grabbed Ned by the shoulders. "I'll never quit looking," he said softly, "but until then, I'm your family."

Ned's dirt-streaked face broke out into a smile.

"Now, I gotta go talk to Aunt June. Aren? Can you read these guys a bedtime story?"

As Aren dug up one of their old, tattered books and started to read, the kids unwrapped themselves from Darius's legs and flounced off. Darius watched as they circled Aren, pulling their tiny feet beneath their legs. Darius gave a soft, sad smile before he took a deep breath and headed away.

The bar had once functioned as both a business and a home. Off of the main room was a hallway with a nonfunctional bathroom, and just at the end was a staircase leading to an upper-level apartment. To call it an apartment was generous, though. It was nothing but a single room, a tiny kitchenette, and another bathroom that didn't work. This is where they quarantined the sick children, and where Juniper had gone.

When he opened the door to the studio, he found Lindsay awake, curled up in Juniper's arms. Her brown eyes were glassy and tired, but all the same, when they landed on Darius, they lit up. She didn't say anything—she just raised her hands and reached out for him.

Lindsay was probably three. Maybe four. It was hard to tell. She was small for her age, and so slender the bones in her wrist swelled into tiny, graceful domes beneath her pale skin. A couple of months ago, Darius had found her sleeping behind a trash bin. Since then, she'd become the joy of the orphanage. She was kind and generous, always sharing her toys and food with the older kids around her. Everyone loved her.

Losing her was going to be hard for all of them—Darius just hoped that loss was to a new family and not to the familiar grip of death.

"Hey, honey," Darius whispered gently as he came and sat beside her and Juniper. Lindsay wiggled her way out of Juniper's arms and fumbled onto Darius's lap instead. Juniper watched sadly as the little girl curled up into a tight ball and cuddled in close to Darius's chest. She was hot. Her caramel hair was matted to her forehead with fever. "How are you feeling?"

"I'm cold." Lindsay shivered against him, and Darius reached over Juniper for the blanket and wrapped it around the little girl. It didn't stop her from shaking. She coughed so hard her tiny body felt like it was going to fall apart in his arms.

For several long minutes, Juniper, Darius, and Lindsay sat there in silence, Darius cradling the small, sick girl against himself while Juniper simply watched with a mixture of pointed pain and deep sadness. Before long, Lindsay had drifted off into an uneasy sleep. Juniper reached out and put her hand against the girl's forehead.

"She's burning up," Darius said. He turned to face Juniper again and found she was avoiding his gaze. "I'm sorry, June, but we *need* those antibiotics."

"There's no guarantee they'll even work," she whispered. Her voice was so quiet it hardly passed the distance between them.

"It's better than not doing anything at all," he said. He kept his focus on Juniper's face, waiting for her to finally look at him. She seemed to feel him staring, because eventually she glanced up and met his eyes. "You know it is."

"I know," she conceded. Her voice was choked and tight.

"And then," Darius continued. He looked down to the small bundle in his arms again, and his heart gave a painful, sad flip. "Lindsay can have a real home."

"I just sometimes wish," Juniper said after a dense silence, and a couple of stray tears fell from her eyes, "that we could be that real home."

And in that moment, Juniper looked small. She was hunched down around herself, tight and full of deep longing and sorrow. Darius reached his arm around her shoulders. She leaned into him and gave a single, throaty sob.

"I know," he murmured. "Me, too."

The next afternoon, after finishing a rough, distracted day bartering for more necessities at the Williamsburg Bridge Street Market, Darius sat in a dingy, empty park near the East River. This was where he and Max had agreed to meet. So far, Darius was the first to show up.

He wasn't surprised. Every time he'd ever had a meeting with Max, the guy had kept him waiting. He liked to be in control, and he knew showing up late made people nervous. When people were nervous, they made bad decisions in a negotiation.

But for Darius, the negotiations were already done. Now, it was a time to see if Max would follow through.

Darius took a deep breath and sat down on a grimy, corroded aluminum park bench, and he waited.

Max didn't show up for thirty minutes. Darius was just starting to worry he wasn't going to come at all when he finally saw two figures walking toward him from the other edge of the park.

Max Douglas was a potato of a man—short, squat, and bald, dressed in an ill-fitted suit which somehow made him look even more like a vegetable. On his left was a tall, muscular man, his hair slicked back, his thick arms showing through the short sleeves of his black t-shirt.

"Darius Jones." Max's high, silky voice was crystal clear in the warm, fall weather. It carried across the space between them like a cold wind. Darius got to his feet. "I hope you haven't been waiting long…"

He smiled a gross little arrogant smile and stopped five yards away. His guard came up on his side and crossed his arms. Darius ignored him.

"Do you have the antibiotics?" Darius asked.

Max's smile widened a little. He drew a heavy, plastic bottle out of an inside pocket, held it out, and gave it a little shake.

"Right here."

Darius's heart fluttered, and he took a few steps forward. Max pulled the bottle back in against his chest, and Darius stopped walking.

"But," Max said with a sigh, "I'm afraid I can't just give these to you."

Before he could stop himself, Darius's mouth fell open. "We had a deal."

"Deals change," Max said, and he slipped the bottle back into his suit jacket. "I have never provided payment upfront of service, and I am not about to now. You will get these antibiotics at the end of your first week."

Darius frowned and took another couple of steps. Max's guard came forward.

"I can't wait a week," Darius said. "I need them *now*."

"Then I guess you'll have to fork over the cash."

Max moved to turn away, and Darius's stomach twisted. He jumped forward and reached out, but Max's guard stood in front of him and blocked his path.

"We had a deal!" Darius shouted.

Max paused and turned back around. His wormy little smile twisted even further, and he came right up to Darius's face. His guard stepped to the side, just enough for Max to stare up at Darius. That cocky grin finally cracked open to show his yellow teeth.

"I don't care about our deal," Max murmured. "You are a nobody here, Darius Jones. You have nothing but a bunch of snot-nosed kids. It's time you learned your place. So, you either *pay me*… or you wait until next week to get these antibiotics."

He reached up, patted Darius condescendingly on the cheek, and moved to turn around again.

This time, Darius's hand darted out, and his fingers wrapped around the soft, squishy flesh at Max's wrist.

The man yelped and turned as Darius yanked his arm back. His guard's broad, heavy hand grabbed Darius by the shoulder with such a firm grip it made his muscles ache, but he didn't let go.

"Listen up," Darius hissed through his teeth, and Max's eyes went wide. The guard tugged Darius back, but Max just moved with them. Darius was wild with panic and desperation. He felt like he was bared open, naked and exposed, but he didn't care. "My little girl is going to *die,* and I'm *not* leaving. We had a *deal* and, so help me, you will *stick to your word* and give me those *damned antibiotics*, then you will leave."

The guard's other arm whipped out and caught Darius around the throat. He pulled him upward, backward, and he lost his grip on Max's wrist. Darius found himself thrown onto the dirt, a hulking figure hovering over him, ready to pummel him into the ground—

Then Max stepped in. His beady eyes were glassy and dazed, but he grabbed his guard by the bicep and stopped him just before he was about to punch Darius square in the nose. Then, to Darius's astonishment, he held out the antibiotics.

"I'll stick to my word," Max said, but something about

the way he said it was off. As soon as Darius's fingers wrapped around the bottle, Max turned around and walked away. His guard stared after him, confused for a moment, before he followed.

Darius watched them go until they disappeared around a corner. He looked down at the bottle of antibiotics in his hand, blown away to see it sitting there. His heart pounded rapidly against his ribcage. He couldn't believe that *worked.* It felt too easy, like it was going to come back and bite him in the ass later, but Darius couldn't worry about it now. He needed to get home—fast.

Lindsay was going to be okay.

The walk back to the orphanage felt longer than usual. Darius rushed so quickly a sweat broke over his forehead. The small bottle of antibiotics swung like a pendulum in his pocket as he hurried down the street. He darted between people, through the crowds, and the closer he got to home, the more anxious he felt. He told himself it was his excitement, that he was just eager to show off his win over Max Douglas, but he knew there was more than that.

He wanted to check on Lindsay. He wanted to make sure it wasn't too late.

Almost unconsciously, he sped up. He was close, so close he could see the partially caved-in roof of their home over the crest of a nearby car. He turned into the alley. Two panels from the back fence had been knocked down into the yard. The hairs on the back of his neck stood on end.

Darius crossed the space in three strides and stopped at the base of the steps. The door to the kitchen was open. They never left the door open. He held his breath. A painful lump formed in his chest as he climbed up the back stairs and walked into the building.

Then he paused.

Thad lay sprawled across the threshold between the

kitchen and the main room. His beard was the color of rust. His eyes wide open, empty. Crimson lines seeped in the divots between the cracked tiles beneath him. They stretched out, fingers of dark red death reaching for Darius at the other side of the room.

This was all wrong.

Darius took a step forward as a deep, horrified weight swelled in his throat. The metallic scent of blood clouded his nostrils. He winced and wrinkled his nose as he knelt by Thad's side.

"Thad?"

He went to search the old man's throat for a pulse. His fingers slipped between folds of skin—warm blood coated the tips.

Darius stopped breathing.

He leapt to his feet, rushed into the main room. Blood. There was blood everywhere. And the kids… Their crippled and maimed forms were spread out, left inhumanely thrown across the red-stained floors. Eyes and mouths opened. They watched Darius, pleaded with him for help.

He retched. As he fell to the ground, overcome with nausea, the wide and empty faces followed him. Darius reached out and touched the nearest child. Alejandro. Lifeless. His little brown fingers wrapped tightly around a bloodied gray rabbit…

"Oh my *god.*"

The world started to spin. Darius's vision was red, colored by the massacre around him. His hands and knees were warm against the blood-soaked rug. The thick liquid seeped through his pants, touching his skin.

Darius vomited again.

And then—a noise. Behind him. Darius jumped to his feet. His heart caught in his throat as though it meant to suffocate him. He swallowed hard. More bodies. Oh, *god,* Aren. More blood—a death trail down the hallway and up the stairs. Children, face down—their backs open and bleeding. The steps dripped with red columns like wet paint.

A little girl's dead gaze watched him. Her mouth was open, revealing a gap from a lost tooth between her front teeth.

Someone cried out from the second story.

Darius leapt the stairs two at a time. He avoided the tiny bodies, ignoring them as best he could. At the top, sprawled out, was Eva. Eyes fluttered beneath her closed lids.

Her shirt was soaked in scarlet. Her skin was white and tacky.

"Eva?"

She only moaned.

Darius picked her up and grabbed her close. He tried not to think about the blood spilling from her stomach and onto his chest as he almost stumbled down the stairs. He heard the crunch of bodies beneath his feet. He couldn't think about it.

But when he reached the end of the hallway, he stopped. A man stood in the center of the room. Had he been there the whole time? Darius couldn't remember. His shined, leather shoes glistened with blood.

And then Darius recognized him. His suit. His stature. His steely gray eyes.

The man from the market.

A wide, wicked smile spread across his face. The sleeves of his button-up shirt were rolled up to his elbows, and blood was slick on his flesh. He held a knife in his right hand. The blade dripped heavy, crimson droplets onto the floor. A strange black tattoo, like a gaping serpent's eye, sat just below his wrist.

Darius took a step back. Eva moaned again.

Suddenly, the front door to the bar crashed open, and splintered wood sprayed into the room. The man didn't have the chance to react as a woman tackled him to the ground. Bodies crumbled beneath their weight.

As they struggled, she looked over her shoulder. Her black, void-like eyes met Darius's. She screamed, *"Run!"*

For a moment, Darius couldn't move. It was *her*.

She screamed at him again. "What the *fuck* are you doing? *Run!*"

The world snapped back around him, and he ran. Eva's limp body dangled from his arms as he hurried around them and into the street. Several black SUVs were parked in front, and people swarmed the building. A handful of men and women dressed in body armor and carrying guns screamed orders and commands as more people barreled toward them from the street. Civilians, in plainclothes, with disconnected and mechanical looks on their plastic, emotionless faces.

Darius gawked. His chest constricted as he was filled with a sense of dread.

A hand came down on his shoulder and shook him. Darius turned. He could barely see a pair of grave, brown eyes through the tinted visor.

"Let's get you out of here," the man said. "Carter! Grab the girl!"

Another man swooped in. Huge and bulking. He lifted Eva out of Darius's arms as though she weighed nothing. "Where's Rose?" he asked gruffly. A flurry of gunshots went off around Darius, and he jumped. The armored men and women made a circle—keeping the civilians out.

"Inside," the first man said, and his fingers tightened around Darius. His other hand gripped a rifle close to his side. "We've gotta get them out. *Now.*"

But Darius didn't move. He couldn't. The antibiotics in his pocket felt like an anchor. He turned back toward the bar. Civilians had broken the line. They climbed toward the door like drones.

Darius ripped himself out of the man's grip and started sprinting back.

"What the hell are you doing? *Get in the car!*"

Darius hardly heard the order. He pushed through the people—both armored and not—and back into the main room. The man and the woman were still wrestling for control of the knife on top of bodies and blood. They didn't notice him as he climbed the stairs again and threw open the door to the apartment.

He wasn't sure what he'd been expecting to find when he burst into the studio. Lindsay wasn't there. Instead, the floor was streaked in blood. Thick dark lines extended from the center of the room to the doorway. A woman stood by the window, her mousy hair flat and lifeless against her shoulders. As he entered, she turned toward him. Her face was plain, almost boring, but contorted in hate. She, too, had a knife in her hand.

Without even thinking about it, Darius said, "Where is she?"

The woman didn't respond. She simply took a step toward Darius. Then another. Her flat lips curled up in a smile, and Darius realized she meant to kill him. Before he had the chance to turn away, she attacked.

She was quick. Darius barely managed to dodge as she thrust her knife at his stomach. He turned, and she lashed out. He blocked the blow with his arm. The blade bit into his skin, and he cried out. Warm blood rushed down to his elbow. Darius tore away as she slashed again, and he stumbled to the floor. She raised the knife above him—

He panicked, kicked out, and scrambled backward. His heel collided with the outside of her right ankle, and she let out a gut-wrenching, excruciating scream and collapsed. The knife fell out of her hands, and Darius kicked it, too. It spiraled across the ground and clattered down the stairs.

Then he turned to get to his feet, but before he had the chance, the woman grabbed onto his shoulder and forced him around. Her nails dug so hard into his muscle it made his arm go numb. He opened his mouth to scream out, but her other hand reached out and wrapped around his throat.

Her grip was strong… then *too* strong. Darius gasped as her fingers dug so far into his flesh that he couldn't speak. She got to her feet and lifted him off the ground with one hand. His eyes widened as, in one swift movement, she hurled him backward.

Before he knew what was going on, Darius's back

collided with the window. The glass behind him shattered, and he fell.

The last thing Darius remembered was the sunset sky. The clouds were stained the color of blood. Then, everything went black.

CHAPTER FOUR

A low, resonant hum woke him. Cold, clammy sweat coated his cheek and plastered his skin to a sticky, leather seat. Everything moved—the surface beneath him bounced and swerved. His body ached. A slash in his arm throbbed with each heartbeat. Above the hum, Darius heard voices.

"Are you sure he's not dead?"

"Positive. I checked his vitals twice."

"Did they see him?"

"When Envy looked out the window, he was unconscious and covered in blood."

Blood. Darius's mind flooded with the color of blood. The dry, metallic scent bombarded his senses, and his stomach buckled. Before he had the chance to get a grip on himself, Darius dry heaved. The voices abruptly stopped. Darius could feel at least one set of eyes on the back of his head as he gagged over the edge of the seat.

When he opened his eyes, he was staring at the floor of a vehicle. Darius's mind spun, and he heaved again. A warm, firm hand came and rubbed his back, between his shoulder blades. Somehow, it comforted him.

"See?" It was the second voice. A woman's. "He's not dead. How are you doing?"

Those words were directed at Darius. He closed his eyes and groaned as he tried to fight off the nausea and the memories. The man driving said, "Probably not great. He *was* thrown out of a second-story window."

"Shut up, William," the woman said, but there was a lighthearted, if somber, note. Then she addressed Darius again. "My name is Chris Silver, and this is my partner, William Michaels. Are you hurt?"

At last, despite his pain, exhaustion, and nausea, Darius looked up. The man, William, was driving, craning his neck to look into the rearview mirror at Darius. The woman was turned around in her seat. She watched him with bright green eyes. Her blonde hair was pulled into a loose ponytail. Clipped to a belt in her beige cargo pants was a gun.

Darius's mouth went dry. It stuck together, so he just shook his head.

"From what I can see, you've just got some minor injuries," Chris said. "A few stitches and an ice pack and you'll be fine."

Darius reached up and gingerly touched the cut on his arm. The bleeding had stopped—now it was sticky and hot.

"We're lucky he landed on you," William said, and he smiled.

She rolled her eyes and stretched her neck to the side. Her long-sleeved, black shirt reached up to the top of her throat. Her hands, Darius noticed, were stained red.

He looked down at himself. He was coated in it.

Darius vomited again.

Images from the orphanage came roaring back in bright red streams. The lifeless faces of his children—the feeling of his fingers inside Thad's throat.

The man with the wicked smile and the blood-covered knife.

The woman in the upstairs loft…

And Eva.

Darius's eyes snapped open again. He moved to sit up in the car, but the motion made his nausea worse. He curled over onto his knees, holding his face in his hands as his body rocked back and forth in the movement of a vehicle he wasn't familiar with anymore. When was the last time he'd been in one? He couldn't even remember. He ran his hands through his shaggy hair. It was matted—Darius didn't want to think with what.

Then he opened his mouth to speak, and all that came out was a raspy cough.

"Here."

Chris's hand gently touched his, and he lifted his head to see a plastic water bottle just inches beyond his frame of view. She pressed it into his palms and unscrewed the cap. Darius poured a little between his lips and swallowed it down. His mouth and throat opened up and sucked in the moisture. He did it again and handed the bottle back to her.

When he tried to speak a second time, his voice broke through. It was so ragged and desperate, it hardly sounded like his own.

"Where's Eva?"

William's eyebrows raised, and he looked Darius over in the mirror. "The woman you carried out?"

Darius nodded before he dipped his head back into his palms. The water in his stomach swirled uncomfortably. Now that he had something to throw up, he wanted to make sure it stayed down.

"She's ahead of us, in another vehicle," Chris said. "We're getting her to a doctor."

Darius shook his head. "We don't have money," he said, and he cleared his throat. It didn't make his voice sound any more natural. "We can't pay a doctor."

"Hey," William said. "Don't worry about it. We've got this covered."

Darius would have felt grateful, but his chest was tight and heavy. He glanced up between the man and the woman again. Maybe he was just in shock, but the two of them seemed remarkably calm for having just seen what they'd left behind.

"So, what's your name?"

William peered at Darius in the rearview mirror again. He looked up, made contact with those kind, brown eyes, and said, "Darius."

The air in the cab grew dense. William glanced at Chris, and her bright eyes widened almost imperceptibly. Then, he turned fully around, not bothering with the mirror this time, and looked right into Darius's face. His expression seemed almost *happy*.

"Darius *Jones?*"

William drove them outside of the city, southbound, until the buildings were spread between miles and miles of empty land. At last, he pulled into a gas station. It was an isolated little building on a lonely stretch of highway. Its dark green roof made it almost blend into the trees around them, and if it wasn't for the lights in the windows, Darius wouldn't have noticed it at all. The parking lot moved around the station in a big U-shape, and the only way to drive a circle around the white building was to go through the carwash attached to the southern wall. William brought them around to the car wash entrance and swiped a card through the credit slot. It roared to life, and they drove into the curtain.

On the other side, though, there wasn't any water. Instead, the doors on either side of them closed and enveloped them in darkness. Then the floor rumbled and slowly slanted downward. William pulled them onto the ramp, and they began to descend into the ground.

Darius hardly had the sense of self to be surprised.

They seemed to drive downward forever. They slowly spiraled, deeper into the ground, until they reached a large, dimly lit parking lot. It would have been possible to park a hundred vehicles down here, but at the moment, there were only a couple dozen identical black SUVs and a handful of coupes. William pulled up to a small loading station beside a set of double doors.

As soon as they parked, the vehicle was swarmed. Men and women in green scrubs whipped out of the doors and opened the car. They pulled at Darius, gently and not-so-gently leading him from the vehicle and onto a wheelchair. One of them introduced herself to him, but he didn't know what to say, so he said nothing. They called codes at one another, speaking in a medical language Darius didn't understand, as they wheeled him into a triage room with a single bed. A few nurses carefully helped Darius up onto it.

"Can you undress?" an older woman asked. Her mouth was hidden behind a mask—her fingers, behind blue latex. Darius just stared at her. Her eyes were kind and tired. "If you can't undress, we're going to do it for you. We need to make sure you're okay."

All Darius could do was nod.

They moved like ghosts. Their faces were as pale as the sterile, white walls around them as they carefully peeled away layer after layer of dirt- and blood-soaked clothing to get to his skin. Darius helped by pulling his arms through sleeves or lifting his legs, but he felt distant. Disconnected. Inhuman. His clothing was thrown into a biohazard container. The bottle of antibiotics and his wallet, both blood-stained, were zipped inside a plastic bag. Darius watched them take the bag away and deposit it on a tray across the room with a numb awareness.

When they finally had him stripped down, they wiped him down with antiseptic rags to scrub away blood and dirt. Fingers and stethoscopes searched his body for injuries and measured his vitals. Satisfied that all he had was a cut on his arm, all the nurses left but one.

The young brunette woman took his arm and sanitized and stitched his wound. She spoke to him, and Darius realized she was the same one who had introduced herself earlier, but he couldn't remember what she'd said her name was. Something with an R? He just nodded, accepted her apology for "what had happened," and when she finished up, she gently led him to another room.

"You'll want to clean up," she said. She looked him up and down before adding. "The doctor will be out to see you as soon as he can."

It finally dawned on him to ask. He looked up, as though really seeing her for the first time. "Eva?"

The nurse smiled. Her pretty, brown eyes glistened with sympathy as she said, "She's in surgery now. Don't worry. Dr. Harris has seen worse than this. There are spare clothes in the cupboard."

Then she opened the door to a bathroom, coaxed him inside, and shut it behind him.

Darius turned on the light. A skinny, haunted-looking man with deep eyes and hollow cheeks stared at him from across the room. Darius jumped and opened his mouth to apologize for not knocking—

Then he realized it was a mirror, reflecting back at him from above the pedestal sink. His scrawny, nearly naked body was covered in a faint, swirling mix of cleaning solution and…

Blood.

It matted in his hair. Caked beneath his fingernails. Lined the tired creases in his forehead and under his eyes.

Nausea overwhelmed him. Darius lunged for the toilet and fell to his knees as he threw up a syrupy, hot mix of acids and water. It dribbled into the bowl, catching to the stubble across his chin and the dry cracks in his lip. The sound of his sickness echoed back at him like a laugh.

A shudder racked his body as disgust overwhelmed the nausea. He *needed* to get clean. Darius tore what remained of his filthy clothing off and threw it into a mangled and bloody pile in the corner of the room. He turned on the shower and stepped into the stream before it turned warm.

Then he slumped back against the cold, tiled wall. Darius wound his arms tight around his knees and watched the water carry filth and blood off his skin and down the drain. It swirled around, a blur of pink and tan at his feet. Darius sat, numb to the water's pounding against his head and shoulders. As he watched the colors gather in sharp contrast against the clean, white tile, the images returned.

The children and Thad.

The man with the knife. The man from the market.

Bodies, crunching beneath Darius's feet as he stumbled down the stairs…

Darius's chest constricted tight around his lungs. His heart. The aching, pitted *loss* nestled deep within his very soul. He couldn't breathe. Everything came crashing down around him, and the numbness melted off like hot wax, exposing him, making him feel raw and cut open.

Everyone he had worked for, everything he had built, was gone, swirling down the drain in a slurry of blood and dirt.

Shivering, naked, and alone, Darius cried.

"Here. Take this."

Something warm was forced into Darius's cold hands. He looked down into a ceramic mug. Steam wafted up from some golden-colored liquid. It brushed against his face in a way that should have been welcoming, comforting, but Darius didn't feel anything. The scent of sweetened tea did little to take the edge off the bitter stink of blood caked inside his nostrils. No matter how hard he'd tried, he couldn't get clean enough.

He was in some kind of waiting room. It was large and empty, which somehow made Darius feel tiny and alone. After he'd recomposed himself and dressed in the gray sweats and plain t-shirt the hospital had provided, he'd been led here and told to wait for the doctor. When the nurse dropped him off, a man had been waiting for him with the mug in his hands.

Now Darius simply stared into it. His shadow reflected

in the liquid and stared up at him with dark circles where his eyes should have been. The air here felt thick and confining. It crowded in around Darius, steeped in so much tension and anxiety that he couldn't help but breathe it in like noxious fumes until he felt hazy and disconnected.

"My name is Abraham Locke."

The man's voice stirred Darius's attention upward. His hands had stopped shaking quite as badly. The warmth from the tea flowed up his arms. The white walls of the room seemed to close around him even more. Abraham sat in the chair cornered beside Darius's, leaning forward with his hands clasped between his knees. He was different from the people who had shown up at his orphanage. Abraham's curly hair was neatly styled. The sleeves of his casual, button-up shirt were rolled to the middle of his forearm. He reminded Darius briefly of the school therapist he'd been sent to see after his mother had died. Clean cut. Put together. Well-intentioned, but unprepared. How could you be prepared to talk someone through something like this?

It seemed he was determined to try. "Are you okay?" Abraham asked.

Darius's mind chewed on the question.

Are you okay?

Images from the bar darted through his brain. They made his stomach bubble, his chest broil, and he tried to blink them away.

"No."

It was all he said. It was all he *had* to say. His voice was hoarse, and his throat burned. It was still sore from his crying, from vomiting.

Abraham nodded, and silence fell again; the kind of silence that said so much more than words ever could, but there was one thing it did *not* say:

"Everything is going to be all right."

Darius's world had crumbled around him. It took all his self-control to keep from crumbling with it.

"Where am I?" Darius looked around and cleared his

throat, trying to loosen the rasp and sound like a human being again.

"Somewhere safe," Abraham said.

Darius glanced at him again. The look on Abraham's face made it very clear just how aware he was of his non-answer. Darius opened his mouth, about to speak, but Abraham went on.

"I can't answer all your questions," he quickly interjected. "And I know you probably have a lot of them."

That was an understatement if Darius had ever heard one.

"But you'll see someone who can, okay? Soon."

"How soon?"

"As soon as we speak with Dr. Harris," Abraham said. "Unless you'd rather wait to hear about your friend—"

"Eva," Darius said. The word came out more aggressively than he'd anticipated. "Her name is Eva."

"Yes, of course. Eva—"

"Don't talk about her like she's just another *patient* who doesn't matter," Darius pressed on. The words stumbled out of his mouth, throaty and harsh.

"You're right," Abraham interjected, and he raised his hands awkwardly. "I'm sorry. I know you've been through a lot today, but I am *not* your enemy, Darius. I'm here to *help* you, and Eva."

Darius said nothing. He leaned back in the chair and placed the tea, still untouched, on the single corner table beside him. Silence spread until the room was cloaked in an awkward, tense quiet. This place carried no background sound—no people laughing or feet shuffling. Just the senselessness of stagnant air.

For the next several minutes, they waited. Abraham awkwardly fiddled with the sleeves of his shirt, but Darius hardly paid any attention to him. He was desperate to focus on anything other than the motionless doors to his left and how Eva may be dying, just on the other side of them—

The door to the hospital swung open. Darius's heart

leapt into his throat. With it came all the anxiety and fear he'd been choking down, and suddenly he couldn't breathe. A man walked into the room. The doctor. He was wearing green scrubs and a white lab coat. In his hands, he carried a clipboard.

Dr. Harris looked around the room, his firm gray eyes falling on Abraham first and, at last, Darius.

Darius jumped to his feet. The world felt like it was moving in slow motion. He could hear the blood pounding behind his ears in rapid, erratic pumps. The sound was so overwhelming, he nearly missed the doctor's next words.

"Mr. Jones, my name is Dr. Elijah Harris." He held out his hand, and Darius took it almost too eagerly. His hands were shaking so badly he could hardly present a strong grip. Despite that, Dr. Harris's fingers were firm, secure, and comforting. "Eva was very lucky," the doctor continued. "The wounds in her stomach lacerated several of her internal organs, but we were able to put her back together. They also carved a word into her stomach. It's going to leave some ugly scarring, but she should make a full recovery. I want her to get plenty of rest, and she'll stay here for observation for at least a week. Tonight, she needs to sleep, but you can see her in the morning."

Before he realized it, Darius was sitting on the chair again. His legs had fallen weak beneath him, overcome by relief and exhaustion. He dropped down and put his face into his shaky hands. Tears stung at the corners of his eyes, but he brushed them away. A tight, heavy breath, trapped between his ribs for the last few minutes, freed itself with a grateful, almost desperate laugh.

Eva was alive.

But something was off. Something about what the doctor had said…

"Did you say they *carved* something into her?" Darius asked, and he glanced up, over his fingers, at the doctor again.

Dr. Harris's spine stiffened. Disgust curled the corner of

his lip. "Yes. The word 'bitch.'"

Darius's chest flared. His bright, green eyes darkened as he dropped his hands into his lap. "They cut that into her *stomach?*"

Dr. Harris just nodded.

And the world around him fully collapsed. Darius had lived on the streets from the time he was eleven. He'd spent eight years on the Bridge Street Market. He'd seen some horrible things, met some horrible people, in his twenty-seven years of life, but nothing had prepared him for this.

He choked back furious tears as he said, "What kind of person does this?"

"Monsters," Abraham said. He and Dr. Harris exchanged a dark look. "But she's lucky."

Darius shook his head and cleared his throat to try to keep from breaking down again. *"How?"*

"She is alive," the doctor said.

Darius's stomach flipped. He covered his mouth with his fist and bit back the new wave of nausea. After he regained composure, Darius stood up and squared his shoulders.

"Okay," he said. "I want some answers."

Abraham gave him an awkward, sad smile. "Of course. Mr. Blaine is expecting you."

The walk to Mr. Blaine's office was quick—much quicker than Darius had assumed after seeing the size of the parking lot. This structure, whatever and wherever it was, must have extended out further, or maybe even deeper, into the ground.

Abraham led Darius from the waiting room down another long hallway, passing a handful of solid oak doors labeled with words like "Tactical" and "Conference Room A." The absence of sound followed Darius as Abraham brought him toward this "Mr. Blaine." Darius's life had been filled with color, sound, and smells so vibrant and exciting that now, enveloped in a distinct lack thereof, Darius didn't know what to make of it. The floors here were covered with off-white tiles. The beige walls reminded Darius of those he saw through office windows when he and his father first began living on the streets.

Abraham said very little as they walked. Darius couldn't stand the silence, so he broke it. "Who is Mr. Blaine?"

"He's the man in charge," Abraham said.

"In charge of what?"

"He'll explain."

Darius sighed.

The two of them went around a corner to a much shorter hallway with five doors. Four of them were labeled with names, only one of which Darius recognized. "Locke." He glanced at Abraham. Was this where he slept? It couldn't be. The fifth door was the only one without a name plaque, and it sat at the end of the hallway. Abraham opened it.

They walked through to another waiting room. This one was far more comfortable than the desolate place outside the hospital. Here, the floor was covered in a rich, creamy carpet. There was a couch across from them and two doors on either side. The left one had the name "Rose," and the right, "Blaine." That was the one they approached.

And it occurred to Darius… This was crazy. He didn't know where he was or who these people were. Everything felt just a little *weird*. Corporate, affluent, organized… but also dark and secretive.

Abraham reached out to knock, but Darius grabbed his wrist. He frowned as he looked up at the embossed name on the door.

"Wait," he said. "How do I know I can trust you?"

Abraham glanced over his shoulder and looked Darius over. "You don't," he said after an uncomfortable pause.

That was the most straightforward thing Abraham had said to him. Darius released his wrist and took a deep breath. "Looks like I don't really have much of a choice right now anyway," he murmured.

"You've always got a choice," Abraham said, and Darius turned to him. "If you want, I can take you back—"

"No," Darius said. "I need to know what the *hell* happened today."

Abraham passed him a kind, sad smile, though he seemed torn, as though he didn't know what to say. "I'm sorry. You've stumbled into something pretty messy."

"What's that?" Darius asked.

"The world's gone to hell, and it's only getting worse…"

Then, Abraham knocked.

CHAPTER FIVE

"Mr. Jones. Please come in."

Mr. Blaine towered in the doorway. The man was slender and fit, at least four inches taller than Darius, and his flawless porcelain skin made Darius feel filthy, despite his recent shower. He was cloaked in a long, black trench coat, which only made him seem taller. Beneath it were pressed slacks and a rich, red button-up. Darius stared up at him as Abraham quietly excused himself and exited into the hallway. Mr. Blaine gave a small, polite nod and gestured his long arm into the room in a powerful sweep.

Unlike the rest of the building, Mr. Blaine's office was fitted with plush red carpeting and tawny-painted walls. A large mahogany desk sat before a wall of bookshelves and glass display cases so tightly packed with volumes and artifacts Darius could barely see where one ended and another began.

A massive, wolf-like dog sat to the side of the desk. It was so large that Mr. Blaine didn't even need to bend as he gently touched its forehead and moved around to his chair. Instead of following its master's movements, the dog looked straight at Darius. Its eyes were bright blue, striking against its rich, dark fur, and they glistened with intellect.

Darius looked away. Then the dog laid down and curled into a tight ball. The tip of its tail rested just below its shining black nose.

"Don't mind Rae," Mr. Blaine said as he removed his coat and draped it on the back of his chair. The dog closed its eyes. "Have a seat."

It was offered almost like a suggestion, but Darius knew better. Mr. Blaine's voice commanded a power that seemed as natural as it was compelling. Darius took one of the two cushioned chairs in front of him.

Mr. Blaine did not sit down. He moved like a shadow behind the desk, silently searching the bookshelves for specific items, which he pulled down and tucked beneath his arm. His sharp face was almost hidden from Darius's view by a curtain of pin-straight black hair that fell just barely to the top of his shoulders. Darius bounced his legs and cracked his knuckles—impatient, anxious—until finally, Mr. Blaine turned around, set a small stack of albums on the desk in front of him, and took a seat. He put a pair of reading glasses onto his long nose, picked up a report from a stack of papers to his left, and stroked his rich, black goatee as he read it quietly.

At last, he looked at Darius, really, truly looked at him, for the first time. His eyes were striking. They were deep black, half-empty. When he finally put the report back on the table and removed his glasses, it was as though those eyes could see into his very soul.

"It's unfortunate we're meeting under such circumstances," he said. "My name is Alan Blaine. I'm in charge of this organization. I'm sorry for all you have had to endure today, Mr. Jones."

Darius murmured an incoherent thank you, which he followed with words mumbled so quickly and awkwardly he didn't know if they'd made any sense at all. "Did… did anyone else…?"

He couldn't even finish the statement. He didn't have to. Alan Blaine just shook his head. "You and Miss Torres were the only survivors," he said. "My team is recovering the remains of your loved ones to provide them a more proper resting place. Do you have any ceremonies or customs you would like us to follow in regard to burial?"

Burial? The word was almost meaningless to Darius. He'd never had the *means* to bury the dead before. The best he could do was wrap them gently in blankets and leave them somewhere the proper authorities would find them. He shook his head—said nothing.

Alan seemed to understand. "If you would like," he went on. "We can arrange a time for you and Miss Torres to say your goodbyes."

Darius nodded. A surge of emotion painfully cramped the muscles along his neck and down into his chest. Tears swelled behind his eyelids. He blinked them furiously away, tilted his head back to stare, aimlessly, at the ceiling. The room was moving slowly. Everything felt dull and numb.

"I don't understand why this happened," he finally said.

"It is difficult to understand tragedies like this."

It sure as hell was. But there were other things Darius could understand—or try to understand—like what was happening *now*.

"You said you're in command of this—this place?" Darius went on, clearing his throat and looking back down at Alan's deep, dark eyes. Alan nodded quietly. "What is it? I thought we were coming to a hospital, but it sure as hell doesn't feel like any hospital I've ever seen."

"It's not a hospital," Alan said. "We are in a hidden safe house."

"A safe house?"

"Yes. Welcome to the Martyrs," Alan said calmly and plainly. "We are an organization dedicated to combating the evil of this world—specifically, the evil that descended upon you and your home this evening." A flame of rage lit itself in Darius's stomach. "The people you met today are very dangerous. We're trying to… neutralize the threat."

"Neutralize it?" Darius said bitterly, "Well, you're doing

a pretty shitty job."

Alan gave a conceding nod. If Darius was in a better mood, he might have been impressed with Alan's composure. "It's a challenging fight," Alan said evenly.

"Why did they come for us?" Darius asked. He was getting angrier, and he took a breath to even himself. "We don't have *anything.*"

That was truer now than it ever had been before.

"I'm afraid," Alan said with a sigh. "They found you *because* of us. We made a mistake, and that mistake, directly or indirectly, led our enemy right to your doorstep."

"What?" Darius frowned. "How?"

"Cyrus Murphy."

Darius's heart dropped. The boy he'd taken off the streets six years ago—though Cyrus wasn't a boy anymore. He was a young man, and the first of the kids Darius had taken in who had been able to get out of their miserable situation. A couple of months ago, Cyrus had been working at a convenience store when he'd been killed in a robbery.

Or, at least, that's what Darius had believed.

"What does Cyrus have to do with this?" Darius asked. A hard, painful lump lodged itself in the base of his throat. He swallowed, but the lump stubbornly stuck.

"Cyrus was wounded in a conflict involving my men," Alan said. "We couldn't leave him there to die, so my people took him, and Dr. Harris tended to his wounds. He made a full recovery, and he was eager to leave. His work with you was very important to him."

Alan attempted to smile, maybe as a way to pay Darius a compliment, but it didn't help. It felt as though Darius's tongue had glued itself to the top of his mouth, and he could only watch and listen as Alan went on.

"We returned him to the city," Alan said. "He would not tell us anywhere specific to drop him off. He was very concerned with the privacy and safety of his home. So, we returned him to the store he had been at when the incident occurred, and he disappeared. But, I'm afraid, our enemies tracked him down before he made his way to you. They recognized him from the conflict and assumed he was with us. We tried to get him back, but it was no use. They forced him to tell them where he lived. They believed he'd lead them here, to the Underground—" Alan gestured around them. "But instead… they found you."

Darius's eyes had filled with tears again. He hadn't even realized it. He tilted his head back a second time, but now, he let them fall silently down his cheeks.

Alan continued. "Our mistake," he said, "was letting Cyrus go unguarded—maybe letting him go at all. Our enemies are ruthless. Merciless. If I had been more careful, if I had insisted Cyrus stay, maybe this whole thing could have been avoided."

Darius said nothing for a while longer. He didn't know what to say. He just continued to stare straight up at the ceiling.

"So this is your fault?" Darius whispered, but he didn't feel any angrier than he already had. Instead, he felt numb.

"I do take responsibility," Alan said quietly. "And I am working to rectify it—in whatever way I can."

Was that even possible?

Darius cleared his throat. "So those people I saw—the ones in the armor?" he asked, and he looked down at Alan again. "They were your people? Not police?"

Alan nodded.

"And they got them?" Darius went on. "They got the bastards who did this?"

The look in Alan's eyes was betraying. Darius's stomach dropped uncomfortably before Alan even said the word. "No."

Darius was dumbstruck. "You didn't get them?" The words came out in almost a whisper, followed by a roar. *"There were over a dozen of your guys there!"* Darius got to his feet and ran his hands through his hair. He pulled so hard it hurt. "And two of them—*just two!* How the hell did you *not* get them?"

"It's not that easy—"

"How isn't it easy? They were outnumbered!"

"You must understand, Mr. Jones, how incredibly difficult it is for my team to take these people down," Alan said. Now his calm demeanor was beginning to irritate Darius even further. "I dispatched six of my Tactical Units to surround and overtake your premises tonight. Twelve people. They were armed with automatic weapons and were given orders to fire at will, to protect you and any other survivors with whatever means necessary. They hardly made a *scratch.* Both perpetrators were able to escape, despite our best efforts, and now four of my men are sitting injured in my hospital while another three are *dead*—just from taking on *two people.* This is the closest we've come to taking one of them out in *years,* and it was still not good enough. We have *failed* here, and trust me, we do not take it lightly."

Darius's anger hedged him dangerously close to nausea again. He grabbed the back of the chair and dipped his head down to stop the room from spinning and the stinging bile bubbling up his windpipe from reaching his mouth.

"I don't understand how this can *happen,*" Darius growled at last.

Alan Blaine hadn't moved at all. His hands still lay clasped calmly on the desk in front of him, and he watched Darius until he finally looked up again. Then he said, "Mr. Jones, I could tell you everything, and if that is what you want, I certainly will, but I must warn you: the more you know about what's going on here, the more difficult it will be for you to get out of it." He paused and watched Darius intently. "Is that what you want?"

Darius just stared at him, confused, furious, and broken. He didn't know what he wanted anymore—everything he had, everything he was, had been destroyed. All he knew was he wanted to get back at the people who did this, no matter what it took.

"Tell me," he said at last.

Alan gave a short, polite nod and said, "We're at war.

The enemy we are fighting is not like any enemy you may have seen before. You asked me why it isn't easy for us to 'get' them. The answer is, because even if we wanted to kill them, we couldn't."

It was as though a hand had reached into Darius's chest and trapped his breath there, crushed between two tired lungs. "Why not? Is this some strict, moral code?"

"Nothing so easily broken, I'm afraid," Alan said. "The man and woman who came into your home today are not ordinary people. They are not like you or your family. They are Sins."

The word played around in Darius's head. He stood up straighter. "Sins?"

"The Sins run this city," Alan continued, as though that answered Darius's question. "They control everything: the media, the police force, even the government. They have desecrated our world and are demolishing our society. They aim to corrupt mankind so thoroughly that they become invincible. Today, they went into your home and murdered your family, and in doing so, they've brought you into my world. In my world, Mr. Jones, it's much larger than the loss of *human lives*. It's the loss of humanity itself."

But hardly any of that had stuck. Darius rubbed his eyes and took a deep breath through his nose. *"Sins?"* he said again. "I don't understand. Is that the name of some underground crime group or something?"

Alan gestured to the chair again. "Please, sit."

Darius, begrudgingly, did.

"You probably imagine I mean 'Sins' in the same way people use the term 'monsters,'" Alan began. "As a way to describe human beings who commit horrifying crimes. Or, maybe, you think of it more like what you've just said—an organization of ordinary people trying to do extraordinary things. That is not the case. As I said, the Sins are not ordinary people."

"But they *were* people," Darius said. "I saw them."

"I did not say they were not people. I said they were not

ordinary."

Before Darius had the chance to object again, Alan put his reading glasses back on and selected the top book from the stack of volumes he'd pulled down earlier. This was the oldest book he'd collected, bound in cracked leather and speckled with gray dust.

"The Sins are their Christian titles, more commonly heard of as the 'Seven *Deadly* Sins.' Of all the names they've been called over the centuries, that's the one that stuck. This is likely because Christianity became a pervasive, systemic religion around the majority of the world. It spread like the plague…"

He leafed through the volume slowly, carefully, as he spoke. The pages were stiff from age and creaked like worn wood when Alan turned them. "At one time, there were more than seven. Several more. We don't know how many of them originally existed. Throughout history, many were destroyed, and the ones that survived grew into the noxious personalities we know today."

Alan tenderly opened the book and turned it around on the desk toward Darius. There was an image on the page—an archaic woodblock print depicting a scene of naked men and women being tortured in the fires of hell by strange, goat-like creatures. Each creature had a word printed on its chest: *Superbia, Acedia, Gula, Luxury, Avaritia, Invidia,* and *Ira.*

"This edition comes from the writings of Pope Gregory. He translated these from a monk who had written them two centuries prior." Alan flipped the page. The names were listed and described in a language Darius could not read.

"It's Latin," Alan explained. "You may recognize the English titles." He placed a long, slender finger on the first name, *Superbia*, and translated down the list. "Pride, Sloth, Gluttony, Lust, Greed, Envy, and Wrath."

Alan turned back to the previous page. The image stared up at Darius like a looming golem. The cold, lifeless eyes of *Invidia*—of Envy—watched him from the parchment.

"These Sins are not a work of fiction. They're not just

stories medieval Christians told their children to keep them in line. They are very real, and you met two of them today."

For several long seconds, Darius grappled with the concept in his grief-fogged brain. Sins—little goblins—running to and fro in the gutters of New York City. Demons, with horns and wings and sinister smiles, flying through the buildings. But they weren't demons. They were people. He examined the picture, and finally, he shook his head.

"This has to be a joke?"

For the first time, Alan's expression faltered. A flash of anger, pure and full, crossed his face. The dog by the side of his desk growled, and Darius jumped. He'd forgotten she was there, and now both she and Alan were watching Darius with the same unfiltered expression. Alan's sharp, soul-piercing eyes drove into his like a dagger. Suddenly, Darius became afraid, as though this man was capable of things he couldn't even imagine.

But as quickly as it appeared, it faded. Alan's face softened, and the wolf-dog laid her head back on her paws. Alan simply said, "I do not joke about the slaughter of children."

"I'm sorry," Darius said, and he meant it. He covered his face with his hands and fell back into the chair. "But… this? These things—" he gestured roughly to the book on the desk. "That's not what I saw today."

"No," Alan said. He gently closed the book and put it to the side. Now, he pulled out a file folder from a drawer in his desk. He opened it, pulled two sheets from it, and placed them on the table. "You saw *these* people."

Darius's heart jumped to his throat, and he quickly swiped the pages up. His hands shook as he stared down at the cold, steely eyes of the man from the market. Derek Dane, the sheet said. Darius's nostrils flared.

"That is Pride," Alan said. "And the woman, Envy. They were the two Sins at your home today."

Darius glanced at the other page, too. Cassandra Smith, the plain, mousy woman who had single-handedly lifted him from the ground by his neck and thrown him through a second-story window.

He reached for his throat and swallowed a lump that had grown there. The places where her fingers had pressed into his flesh were tender to the touch.

"They are only two of the seven." Alan reached across the desk and handed Darius the rest of the file. He flipped through the pages and looked into the faces of people he would have never taken as anything but normal men and women. And here, the man behind the desk was asking him to believe they weren't.

To believe, instead, they were Sins.

"Okay," Darius said, and he closed his eyes and pinched the bridge of his nose. "Then explain it to me—explain everything—because Sin or not, I still don't see any damned reason these two can't be dead."

"Killing these bodies would be a temporary solution, and while it provides us a slight reprieve from the constant fighting, it's not enough to solve the problem at large," Alan answered. "The Sins themselves are not actually human. They are simply energy—or spirits, if that fits better with your personal belief system. However you want to look at it, the Sins are an ethereal essence that relies upon corporeal hosts in order to take form and exercise their power in this world. This is how the term—and likely even the general myth of—possession came into being. For lack of a better term, a Sin's *'energy'* possesses a host.

"The bodies they take over then undergo some kind of change on the molecular level. To be completely honest with you, we're not exactly sure how this change even occurs. We've had doctors and scientists looking for an explanation for years. Once a Sin overtakes a human being, the host body no longer ages, and it heals from wounds extraordinarily quickly. Additionally, they become stronger and faster than an average human being, and they gain the ability to Influence people by simply being in the same room as them. All we can imagine is this Sin energy is an infinite resource, which provides host bodies with an excess of tools the rest of us simply don't have."

Darius shook his head. "This can't be real."

"Oh, I assure you," Alan said. "It is very real. Let me show you."

Then Alan turned to his computer and brought the monitor to life. Bright light flashed up against his face, casting his sharp, angular features in deep shadows. He clicked around a few times before swiveling the monitor around to face Darius.

"This is a video taken by a Martyr doctor decades ago," Alan said. "He was conducting experiments on the Sins, trying to identify how their healing properties worked."

He then pressed play, and the video came to life.

"My name is Dr. Simon Reed," the man in the video said. He was young, his smile wide and eyes bright and eager. The quality of the footage was grainy, and the sound of Simon's voice was noisy and rough, but Darius could still hear the excitement in his words. "The date is February 6, 2018, and today, we're looking at the Sin's healing factor."

The video hard cut to a new scene where Simon was standing in front of a hospital table. Behind him was the bare back of a slender man with short, dark hair and a strange, black tattoo at the base of his neck. Darius frowned. Had he seen that tattoo before? Simon took a scalpel to the subject's right shoulder blade.

"As you can see here," he said as he poked the point of the blade into the man's flesh and drew it down to create a shallow, three-inch gash. The man on the table didn't even flinch. "The Sin's healing factor is approximately three hundred times faster than the standard human rate of regeneration." He took a white cloth and blotted the blood away, and Darius watched in awe as the skin began to stitch itself back together. He leaned in closer toward the screen and squinted. Simon plunged the scalpel back into his subject's back and created a brand new cut as the first sealed itself and faded into nothing. "The cells in the Sin's body seem to react independently *of* the body. When they're agitated, the cellular repair rate multiplies by several hundred—"

Alan shut off the video and turned his monitor back around. Darius sat quietly for a moment. He looked down at the file folder in his hand and stared darkly at Derek Dane's cold, smug face.

What the hell had he just watched?

Darius carefully put the file back on Alan's desk. He clasped his hands and rested his lips against his thumbs. "I can't believe it," he murmured against his fingertips. "Who was that? That he was cutting?"

"Wrath," Alan said after a brief pause.

"Did they kill *him?"*

Alan shook his head. "No."

"Do you still *have* him?"

"He managed to free himself."

Darius nodded absently, but he wasn't really paying attention anymore. He stared at the face looking up at him from Alan's desk. Derek Dane. The man—no, the *Sin?*—who had destroyed everything Darius had worked for in the last decade. "If you can hurt him," Darius said quietly, and he moved one of his hands to point right at Dane's smug, hateful face. "Then you can kill him. There has to be a way."

Only a few days ago, Darius would have been surprised at himself. He'd never wanted anyone dead before—not even the men responsible for shooting Cyrus or the drunkard who had swerved onto the sidewalk and mowed his mother down. He'd wanted justice, maybe karma, if he'd believed in such a thing. But this… this was different.

A dozen children were dead.

Eva had the word "bitch" carved into her stomach.

Darius's gut twisted. He wasn't sure if he was more uncomfortable with the idea of Eva's disfigurement or his own.

"It *is* possible to kill the body," Alan said. "The host. Difficult, yes, but possible. You must damage the body beyond the point where the accelerated healing can prevent death. But killing Derek Dane will not destroy the Sin. All it will do is release the energy back into the world to possess again."

"So kill that," Darius said simply. "You can do that, can't you? Kill the… the energy, or whatever."

Alan sighed. "Unfortunately, we do not know how."

Darius groaned and threw his hands up in the air. "How can you *not* know how? Aren't you trying to tell me that's the whole point of this place? Of—of these Martyrs?

"It *is*, however—"

"And you said there used to be more than seven and that many had been destroyed already! How can you *not know how* if it's already been done?"

Alan held up his hands. "Let me speak." He hadn't raised his voice, but all the same, it reverberated around the room in a way that demanded silence. Darius was caught off guard. The dog beside Alan's desk twitched her ears but otherwise remained motionless.

When the tension had faded a bit, Alan spoke.

"We have evidence of the existence of many Sins thanks to the Influence they had upon ancient cultures and mythologies for centuries, well before they made an appearance in Christian lore." Alan pulled a book down from his stack again. This one read "Anthology of World Religion" on the spine. "We have reason to believe many ancient religions revered the Sins as gods, especially within Egyptian and Greek cultures. This explains the more human-like characteristics of their deities. The majority of ancient polytheistic faiths were likely led by several Sins posing as gods to gain power and exert their will on others. The stories of people coming into contact with a god? They were based in truth—though the god they believed they were meeting was, in fact, one of these malevolent energies. How familiar are you with Greek mythology?"

Darius just blinked. What the hell kind of question was that? "I had to drop out of school when I was twelve."

"Ah," Alan said, and he nodded. "Then let me show you what I mean." He opened the book and flipped to a page about Greek gods and goddesses. There were dozens of names written down. Beside many of them were hand-jotted notes. The word "Lust" was beside a picture of Zeus. The other seven were there, too, but there were more than seven gods. Many more. Every single ancient deity had notes written beside it, encapsulating other negative traits unique to humanity.

"We have the Sins we are familiar with here," Alan said, pointing to Zeus, Hera, Dionysius, and a few other names on the list. "But then, these others? We believe many of them were Sins who have since been destroyed."

"Yeah, but *how?*" Darius asked. "Knowing there *were* more doesn't help you figure out how to get rid of them."

"No," Alan agreed. "But it means someone, at some point, did."

"Then what happened to that information?"

Alan closed the book. "The Sins spent centuries trying to decimate that knowledge. These other books here?" Alan gestured beside him. "They are filled with all the wars and conflicts mankind has waged since the dawn of history. From the Battle of Kadesh in ancient Egypt over three thousand years ago to the Corinthian War, from the Roman conquest of Britain to even as recent as the World Wars of the twentieth century. The Sins were likely at the heart of many of these conflicts—not only in their attempt to keep humanity filled with hate and loathing of one another, but to also destroy those who knew who they were and how to stop them.

"However, we believe the knowledge was truly lost around the time Pope Gregory was translating the monk's writings, when the final seven Sins we have today were all that remained. At this time, Europe was falling into the Dark Ages," Alan said. "Many great texts and technologies were lost in the wars and plagues that ripped through the continent. The last remaining scholars seem to indicate the

Sins were in Europe at this time, and most of those scholars were killed. The knowledge to destroy the Sins was lost."

If Darius had been grasping at hope, it disappeared. The empty feeling in the pit of his stomach swelled, and his anger returned. He wanted to lash out and break something—maybe one of the many cases with ancient artifacts behind Alan Blaine's desk.

"So, we're screwed? These guys—" Darius whipped a hand at the open folder showing Derek Dane's face again "—they just get to kill my family and get away with it?"

Alan shook his head.

"No. I do not believe they will."

"No? What can you do if all knowledge on how to destroy these things was lost?"

Alan raised a finger. "Ah, I did not say *all* knowledge on how to destroy them was lost. The exact methodology, yes, but not the tools."

Darius raised an eyebrow. "What, like a weapon?"

Alan wrinkled his nose a little at the phrase and shrugged. "Not exactly. I think of weapons as manmade, and nothing mankind has ever constructed in our entire history can destroy the essence of a Sin. No, I suppose a better word would have been 'keys.' We know what they are, even if we don't know who."

"Who?"

"Yes," Alan said. "The keys to destroying the Sins are human beings. Again, going back to the names Pope Gregory gave to them, the Virtues are humanity's response to the Sin's evil energy. They've shown up across ancient texts, as well. We believe many human heroes, such as Gilgamesh and Odysseus, may have actually been Virtues."

"So," Darius said. He was having a hard time following. "They're like 'good' Sins?"

Alan shook his head. "Yes and no. Virtues are human energy, born and reincarnated over and over again until their Sin is destroyed. Again, this is likely where the very myth of reincarnation even originated. Like the Sins, we don't know how or when they came into our timeline. For all we know, the Sins and Virtues have coexisted in our world since the dawn of time. What we *do* know is the Virtues are a force equal in power to the Sins, and they have some ability to obliterate the true energy of a Sin. However, tracking Virtues down is… difficult."

"Why?" Darius asked. "Wouldn't they be trying to find the Sins, too?"

"Unfortunately," Alan said, "the Virtues are not born *knowing* they are Virtues, which makes them just as much of a challenge to find as the Sins are. There is also no way to guarantee they even *want* to help if we do manage to track one down. I am not a god. I cannot force someone to fight for me and my cause."

"And you don't have any?" Darius asked. "You can't find them?"

Alan watched him for a moment, steepled his fingers, and pressed his lips against them. "We have not found a new Virtue in decades," he said at last.

"So that's it?" Darius said. "You can't kill these bastards until we track down these hidden Virtues and convince them to do it for us?"

"That's a very rough summary, but yes."

Darius heaved a sigh and rubbed his eyes. They burned behind his lids, tired from exhaustion and raw from crying. It seemed more and more unlikely Darius would ever—could ever—see justice brought against the people who tore his life to shreds.

Alan went on. "It's important to not lose faith," he said. "The Virtues are a very potent force—much more potent than the Sins, which is probably the only thing that has saved our species so far. We will find more, in time. They always seem to creep up again. At one point, there was even an Order dedicated to the discovery and Initiation of the Virtues, but the Sins destroyed them during the Spanish Inquisition. Their teachings were considered witchcraft by the church, and they, along with the Virtues they were working with, were destroyed."

"Let me guess," Darius grumbled. "The Sins were behind that, too?"

"What better way to corrupt the masses than to convince them you are doing good work in the name of a god? You would be shocked at how many leading world religions were heavily driven and Influenced by the Sins. For centuries, that alone was enough to keep the majority of people from thinking for themselves, and it has cost us dearly.

"Regardless." Alan flicked his wrist. "The Virtues are our only hope in destroying the Sins, or else they will continue to move throughout our world and destroy us, bit by bit, robbing from us our empathy and our grace, until we are nothing but corrupted shells to fuel their hatred. Our goal is to neutralize the threat by destabilizing the Sins' hold on humanity." He then let silence fill the space between them for a moment. "Welcome to our war, Mr. Jones."

All Darius could do was stare. This was crazy. He knew it was. Every logical part of him told him this was all too insane to be real, that he should run away as quickly as he could and get as far away from Alan Blaine and the Martyrs as possible. Every part of him that everyone else in the world would have listened to told him to leave this place behind him and these memories as a dark part in his history.

But he couldn't argue with the evidence sitting right in front of him:

A woman who was strong enough to lift him single-handedly into the air and throw him out a window.

A video showing footage of a man healing so incredibly quickly he'd be almost impossible to kill.

A room full of dead children.

Darius groaned and put his face into his hands. "I'm gonna need some time to process this," he said.

"Of course," Alan Blaine said in the same calm and unreadable tone he'd said almost everything else, and Darius looked up to him. He'd always relied on his ability to read people, but Alan Blaine was an enigma. Darius couldn't read him at all, and that unsettled him almost as much as his story of the Sins did.

Believing what he had to say was one thing, but trusting him was another, and Darius wasn't sure he did.

She sat on the doorstep to the bar—the orphanage? Whatever it had once been—and she took a slow drag on her cigarette. Her long, pale fingers were stained in blood. The whole place reeked of it. The metallic stink clouded her even from out here.

The Cleaning Crew had cleared out hours ago, dragging with them duffle bags filled with the bodies of dead children and decades of nightmares. The faces of the men and women who had picked up the mess inside had looked just as white and lifeless as those of the kids they'd had to carry out. They'd seen some horrible shit, but this had to be at the top of the list. It made her blood boil.

Not much pulled at her trigger more than the deaths of children—nothing much, except maybe fucking up as badly as they had today.

This was the first major conflict they'd had with the Sins in years, and it showed. They'd been outsmarted. The Sins had gotten here hours before they'd even tracked the place down. By the time she'd gotten there, nearly everyone was dead. What a waste of human life.

And when backup rushed in behind her, hoping to slow down Envy and Pride so the others could get the survivors out, the Sins had shredded through them like paper dolls. Even full of bullets, they'd managed to take out a bunch of her people as they fought their way out of this slaughter-house. Killing just one of them would have made a huge difference for the Martyrs. Now, instead, the Martyrs were down another seven people—three of them permanently.

She pulled her long, black hair over one shoulder as she shook her head and flicked the ashes from her cigarette down onto the steps beneath her feet. Long after her crew had gone, she stayed behind. She said it was to keep an eye on this place in case the Sins tried to come back, but really, she needed to be alone with her thoughts and with the monstrous anger welling up inside her gut. It thrashed against her ribcage like a living, breathing creature.

She needed to cool the fuck down before she went back to the Underground. The last thing she needed to do was punch someone else today—somebody who didn't deserve it. She glanced down at her swollen, red-stained knuckles.

It *had* felt good, though.

The late sun was setting beyond the silhouette of the city. Tall, black shadows were fringed in red and purple, like even the skyline was bruised and beaten. She took another long drag on her cigarette. The smoke burned all the way down, against the sides of her throat and deep into her lungs. She held it, closed her eyes, and sighed. The nicotine sedated the beast, calmed her down, if only for a moment.

That man's face stuck out in her mind. Dirty. Scared. Determined. That last one was what got her. He could have let himself fall apart. He could have given up.

But he didn't. Instead, he got himself thrown out of a god damned window. All her hard work, wasted.

The thought just made her angry again. She swore, sucked her cigarette down to a pillar of red-hot ash, and lit another.

They'd spent weeks tracking him down—stressful, anxious weeks as they tried to stay ahead of the Sins, and in *minutes* he'd thrown it all away.

All the same, he had guts, and she liked that. At least, she'd like it if he managed to live through this.

The last hints of warm light faded into the cold, heartless dark of night as she sat there. Her rage boiled and died and boiled again in a cycle she could almost time her watch by. A cell phone trilled in her pocket, and she answered it without looking at the screen.

"Is he dead?" she asked without saying hello.

Alan Blaine responded with a single word. "No."

Her heart, for the first time in what felt like decades, flipped. She sat there, alone on the stoop of an abandoned and blood-soaked bar, her cigarette held just centimeters from her thin lips. She brought it down and leaned forward. Her black, void-like eyes stared out into the starless sky.

"Do the *Sins* know that?"

"No."

She nodded. Slowly.

"I'll be damned."

CHAPTER SIX

"Good morning, Mr. Jones."

Elijah Harris came around the corner from the elevators and into the waiting room outside of the hospital. Darius jumped. He'd been sitting there for thirty minutes now, ever since Abraham had shown him the way back, too nervous to go in on his own and too absorbed in his own thoughts to hear the doctor's footsteps coming from down the hallway. Dr. Harris was carrying a bowl of steaming oatmeal. The smell made Darius's stomach rumble. Abraham had offered to help him make breakfast, but Darius had declined. Only now, when faced with the sweet scent, did his mouth water, and it occurred to him he hadn't eaten since the previous afternoon.

"Good morning," Darius said, and he got to his feet. Now that he was face to face with someone else, he felt stupid for sitting out here for so long.

Dr. Harris seemed to be wondering about that. He paused and glanced over Darius for a moment before ultimately deciding not to comment on it. Instead, he opened the door to the hospital and said, "Miss Torres is anxious to see you."

Darius felt the same way.

After he met with Alan Blaine, Abraham took him to a dormitory room to get some rest. The very last thing he'd done that night was "rest."

To say his first night in the Underground—is that what Alan had called this place?—had been challenging would have been an understatement. The night had passed slowly, agonizingly. For hours he cycled between crying until his eyes were swollen and screaming until his throat was raw. He dreaded seeing Eva, explaining to her why someone would want to cut something so hateful into her beautiful body or why they'd murdered her brother. All he wanted to do was forget—forget the blood and the bodies and being picked up by his throat and thrown out a window.

But mostly, and maybe most frighteningly, Darius had spent large chunks of his night imagining what it would feel like to throttle Derek Dane—to punch him in the face, over and over, until Darius's knuckles were bruised, and the Sin was unrecognizable.

Those hateful thoughts were what bothered Darius the most.

When he finally had fallen asleep, he didn't get to sink into it. It was fraught with nightmares and memories, and Darius kept waking up, drenched in sweat and tears.

Now here he was. Still tired. Still sore. Still not sure he was ready to face Eva, to relive the experience through her.

But would he ever truly be ready?

Darius thanked the doctor and walked into the open hospital ward. It was a lot like it had been the previous day, except for about a half-dozen curtains had been pulled up around beds to give their occupants privacy. Today, the energy was different. Relaxed. There were no tense, busy people rushing around him. No beeping alarms. No shouting. The nurses on staff were quietly tending to their duties, as though just yesterday they hadn't had to rush Eva into emergency surgery to save her life. When Darius entered, people looked over to him, and the quiet conversations died down. A nurse no older than Darius himself, with her brown hair pulled back into a messy bun on the top of her head, came up and reached out her hand. Darius took it. He tried to present a strong grip, but he just didn't have it in him right now.

"Hi, Darius," she said warmly. "My name is Raquel. We met yesterday, but things were so crazy in here I wanted to introduce myself again." Darius appreciated it because he only vaguely remembered her. "I'm Eva's nurse, so I'm sure we'll be seeing a lot of each other in the next week or so. She's awake and doing well, and she's been asking about you." Raquel smiled, and Darius tried to smile back, but he wasn't sure it came off right.

"Is now a good time?" he asked.

"Absolutely," Raquel said. "She's in the bed at the far end of the ward. We wanted to give her some privacy. Just be gentle with her, okay? She's been through a lot."

There was a warning tone to her voice, but Raquel smiled all the same and gestured down the hall to the very last curtained bed. He thanked her for her help and made his way down. It felt as though his heart beat harder with each step he took, and by the time he pulled the curtain aside, he was sure Eva would be able to hear it.

But seeing her melted his anxieties away.

There Eva was, tethered to the station by wires, IVs, and catheters. She was propped up by pillows, and her thin face looked sallow and sick. The hollow spots beneath her cheekbones were dark, and the rings beneath her eyes darker, but all the same, Eva was smiling.

Everything from the night before faded away as he rushed up to her. He grabbed her face in his hands and took her in. The matted sweat caked and tangled in her dark hair. The dry film across her lips.

But those lips were still *smiling*, and it was beautiful. For the first time in what felt like years, Darius did, too.

"Darius."

Eva's voice was quiet. There was an uncommon rasp of thirst and fatigue, but her eyes shone with relief. She reached forward and winced, but nonetheless, Eva grabbed Darius and pulled him into her for a long, desperate embrace. Darius dipped his face into the crook of her neck. She smelled of sanitation—of hospital chemicals Darius hadn't known he remembered—and her skin was cold to the touch, but Eva was alive.

Then they cried.

He and Eva sat there for a few long minutes, and Darius was so grateful for the curtain separating them from the rest of the room. The tension, the shock, and the vast *relief* overwhelmed him. His body slumped and shook as he wrapped his hand around the back of Eva's head and gently cradled her face against his neck.

Soon, his exhausted body ran out of tears.

Eva collected herself as Darius pulled away. He sat on the edge of her bed. His muscles felt tired; they wobbled beneath his weight.

"The doctor told me you were alive," Eva said. She dabbed tears out of the corners of her eyes with the hospital's white sheet. Her movements were careful and slow. Darius glanced down at her stomach, covered by her gown, and back up to her face. "But I had to see for myself."

"Alive and well," he said.

"Are you hurt?"

"Just a cut." Darius lifted the sleeve of his shirt to show her the bandage. "A few bruises. Nothing serious. Not like you. You're a damned *fighter*."

Again, he glanced down at her stomach, and this time Eva wrapped her arms around herself. She looked away from him, and he reached out for her hands. He wanted to say something, but he didn't know what.

Then, suddenly, like she just needed to hear it from someone she knew, Eva asked, "And the others?"

She still didn't look at him—instead, she stared at the seams between the white tiles on the floor. Darius watched the side of her face for a long minute before whispering, "They're gone."

There was silence.

Eva's focus shifted. Her gaze was distant, lost in places only she could see. The fear and sadness had abandoned her expression. She went blank. Empty. That emptiness was terrifying. He squeezed her fingers. She didn't squeeze back.

She just said, "I was afraid of that." She didn't sound afraid.

"If you want," Darius said. "We can go say goodbye. Their—" he was going to say, "their bodies," but the word caught in his throat, and he found he just couldn't do it. He cleared his throat. "They were brought in for a proper burial."

Eva nodded, and a few silent tears fell from her eyes. "I'd like that," she whispered.

A few tears fell from Darius's as well. His grip tightened around Eva's hand. "I'm so sorry."

She looked at him at last. "This is *not* your fault."

Even though he knew that, he didn't feel it. He *knew* being there wouldn't have solved anything. He knew he'd have just been butchered along with the rest of them. He knew nothing would have changed, not really, except two more bodies would have been added to the pile that night.

He felt guilty to be here, alive and breathing, when so many others were not.

"I know," he said, and he shook his head. "But maybe I could have *done* something…"

"You couldn't have," Eva said quietly. "They were so *awful*… so *vicious*…"

"Eva, don't," Darius said quietly. He remembered what the nurse, Raquel, had said. "We don't need to talk about this right now—"

"No. We do," Eva cut him off. She drew her hands out of his and rubbed her eyes. "We have to, because *no one else* will tell me what the hell happened."

Darius just watched her for a moment. His brows furrowed, his jaw *aching* from how tightly clenched his teeth were. "Because we don't *know*," he said at last. "We weren't there…"

"God, it's so hard to remember," Eva muttered, and she shook her head again. "Saul and Juniper were giving Lindsay a bath in the sink in the kitchen, and I heard June scream. Thad went out to check… then it was crazy. It doesn't make any sense. It was just two people, Darius. All they had were a couple of knives… but they moved *so fast*…"

Darius squeezed her hand. He remembered what Alan Blaine had said the day before about the Sins: *"They become stronger and faster than an average human being."*

Eva suddenly sat up a little straighter again, winced, and said, "Oh, my god, and they had Sophie!"

The room seemed to go colder. Darius frowned, and his mouth fell open. "What?"

"Yes," Eva said, again looking far away, her eyes narrowed, not really seeing, as she tried to remember. "Sophie came in with them, but she was… different. Distant. She didn't react at all as they attacked us. She just watched, until…"

Her voice drifted off. Darius thought he knew what she was going to say.

"Until they killed her, too?"

Eva just nodded.

"Then I ran upstairs. That woman followed me. And, after that… I don't remember anything until I woke up here." She gestured around her, then looked back to Darius. "Where are we?"

"I don't know," Darius said. "They call it the Underground."

"Who are 'they'?" Eva's eyes narrowed.

"The Martyrs," Darius said. "They got there just in time, picked us up, and brought us… here. We're somewhere south of the city. I'm not really sure exactly where. I was thrown out the window and was knocked out for more than half the ride."

Eva's eyes widened. "You were thrown out a *window?"*

"Yeah, the same woman who hurt you just picked me up

and threw me," he said. "I'm lucky I didn't break my neck."

Eva grabbed his hand with both of hers and held it tight. "Thank god. Darius, this is crazy. Those people were *not* normal."

"You have no idea," he murmured. "I met with the guy who runs this place yesterday, and Eva, I think we're in way over our heads here."

She narrowed her eyes and pressed her lips together, like she was deciding if she wanted to ask. Then she said, "As long as we're in it together. What's going on?"

So Darius told her. He told her everything he could remember from his meeting with Mr. Blaine—about the Sins and their history, about the Martyrs' goal to destroy them. He told her about Cyrus and how this whole mess had even come to their doorstep to begin with. He told her about the video he watched where the man's skin sewed itself back together. He told her every detail, every tiny, little thing he could possibly think of because he knew she deserved the truth, because she was the last person on Earth he had left, and because, even though it all sounded insane, he was pretty sure he believed every word of it was true.

When he was finished, neither of them spoke for a long time. Eva's eyes were wide, her mouth open. He understood why. He knew it was a hard pill to swallow.

"Honestly," Eva said at last, "I thought it had to do with some kind of drugs, that they were high on some crazy shit… *Sins?*"

Darius nodded. "That's what he said."

"And you believe him?" Eva pressed.

Darius paused for a moment. "I believe he was being honest," Darius said. "He believes what he told me. I think I do, too. When that woman grabbed my neck… She picked me up like I was just a toy. But even if I do believe in this Sin stuff… I'm not sure I really trust what's happening here."

Eva frowned. "What do you mean?"

"It's hard to explain," Darius said, and he crossed his

arms and leaned forward toward Eva. He lowered his voice. With the curtain, he couldn't tell if anyone was close enough to overhear him. "Mr. Blaine wasn't *lying* to me, but he wasn't telling me the whole truth, either. There's something else going on here—something he didn't want me to know. I dunno… He was hard to read."

A couple of tense, silent seconds hung in the air between them. Then Eva sighed. "I don't like this."

Darius shook his head. "I don't, either, but these people are working on killing the monsters who did this to us. If I can—"

"Can't we just leave?" Eva cut him off. Her request was almost desperate. Tears welled up in her eyes again. "Whatever this is—Sins, PCP, whatever—I don't want to have anything to do with it."

The weight of what she said sank in, and a surge of guilt swept through Darius's chest. "Hey," Darius soothed. He grabbed her hands up in his again and pressed them against his lips. "Hey, it's okay. Of course we can." Eva's eyes lit up, and her shoulders relaxed. "I'm sorry, you're right. We don't belong here. But I do think we need to stay just a bit longer. I need to know you're going to be okay. The doctor said you'd be in here for a few days to make sure you're not going to have any complications, but as soon as you're back to feeling one hundred percent, we can make our next plans, okay? Let's just take this one day at a time."

Eva nodded and wiped the tears from her eyes.

"All right," she said. "I can do that."

Darius wrapped her up in a hug. She sank into his embrace with a deep sigh. He ran his hand over her hair and took in a heavy breath.

He had a few more days, and he planned on using those days to dig more into this "Martyrs" organization.

When Darius had assumed the Underground had to be

much larger than it appeared at first glance, he wasn't wrong.

With Eva stuck in the hospital for several more days and Darius determined to figure out more about the Martyrs before they took off, he spent a lot of his spare time wandering the structure looking for… anything. Any scrap of information he could find about the Martyrs and the work they did here.

But all he learned was the Underground was massive… and most of it was totally abandoned.

Darius found three distinct floors. The uppermost floor was where they'd come in. The large parking lot came into a main entrance, which opened to the waiting room just outside the hospital. From the waiting area, hallways branched out to the right and straight ahead. The right hallway led to a foyer for the stairs and elevators. The hallway straight ahead led to the alcove of offices where Darius had first met Alan Blaine. Along the way, there were a couple of doors for conference rooms, smaller offices, as well as a large tactical room, which was always locked, so Darius had no idea what was inside.

The bottommost floor was also a mystery. It wasn't accessible by the elevators, and the door at the bottom of the stairs was locked as well.

But the middle floor—this was the floor where the members of the Martyrs lived, and it was *huge*.

Right outside the elevator doors stood a large, open courtyard with tall, vaulted ceilings and colossal lights, giving the illusion of sunlight. It had room enough for hundreds of people to comfortably walk around without bumping shoulders. A handful of concrete planters were placed around the area, but they were all either empty or held nothing but the skeletal remains of small bushes or trees that had long ago been neglected and left to die.

Across the courtyard were dozens of tables and chairs. Most of them hadn't been used in ages—covered in dust, empty and alone. In fact, most of the courtyard felt that way, except a small area to the right. A huge, industrial kitchen nestled into the wall on the far side. The tables and chairs were more concentrated here, set close together and kept clean and tidy. It seemed like this was where most, if not all, of the activity in the courtyard took place. It was one of the only areas Darius regularly saw other people. Abraham, for example, was always eating a late lunch (or an early dinner) around three in the afternoon. Every time Darius found himself in the kitchen when Abraham was there, the other man tried to engage him in conversation. He was friendly, but awkwardly personal, so Darius started making his trips at different times or in the middle of the night.

Beyond the kitchen, the rest of the courtyard felt dead and empty. A handful of alcoves sat nestled along the outer edges, dreary rooms filled with boxes or abandoned furniture. Darius had asked Abraham about them during one of his trips to the kitchen when he *hadn't* been able to avoid him. Abraham explained these had once been set up as a variety of community spaces, perhaps a school or art studio, for the Martyrs to enjoy on their time off. He didn't go into when, or why, they'd stopped using them.

On the far left side, opposite of the kitchen, was a recreation room. Darius had never actually set foot in there. He figured that was one of the most likely places he'd run into someone, and he'd much rather be left alone. But the door to the recreation room was almost always left ajar, and the flickering lights and canned laughter from a television set spilled out into the courtyard. Darius found this unnerving. It felt misplaced in this strange, forgotten space.

Across the courtyard, opposite of the elevators and stairs, was a gym behind another set of double doors. Abraham had told him this was used primarily as a training area for combat units, but he insisted Darius was welcome to it whenever he wanted. Darius was pretty sure that was never going to happen, and he'd never done more than peek through door windows to see mirrored walls, workout equipment, and a large, open area with a padded floor.

On either side of the gym, two short hallways led to the living quarters. When Darius was doing his exploration, this is where he spent most of his time.

There were hundreds of bedrooms in the Underground. Literally hundreds. Just looking down the hallway from his own door in the west wing, Darius could count dozens of rooms, with more hallways branching out, leading to even more empty rooms, more empty hallways. It would have been easy to get lost here. The hallways were long and monotonous. Beige tile and brown walls for miles, with each door looking exactly identical to the one next to it. There was a peculiar lack of personalization everywhere. If not for the occasional door he found labeled with a name plaque and decorated with personal effects, Darius would have never assumed people lived here at all. These decorated doors were few and far between, like small oases in a desert of lifelessness.

There was a community bathroom for every twenty dormitory rooms, equipped with just a toilet, sink, shower, and mirror. They all looked the same: white tile, white walls, white towels. Even the toiletries provided were in plain, white packaging. Darius peeked into a few of them toward what he assumed was the back of the west wing of rooms and found them covered in dust. He also discovered two large, industrial laundry rooms, one in either wing. They were set up with dozens of washer and dryer units and cupboards full of useful things like extra soap, spare towels, flashlights, bath sponges, and spray bottles full of mysterious cleaning supplies.

He took the liberty to peek into a few unlocked bedrooms as well. The rooms varied in size. Some, like Darius's, were singles, set up with nothing but a long twin mattress and a solitary dresser. Others were set up with two beds or maybe a larger mattress. A handful even had bunks, providing enough space for four individual people to sleep. If Darius had to make a guess, he'd assume over four hundred people could have comfortably lived here.

So. Where the hell were they?

Though Darius had taken care to avoid running into others, he'd found it shockingly *easy* to do. He'd see people sitting at the tables in front of the kitchens, and men and women with black turtlenecks and beige cargo pants filtered in and out of the hospital to be treated for minor, but mysterious, injuries. Besides that, he didn't see a soul. Not in the courtyard. Not in the hallways.

Not outside of Alan Blaine's office, at 9:00 p.m…

About the only thing he'd been able to learn about the Martyrs by wandering around the Underground was, at one point, there had been a whole hell of a lot more of them than there were now. Otherwise, it seemed all of the Martyrs' personal information was kept somewhere under a tight lock. That left three places: the tactical room, the lowest floor, or Alan Blaine's office. If Darius wanted to learn more, he was going to have to do it the hard way.

Darius had taken to observing Alan's schedule. Soon Eva was the only patient still in the hospital—apparently, all the Martyrs who had been injured had been easier to mend than Eva was. When the last man, who had the bed closest to the door, had been discharged, Darius had requested Eva be moved to that bed so he didn't have to walk quite as far when he brought her food from the kitchen. That gave him a perfect place to sit and watch through the glass windows in the doors into the waiting room… and the hallway that led to Alan Blaine's office.

Alan Blaine wasn't predictable. He came and went from his office at odd hours throughout the day. It didn't seem like he kept to a particular schedule at all, instead ebbing and flowing with the waves of the Martyrs' business. The only thing Darius seemed to be able to rely on was Alan never returned to his office after eight.

He'd have to break in after that.

While Eva had slept and Darius had scoped out the Underground, he'd also been preparing for this. He snagged a flashlight from the laundry room and rummaged through the bathrooms until he found bobby pins in one of the ones that saw regular use. In the kitchen, he'd grabbed some cooking shears. Pliers would have been better, but he hadn't found any source for tools yet, so the shears would have to do.

Darius's work was clumsy. With the flashlight propped up in his teeth, he worked on the doorknob. Picking a lock wasn't something he had a lot of experience with. Saul had been a master, but he didn't have Saul. Not anymore. All he had were the tricks Saul had taught him over the years and the tenacity to find out what the hell was going on here. He'd have to hope it was enough.

It was, but only just. After thirty minutes, a handful of broken bobby pins, and very sore fingers from bending and twisting tiny pieces of metal over the cooking shears' blades over and over again, Darius heard the lock "click," and he breathed a sigh of relief.

Even though he knew Alan was done for the day, the whole situation made Darius's heart beat hard against his ribs. He'd always tried to do things morally, even when he was living on the streets, and breaking and entering was definitely something that was ordinarily against his personal code.

But these weren't ordinary circumstances.

He hastily shoved the bobby pins back into his pocket, grabbed the flashlight, and stepped into Alan's office. Then he closed the door behind him.

Now that he was here, he wasn't sure where to start.

The shelves and cases behind Alan's desk were packed with hundreds of books, most of them historical or biographical. Darius pulled a few down and thumbed through them, finding the pages scrawled with handwritten notes. Not all the handwriting seemed to belong to the same person, so he could only assume Alan wasn't the only one who had taken them. Maybe he hadn't taken any at all. Darius picked up an invoice from Alan's desk—some purchase order for the gas station sitting hundreds of feet above their heads—to see Alan's signature and compare it to the notes he found in the books. It didn't match.

Alan must have inherited this collection. But from whom?

The books didn't give him much new information about the Martyrs organization itself. Most of it revolved around the Sins' suspected movement throughout history. Some of the notes revealed interesting tidbits of information. *"Most Sins prefer to possess accessory hosts to Influence from a distance. Pride may be the only exception."* The word "Influence" was capitalized. Darius wondered if that had any significance. *"When a host is destroyed, Sins prefer to leave just before the point of death to preserve their memory integrity,"* another scrawled. *"Sins appear to be conscious while they are disembodied and searching for a host. However, once the possession has begun, they seem to enter into a catatonic state and remember nothing concrete until the possession is complete."*

The collection was fascinating, and it took a lot of self-control for Darius to pull himself together and focus on what he was really here for. If he got sucked into a rabbit hole learning about the Sins, he'd never learn about the Martyrs. He put the books back where he'd gotten them and turned to Alan's desk.

There were four drawers. The one on the bottom right was locked, but Darius was able to rifle through the other three. Holding the flashlight between his teeth, he started searching. One was full of nothing but financial details. Darius glanced at them just long enough to learn the Martyrs were *loaded.* The money was hidden well, spread out between dozens of individual accounts and investments in the States and overseas. He found records going back as far as 1956, almost one-hundred and thirty-five years ago, when a woman named Judith Gladstone had divided her solitary fortune, worth millions of dollars, into the assets the Martyrs still had access to today.

Another drawer was dedicated to information about the current Sins running around New York City. Darius found the file Alan had shown him during their first meeting, as well as individual binders on each of the seven. Darius couldn't help himself. He lifted Derek Dane's binder and opened it.

Just seeing Dane's face made him angry again. The smug smile. The cold, gray eyes. Darius thumbed through the first few pages, and his stomach flipped. Newspaper clippings were tucked between the pages, revealing stories about how Derek Dane had risen up in the ranks of the Pfizer pharmaceutical company. About four years ago, as the CEO, he'd made the call to raise their prices. Other companies had followed suit.

Darius hadn't thought he could hate the man any more than he already did.

He angrily shoved the binder back in and moved onto the third drawer. This one wasn't anything special—pencils, stationary, and other standard office items, though, peculiarly, it also had some basic first aid supplies, like bandages, ointment, and medical-grade tape.

All that was left was the locked one. What kind of information did Alan need to protect?

Darius reached into his pocket for the bobby pins again, but something made him pause. All the hairs on the back of his neck stood up. He stopped, turned off his light, and listened.

The door to the waiting room outside opened. He heard muffled voices. One of them was Alan Blaine. The blood drained from Darius's face.

He swore beneath his breath and looked around the room. There was no way he could just hide out behind the desk—what if Alan decided to sit down? No, his only option was a closet on the left wall. He quietly darted over and pulled the bi-fold door open just as he heard a key hit the lock. He barely squeezed himself behind and it when the office opened, and Alan Blaine walked in.

Darius held his breath. He hadn't had the chance to close the closet door all the way, so all he could do was pray Alan didn't find a reason to take a close look inside. He peered through the slats in the door, watching as Alan turned on the light and ushered in someone Darius recognized: Chris, the blonde woman who had been in the car when he'd first come to the Underground. Alan's dog followed behind her.

"I'm sorry for calling you so late," she said.

Alan calmly raised his hand to quiet her. Darius thought how odd he looked, dressed down from the red button-up and black slacks he'd been wearing when Darius had first met him. Seeing him in lounge pants and a simple t-shirt was off-putting. "It's not a problem, Christine," Alan said. "Though I do wish you had visited the hospital ward first. Elijah will need to stitch that up. Here."

He gestured her forward as he leaned back across the top of his desk. Darius's heart lodged in his throat as Alan's head appeared in the opening in the closet door, but the Martyr leader didn't look his way. He just opened one of the drawers and pulled the gauze and medical tape out. Then he turned back to Chris. She pulled her turtleneck over her head, revealing a black camisole underneath. Her bicep had a deep gash. This wasn't the first. Blood dribbled down her muscular arm and settled into a dozen other scars from similar injuries. Alan opened a clean bandage and pressed it against her wound.

"You are ordered to go see him as soon as we're done here," Alan said, and he threw her a stern, almost paternal look. "Wake him up if you have to."

"I will," she said. A wince briefly crossed her face, but she spoke through it as Alan wrapped the tape around her arm to keep the gauze in place. "But I needed to talk to you as soon as I could."

Alan gave a curt, polite nod. "Please, sit."

He gestured to the chair, and for one panicked moment, Darius was sure Alan was going to walk around his desk to sit behind it. From there, he would easily be able to see Darius inside the closet if he looked closely enough. Instead, he sat on top of it and faced Chris. His dog went and laid in her spot beside his chair. Darius's heart was pounding so hard he was sure the dog would hear it, but she kept her focus intently on Alan and his guest as though she were a part of the conversation.

"So, what happened?" Alan asked.

"Thorn and I were at the street market," Chris said. The mention of the market made Darius's stomach twist uncomfortably. He turned his attention away from the dog and back on Chris. She hadn't taken a seat, like Alan had asked, but instead remained standing where she had first come into the room. She folded her ruined turtleneck and held it tight to her side. Her arms were rigid and formal, her shoulders straight, and she spoke to Alan like she was giving a report. "There have been recent violent attacks there in the last couple of days. Gangs that normally have no interest in the area have been showing up and causing problems. Thorn suspected Autumn Hunt, so we went to check it out."

Autumn Hunt. The name was familiar to Darius. He'd read it on the notes about the Sins. Which one was she? He couldn't remember...

Alan's eyes darkened, and he crossed his arms. "Why would Hunt have any interest in the market now?"

"That's what we went to find out, sir," Chris said. "Thorn was right, of course. Hunt *was* at the market today."

"And I assume that is a parting gift," Alan said. He gestured to Chris's wound.

"Yes, sir."

"And the market? How much damage has been done?"

Darius had been hoping he would ask that question. His hands were clenched into such tight fists his fingers felt numb.

"The damage is substantial," Chris admitted. "There have been a handful of fatalities. I expect the number will only go up. Most of the regular street market customers do not have access to professional medical care, so their injuries may worsen over the next couple of days. However, it could have been much worse. Give it a few months, and the market should return to normal."

Fatalities? Darius's stomach churned. How many more people were going to die over this? How many people Darius knew? He found himself thinking of Jalal, Miguel, and all the other innocent people just struggling to survive out there.

The first thing he'd do when he and Eva left was return to the market and see if he could help.

Alan sighed and shook his head. "Did you learn why Hunt is still interested in the market?"

For the first time, Chris hesitated. She looked down at her feet and took a deep breath before responding. "We believe so, sir," she said. "Thorn tracked everywhere Hunt has been in the last week and linked her to Midtown—"

The door to Alan's office flew open. Darius startled as two more women stormed in. The first had clearly been sleeping. She was wearing pajamas, and her feet were bare. Her short, platinum blonde hair was spiked up in messy disarray, as though just a few minutes ago it had been pushed against a pillow.

The other woman was shoving her forward by the arm, and Darius had to stifle a gasp.

It was the dark-haired woman from the market! The woman who had come into their home, attacked Derek Dane, and saved Darius's life.

And she was *pissed.*

Her black hair was pulled back in a low ponytail, but it had begun to fall out in long, haphazard wisps around her shoulders. Her pretty face was distorted in rage as she roughly shoved the blonde woman toward Alan. She had a smudge of something dark on her cheek—Darius wondered if it was blood.

"Tell him what you did!" she screamed.

Chris stepped up between the two of them and grasped a firm hand on the dark-haired woman's arm to keep her at a distance.

Then something crazy happened. A flash of blue and red whipped through the open doorway, and a winged creature landed upon the woman's other shoulder. Darius gawked and tried to get a better look, but the animal was so small beneath its massive, leathery wings it was hard to see it from between the slats in the closet door.

It wasn't hard to hear, though. It let out a high-pitched, reptilian screech.

At this point, Alan was standing. He helped steady the woman in the pajamas. "Damn it, Thorn, you could at least let her get dressed! Alexis, I am so sorry."

"Don't apologize to her!" Thorn screamed. To say she was furious would be ludicrously misleading. She absolutely seethed with rage, the emotion permeating the room. When her voice roared to life, Darius felt a flame of fury grow up in his own chest. "She doesn't deserve it! She *told* them!"

Darius leaned forward and pushed himself as close to the door as he could. His hands and feet tingled with anticipation—or maybe it was just the awkward way he was forced to stand in the closet.

"Told them what?" Alan asked. He looked down at Alexis. She made a point not to look back.

"I didn't mean to," she defended, and she cast a loathing look back at Thorn. "We weren't *talking* to them. Some Sentry must have overheard us! *And* we were never briefed that it was some big secret!"

"How the fuck is this not a secret?" Thorn shouted.

Alexis rounded back and faced Thorn head-on. "You didn't tell me they didn't know Jones *survived!* Don't blame me for your bad managi—"

She didn't get the chance to finish. Thorn ripped away from Chris's grip and flew across the room. She grabbed Alexis by the collar of her pajama shirt and slammed her into the wall with such force a framed map of the New York City subway system fell and landed with a dull *thud* on the crimson carpet. Alexis gasped and clawed at Thorn's wrist, but Thorn's forearms were covered by long, fingerless gloves so Alexis's fingernails couldn't find skin. The creature on Thorn's shoulder hissed. Its wings flared out behind

Thorn's head like a halo.

"ENOUGH!"

Alan roared. Everyone in the room jumped, including Darius. He lost his footing and stumbled backward into the heavy coats behind him. He was lucky Alan and Chris were too busy pulling Thorn and Alexis apart to notice, but somebody did. Alan's dog suddenly jerked her head in his direction, and their eyes met.

Darius froze. The dog stared at him. Her bright blue eyes were alert with recognition.

"I can't *believe* you let it slip Jones survived," Thorn was snarling. "Now they're going to be *looking* for him!"

Darius's heart flipped. He tore his eyes away from the dog and looked back through the slats at Alan and the others.

The scene was strange. Alexis was holding a hand to her throat and glaring at Thorn, while Chris was standing almost entirely in front of Thorn to keep her from lunging forward again. But Alan—it was as though Alan had frozen, too. He threw a quick glance over his shoulder. For a moment, Darius was terrified he'd find his dog looking back into the closet, but to Darius's shock, the dog had laid her head back down on her paws and closed her eyes.

"Alan?" Thorn seemed annoyed by Alan's lack of concern. "Did you hear what—"

"Enough," he said again. His voice was quiet now. That was somehow more unnerving. "Miss Claytor, this is unacceptable, and this incident will be investigated further. Talking so candidly about any classified Martyr matter is against protocol *and* against your better judgment." Alexis glared down at her feet. Her face flushed a deep red. "I need time to assess the damage that's been done tonight and plan for how to move forward."

"That's *it?"* Thorn was incredulous. She stepped up, face to face with Alan. Her black eyes glittered with rage. "This is going to—"

"I am aware of the situation," Alan snapped, and Thorn

seemed genuinely taken aback. Her eyes narrowed, her lip curling into a snarl. "Talking about it tonight is not going to change anything. I will call a meeting tomorrow to discuss our options. I suggest you stay here tonight so you don't miss it." He cast Thorn a dark look. "Now *leave,* all of you."

"But—"

"I said *leave.*"

And they did. First Alexis, who rushed out as quickly as she could. Chris gave a short bow and said goodnight to Alan on her way out. Thorn simply turned on her heels and slammed the door behind her. Then it was just Alan. He stood in the center of the room for a minute or so, with one arm crossed over his chest and the other hand pressed against his lips as he thought to himself. At last, he and his dog left as well.

Darius waited another ten minutes to make sure they had all had plenty of time to get to the elevators and back down to the second level before he booked it out of there as quickly as he could.

He'd been looking for answers, but instead, he left with more questions. Like why the hell the Sins would care if *he* survived?

CHAPTER SEVEN

Soft, quiet voices fluttered through the courtyard as the regular "rush" of morning traffic filtered out. Martyrs quietly shuffled into the kitchen, washed their dishes, and made their way to the elevators and out of sight. Darius and Eva sat at a corner table, and Darius watched as the room slowly emptied. A weight of anxiety lifted a little off his lungs as the space cleared out.

"We should go grab some more water bottles," Eva said, and Darius glanced at her. "You think they have any of those water filtration things? Seems like the kind of thing this place would have..." Eva frowned and looked broadly around the room, and Darius shifted uncomfortably beside her.

"Maybe," he said, "but I wouldn't know where to even find one."

"It would be nice to have when we leave," she said. "How great would it be not to worry about safe drinking water anymore?"

Ever since Eva had been released from the hospital a few days ago, she and Darius had been planning their return to the city. She wasn't cleared to leave just yet—Dr. Harris wanted her to return once a week for the next month or so to monitor her progress and make sure she didn't have any lingering problems or infections—but she was one step closer, and she was eager, almost desperate, to get the hell out of here. It was all she could talk about.

"It would be nice," Darius agreed, "but I don't want to steal more than we have to."

Eva frowned. "It's not *stealing*," she said. "This stuff is just out in the open for all of us to use."

Darius just shrugged and looked down at the coffee in his hands. While that was true, he was pretty sure the Martyrs didn't really intend for people to collect a stockpile of goods in their rooms, either.

But that was exactly what he and Eva had begun to do. They'd filled the dresser in Eva's room with essentials, from foodstuff to hygiene products, blankets, and spare clothes. Darius had even found a first aid kit tucked behind the sink in one of the bathrooms. That was the only thing he didn't feel guilty about taking.

"Darius," Eva said, and her voice was quiet and compassionate, but stern. Darius looked back up to her, and her rich, brown eyes were heavy with conviction. "This is about *survival.* We need to take advantage of anything we can."

Darius's heart leapt painfully into his throat. She reminded him so much of Saul in this moment, and it carved a pit in the center of his chest. Maybe it was the way he was looking at her, but Eva seemed to sense what he was thinking, and she cleared her throat and glanced away from his face.

After that first day, when Darius had visited Eva in the hospital, they hadn't talked about what happened again. Instead, they kept themselves distracted by planning their lives outside of the Underground and "collecting" the things they needed to make it work.

But just because they ignored their grief didn't mean grief didn't find a way to haunt them. Eva had been assigned a room right beside Darius's, but she didn't stay there. For the last several years, neither of them had slept alone, and now that Eva was out of the hospital, they found a codependent comfort in laying side-by-side, clinging to a sense of normalcy in an otherwise abnormal situation.

But the evenings were long and sad. Almost every night, after she thought Darius had gone to sleep, he would hear Eva quietly cry until she eventually fell asleep, too. For Darius, though, sleep just wasn't an option. He was struck with insomnia, trapped awake for long hours in the night and only passing out when his body just couldn't keep going. When he did sleep, it was restless and full of weird, uncomfortable dreams.

Dreams he'd rather not talk about or think about—just like he didn't want to talk or think about the orphanage.

"You're right," he said at last, breaking himself out of dark thoughts and focusing on his distraction again. "Once we get back to the market, I can focus on doing the work I *know* how to do."

He didn't mention the other reasons he wanted to return to the market. What he'd overheard Chris tell Alan was weighing heavy on his shoulders. Sin activity. Fatalities. More chaos and damage in *his* community. In his *home*.

Eva didn't know about any of that, though, and Darius didn't want to worry her. It was the same reason he hadn't told her he'd broken into Alan's office in the first place. She had enough on her plate as it was between recovering from major abdominal surgery and losing their family. Adding more trauma to that felt gross and unnecessary.

Darius could bear the burden alone.

"I'm not sure I want to go back to the market," Eva admitted. She looked down and poked at her breakfast. She hadn't had much of an appetite, and her oatmeal was beginning to get cold. "I think it's too close to… It's just too close."

A disappointed bubble swelled in Darius's stomach, and he just nodded and looked around. He understood her concern—the market would be a stark reminder of all they'd lost—but Darius wanted to check in. At least once. He had to know, he had to *see*, how much his world had been torn apart.

Voices from across the courtyard caught their attention. A handful of Martyrs had just come out of the elevators and made their way toward the kitchens. The weight of anxiety fell back upon Darius as they glanced up, spotted him, and exchanged a few pointed looks before they disappeared behind the counter.

Now that he wasn't spending most of his time at the hospital, Darius had begun to see people around the Underground. There were more of them than he'd thought, but still not nearly enough to fill this place. He figured there were just over one hundred active members. They filtered in and out of the recreation room, the gym, and the residence wings throughout the day, and Darius couldn't help but feel like he was the center of much of their discussion.

He first started noticing the looks the Martyrs shared between one another whenever he was around. Then it was the whispers. On more than one occasion, he had walked into a room just to have conversations stop dead as soon as he was within earshot.

It made him uncomfortable, and he'd started insisting that he and Eva only visit the courtyard during times of the day when it was less busy. He wondered if this had anything to do with what that Alexis woman had let slip—about the Sins knowing he had survived the attack.

And if it was, why did it matter?

"Darius?"

His mind had started to wander, and he hadn't noticed Eva talking to him. He shook his head and turned back toward her. "Hmm? I'm sorry."

"I was saying there's nothing keeping us in New York," Eva said. Her tone was sharp and short. "Why don't we go south? We won't have to worry as much about the winters."

Darius took a sip of his coffee and nodded. "That's not a bad idea," he said, but he didn't really mean it. He'd never set foot outside the city before—well, before the Martyrs had taken him to wherever this underground compound was built. He wasn't sure he knew how to survive anywhere else, and he wasn't sure he wanted to figure it out.

He was drawn here, like it was where he belonged.

"Good afternoon."

Darius and Eva turned around to see Abraham walking up to the table. He gave a small, polite bow toward Eva and held out his hand. "Eva, right? It's nice to finally meet you. My name is Abraham Locke. I'm the counselor down here. How are you doing?"

Eva shook Abraham's hand, but Darius could tell by the way her shoulders tensed up she wasn't really comfortable with it. The only people she'd really spoken with from the Underground were Dr. Harris and the nurse, Raquel. Her skepticism of the Martyrs and their whole battle against the Sins was evident in her posture.

"I'm fine," she said. It was short, polite, but also gave the definite air of ending the conversation.

Abraham didn't let it bother him. He turned back to Darius and said, "May I join you?"

Though he was sure Eva would have rather said no, Darius was happy for a change in the conversation. "Of course," he said, and he pulled out a third chair from their table to make room.

"I actually wanted to talk to the two of you," Abraham said, and he cleared his throat. "I'm sorry if this is a little uncomfortable, but it's about laying your family to rest." The atmosphere at the table changed. Eva seemed to shrink down in her chair, and Darius felt a lump form just behind his Adam's apple. "Mr. Blaine expressed you were interested in saying goodbye. I can arrange that for you if you'd like."

Darius glanced across the table at Eva. She wiped a tear from the corner of her eye. He reached across the table to hold her hand. "We would like that. When?"

"We can leave tomorrow," Abraham said. "Meet me in the waiting room at eight, and we'll head out."

They thanked him, and Abraham excused himself and

went off to attend to whatever other business he had. Then an awkward, painful silence fell between Darius and Eva as they were thrust right back into the past they'd been trying so hard to ignore. That night, Eva cried a little longer, and Darius's sleep was even more unsettled.

Landscape flashed across the window. Fading grass and trees tinted with the first signs of autumn blurred together in a swirl of yellow-green and burnt orange. Darius stared out at the world as it passed them by, his forehead pressed up against the window. An anxious monster had settled into his gut as Abraham drove them to what Darius could only assume was a cemetery.

They weren't alone. Sitting shotgun beside Abraham was a woman named Lina Brooks. Darius had gathered she was a director of one of the Martyr's departments, and she was also Abraham's sister-in-law. She was maybe ten years older than Darius was, and she was just barely beginning to get fine lines at the corners of her eyes and mouth. Her caramel-colored hair was the same shade Lindsay's had been, and she had it braided neatly down the back of her head. While Abraham drove and made awkward small talk about the weather and the topography, Lina was absorbed in reading. Her kind, gray eyes quickly darted across the pages of a book held in her delicate hands.

Behind Darius and Eva, sitting in the third-row seats of the black SUV, were two people Darius knew: William Michaels and Christine Silver.

Chris, Darius learned, was the assistant director of the Tactical Armed Combat Unit, or TAC, which primarily handled any violent conflicts with the Sins. William was her partner. TAC was the team sent out whenever aggression was expected or, as in today's case, as security for otherwise unarmed and untrained Martyrs outside of the Underground.

Chris had insisted the Sins had no idea where the Martyrs' memorial was, and they had never once had an incident with them this far southwest of the Underground, but protocol was protocol. All the same, when she and William packed some of the full-body armor Darius had seen them wearing when they'd come to the orphanage, it made him nervous.

Actually, being around Chris herself just made him nervous. It wasn't just her job, or the gun clipped to her belt, but because she reminded him of the conversation he'd overheard in Alan's office—and how he'd even been in the situation to hear it in the first place. He felt dishonest and non-transparent, two things he'd *hated* on the market.

Darius took a deep breath and glanced to Eva. She was sitting still as a statue, eyes focused dead ahead on the road before them. Her hands were clasped so tightly in her lap that her knuckles were turning white. He reached out and grabbed them. She startled a little but passed him a weary smile.

They both had people to grieve, but Eva's loss cut a deeper wound. Darius didn't know much about her life before she and Saul were turned out onto the streets, but he did know Saul had sacrificed everything he could to provide for her. Darius had no idea what that was like—or how hard it would be to lose it.

"How are you two doing?" Abraham asked, peering over at them in the rearview mirror. Eva shifted uncomfortably. She wasn't keen on making friends here. When Alan Blaine had come by to introduce himself to her in the hospital, she had all but ignored him.

"I'm not exactly excited," Darius murmured, and he looked back out the window. He caught Chris watching him from the corner of his eye and glanced up to her. She gave him a short nod that seemed to say, "I feel you," and it was somehow more comforting than anything Abraham had to say.

"I know this is hard for you," Abraham continued. He

spoke quickly, almost nervously—the way new vendors on the market did when they met Darius for the first time and didn't want to make a bad impression. "You never really get used to it—not that you're really supposed to get used to it. We've had to say goodbye to a lot of people over the years—"

"Abraham, hush." Lina Brooks looked up from the book she was reading and gave Abraham a stern look. "You're not helping."

"Right," Abraham said, and he cleared his throat. "Sorry." Then, almost to himself, "This is the worst part of the job."

The car went quiet again. Thank god.

The landscape began to change. The trees thickened for a moment then disappeared almost altogether as they made their way through acres and acres of farmland. After a half-hour, Abraham turned off the main highway onto a twisted and narrow path. This path led them back into another grove of yellowing trees. Before they disappeared inside it, Darius glanced over his shoulder. He couldn't see any signs of the city anymore. He swallowed against his dry throat. The sides stuck together.

He'd never imagined his first trip outside of the confines of New York would be on a trip to say goodbye to the dead. It had been over two weeks, and those scarlet memories were still fresh in his mind.

Eva's fingers tightened around Darius's, and he realized he'd begun to grip her hand a little too hard. He loosened his hold and glanced at her. Tears welled up behind her dark lashes, but she still managed to pass him a smile.

"There it is."

Abraham pulled off the road onto a gravel driveway. A modest, ranch-style house overlooked the drive. It was old. Exterior paint chipped away and revealed the worn wood beneath. Even from the outside, Darius could see the windows were layered in cobwebs and dust. Abraham put the car into park, but suddenly, like he had just remembered something, he turned to Darius and Eva.

"Oh—I feel like I should warn you about Cain. He's a little…"

Abraham struggled to find the words. He winced and shrugged as Lina quietly shook her head.

"Eccentric," she offered.

"More like *weird*," William Michaels said behind them. Lina hushed him, and Darius looked up to the house.

A man was waiting patiently on the front porch as the four of them got out of the car. He leaned back against the doorframe, resting a glass of red wine gently against his palm as he watched Darius and the others walk toward the door. Worry lines creased his face, and his black hair was peppered with gray and white. His clothing wore a strange blend of love and neglect. It fit him well enough, but it was wrinkled in a way that implied it had been grabbed straight from a dryer, where it had been sitting, clean, for at least three days. Once they were near, the man smiled and took a step toward them. A long-coated, brown and black tabby arched its back on the railing by his feet and watched them with alert, orange eyes.

"Good morning, my dears," he said to Abraham and Lina. "It's so good to see you again." The slightest hint of an old accent touched his tongue as he spoke, and he gave a smile that didn't quite reach his eyes. He stepped down and offered Lina a hand up the front steps. When she grabbed it, he kissed her knuckles. "This old house is really quite lonely between your visits."

"Good morning, Cain," Lina said kindly. "Thank you for letting us visit today."

"It's no burden at all," Cain said. The cadence to his voice was almost lazy. Then he looked over Lina's shoulder awkwardly, as though he had been itching to do it but knew he had to go through the formalities first. "And this must be Darius Jones."

The man looked right past Eva, ignored Chris and William entirely, and focused on Darius and Darius alone. He held out his hand as Darius stepped up onto the porch. "My name is Cain Guttuso."

Darius grabbed it and shook. Cain watched him for just a split second too long, gripped his hand just a little too tightly, before finally letting go and offering the same gesture to Eva. "And Eva, I believe?" He glanced over at Abraham; Abraham nodded. When Eva dipped her fingers into his outstretched palm, he brought her knuckles to his lips and kissed them, as he had with Lina. Eva stiffened. Darius could smell the wine on Cain's breath from where he was standing. "It's a pleasure."

"Thanks," Eva said quietly.

"You are here, of course, to say goodbye to your dead," Cain said then, lingering a little on Darius. The words made Darius's stomach flip uncomfortably. Or maybe it was the way Cain said it—casually, without a hint of compassion or sympathy for what Darius and Eva had gone through. "Come, come. I'm really quite proud of the memorial I've designed for them. It's been a while since I've had so much to work with."

Cain turned around and led the way into the house. As soon as his back turned, Lina gently put her face into her hands, and Abraham shot Darius and Eva an apologetic look. Darius, however, was shocked. He had to have misunderstood, didn't he?

Was Cain… *excited* about this?

They filed in after Cain, Abraham and Lina leading the way and Chris bringing up the rear. William stayed behind to stand watch on the front porch. Cain's cat followed in closely behind Darius, watching him with those large, lamp-like eyes.

They walked straight through a small, modest living room into a kitchen. The walls in the home were bare, and a fine layer of dust hung over the tables. A path had been worn into the carpet from years of habit. It led from the kitchen, down the hall, and to a single chair in the living room.

Nothing here indicated Cain had any close friends or family. There were no photographs on the walls, no personal items stuck to the refrigerator. The kitchen was just as impersonal as the rest of the home. A single plate sat in the sink. The windows were discolored. Dead flies speckled the windowsills. Before heading outside, Cain paused. A row of bottles stood beside the sink, and he lifted them one-by-one until he found one that wasn't empty. Then poured the rest of its contents into his glass until it was full almost to the brim.

The kitchen connected with a back porch, and Abraham opened the door and walked out onto it. Darius and Eva followed, and Darius was totally taken aback by what he saw.

He wasn't sure what he was expecting. A yard full of gravestones, maybe? But Cain's estate was anything but an obvious, morbid reminder of death. It was… beautiful. Even thinking that made an uncomfortable, guilty surge catch in Darius's throat. He paused at the top steps of the deck and just *stared.*

The rolling hills were lush with greenery. Delicate walking paths weaved in and out of flower beds, full of rich bushes and so many varieties of flowers Darius couldn't count them all. Large, flourishing trees went back as far as the eye could see, their leaves half-turned to vibrant oranges and soft yellows. The garden extended so far Darius couldn't make out the back of Cain's property at all.

"We had to get creative," Cain said. Darius jumped. Cain had sneaked up uncomfortably close behind him, watching him appreciate the beauty of his property. "With satellite imaging being so sophisticated now, we had to ensure the Sins could not pick us out on a map. Hence, the Martyrs Memorial Garden was born. It's unfortunate you are here in the fall," Cain said with a sigh. "When everything blooms in the springtime, this place is magical."

He led the way down from the steps and onto the walking path. As they got into the heart of the gardens, Darius began to spot tiny hints to what this place actually was. Large stones were set up as memorial place markers for the deceased among the plants. Engraved names and dates of people long since dead peeked out at them as they wandered down a dirt path through the trees.

The further they got from the home, the more recent the dates on the stones. Most of the gravesites were solitary, placed into the garden as stand-alone markers. Occasionally, though, there was a separate, more prominent feature that had obviously been planned as the resting place for a group of people who had died together. Darius noticed a bubbling, man-made pond, full of turtles and frogs, where at least six of the rocks along the edge were dedicated to dead Martyrs.

The path twisted and turned through decades of Martyr history. Separate trails branched off from the main strip and came around in big circles to connect again. The garden was quiet. There was nothing but the soft crunching of gravel beneath feet, the rustling of leaves in the wind, and distant chirping from birds in faraway branches. Darius tried to count the memorial stones, but he lost track well after one hundred. The beauty of this place felt dark and haunted.

He'd known the Martyrs had to have a bloody backstory, but he hadn't expected *this*.

Everywhere he looked was another reminder of this secret war, another life lost. They were getting closer and closer to modern times, and Darius saw a couple of names he thought he recognized. Lance Silver, 2031 to 2069. He wondered if he was related to Chris? Darius glanced back at her to see if she had any reaction to the marker as they passed it, but she remained as impassive as ever.

The longer they walked, the more spread out the garden became. Gorgeous beds full of dense greenery were broken up with pockets of plush grass and clover, areas Cain was undoubtedly saving.

When they had been walking for several minutes, Cain said, "Ah, here we are."

He stopped at one of the open, grassy alcoves. This was

clearly a space in progress. Unlike the rest of the garden, which was mature and established, here things were new. The turf had been cut away in a large, hexagonal shape, and wood beams were set up beside it. On all sides of the hexagon but one, young maple trees had been planted. They were still tied to the posts supporting them in the ground.

"I am going to build a gazebo here," Cain said, and he smiled intently at Darius as he said it. His crowded teeth were stained pink from wine. "It will be a wonderful place to sit and pay your respects when it's done. I haven't gotten to build something this elaborate in quite some time, and I'm excited for the challenge."

There he was again, celebrating a disaster that had brought Darius's life to a painful halt. Eva shot Cain a dirty look. Cain continued on as though he didn't notice their discomfort.

"The stairs will be there, where Crescendo is lying," he said. He gestured to the one edge of the hexagon pattern not flanked by a sapling, where his cat had laid down to roll in the dirt. The animal's tail flicked happily as Cain went on. "Instead of gravestones, I want to embed each memorial stone on the wall inside the gazebo. I can align the stones with the remains by the trees, if you would like."

Darius frowned. "The remains by the trees?" he repeated.

"Yes," Cain said, and he took a step toward Darius. His eyes, which seemed to lack any real substance, glistened excitedly. They were standing a little too close for comfort now, and Darius took a half step back. "I came up with the idea ages ago. Each of these trees was planted above a biodegradable urn containing the remains of your loved ones. Beautiful, isn't it? The dead providing new life, in a way." Darius's eyes widened, and Eva looked back over at the trees, no doubt wondering which one was Saul's final resting place. "Of course," Cain continued with a shrug. "Before I can create the memorial stones, I will need to know the names of the people buried here. I have it all documented.

If you would like, we can return to the house, and you can help me fill in the blanks."

A tense silence fell. Darius glanced over at Eva. He felt it wrong to leave their remains alone, unnamed in a cemetery that didn't belong to them, but the idea of going through Cain's documentation on them made his heart ache.

The garden had made it a little easier for him to forget what a morbid affair this all was.

"Yeah," he said at last. "Yeah, I'll help out. Eva?"

She shook her head. "You can handle it," she said. "I'd rather stay here."

"Excellent," Cain said, and he gave an excited little bounce. The wine in his glass sloshed from side to side and threatened to spill over. "Lina, Abraham, I can assume you are going to visit Stella?"

Lina gave a soft smile. "Yes. We'll keep Eva company, too."

Cain nodded. "And Miss Silver?"

Chris was so quiet and to herself that Darius had almost forgotten she was with them. "I'm going back."

Cain seemed almost annoyed she was joining them. His mouth twisted up into an awkward half-smile, half-grimace, and he began to lead the way back through the garden. Darius glanced over his shoulder one last time to see Eva reach out and touch one of the maple trees before the path twisted and she was out of view again.

He was glad to have Chris with him on the walk back to the house. Cain seemed almost eager for conversation. Now that it was just them and he could walk almost side-by-side with Darius, he wouldn't stop talking. He told Darius all about how he had learned to landscape when he'd taken over the Martyrs' Memorial Garden, and how it had given him an opportunity to get back into stone working, something he had apparently appreciated a lot in his youth but had given up over the years. He had a lot of hobbies, and almost all of them revolved around this garden of death.

Stonework, sculpture, calligraphy, construction, gardening… The list went on and on.

Weirder than his hobbies, though, was the way he talked about the Martyrs Memorial Garden: like it was his baby, his *masterpiece*. His obsession with it, and with everything in it, was unsettling.

So Darius was grateful when they could see the porch again, but something else caught his eye. A small patch of grass was tucked away on the far side of the house, against a side fence, isolated from the rest of the garden. And inside it was…

A headstone.

He was surrounded by memorial stones tucked away and hidden behind beautiful and lush foliage, and brazenly out in the open was a proper headstone. It stood almost four feet tall. Darius couldn't believe he'd missed it the first time he'd walked by. Weeds popped up around its edges, and a dried bundle of flowers lay in front of it.

Donovan Rose
September 19, 2000
December 28, 2024

He'd died almost sixty years ago, but based on the information Darius had found in Alan's office, that was nearly seventy years after the Martyrs started…

"This is the oldest grave in my yard," Cain said. Darius leapt as the older man crept up behind him and looked down at the grave. He didn't seem to notice Darius's surprise. "The first Martyr buried."

"But not the first killed?" Darius asked.

Cain laughed. It was a cold, dead sound. "Oh, no. This organization has been around for over a hundred years. Until Donovan, the bodies of the dead were left behind."

Darius frowned. "Why?"

Cain didn't respond right away. When he did, he simply shrugged and said, "Things changed. Now come. We have a lot of work to do."

Back inside the house, Cain and Darius got set up on the couch in the living room. Chris had given them privacy and stepped out onto the front porch to join William, and the two of them talked in low, hushed voices. Darius kind of wished they'd come inside. Cain's attention was smothering.

He sat beside him, again almost too close for comfort, with a binder in one hand and a pen in the other. Crescendo had joined them, curled up on Darius's other side, making it impossible for him to scoot over and get some space. When Cain looked at Darius, his eyes had a strange, almost hungry look to them. "I have photographs I took in the morgue," he said. "I own a local crematorium, and I must say, getting these remains in to be photographed and cremated without raising suspicions was no easy task. One or two is simple, but thirteen? Anyway, I got it done. We can do this one of two ways: either you can look through the file and give me names, or I can describe the individuals for you, and you can tell me who they are. What would you prefer?"

There wasn't an easy answer to that. On the one hand, he'd be stuck with Cain. On the other, he'd be looking right into the faces of all the people he'd lost that day, revisiting the massacre again. Darius glanced up to see Cain watching him expectantly.

"I'll take the folder," Darius murmured.

Cain seemed disappointed, but he handed the folder over to Darius all the same. Darius excused himself from the living room and walked out onto the back porch. For a long time, he just sat on the step and looked at the blank manila file in his hands. After taking a couple of deep breaths, he opened it.

Thad's face looked up at him.

Though Darius didn't like to admit it, Cain had done a good job with the photos. He'd printed them in black and white and had clearly spent some time editing out the gorier details. While looking through them and assigning names was gut-wrenching, it wasn't the horrifying experience Darius had expected. If he tried hard enough, he could pretend they were just asleep.

Slowly, he thumbed through the images. From Thad, it went to the children. There was Alejandro and Aren. Sophie. He paused on her photograph for a long time. He wondered what had happened to her and why she'd been with the Sins. Had they kidnapped her in hopes she would lead them to the Martyrs, too?

Darius wrote each child's name on the top, right-hand corner of their photograph. He added the birthdays he knew and made up some for the children who had come in without them. He provided personal details where he could, hoping maybe it would give Cain some ideas as to how to decorate their memorial stones. "She loved bears," he wrote on one. "He wanted to be a fireman when he grew up."

By the time he reached the last photograph, his eyes were swelling with tears, but when he turned it over, he paused.

Had he missed some?

Darius's heart skipped a beat. He brushed the tears out of his eyes and flipped back through the pictures, taking extra care to make sure none of them had stuck together. They hadn't. This was all Cain had given him.

And three people were missing.

Abraham, Lina, and Eva were just making their way back around the path. Darius jumped to his feet and rushed up to Abraham, holding the file in front of him.

"Did you get everyone?" he asked. The words came out rushed, almost frantic. "You didn't leave anyone behind, did you?"

"What? No. The team was thorough." Abraham reached out and grabbed Darius by the shoulders. His thick eyebrows cinched together in concern. "Are you okay? What happened?"

"They're not in here," Darius said, and though he knew he was getting ahead of himself, he smiled. He looked over Abraham's shoulder to Eva and pushed his way toward her, waving the folder. "Saul and Juniper and Lindsay. They're not here!"

Eva ripped the file out of Darius's hands and started going through the pictures herself. For the first time since it happened, Darius thought back to the massacre on purpose, trying to remember if he'd seen their bodies among the others. He hadn't stopped to get a good look, but now that he was really focused on it, he didn't think he had.

"They're alive," he breathed.

CHAPTER EIGHT

For the next few days, Darius didn't hear any update on what the Martyrs planned on doing about Saul, Juniper, and Lindsay, and it was driving him crazy. His sleep, which was already broken, became even more sporadic. He spent hours awake at night, thinking about how they could have escaped, wondering where they were now, and worrying that Lindsay had survived the attack only to succumb to her illness anyway.

As frustrated as Darius was, Eva was even worse.

The minute she'd discovered her brother's body hadn't been among the dead, she had become obsessed with tracking him down when they left the Underground—and she wanted to leave *now.*

But they couldn't go. Not yet. Eva's injuries, though healing, still needed to be monitored. Even if they didn't, she and Darius didn't have any update on what the *Martyrs* were planning to do about Saul and the others.

After the incident at the Martyrs Memorial Garden, Abraham had promised Darius and Eva that he would speak to Alan as soon as possible and let them know what he said. After almost a week, Darius was ready to knock on Alan Blaine's door himself.

"You're just going to charge into his office?" Eva asked. She was lying in the bed, curled up in a set of oversized pajamas the Martyrs had provided to her. The tank top was loose on her skinny frame, and she frowned at Darius as he pulled a shirt on over his head.

"Yep," he said. "It's been six days."

"I don't get why you need to talk to him at all," Eva went on. "What's he going to do that we can't do when we get out of here?"

Darius turned to look at her with an almost incredulous look on his face. "Have you *seen* this place? He's got resources we can't even imagine." He didn't want to tell her just *how much* he knew about those resources. He thought back to the financial records he'd seen in Alan's office. "There's probably a lot he can do. It doesn't hurt to talk to him about it."

Eva's face soured in an unhappy pout. She opened her mouth to speak, but before she had the chance, someone knocked on the door.

When Darius answered it, he was surprised to see Alan Blaine himself standing on the other side.

"Good morning, Mr. Jones."

Darius didn't say anything. He had never seen Alan on this level of the Underground, let alone in the residence wings. Eva jumped up in the bed and pulled a pillow over herself, as though trying to hide. Alan did not comment on her presence in Darius's room and passed her a patient smile. "Miss Torres. I hope you are doing well?"

She didn't answer him, either. Darius cleared his throat. "Is this about Saul and the others?"

Alan gave a moment's pause as he looked back to Darius. Darius had forgotten just how tall, how formidable, Alan Blaine was in the weeks since their first meeting. Even holding his shoulders back, he was still vastly overshadowed by the Martyr leader.

"Yes," Alan said. "And no. I have a few things to discuss with my team today regarding Mr. Torres, Miss Foster, and young Lindsay before I have any concrete information to give you, but I would like a chance to discuss it with you both tonight. Over dinner."

Darius frowned. "Dinner?"

Alan nodded. "I enjoy connecting to my people in smaller, more intimate settings, and getting away from the Underground can provide a welcome break to the dreary monotony. If you'll meet me in the waiting room at 5:00 tonight, we can head out. We have… quite a bit to discuss."

Then he gave Darius a pointed look that sent a shiver down his spine.

"Uh… yeah, of course," Darius said. "We'll meet you there."

"Excellent," Alan said. He smiled and dipped his head in a short bow. "I look forward to it."

Then he turned around and walked back down the hallway. Darius leaned out the door and watched him go. When Alan's black trench coat whipped around the corner, Darius turned back to Eva, and she was furious.

"I'm not going," she said. She got to her feet and pulled on her socks and shoes. "No way in hell am I going anywhere with that man, or anyone else here."

"Don't you want to find out what they're going to do about Saul?"

"No," Eva said shortly. "I'd rather be out there looking for Saul myself. I don't think these 'Martyrs' are going to help us. Did you see how many people they've killed? Thousands, Darius. Thousands!"

Darius sighed. He wanted to point out the garden wasn't full of Martyr victims but rather Martyrs who had died in the line of duty, but he had a feeling Eva wouldn't see it that way. "Well, I'm going," he said. Eva crossed her arms and glared at him from across the room. "I want to hear what he has to say. It's been days! Maybe they've already found him!"

"Or maybe they're just trying to keep us here longer," Eva said. "Maybe they're so desperate for new recruits they're going to lie to us to keep us here until we feel like we don't have any other choice. You heard him. He called us 'his people.' I don't know about you, but I don't want to be 'his people.'"

"We're not going to be," Darius insisted. "But we're here for at least another week or two until the doctor is confident you're totally healed, so we may as well take advantage of whatever we can learn."

Eva just considered him for several seconds. "Fine," she said at last, quietly, defeated. "Fine. But I'm still not going. You can fill me in when you get back."

And there was no arguing with her, so Darius agreed.

"It's a shame Miss Torres didn't want to join us," Alan said. "I was looking forward to getting to know her better."

He and Darius made their way from the glass doors of the waiting room and into the Martyr garage. Darius followed behind as they came up beside a sleek, black sports car. It was so clean it was reflective. Darius saw his own image looking back at him in the dark sheen. His olive skin looked darker—his green eyes, shadowed.

"Well," he said as Alan moved around the car and unlocked the doors. There was a strange tension to Alan's expression—an almost uncomfortable look as he climbed into the driver's side. Darius got into the other seat. "She doesn't want to stick around here long enough to get to know anyone better."

"Oh?" Alan didn't seem surprised by this. He said it casually, almost disconnected. "I can certainly appreciate that. We are quite a bit removed from what she is accustomed to. How do *you* feel about it?"

Darius just shrugged. He didn't want to let it slip that he was looking forward to leaving, too, probably because part of him wasn't. While the idea of being out with Eva, searching for Saul and the others, was enticing, the Martyrs could offer him something the streets of New York never could:

A chance to get back at Derek Dane.

He could feel Alan's eyes on the side of his face—could feel him trying to read what Darius was feeling—but he didn't say anything about it. Instead, he'd just turned the car on—with a button, not a key. There was no engine roar. It just silently came to life.

Then he pulled them out of the garage, up the ramp, and into the real world.

When Darius had imagined going back to New York City, he'd assumed it would be on foot, a pack of stolen Martyr goods over his shoulders, and Eva by his side—*not* in the front seat of *another* Martyr issue vehicle on the way to *dinner*.

It felt almost *domestic*.

Darius shifted on the leather seat. It squeaked beneath his thighs, and in the quiet around them, the sound felt awkwardly loud. This car was different from the black SUVs Darius had ridden in so far. It was sleek, fast, and hugged so tightly to the ground Darius was amazed they didn't scrape the bottom on every little bump on the highway into the city.

The relatively rural road began to shift. New York's silhouette grew larger and larger as they approached, jutting up into the orange and magenta autumn sky. For a moment, he was struck by the surreality of watching the city from a distance, in the cab of a car more expensive than all the goods he had acquired in his lifetime, with a man who told stories about Sins and Virtues.

A man who hadn't said two words since they'd left the Underground.

The silence was making Darius uncomfortable. Alan was as unreadable as ever. He drove, eyes focused forward, with his thin lips shut tight in thought. Darius cleared his throat. "So. If you don't mind my asking, how can the Martyrs afford to… well, to do what you're doing? I can't imagine you're getting paid." Darius already had an idea of the

Martyr's financial situation from his snooping in Alan's office. He wanted to know if he could trust Alan, and the best way to determine that was by testing whether or not he'd tell the truth.

"We've made very wise investments over the decades," Alan said with a half-smile. "The men and women who started this organization, oh, a hundred years ago or so, came from significant wealth. They built the Underground, established our accounts. Since then, we have been tactful and quite successful. The interest on our assets alone is enough to maintain our baseline expenses."

Darius simply nodded. "Makes sense," he said. He was admittedly a little surprised Alan had been so candid, but then again, the Martyrs' finances were probably not a big secret. Anyone could tell by looking at their fleet of vehicles and the massive underground complex they'd built they had to have a big, fat bank account hidden somewhere.

"Though," Alan said, almost casually, but there was a knowing tone to his voice, "I believe you already knew the answer to that question."

Oh shit. Darius's heart skipped a beat, and he froze. Alan cast him a slow, unreadable sideways glance. Darius didn't know what to say, so he cleared his throat and settled on, "What do you mean?"

"Mr. Jones," Alan said shortly, "we have cameras around the Underground, and that includes the waiting room to my office." Darius's stomach churned. He should have considered that. Saul had always told him the first key to breaking and entering was to sweep for cameras, and Darius had totally forgotten. "I understand you are curious about us, maybe even distrustful, so I can appreciate the temptation to understand more about who we are and what we do. I am not angry you broke into my office, but let me be clear: if it happens again, I will be."

A glint crossed Alan's expression then, and Darius looked down at his hands.

"To be honest with you," Alan continued with a sigh. "I

am disappointed in myself. I had hoped to make you feel comfortable enough to ask me questions directly instead of sneaking around. Apparently, I have failed. Tonight, I want to address it."

Darius looked back up to Alan. The tension in his chest was beginning to dissipate. "How?"

"I'll answer any questions you may have," Alan said. "I suggest you take some time to think about them. I assume you'll have many."

That was an understatement.

The transition from hillside to cityscape was so subtle Darius almost didn't notice it. Fields became parking lots—bushes, buildings. The city sprang up around them, growing larger and busier the further in they got. Massive structures dominated the skyline. Tower Fifth pierced up so high its top was hazy and hard to see in the backlit glow from the lights below. By the time they crossed the Hudson, they were enveloped by hundreds of cars—hundreds of people. Advertisements flashing on big, electric billboards. Sirens wailing in the background…

The restaurant they were going to was along a busy Queens street. Alan pulled up, they got out of the car, and he handed the keys to a young, pock-faced valet. As the kid took their vehicle, Alan led the way up a brick-paved path to the front entrance.

As soon as Alan opened the door to the restaurant, Darius was bombarded with the savory scent of hot, buttered garlic bread and sharp marinara sauce. Alan spoke with the hostess casually, naturally, as though he was just another man here for a meal who didn't also happen to run an illegal, underground operation miles outside of the city. "Devlin," he said. "The reservation was for four, but we actually only need three places now."

Darius frowned. "Three?" he asked as the hostess led them away from the waiting area and toward a table in the back corner. The window overlooked the street. Night was closing in, and the blurry lights of passing cars sped by, sending long streams of orange and yellow across the pavement outside.

"Ah, yes," Alan said. He gestured for Darius to sit, and when he did, he situated himself across the table. The third chair was set up to Darius's right, across from the window. "My second-in-command is going to join us. I believe you've already seen her from the closet in my office." That glint crossed Alan's eyes again, but this time it was accompanied by a good-natured smirk. "Her name is Thorn Rose. She's my niece."

Well, if that didn't raise a whole lot of questions, Darius didn't know what did. Despite the clear similarities in their appearance, he hadn't even considered the possibility this Thorn person and Alan Blaine could be related. Now that it was out in the open, he felt kind of stupid for not noticing. Their jet-black hair. Their dark, empty eyes. Even the way they carried themselves—with an air of innate authority and status. At the same time, though, he never would have pegged Alan as her uncle. He looked, at most, seven or eight years older than she did.

"Your niece?" Darius said. Alan nodded. "Okay, so I have my first question." He leaned forward a bit, resting his arms on the table in front of him. "Your sister—brother?—whoever, really named their daughter *Thorn Rose?*"

Alan didn't laugh. He didn't seem amused at all, which caught Darius off guard. He'd been trying to lighten the mood, but Alan didn't seem to find it very funny. He took a deep breath and said, "No. My sister did not name her Thorn, but her birth name has come to have some very negative associations for her. Instead, she chose a new one—one that empowered her. Inspired her. I've found in my time the names we give ourselves are so much more important than the ones others provide for us."

Darius was a little ashamed. He hadn't meant to be offensive. He started to apologize, but Alan cut him off.

"No, no," he said, raising a hand. "Don't be sorry for asking questions and educating yourself. This war we're fighting has had many casualties, my sister and brother-in-law among them, but in many ways, the little girl they had together was lost, as well. She rebuilt herself into the woman she is today, and while she's… rough around the edges, I am very proud of her."

"She's been involved here since she was little?" Darius asked. "Your niece?"

Alan gave a short, single nod. "She was tied up in this battle from the moment she was born."

"I'm kind of surprised," Darius said, this time more cautiously, as he didn't want to slip up again. "She's the second-in-command? She seems like a loose cannon. The way she—"

He stopped himself. Though he knew Alan knew about the break-in, he didn't want to incriminate himself by admitting too many details. Alan seemed to catch onto what he was saying, though, and he nodded.

"She can absolutely be a loose cannon," Alan said. "But she has dedicated more of herself to this organization than anyone else I know. Thorn has a vast array of useful skills and connections in the city. She's a combat specialist, as well as a first responder. She has single-handedly taken out more of the Sins' hosts than anyone else on my team. And at the end of the day, she's the only person I can really count on to be here, no matter what."

Darius didn't really have any response to that. Of course he could count on her. She was family—probably the only family he had left.

But Thorn—the image of Thorn—brought more questions to Darius's mind. He remembered that flash of blue and red…

"Okay," he said. "Then what was the… the thing on her shoulder?"

Alan chuckled. "His name is Sparkie," he said. "Yes, another odd name, I know, but he came about when Thorn was a child, and you know how children name things."

"What *is* he?"

"We never really figured it out," Alan said. A waitress came by with water and asked for their drink orders. Alan got an iced tea for himself, and Darius declined. Alan continued, "But after dealing with the Sins for as long as we had been, we didn't really question it. This world is full of things I never knew existed." He cleared his throat, pulled a pair of reading glasses from the chest pocket of his jacket, and opened his menu. "What will you be having?"

Darius opened the menu and frowned behind it. Alan was clearly trying to change the subject, and Darius knew he'd be wasting his breath trying to dig deeper into it right now, so he looked down at the menu instead. He hadn't held a menu like this in his hand since before his mother had died, and now that he was here, really considering it, he felt out of place. He glanced around the room. Everyone else here fit in. Clean cut, well dressed, and soft-spoken. With his borrowed, oversized clothing and scrawny limbs, Darius felt like a child again—a child who had no place in a fancy restaurant like this.

"Is everything all right?"

Darius snapped out of his thoughts and found Alan watching him. He rubbed his eyes, shook his head, and said, "Yeah, I'm good."

Alan didn't let on if he knew Darius was lying or not. Instead, he simply said, "I was concerned you were uncomfortable returning to the city."

Darius's stomach turned into a knot. He looked back down at his menu. "No," he said, and he meant it. It wasn't the city that made him nervous. It was *this* part of the city. This kind of life. The last time Darius had eaten restaurant-quality food was from a dumpster out back, not sitting at a table on the inside. "I just haven't done this kind of thing in a while. Feels weird."

Feels wrong. Like he didn't deserve it.

"So," he said, and he cleared his throat and shifted in his chair. He didn't want to dwell on his own upbringing or his life in Alphabet City. Those thoughts just led to memories of the orphanage, and he'd rather not get lost in that sorrow right now. Now, he was here to learn more about the Sins, about the Martyrs, and about Saul, Juniper and Lindsay. But before he got into that, there was one thing nagging at him. "You said I can ask anything, right?"

"Of course," Alan said.

"You know I was there," Darius said bluntly. He put the menu down and looked intently across the table at Alan. "That Alexis woman—she told the Sins I survived, right? And I've been wondering, why the hell would that matter?"

Alan seemed to have been anticipating this, and his answer came out almost as though he had rehearsed it. "If the Sins had assumed you had died," he said, "then you would be out of danger. They wouldn't be on the lookout for a dead man. However, now that they know you and Eva survived, they *will* be looking for you. They know we took you with us. They know you've been to the Underground. They will do anything they can to get ahold of you in the hopes they can use what you know to get to our home base and eliminate us."

For a few seconds, Darius just considered this information, but he did notice a very subtle change in the narrative. Alan had said the Sins knew he *and* Eva had survived.

"They can't possibly find us that easily," Darius said. "New York is a huge city."

"They found you once before," Alan reminded him. "And the Sins have heavily Influenced much of this system's infrastructure—the police force, the fire department… Even the local news media. They control most of the city, as well as many of the cities surrounding it. Living outside of normal society kept you out of sight, but now that they've seen you and know who to look for, it will be much, much harder."

Darius shrugged. "There are only seven of them. How much can they do?"

"They can do quite a lot," Alan said. "Their corruption goes beyond their physical bodies. When I say they have

Influence, I mean they have a real, physical presence that affects those around them. Their Influence makes it easy for them to take over an entire city."

"That's another thing," Darius said. "I read something about 'Influence,' and it was capitalized, like it meant something specific. What is it?"

Alan did not answer right away. He paused to think, and he watched Darius carefully. "There are three kinds of Influence," he said at last. "Indirect, Direct, and Programmed. If I were a Sin, my Indirect Influence would spread into everyone in this room. Given enough time, these people would then spread my Influence for me, extending it far beyond my physical reach."

Darius's eyes widened. "Seems serious."

"Very serious," Alan said. "It's like an infection. When others come into contact with a Sin, they become corrupted, and they, in turn, corrupt others. Indirect Influence is not particularly potent. It takes years in the company of a Sin for that Influence to become extremely damaging. And, when the Sin has lost its host, it wears off relatively quickly. Indirect Influence is not meant to control, but rather to spread the Sin's maliciousness through a population. It also works like a battery. The more a Sin's Indirect Influence has spread, the more powerful that Sin seems to become.

"Direct Influence, on the other hand, allows a Sin to actually control a person—or many people, if he is so inclined." Alan leaned forward and took a drink of his water. Then, to accent what he said next, he pushed his glass away from him on the table. "They can *force* their will into people. Usually, Direct Influence is only meant to sway decisions, nothing more than a quick, subtle control, but occasionally, they take over entirely. People under this kind of Direct Influence, where a Sin controls everything, are called *Puppets*. Any time a Sin has that much control, the person will lose patches of memory of what they did, and why they did it."

"I can't believe the Sins have that kind of power," Darius said. "How can you fight that?"

"Puppets are easy to recognize," Alan said. "They look, for lack of a better term, *like* puppets. Emotionless. Puppets are also not common. Maintaining total control is draining for the Sins. Typically, Puppets are taken for specific situations and then abandoned. Sometimes killed, depending on what they had to do. The scariest form of Influence is the Programmed Influence.

"Sins can actually get into your mind," Alan said, pointing a finger at his temple, "and place cues there to get you to behave a certain way or take a certain action. It's not sophisticated—usually just triggered by a face or a name—but effective enough to give the Sins eyes all over the city. This is the Influence that makes it dangerous for you and Eva to come back here. It's likely that the Sins have already Programmed people all over New York to recognize your name or your face. You'll notice that I provided a false name for our reservations? That's because my name has been Programmed, as well. When these people recognize us, they will alert the Sins to our location without even wondering why they're doing it."

Alan paused for a moment, watching Darius with a genuine, concerned expression. "I understand you may not want to stay with the Martyrs," he said, "but I believe, if you return to the city, it's only a matter of time before the Sins track you down and kill you."

Darius didn't say anything. He didn't know what he could say. Eva would be devastated. All she wanted to do was come back to the city and search for her brother. Darius groaned and rubbed his eyes. New York was his home, and he hated that the Sins were taking that away from him—like they'd taken everything else.

"For this same reason," Alan went on, "we are launching a search for the others who survived the massacre of your home."

In all the talk about the Sins, Darius had almost forgotten to ask about Saul, Juniper, and Lindsay. He straightened up in his chair. "Do the Sins know about them, too?"

"We cannot be sure," Alan said. "If they saw them in the home, they are probably on the lookout for them as well. They have not started any obvious hunts—if they had, we would know about it—but that does not mean they are not keeping an eye out. We are hoping they realized you were not actually associated with us or the Underground after the failed attack. That may keep your friends safe. All the same, we are going to look for them."

It was like a weight had been lifted off Darius's shoulders. He heaved a sigh and relaxed a little bit. But he still had questions he needed answered.

"But wait," he asked. "If the Sins have so many people hunting for us in New York… why are we back here now?"

He glanced around the room. It just dawned on him how exposed they really were. It wasn't just the Sins he had to look out for. It was everyone. Any of these people could have been Programmed.

"The Sins tend to work in a relatively predictable system," Alan said. "They can't possibly Program everyone in the city. There are simply too many of them. Additionally, every time a Sin loses its host, the Programming made under that host is erased, so they have to start all over again once they've made another possession. I know their systems well enough to get around unnoticed, but for you and Miss Torres, it would be especially challenging. The city you know does not exist anymore, Mr. Jones. Your city was safe. Anonymous. *My* city, the one to which you now belong, whether you like it or not, is more dangerous than you realize. I can only get around the way I do because of the knowledge I have."

"But that can't be foolproof," Darius said.

"It's not," Alan agreed. "Another thing I have that you would not, were you to leave, is a team. My people are watching us." He glanced at the security camera on the ceiling in the corner of the room. Darius frowned. "They are watching the Sins. They are watching the men and women in this restaurant—*around* this restaurant. If there is suspicious activity anywhere within five miles of us, we will hear about it and be able to make our way out."

The beady, black camera lens was pointed right at them. Darius watched it in awe. He never realized how much he had taken anonymity for granted before—until he didn't have it anymore. "It's not just the Sins who have eyes everywhere."

Alan smiled. "No. It's not."

"So," Darius said, tearing his focus away from the camera and back to the table. "You mentioned them losing a host. What happens then? How can you keep an eye out for a Sin if you don't know what it looks like anymore?"

"It is difficult," Alan conceded. "It can take several months for a new possession to complete. Sometimes much, much longer. The longest possession on record took seventeen years." Darius whistled. "We have no way of knowing for sure when a possession has been completed, so we have to look for certain clues as to where the new Sin may show up. Usually, the new host ends up inside of the same circles the Sin ran in beforehand. That's because these communities have already been saturated in their Influence, and the Sin has the most power there. Like I said, they work in somewhat predictable systems.

"And," Alan reached across the table and grabbed a napkin. He pulled a pen from his jacket pocket and began to draw a simple sketch. "All Sins have a mark that sets them apart… Here." He handed the napkin to Darius.

Darius recognized the symbol. He'd seen it on the man who had killed his family and in the video Alan had shown him in his office, at the base of the Sin's neck. He leaned forward and took a closer look. "What is it?"

"It's called the *Peccostium*," Alan said. "All the Sins have one. Once the possession is completed, the mark appears, almost as though it is burned into their skin."

Even in all its simplicity, the tiny symbol was daunting. The look of it, all it represented, sent a chill up Darius's spine. "Like a brand?"

"Yes," Alan said. "When we suspect we've found the new Sin, this mark is what we look for to verify we are correct."

Darius's eyebrows raised. "*How*? You've got to get really close to them, don't you?"

Alan heaved a sigh. "Yes. There are five places the *Peccostium* can manifest on a Sin's host body: on either wrist, on either ankle, or at the back of the neck. The mark moves cyclically, so if one host has it on the back of his neck, the next will have it on her left wrist, then down to the left ankle, and so on. This, at least, makes it easy for us to know where to look for the *Peccostium* when we suspect a new Sin."

"They could just hide it," Darius said.

"Often they do," Alan concurred. "On top of being a mark to identify them, it is one of their largest weaknesses."

Darius frowned. "How?"

"The mark is sensitive," Alan said. "It is a direct tie to the essence of the Sin itself, not just the host. In fact, it marks the *entrance* the Sin took to possess the host in the first place. The very word '*Peccostium*' translates to 'Sin's Doorway.' This connection to the Sin's essence makes it more vulnerable than any other part of their body. If it is grabbed, it sends pain through their nervous system and weakens the muscles. In rare cases, if it is damaged more thoroughly, it may even disrupt the Sin's powers. This is exceptionally challenging, however, as their healing abilities make this kind of injury difficult to inflict."

"So, it's not a *real* weakness, then," Darius said.

Alan shrugged. "It is as much of a vulnerability as, say, the groin. It is easier to hurt than the rest of them, but it will likely not totally disable them. When the opportunity to hurt the *Peccostium* presents itself, we take it. Not only does it make it more likely for my men to destroy the host, but it also provides them a chance to *escape* if destroying the host is not on the table."

For a moment, all Darius could do was look down at the mark scribbled onto the napkin. It was so simple, but just the shape of it made him uncomfortable.

"Ah, there she is."

Alan's voice snapped Darius out of his thoughts again, and he looked up to see a familiar face enter the restaurant. Thorn. Her dark figure moved like a shadow across the room, walking through the crowd in long, fluid steps. Keen, black eyes fell on Darius. Alan got to his feet, and Darius hastily did the same.

"Mr. Jones," Alan said, gesturing to his niece as she approached, "Thorn. Thorn, this is Darius Jones."

Darius held out his hand, and Thorn reached out and shook it. Her hands were icy, and he noticed she was wearing long, fingerless gloves again. Her grip was so firm it bordered on painful.

"It's nice to meet you," Darius said. "Officially."

After all, he had seen her three times now: once at the market, once at his home when she attacked Derek Dane, and once when he'd been hiding in her uncle's closet.

She didn't return the formality. She just nodded to him and then turned to Alan. "Sorry I'm late." She didn't sound sorry. "Did you order?"

"No," Alan said. "We were waiting for you." They all sat down again and took a few minutes going through their menus. Darius chanced a couple of glances at Thorn. She had a fierceness about her. Her thin eyebrows seemed to have settled into a permanent furrow, and her thin lips were set and stern. Something in her jacket moved, and Darius saw the tiny, blue creature's head pop out of her pocket. It was scaly, smooth, and almost childlike, and it watched Darius as though it was trying to read him.

Then Thorn suddenly turned his way and gave him a sharp look. Startled at being caught, he turned his attention back to his menu.

If Darius and Alan had finally achieved a more relaxed atmosphere, it disappeared almost immediately with the arrival of his niece. For the next several minutes, the three of them sat in silence, only speaking when the waitress returned to take their orders. Thorn got more than just her dinner—she also ordered a neat scotch, and she sipped it as smoothly as though it was water.

When the waitress left their table, Alan cleared his throat and started the conversation again.

"I asked Thorn to join us tonight because she is in charge of our Intelligence Department," he said. Thorn glanced at him, just with her eyes. They darted up to Alan's face over the rim of her glass in a quick, sharp motion. "Primarily, her agents focus on tracking the Sins within the city and gathering intel. It was *her* team that discovered the Sins had captured Cyrus and learned of his connection to you and the street market."

Darius turned to look at Thorn. She said nothing as she lifted her scotch to her lips again and took in just enough to wet her tongue.

"However," Alan went on. He was watching his niece still, as though waiting for her to take ownership of this part of the conversation. She seemed content to let him do the talking. "We are going to be reallocating the Gray Unit—that is, our intelligence agents who work within the city—to search for your surviving friends instead. Thorn, would you tell Darius a little bit about how we are going to do that?"

Thorn didn't speak right away. She took her time in lowering her scotch back to the table and squaring her shoulders before she finally turned and took Darius in. Her black eyes were hot and piercing, focused on him with an almost unsettling precision. Then she turned to Alan again.

"You pretty much covered it," she said shortly.

Alan just watched her with a small frown.

"Surely you can provide Darius with *details*."

Then Thorn took in a deep breath, threw Alan a hot glare, and looked at Darius again.

"What would you like to know?" she asked him.

He blanched for a moment. He felt his mouth fall open a little stupidly at the broadness of the question and the inevitable broadness of his answer.

"Everything," he said.

So Thorn went into it. She explained, with short sentences and quick summaries, how her team was going to search for Saul. Every so often, Alan would interrupt and insist she elaborate on a point, and she would do so with a curt, matter-of-fact attitude.

The answer was overwhelming. Thorn indicated software used to search for faces, systems designed to ping off names, and people with their ears on the ground. She didn't sound hopeful, but she didn't sound hope*less*, either. She just laid it out for him like she was telling him the weather.

And when she was done, she turned to Alan with her eyebrows raised.

"Thank you," Alan said with a tone that seemed to say, "Now that wasn't so hard, was it?"

Thorn just nodded back, but the tight muscles on her throat, and the look she threw Alan, let Darius know she caught the snark.

Then their dinner arrived, and the conversation evolved to less *important* matters.

Darius was fascinated by the pair. As the three of them discussed Darius's time in the Underground and Eva's healing, he paid attention to the way Thorn and Alan interacted. Particularly, he paid attention to *Thorn*. She contrasted her uncle's calm and patience. She was a tight knot of pure, angry, untethered energy. It seemed like every muscle across her body—from her shoulders to the slender fingers gripped around her scotch glass—was ready to fight. Darius got the distinct feeling she lacked a sense of control that came so easily to her uncle.

But on the other hand, their similarities were haunting. They shared the same cold, half-empty black eyes and dark hair, the same angular features. Even their *moods* were similar: a combination of melancholy and cunning, wisdom and spirit, that shouldn't have worked together as well as it did. Every so often, they'd exchange a look and communicate silently through body language alone, and the messages were so subtle, so well-crafted, that even Darius, who prided himself on his ability to read people, couldn't figure them out.

Whatever it was, Darius couldn't shake the feeling both Alan Blaine and Thorn Rose were somehow aged, as though years of death and loss had shaved precious minutes from their short lives and given them wisdom far beyond their years.

And as quickly as she had appeared, Thorn was gone. Once the meal was done, she excused herself and took off. Darius watched her dark form slowly merge into the evening crowd on the sidewalk outside. She pulled her hood up over her head and disappeared into anonymity on the bustling streets of New York City.

Darius didn't know how to place his feelings about her. She was hardened, cold, and private, but something about her drew him in. Despite all the reasons he had to dislike her, he didn't.

Almost immediately after Thorn had gone, Alan led Darius out from the restaurant, too. The walk to the car was short, but Alan was keenly observant of the streets around him. At one point, his attention was drawn eastward—and if Darius wasn't mistaken, there was a sense of urgency in his voice as he asked the valet for his keys.

"Thank you for joining me tonight," Alan said, then, and he turned and provided Darius with a small smile. "I hope you are feeling more comfortable with the Martyrs. Did you have any other questions you wanted to ask?"

Darius shook his head. "No, I'm good," he said, and he was. He had a lot of new information to take in, and the weight of it was giving him a splitting headache at his temples. "Thanks for doing this."

"It was a pleasure," Alan said, and the valet pulled up with their vehicle on the side of the road. Alan opened the door for Darius before he moved around to the other side. As he got into the car, he turned to Darius and said, "I do hope Miss Torres will join us next time. I was looking forward to getting to know her, as well."

Eva. Darius's stomach flipped as they made their way out of the city again. Now he had the dilemma of talking to Eva and explaining to her why leaving the Underground was going to be a lot more complicated than he'd initially thought.

And he felt a little guilty, because he was grateful for the excuse to stick around longer.

Eva was waiting for him in his room. She had tracked down a map of New York and was looking over it when he opened the door and walked in. Her expression was tight as she asked, "How was dinner?"

"It was… educational," Darius said.

"What's the plan about Saul?"

"They have a team looking for him," Darius said. "And they're using some computer program or something, too, but that's a lot harder because they don't have a photograph of him to base it on. Some face recognition stuff? I'm not sure."

The tension in the room faded a bit. Eva's shoulders relaxed, and she leaned back on the bed. "Oh, good," she said. "But I'll feel a lot better when we're out there looking for him ourselves. I've been circling the places I think he's most likely to take June and Lindsay to. I think that—what?"

His expression must have been a dead giveaway because Eva took one look at him and stopped in her tracks. Darius sighed and looked down at his feet. "Eva, I don't think it's a good idea for us to be out there right now."

The tension returned. Eva's eyes darkened, and she crossed her arms. "You're kidding! Why the hell not?"

"Because the Sins know we survived the attack," he said. "And they know we know about this place." He gestured widely around him—at the room, at the whole Underground. "They have people out there looking for us, and if they find us, they'll do more than just kill us. They'll use us to find the Martyrs. I don't think we can take that kind of risk. Not yet."

"You said we could leave," Eva growled. "You told me we could leave this place and start out on our own. Now you want to *stay?*"

"I don't *want* to stay," Darius said. That was only half a lie. "But I don't want to go out just to get ourselves killed, either. If the Sins really have the kind of power they seem to have, we're in a lot more trouble if we try to find Saul ourselves. Why don't we let the Martyrs—"

"Do you even *hear* yourself right now?" Eva jumped to her feet and threw her hands up in the air. "'If the Sins have the kind of power…' Damnit, Darius, did you just go full in on this cult?"

That caught him off guard. For a moment, all he did was blink and stare. "This—what? No. No! It's not a cult—"

"It sounds like one," she said. "And even if it's not, I don't really give a damn! I don't care about what's happening here. Saul is *alive,* and I just want to go out and find him!"

"I'm not saying we can't go look for Saul," Darius said hastily. "Or June and Lindsay. I'm just saying we might not be leaving as quickly as we thought—"

"If we wait much longer, they could die!"

"And if we go right now, *we* could die! All the Sins want is to find this place, and now that they know we've been here, we're targets."

"Look." Eva exhaled hard and covered her eyes with one hand. "We don't know if anything these people are telling us is even *real,* but we *do* know Saul, Juniper, and Lindsay are out there somewhere, *right now.*"

"Eva, they have a video—"

"Videos can be faked!"

Now he was starting to get angry. He felt it constricting around his chest and rising color to his cheeks. Eva was poking at all the little insecurities he'd had about the Martyrs and putting it into sharp light that Darius had no real, concrete evidence to explain why he believed in the Sins. Nothing except an old, grainy video and that it explained why someone was able to slaughter a room full of children in cold blood.

"What *point* do they have in lying to us?" Darius shot back. "And how do you explain everyone who has believed in them? Are they all crazy?"

"Maybe not," Eva screamed. "But I won't be a part of it. All I want to do is find my brother, whether you're coming or not. If the tables were turned, Saul would be out there right now looking for us, and you know that. We're family. I thought that meant something to you!"

Before Darius could say a word, Eva brushed past him and through the door. She slammed it behind her, and he was left alone.

CHAPTER NINE

For the first time since the massacre, Darius found himself distinctly *alone* in the Underground. The next couple of days were the hardest. Eva kept to herself, locked in her room, and she refused to come out. She didn't even come to the kitchen anymore. She must have been relying on the stock of food she and Darius had gathered together and slipping off to the bathrooms as quietly and secretly as she could.

Eva was a ghost in his desolate place, all but invisible and unheard.

Darius didn't push her to reconnect with him. Though he was sad, and he was lonely, he wasn't the kind of man who thought he was *owed* company. Instead, he resigned himself to the idea Eva would seek him out—when she was ready.

Until then, Darius was by himself.

His days were long, his nights became even more frazzled, and Darius felt truly isolated. Down here, miles under the ground, away from the world he knew, he was going stir crazy. He wanted to know how the search for Saul and the others was going. When he wasn't wondering when Eva was going to speak to him again, he was worrying about them.

Did they get hurt in the attack? Where could they have gone? And whatever happened to Lindsay?

Had she died anyway, not from the Sins, but from her sickness? All the effort he'd gone through to get her antibiotics felt infuriatingly pointless now. When he closed his eyes at night, all he saw was Max Douglas's smug, meaty face *laughing* at him for his failure.

Darius did most of this wondering and worrying alone at a table on the outer edge of the courtyard. He'd never been an introvert, and the close walls of his room felt almost suffocating. At least the courtyard gave the *illusion* of space, and even from a distance, the Martyrs were better company than the miserable thoughts inside his head.

But they didn't stay distant.

His presence in the courtyard drew attention. It didn't take long for others to reach out to him and try to make him feel welcome. Occasionally, Raquel would join him, still in her scrubs, fresh off her shift. Sometimes, Chris would be with her. Abraham also made a point to talk to Darius when they were out in the courtyard at the same time, even though Darius always asked about Saul, and Abraham never had any new news on the subject. Darius had even been approached once by a petite, vibrant woman with bright purple hair and an Irish accent—she had seemed so misplaced that, if Darius hadn't known better, he'd almost have thought she accidentally wandered in from the street.

They all asked versions of the same question: How are you—and Eva—liking the Underground?

It wasn't long before *everyone* knew Eva was *not* a fan—of the Martyrs or, currently, of Darius.

"Mind if I sit here?"

Darius had been so caught up in his own head he hadn't noticed someone approach him. He jumped a little and turned to see William Michaels standing over his shoulder. They'd officially met on two occasions. First, when William helped get Darius away from the massacre of his old life, and again when they visited the Martyrs Memorial Garden.

He was older than Chris and Darius—if he had to guess, he'd place him in his early forties. He was fit, broad-shouldered, and wide-mouthed. When he smiled, which he did often, Darius could count most of his big, white teeth.

"No," Darius said. "Go ahead." William pulled the chair out and sat down.

"So," he started, cutting into his grilled chicken breast. "How are you settling in?"

Darius gave the same forced smile he used every time people asked him this. "I'm not really planning on 'settling' here."

He was getting tired of the repetition—and tired of giving docile, polite answers.

William popped a piece of meat into his mouth and gave Darius a curious look. If Darius's curt attitude had bothered him, he didn't show it. "That's a shame," he said. "It's been a long time since we've had any new members join up. It's been refreshing. Given a lot of us a new sense of purpose."

"Oh yeah?" Darius leaned forward across the table. "So, this organization is kind of dying, huh?"

William shrugged. "Eh. *I* don't feel that way. We're not gaining a lot of new people, like I said, and obviously this place is past its heyday." He gestured widely around the empty, echoing cavern of the courtyard. "But we're a scrappy group, and if we *are* going down, I'm gonna smash a few Sin faces along the way."

"Why?" Darius asked. "Why does anyone stick around if things are going downhill?"

William paused and sat up a little straighter in his chair. "Why? Alan told you what we're up against, didn't he?" Darius nodded. "Well, *that's* why. We've seen firsthand how dangerous the Sins are. The rest of the world has no idea, but us? We live in it. Some of us were *born* to it. Like Chris. This battle runs in her blood."

"Well," Darius said, and he raised his eyebrows on his head defiantly. "It doesn't run in *mine*."

"Not *yet*," William said.

Darius didn't respond.

"Tell me." William cleared his throat and went back to his dinner. "What's so important for you to get back to?"

That struck a chord in Darius's chest and made it tight and angry. His mother and father were dead. His home had been decimated. The only person he had left in the world wasn't talking to him. He just stared at William from across the table, and William stared back.

"Some of my friends are out there," he said. William shook his head.

"I know," he said. "And *we* are looking for them—and we stand a better chance at finding them than you do. What *else* you got?"

"Look," Darius said. He felt his fists ball up, and he shook his head. "I may not have much out there, but what the hell do I have in *here*? This isn't my war."

"Isn't it?" William asked. "I was there when we found you, and I saw what the Sins took from you. I don't know, man. If I were in your shoes, I'd be chomping at the bit for the chance to bite back, and I'd fight like hell to make it happen."

A flame flickered to life in Darius's stomach. That was true. Darius couldn't think about the children and Thad without Derek Dane's smug, arrogant face popping up to taint their memories, but the dark, vicious feelings he had made him uncomfortable. "I don't know what I want," he said. His anger ebbed a little at the brutal honesty of it.

Because even if Darius didn't know if he wanted to join the Martyrs, he sure as hell knew he wanted to stop Derek Dane.

William didn't respond right away. He chewed and watched Darius from across the table. "You know," he finally said. "You're not the only person whose life has been ruined by the Sins. Fighting against them isn't just a fight for yourself. It's a fight for all of us. I think it's a worthwhile one."

Darius heaved a sigh. "That might be true," he said. "But

I can't abandon Eva. She's all I have left."

"You guys have us," William said, and he passed Darius a kind, genuine smile. Darius was caught off guard. He hadn't stopped to think that the Martyrs may not just be hoping they decided to stay. They already considered him and Eva a part of the team.

A surge of gratitude snuck up on him. He felt his throat tighten up, and he cleared it. William seemed to sense it, so he gave Darius a graceful way out and continued to talk.

"So, Eva doesn't want to stay, huh?"

"God, no. She doesn't believe any of this is real."

"But you do?"

Darius looked over at William and took a deep breath. "Yeah," he said. "It seems crazy, but yeah. It's the only way I can make sense of what the hell happened... Doesn't do me much good, though. I can't convince Eva."

"Don't be too sure about that," William said. "I'm sure you'll end up finding all the proof you need. Once you've been here for a while, the evidence will be pretty damning."

Darius laughed. "You talk like I'm staying."

William smiled and shrugged. "What can I say? I'm never gonna quit trying to convince you to stick around. I can promise you that."

The way William planned on convincing Darius to join the Martyrs meant *showing* Darius the Martyrs. When he realized Darius had never been given a proper tour of the Underground, he took it upon himself to make that happen.

For the next couple of days, Darius spent his nights sleeplessly tossing and turning, his days waiting for Eva to decide she was ready to talk to him, and his evenings with William Michaels, walking around the Underground and learning more about this organization.

"Alan Blaine obviously runs the whole show," William was telling Darius as they wandered on the upper-most floor of the Underground. He led him through the narrow hallway to Alan's office—and Thorn's. They got to the waiting room outside Alan's door, and William held his hand out toward it. Darius tried to act like this wasn't his third time here—and that the second time hadn't involved breaking and entering. He briefly looked around for cameras, but they were so well hidden in the room he couldn't spot them. William went on. "He's in charge of finances, security, tactical, you name it. The heads of all the departments report directly to him."

"How long has he been in command?" Darius asked.

William just shrugged. "As long as I can remember. Anyway—"

He gestured to the door with the name "Rose" on it.

"You've met Thorn, right?" When Darius nodded, William went on. "On top of being the second-in-command, she runs the Intelligence Department, which includes our Cleaning Crews and the Gray Unit. Basically, any unit focused on *learning* about the Sins or *covering up* the Martyrs is her territory. She's not here a lot—spends a lot of time in the city. She and the rest of the Gray Unit live double lives. They've got aliases and connections in New York to gather intel. She helps out with TAC sometimes, too."

"Helps?" Darius frowned. "How?"

"Well, Thorn's had the most one-on-one experience with the Sins," William said. "And we're short-staffed, so we need all the help we can get."

"Why don't you recruit more people?" Darius asked as they walked back into the narrow hallway outside the waiting room.

"It's hard," William said. "There used to be a more well-established recruitment protocol, way before I was here, but apparently, there were complications with people not being careful enough. The Sins would get valuable information, and the families of the Martyrs who *didn't* live in the Underground were slaughtered. Most of us who join up now? It's *after* we've already lost everything…"

Then William cleared his throat and went on.

"These four offices out here," he said, gesturing around him. "They belong to the *other* members of the Martyr leadership."

Beneath Thorn and Alan, there were four directors. Jeremiah Montgomery commanded the Tactical Armed Combat Unit; Lina Brooks and Mackenzie McKay together ran the Virtue Research and Discovery Department; and Abraham Locke functioned both as a counselor to the Martyrs and brought morale issues to the table inside of leadership meetings.

William knocked on three of the four doors—Lina's, Mackenzie's, and Jeremiah's—but the only one who answered was Lina. Darius recognized her. He'd met her on the drive to Cain's estate. When she saw them, she smiled. Her gray eyes were little half-moons, smiling themselves.

"William," she said. Her voice was soft. "Darius! Can I help you?"

"I'm just showing Darius around," William said, and he crossed his arms around his chest. "Teaching him about what we do here. I was hoping you or Mackenzie could give him a look into what you're working on."

"Oh," Lina said, and she opened her office to them with a wide, swooping arm. "Of course! Come on in."

Lina's office was small and cramped. There were four desks set up around the room, and at each desk, a Martyr sat diligently working. The spaces between desks were crammed with books, papers, binders, photographs, and artifacts, and the desks themselves were piled high with more of the same. High-tech computer screens blared harsh light into the room. A few eyes glanced up as Lina closed the door and walked to her desk, which sat in the center of the chaos. Then she spread her arms and smiled.

"Welcome to the 'research' side of the Research and Discovery Unit!"

The Research and Discovery, or R&D, Unit was fascinating. Their job—their *only* job—was searching for Virtues.

There were two teams. Lina's team, the research units, focused on looking for clues indicating the presence of a Virtue in the area. When they found a lead worth following, it was passed to Mackenzie's team—the recon units—who would go out and see if they could actually find one.

"How many Virtues have you been able to track down?" Darius asked. Lina cast William a defeated little look before she sighed and turned back to Darius.

"None," she said. "There are only seven of them, in a world of almost ten billion people. We're essentially looking for needles in a haystack the size of New York City itself."

Darius's chest tightened. He'd known the war was going to be a challenge, but the numbers behind it were stacked staggeringly high against the Martyrs.

After explaining the leadership structure to Darius, William took him through the rest of the Underground and introduced him to the other Martyr units—smaller, more specialized groups with more technical jobs. Of course, there was the hospital staff. Darius was already familiar with Dr. Harris and most of his nurses. William also tracked down the maintenance team who handled cleaning and care for the Underground's systems. Then the two of them climbed up the stairway beside the elevator—all the way to the top. It was long and grueling. Darius was sweating through his shirt by the time they reached the threshold.

Here, the door was locked.

"This leads out to the gas station," William said. He put his thumb against a pad in the door lock, and it beeped open. He led the way through. "It's also the emergency exit."

"Are we allowed up here?" Darius asked as he poked his head out and found himself in a back storage closet. Brooms and buckets lined the walls.

"Well, *I* am," William said with a chuckle. "You'll have your thumbprint registered in if you join up, too. This station is owned and run by the Martyrs. The six employees who work here? They're specialized TAC agents trained both to run the station and handle any Sin attempts to get Underground."

Darius's face paled. "Has that happened?"

"Oh, god, no," William said. "If it had, we wouldn't be here. The Sins have never tracked us down."

Then he ushered Darius into the room and shut the door behind him. He walked to the other door, which was also locked, and he pressed a button beside the handle. While they waited, Darius frowned.

"It's amazing they haven't found this place," he said.

William shrugged, but he didn't look Darius in the eye as he said, "All Martyrs go through anti-torture procedures. The Sins can't get anything valuable out of us."

He didn't elaborate—and didn't give Darius the chance to ask. Someone finally came to the door and opened it from the other side. William seemed almost grateful for the reprieve as he brought Darius out and introduced him to even *more* of the people dedicated to eradicating the Sins. More seemingly ordinary people, living this secret life, with a secret mission, that kept them somehow just as isolated as Darius had found himself feeling.

"It's a lot, huh?"

Darius filled his mouth with air and released it in a popping huff.

"You could say that again."

After coming back down from the station above, William had insisted Darius join him for a beer in the break room. Now the two sat side by side on an overstuffed sofa while the television blared from across a coffee table. This space was set up almost like a bachelor pad. Beside the huge television were floor-to-ceiling shelves, and those shelves were packed with books, board games, and movies. In the back, there was a pool table, a dartboard, an old pinball machine, and a streaming stereo. William laughed and took a sip of his drink. Darius held his awkwardly. After losing both his mother and father to alcoholism, in one way or another, he'd never cared to try the stuff. All the same, he hadn't known how to say that to William when he'd handed him the bottle, and now he was stuck with it.

"See, we're not half as dead as we look," William said, and he playfully nudged Darius with his elbow.

"How many Martyrs are there?" Darius asked. "There are a lot more departments than I expected…"

William frowned as he thought about it. "About a hundred," he said with a shrug. "Give or take. Almost half of those are in TAC with me. We're the largest group since we're sent out on operations to take down Sin hosts—or to stop the Sins from doing damage."

Darius sucked in a thin breath through his teeth. "God, I wouldn't want *that* job."

He regretted saying it almost as soon as it slipped from his mouth. Darius saw William latch onto the opportunity like a starving child waiting for dropped scraps. His eyes glinted, and he leaned in toward Darius with a smirk that seemed to say, "I got you now!"

What he actually said was, "Which job *would* you want?"

Darius couldn't help it. He laughed and scratched the back of his head. He'd walked right into that one, and though he still didn't want to commit to anything—not without Eva—he had to admit, this time with William had helped distract him from the agony of waiting for her to talk to him. It didn't hurt to play along.

So he said, "I mean, probably the Gray Unit. They get to live in New York, yeah?"

But William's face fell a little bit. He nodded and said, "Yes, but you can't be on the Gray Unit."

Darius frowned. "Why not?"

"Because the Sins have marked you," William said. "Pride and Envy saw your face. Since they've seen you, they've got people Programmed to look for you. The Gray Unit can only include people the Sins haven't identified as one of us. The only—and I mean *only*—exception to that rule is Thorn herself. Even though the Sins have had her marked for forever, she's the head of the department, so she gets to do what she wants. And honestly, she's too good at what she does to stay in the Underground. But you? There's no way she'd take chances letting you out there."

Darius's heart sank a little. Even though he wasn't sure he even wanted a place anywhere in the Martyrs, it was still disappointing to know he couldn't have joined the team looking for Saul and the others.

William seemed to sense that. He watched Darius for a moment before he shrugged and said, "Besides, Thorn hand selects the agents, and she's really particular. Only certain people make the cut for the Gray Unit."

"What kind of thing does she look for?"

"A big one is their ability to blend in," William said. "She selects different people for different parts of town, so they need to fit into the scene there—*really* fit in. They spend half their time living out in the city, working in the same spaces the Sins work in, so it's gotta be convincing. They've also got to be driven and detail-oriented. Unfortunately, though, there's a lot of turnover."

Darius frowned. "Why?"

"Because the Sins know we've got people out there keeping an eye on them," William said with a sigh. "They're on the lookout for suspicious behavior. A year ago, my buddy, Peter, transferred to Gray from TAC because one of the field agents was marked by the Sins. They burned his apartment down—with him inside. We only found pieces of him."

"Oh my *god*," Darius breathed. Maybe he *didn't* want to be a part of the Gray Unit.

"Yeah," William said. "Alexis and her brother Caleb are some of the longest-lasting Gray Unit agents I've heard of. I think they've been there for five… six years?"

"*Alexis* is part of the Gray Unit?" Darius asked, shocked. "I thought Thorn hand-picked her people?"

William laughed. "Oh, so you've met Alexis?" he asked.

Darius felt heat rise to his cheeks, and he cleared his throat. "Well, not *technically.*"

"You get the gist, then," William said. "She and Caleb are hard to get along with. They were here for four years before joining up with the Gray Unit, and they never really connected to anyone down here. I personally think it's because their dad's a Sin—"

"What?"

"Oh, yeah." William said it casually, like it was a normal thing for conversation around here, but Darius could tell he loved having a story to tell, and an invested audience to listen. "Anton Claytor. Greed got in and tried to kill the whole family. His wife didn't make it, but we got there in time to save the kids. Alexis was nineteen and Caleb sixteen, if I remember right. It was one of my first big incidents with TAC—pretty wild ride."

Darius couldn't believe it. "And he's *still* Greed?"

"Yup," William said. "So I think they feel weird fighting against him."

"That's got to be a conflict of interest," Darius said.

William just shrugged. "I mean, by default it is, sure. But we're short-staffed, and Alexis and Caleb are great at what they do. Alexis is the second-best Gray Unit agent we've got, or so I've heard. Plus, they're not assigned to follow Greed. Alexis is on Gluttony, and Caleb on Lust, so there's no overlap. Like I said, Thorn picks her people, and she picked them for a reason."

"I thought they couldn't be in the Gray Unit if the Sin had seen them, though?" Darius asked.

"He didn't see them," William said. *"He* didn't go to kill his family. He sent some Puppets. It was chalked up as a random attack—robbery gone wrong. We saved the kids, forged their deaths, and gave them a new life here. All the same, I bet it's hard for them. They were raised in a pretty privileged household, and they come to find that privilege kind of came about because their dad sucked so much that he was targeted by the Sins as a new host. Speak of the devils…"

Motion at the door had caught William's eye, and he and Darius turned to it to see three people walking in. One of them was familiar: Alexis Claytor. She scanned the room, and when her icy blue eyes landed on Darius, she frowned. Darius wondered if she knew he'd been hiding in that closet, watching her get berated by Thorn. The look she gave him made him think so. It was full of venom and anger. Then she turned away and walked back to the pool table.

She was followed by a man who looked remarkably like her: same cold eyes, same slender form. His platinum blonde hair even had a similar haircut. That had to be Caleb.

Bringing up the rear was someone Darius hadn't seen before. From the outfit he was wearing—the beige cargo pants and black turtleneck Darius had learned was the Tactical uniform—he could assume he worked with William. He was older than Alexis and her brother by at least fifteen years, and where they were tall and slender, he was lined with bulky, undefined muscle. With a snort, he hacked up a wad of chewing tobacco and spit it into an empty plastic water bottle. Then he caught Darius watching him, and he offered a stiff nod of acknowledgment.

"Hey, Conrad," William called across the room. "Alexis, Caleb."

The big man grunted in response while Alexis and Caleb all but ignored them. Conrad pushed another pinch of tobacco in between his gums and cheek. He grabbed a pool stick from the rack on the wall. Alexis was already chalking hers while her brother swiped around on his phone in the corner. They didn't even look up from what they were doing.

That didn't seem to bother William. He cast Darius a quick look—one with a kind, concerned note to it—before he turned fully around on the couch and looked across the room.

"Hey, Alexis," he said. A couple of empty card tables stood between them, and her eyes darted up to William to acknowledge she'd heard him. "How's the search for Darius's buddies going? Any updates?"

Alexis didn't respond right away. She was lining up to take the opening break shot. She rolled her shoulders, sighed, and said, "It's a lost cause."

Darius's heart sank into his stomach, and Alexis took her shot. The cue slammed against the rest of the balls and sent them sprawling across the table. William frowned.

"The hell do you mean?"

"I mean," Alexis said irritably, "it's been over a month. If the Sins didn't track them down and kill them, chances are they left the city. That's what I would have done. I don't know why we're even wasting our time. Conrad, you're up."

As Conrad came to the table, William said, "You're not serious? We're looking for them because they could be in danger. If the Sins find them—"

"Look, Michaels, you asked for an update, and that's the update. We haven't found jack shit, and we probably won't. Remember how long it took us to find *this* guy?" She jabbed her pool stick in Darius's direction. "And he wasn't a moving target. Don't get your hopes up. They're gone."

She turned back to the table. Conrad looked over her back to William, and the two of them shared a look of exasperation. Then William and Darius turned back toward the TV. "Don't listen to her," William murmured, but Darius already had, and the words had sunk like lead into his gut. "Thorn won't give up."

But Darius wasn't so sure about that, either. He'd met Thorn, and while she didn't seem like the "giving up" type, she also didn't seem like the kind of person to go chasing the desperate hopes of a man she'd just met.

"Yeah," Darius said, but he said it just to fill the silence building in the air between them. "You know, man, I'm tired. I'm going to go see if I can convince Eva to talk to me and then head to bed."

William didn't even try to stop Darius from going. He reached out and gave him a firm thump on the shoulder and wished him good luck. Darius didn't look up to the three playing pool at the other end of the room, but he felt their eyes on the back of his head as he walked through the door.

It was late. The lights in the ceiling had been dimmed to let the Martyrs know it was past 9:00 p.m. The courtyard was all but empty—a few people were eating late dinners by the kitchen, and others were filtering back to the living halls. As Darius was walking back to his room, the door to the gym opened, and for the first time since arriving at the Underground, he saw Thorn Rose on the second level.

She was alone. Her wet hair was combed back from her face, and she wore loose lounge pants and a blood-red, cotton camisole. A white towel draped around her bare shoulders, and a black gym bag hung from the crook of her arm. Even here, all by herself in the empty courtyard, Thorn held herself high, with a sense of drive and power. This time, though, Darius also got a sense of clarity and calm he hadn't seen in her before. Her dark eyes swept around the room and landed on Darius. She seemed almost taken aback to see him. Her brows pinched together, then she pulled down her towel, draped it over her left forearm, and abruptly, she made her way toward him.

There was no sense in pretending he hadn't seen her or noticed she'd changed course to intercept him, so Darius just stopped where he was and waited for her. As she got closer, Darius caught the distinct smell of chlorine. Was there a *pool* down here?

"Jones." The word came out curt and sharp but somehow polite all the same. She paused a bit, almost like she wasn't sure how to talk to him. It seemed like she had a specific agenda in mind, but instead of jumping right into it, she attempted small talk. "What are you doing out here?"

"I was just having a beer with William," he said. He held up his bottle, which was still nearly full. Thorn glanced down at it, and one of her thin brows raised high on her forehead. Darius felt his cheeks flush. He dropped the bottle back down and wished he'd thought to throw it out in the rec room. "Now I'm going to go talk to Eva."

"If she'll talk to *you*," Thorn said.

"Ah," Darius said. He shouldn't have been surprised the news moved this high up the food chain. "Everyone knows about that, huh?"

Thorn didn't respond in the same humor. She just watched Darius with that familiar furrowed expression and said, "This is a hard place to keep secrets." Then, just briefly, she broke eye contact and glanced down at the towel over her folded arms. Her brows pinched together just a little bit harder as she looked back up to him and said, "Alan has been looking for you." Her tone darkened, and the clarity and calm that had washed over her face seemed to fade away. A sliver of anger reappeared in her black, half-empty eyes. "Where have you been?"

"With William," Darius said, gesturing with his full beer bottle back toward the rec room. "He was showing me around."

Thorn nodded. Darius couldn't tell if that answer was satisfactory or not.

"Well," she said, "Alan thinks he found a way to '*help*' with your problem."

Thorn clearly didn't believe in this solution. The subject change reignited the mood Darius had come to expect from her. Whatever fragile calmness she'd had shattered, and the embers behind it flickered to life.

"He's probably still in his office," she said, "making arrangements. Go talk to him."

She didn't even give Darius a chance to thank her. She just excused herself and walked across the courtyard toward the East Wing dormitories.

Heading to Alan's office now felt odd, like he was returning to the scene of a crime. Darius made sure to pour the undrunk beer down one of the kitchen sinks and put the bottle in the recycling bin before he made his way to the elevators and back to the top level. Sure enough, when he got to the waiting room outside Alan's office, he found the door open and Alan sitting patiently behind his desk. He got to his feet as soon as he saw Darius in the doorway.

"Mr. Jones," Alan said. "It's good to see you again. Please, shut the door."

Darius did.

Alan came around his desk and leaned back against it. He steepled his fingers and pressed them against his lips. After a brief silence, he said, "I've gotten the impression Miss Torres does not trust the Martyrs."

Darius had no idea how to respond. He just raised a single brow and said, "Well… can you blame her?"

"No," Alan said with a small, ironic smirk. "I suppose I can't, but I would like to change it. I have been pulling in some favors, connecting with old contacts in the Martyrs books, and I believe I can provide Miss Torres with something that will show her we are here to help."

"What is it?" Darius asked.

"I know someone who may be able to aid in Eva's healing," Alan said.

That wasn't what Darius was expecting. He raised his eyebrows and crossed his arms. "*Really?* How? Dr. Harris said she's almost totally recovered."

"This person," Alan said cryptically, "has different specialties than Elijah's. Elijah is a skilled physician and surgeon, certainly, but he tells me the mutilation in Eva's stomach will scar quite badly. I believe we can minimize this scarring if we act quickly."

"How quickly?"

"I've already set it up," Alan said. "We leave tomorrow morning."

Darius took a deep breath and exhaled it slowly before he said, "Eva's not even talking to me. I don't know how I can convince her to go."

"Please try," Alan said with a smile, but there was a sense of urgency in his voice so subtle Darius wasn't sure if he was imagining it or not. "And meet me in the garage tomorrow morning."

Darius agreed, but he was pretty damn sure he knew what Eva was going to say.

CHAPTER TEN

Darius had been right. Eva had just ignored him as he talked to her through a closed door. No matter what he said, she didn't respond except by turning off the light. When the sliver of yellow disappeared from the crack under the door, he knew it was time to give it up.

By the time he'd gotten back to Alan's office to break the news, though, the Martyr leader was gone for the night. Darius would just have to tell him in the morning.

At 7:00, Darius found Alan closing the back of his sleek sports car. He was dressed in his typical black trench coat, with a pressed, red button-up and slacks beneath it. He looked almost excited as he turned to see Darius walking across the parking lot. His expression faltered a bit when he saw Darius was alone.

"I take it Miss Torres has no interest in my offer?" He asked it out of formality only. It was clear Alan already knew the answer.

"I'm afraid not," Darius said. "I was just coming to tell you the trip's off."

Alan's reaction surprised Darius. He was almost flustered. Alan took a deep breath and shook his head, glancing over his shoulder at the car he'd just finished packing. It seemed he was debating with himself on what the best course of action should be. Finally, he turned back to Darius and said, "No. I think, once you meet this person for yourself, you will be able to convince Miss Torres how much we can help her. Let's go."

"What?" Darius blinked a couple of times and frowned. "How long will we be gone? I haven't told Eva I'm leaving."

"I had Abraham pack you an overnight bag," Alan said dismissively as he climbed into the driver's seat. "We'll be back tomorrow evening. Miss Torres may not even notice you've gone."

Darius hated to admit that Alan was probably right.

So, without much else to do and nothing really keeping him at the Underground, Darius climbed into Alan's car, and they left.

They drove north, hugging close to New York State before veering to the west, up into the Appalachian Mountains. The evidence of fall had officially set in. Trees boasted colorful leaves: orange, red, yellow, and gold. They fell and coated the earth in a vibrant, fiery blanket, illuminated by the bright light of morning. The very air smelled of autumn. Musky, earthen, and crisp.

The first hour of the drive passed in quiet, albeit somewhat awkward, peace. Alan still seemed irritated Eva had decided not to join them. His thin lips were set into a fine line behind his black goatee, and his brows were furrowed heavily over dark eyes.

He was also driving faster than he had when he had taken Darius into the city for their dinner together. They flew around a corner so quickly Darius gripped his armrest for support. It was almost like Alan was eager to get to where they were going, which, now that he thought about it, Darius didn't even know.

"So," Darius said, "how long will it take to get to… wherever we're going?"

"We're going to a small town in northern Pennsylvania," Alan said briefly. "The drive will take just under five hours."

Darius's eyes widened. Five hours? Maybe he should have insisted on staying in the Underground. "And this person," he went on. "Are they, what, a plastic surgeon or something?"

At this, Alan gave Darius a quick glance and a smirk. "Or something."

Darius frowned. Clearly, he wasn't going to get a lot of information out of Alan here. It was like he was relishing the surprise.

They rounded another corner. Suddenly, Alan swore and let off the gas. Their car began to slow, and Darius glanced out the back window to see a highway patrol sitting on the side of the road. Alan watched the cop in the rearview mirror, his knuckles tight on the wheel.

When the cop turned out onto the road and flashed his lights, Alan swore again, this time much more loudly.

"Put your hood up," he said. He didn't pull over immediately. Instead, he waited until he could exit the highway and stop on the side of a quiet, country road. Here, no cars passed by, and the highway sat several yards above them. Alan put the car into park and tossed Darius his phone. "Pretend you're reading something. *Do not* look up from the screen."

The whole tone of Alan's voice shifted. It was quiet and tense. Darius did as he was told as Alan firmly planted both hands on the wheel. A police officer came up to the side of the car. Another one appeared on Darius's, just outside his field of view. Darius glanced out of the corner of his eye as the first officer tapped on the window. Alan rolled it all the way down.

"Do you know how fast you were going, sir?" the officer asked Alan. His voice was stern and annoyed. In his peripheral vision, Darius saw him raise his sunglasses to look Alan over. Then, if Darius wasn't mistaken, his body language shifted. He seemed to get *more* guarded. The hairs on the back of Darius's neck started to tingle. The officer pulled a phone out of his pocket—

What happened next occurred so quickly Darius could hardly keep up. Alan reached through his open window, grabbed the officer by the collar, and pulled him down—HARD. The man's head slammed onto the roof of the car, and he stumbled off to the side. As Alan hurled his door out and into the officer, the other cop ripped Darius's open. It caught him so off guard he dropped Alan's phone onto the ground. Hands roughly grappled with Darius, tugging on his shoulders, attempting to pry him loose from the seatbelt.

Darius struggled against the officer, batting at his face with his fists and working to twist himself out of his grip. He tried to lunge across the seat to the driver's side of the car, but the cop was too strong. He pulled Darius back, his fingers fastened around Darius's sleeve as he tried to drag him out onto the side of the road.

Suddenly, Alan was upon him. He grabbed the cop in a chokehold and yanked him backward. The cop's feet flailed as he tried to get out of Alan's vice-like grip, and he kicked the passenger side door. It snapped back to the car—catching Darius's fingers as it slammed shut.

He swore loudly as he tore his hand out of the door. Skin flayed back, and blood began to pour into his shaking palm.

The scuffle outside the car went quiet. Darius yanked his sweatshirt off and wrapped the sleeve around his injured hand. Alan's head appeared in the window, and he opened the car.

"What the *fuck* was that?" Darius screamed. He clenched his teeth and held tight onto his wrist.

Alan's pale face had gone even whiter. "They're Sentries," he said, a little breathless. "Programmed by the Sins. Most likely to apprehend me. This is the furthest I've seen them—their Influence must be spreading…"

That meant almost nothing to Darius. He gritted his teeth and curled up over his injured hand. "Yeah," he grumbled. "Great. What the hell do we do now?"

"I need to do some damage control," Alan said. "As no

other cars have passed by, it should be easy, but we must assume they contacted their precinct, and the Sins will learn of this stop. I'll be right back."

Then Alan disappeared again. He grabbed both cops, who were now unconscious, and dragged them back to their cruiser. There, he spent some time inside the vehicle, turning off the lights, and doing god knew what else before he came back to his car and climbed into the driver's seat. By this time, Darius's wounds had soaked through the light gray fabric of his sweatshirt. The fingers of his uninjured hand were hot and sticky with blood.

Darius was sure they were headed back to the Underground, but Alan pulled back onto the freeway, took an odd off-ramp, doubled back onto a smaller, less busy highway, and then pulled over under a small clump of trees. As he got out of the car, Darius called after him. "What are you doing?"

Alan ruffled through the trunk for a moment before returning to the cab with an old first aid kit. "Tending to your injuries. Let me see."

Darius gingerly unwrapped the fabric from his mangled hand. He winced as the last layer stuck to his oozing, open flesh. The sight of his own fingers peeled open made him a little nauseous, and he turned away as he placed his hand in Alan's open palm.

Alan was less gentle than Darius would have liked as he turned Darius's hand this way and that to look at the wounds. Then he began to bandage them up. "You've got two broken fingers," he said. "As well as some pretty significant trauma. I've applied antiseptic and numbing gels. I have some painkillers here, too. That should be enough to get us to where we're going."

"*What?*" Darius was dumbfounded. "You just said my hand is *broken*."

"Your fingers are broken," Alan corrected. Darius glared.

"Shouldn't we head back? Dr. Harris should take a look

at this!"

Alan sighed and shook his head. "Trust me," he said as he put the first aid kit back together and hid it under the back of his seat. "We can help you more where we're going. Just remain calm and take some ibuprofen."

That was the last thing Darius was going to do right now. Alan started them back on the road, and Darius was horrified. It wasn't enough that they'd just run into two men who had maybe been Influenced by the Sins, but now Darius was sitting there with a painful, *broken* hand.

"What about the cops?" he asked incredulously. "They'll send people out looking for us!"

"It's possible," Alan said. His face was still whiter than usual. "I got into the computer to erase all data about the stop, but they called in with a description of the car. We must be careful."

Darius had his doubts, but he didn't have the chance to voice them. A sudden trilling from the ground by his feet distracted him. He winced as he leaned down and found Alan's phone. It was ringing. Thorn's name and face looked up at him from the screen.

Alan quickly snatched it out of Darius's hand and ignored the call.

"Please, Mr. Jones," he said with an air of exasperation. "Trust me."

Darius frowned.

The drive took longer than Alan had anticipated. He was clearly nervous about running into more people who had been Influenced by the Sins. The path they were taking had become a lot less direct. Alan was getting off the freeway and doubling back occasionally or taking obscure side roads that took him well off the beaten path. Darius was getting increasingly agitated. Within an hour of being back on the road, he was starting to bleed through the bandages Alan had applied. Within two, the numbing gel had worn off, and stinging pain was shooting through his fingers. By the time he finally gave in and took some ibuprofen, as Alan had suggested, it barely took the edge off.

Something else seemed to be at play, too. Alan's phone had rung again almost immediately, and again he'd ignored it. After Thorn's third attempt, he put the phone on silent and tossed it into the center console. Darius could only assume Thorn was calling so many times because it was important. Why wasn't Alan answering?

He hated to admit it, but part of him was starting to worry Eva was right—maybe Alan was crazy. Darius watched him out of the corner of his eye, trying to gauge him. He was usually so good at reading people—Alan had him questioning everything he ever knew.

After an agonizing six and a half hours, they finally pulled into a small, quaint town. "Welcome to Wellsboro, Pennsylvania," the sign said. Darius groaned as he cradled his hurt hand against his chest.

"Tell me this is it," he muttered.

"We're almost there," Alan said.

They drove right on through Wellsboro. Thirty minutes later, well outside the town, Alan turned up the driveway to a large home at the top of a hill. Modeled after plantation estates from the South, the house jutted into the sky and boasted two stories. The white paint was chipping around windows and door frames, but the architecture stood sturdy and ornate. The front porch was larger than Darius's room at the Underground. If he wasn't in so much pain, he might have been impressed.

As it was, though, he was just pissed. Alan parked the car, and Darius got out as quickly as he could. He slammed the door behind him and turned on Alan.

"All right! We're here! Now I want to see a goddamned—"

But then the front door to the house flung wide open, and a small, frail old woman came bustling down the steps. "Oh my god! Alan, what the hell happened?" Her silvery gray hair was pulled back into a messy bun at the base of her skull. She didn't even introduce herself to Darius as she grabbed his hand in hers and started unwrapping the bandages. Her skin felt like soft leather against his fingers.

"The Sins," Alan said flatly. Darius was shocked—so this woman knew about the Sins? "Gluttony's Influence over the police departments is spreading. This is the furthest out we've run into one of his officers. They attacked us."

"How'd they get to you?" the woman asked, sending Alan a reproachful look as she finished unwrapping Darius's injury. He wasn't sure why he let her do it. He couldn't explain it, but she felt honest and good, and something was telling him to trust her. "Were you speeding again?"

Alan provided just one short, guilty nod.

"There," the woman said softly. She moved Darius's hand around in her own to look at the damage. She was much kinder and gentler than Alan had been, and attentive in a way that made Darius feel self-conscious. She clicked her tongue and said, "Oh, it's not so bad. I thought it was going to be a lot worse."

"It sure as hell feels—"

Darius was about to say "bad," but something miraculous happened, and the word disappeared between his brain and his tongue. The tips of the woman's fingers suddenly grew warm, and Darius watched in awe as that warmth moved from her flesh and into his. It wound its way through his nerves to the flayed skin on his fingers. It felt electric. Tingling sensations sunk deep into his flesh and bone, pulling them back into place, stitching them together, and in a matter of seconds, the only evidence Darius had been hurt at all was the blood all over his clothing.

"Holy *shit.*"

"Mr. Jones." Darius was only vaguely aware of Alan's voice, or the firm grip of the man's hand on his shoulder. He was staring hard at his fingers—his formerly bloody and mangled fingers. "I'd like you to meet Teresa Solomon. She's a Virtue."

The next few minutes were a blur as Darius tried to simultaneously process what had just happened to him while also helping Alan bring their things in from the car. Teresa led the way up the porch and into the foyer. The warm light coming in through arched windows danced around the tall ceilings. She showed him to his room at the top of the stairs, invited him to wash up and change clothes, and then they shared a quick and easy meal. Darius just followed silently, flexing the fingers of his right hand, shocked at the transformation he'd seen them go through just minutes before.

When they were finally all settled in the grand room, Darius just sat there and stared at his palm.

"You look like you've seen a ghost," Teresa teased. She was sitting across from him, on one of the plush armchairs placed on either side of her fireplace. Darius was on the couch, and he felt at odds with everything around him. Teresa's house was beautiful, clean, and warm. Teresa, even more so. And here Darius was, awkwardly gawking at a hand that shouldn't be working nearly as well as it was.

He shook his head, frowned, and said, "This is the craziest thing that's ever happened to me."

Teresa's laugh was like a song. It resonated around the grand room, and though Darius was still freaked out and overwhelmed, it calmed him down, and soon he found he was smiling back at her.

"Oh," she said with a wink. "Just you wait. The Martyrs will keep you on your toes. Give it a little bit of time, and this will be tame."

"I thought you didn't have any Virtues?" Darius turned to Alan now. The Martyr leader was sitting in the other chair, beside Teresa. He relaxed back in his seat before answering.

"I said we haven't found a Virtue in a very long time, which is true. Teresa was found by the Martyrs back in 2018—over seventy years ago." Alan looked over at Teresa and gave her a kind, warm smile. Teresa smiled back.

Darius just looked between the two of them, waiting for

someone to elaborate. When no one did, he said, "And? What the hell's been going on since then? That was incredible." He held up his hand and shook it around for emphasis. "Why the hell isn't she at the Underground? Dr. Harris could use the help!"

Alan shook his head. "It's a great deal more complicated than that," he said. Teresa reached across and grabbed a cup of tea off the table. She gently stirred it while Alan told her story. "The 20s were a very bloody decade for the Martyrs. We lost scores of people. The Sins had found out about Teresa and were determined to kill her. It was decided the best course of action was to send her away, for her own safety as well as to mitigate tensions with the Sins. Over time, the Martyrs who knew about her were lost and replaced with Martyrs who didn't, and slowly, they forgot she existed at all."

Darius frowned. "Then how'd you know?"

"Martyr leadership kept the information," he said. "The only two Martyrs alive today who know about Teresa are myself and Thorn—and now, you."

"Why keep it a big secret?" Darius asked. "If the Martyrs knew they had a Virtue to fight for, it would change everything!"

"Because the Martyrs were not the only ones who forgot Teresa existed," Alan explained. "The Sins forgot, as well, and we wanted to keep it that way. If the Sins assume Teresa is dead, they won't hunt for her. If they knew about her, they'd do whatever they could do to kill her." The timbre of Alan's voice changed, and a protective tone came to it. Teresa quietly reached across the space between them and grabbed Alan's hand. That simple action alone seemed to be enough to calm him. He took a deep breath and nodded in her direction before he released her fingers and said, "If the Martyrs don't know about her, it's less likely the Sins will get their hands on the information. The best way to make someone torture-proof is to keep them in the dark."

Darius's stomach dropped. "It was to keep you safe?" he

asked, and he turned back to Teresa again.

"Yes," she said. "But even though I was sent away, I never stopped working for the Martyrs. I studied ancient history and world religion to get as much of an understanding of where the Virtues stood in time with the Sins." Darius watched her as she spoke, captivated. It was like an aura of calm, peace, and warmth emanated from her. She seemed aware of it, and she watched Darius back with a similar rapture as she continued. "Then I spent my career traveling. It was as much to keep safe from the Sins as it was to search for other Virtues, like myself, though I didn't have much success. There are only seven of us, after all."

Darius frowned. "I know—seven people out of ten billion. It's impossible."

"Almost," Teresa said with a smile and a wink. "I'm drawn to other Virtues. Think of it like a magnet. When I'm close enough to one, I feel this pull, right here—" she placed a hand at the center of her chest. Almost without thinking, Darius touched his chest, too "—and if I follow that pull, I'll find another Virtue on the other side."

"But you never did?"

"I only felt the pull on a few occasions, and once, I did meet another Virtue, but nothing ever came of it."

"What?" Darius shook his head. "Why not? Couldn't they feel it, too?"

"No," Teresa said with a sad shake of her head. "Virtues are born naive. They don't know what they are, and until they learn about it and *intentionally* accept it, the Virtue lies dormant. He had no way to know what I was telling him was true, so he naturally didn't believe me. Since I couldn't force him to understand or to be ready to take on this kind of responsibility, I just gave his information to the Martyrs, but unfortunately, the Sins found him first."

Alan, who had been watching the side of Teresa's face with a soft, respectful adoration, looked down at his hands. Darius felt the blood drain from his face.

"How?"

"Because I told him too much, I think," Teresa said softly. "He talked too openly about it, and the Sins caught wind of him. After that… I never found another Virtue in person. Instead, I would send the Martyrs any new leads so they could follow up."

"And they never found another?"

Alan shook his head. "No."

Darius nodded, then he looked down at his hand again. He flexed it. Wiggled the fingers. Shook his head.

"I still can't believe this," he murmured—almost to himself—before he looked back up at Teresa again. "So, there are only seven Virtues?" he asked. Teresa nodded. "Does that mean there's one of you for each Sin?"

"That's right," Teresa said. "Each Sin has a Virtue working directly against it. The Virtue's Influence cancels out the Sin's, and, assuming we can ever unlock the secret, that Virtue can destroy the very essence of the Sin."

"So, which one are you?" Darius said.

"Humility," Teresa said.

"Opposite of Pride," Alan added. His voice carried a note of caution, and he turned to Teresa. "Pride and Envy were the Sins responsible for destroying Mr. Jones's family," he explained.

Teresa let out a quiet little gasp, but Darius hardly heard it. His mood darkened, and the light he felt in Teresa's Virtuous presence flickered. Instead, his mind went back to a dark, bloody room—and the man who stood in the middle of it with a smile on his face.

"The Martyrs have had the Virtue who could have killed Pride for over *seventy years*," he said quietly, and he felt familiar rage bubbling up in his stomach. The unfair reality of it—that the only person in the world who could destroy Derek Dane was a sweet old woman—felt as real as being punched in the chest and having the breath knocked out of him. "And instead of letting her *try*, you've kept her hidden away?"

"Darius, please—" Alan started to say, but Darius shook

his head.

"My family is *dead* because of him," Darius said. He felt his throat tightening up around the words, threatening to strangle them. He let it. A wave of guilt washed over him, and he closed his eyes, but not before he saw Alan and Teresa share a curious but disconcerted look. Then, soft, warm fingers wrapped up around Darius's own, and he looked up again to see Teresa kneeling down in front of him.

"We're not giving up," she said quietly. "I will *never* give up."

Darius nodded—then shook his head—then got to his feet.

"I think I need to go lie down," he murmured.

And he didn't even wait for them to answer as he walked out of the room and back up the stairs. For the next several minutes, he stared at his ceiling and listened to the muffled, unintelligible sounds of Teresa and Alan's voices floating up the stairs. He may not have been able to make out the words, but the mood was clear: they were disappointed.

Darius woke up the next morning to soft light coming in through a set of large, glass doors sitting on the left side of his bed. He opened his eyes and squinted at the sun. Before coming to the Underground, Darius was always up with the dawn, but after just a few weeks of darkness, his circadian rhythm wasn't used to it anymore. He sat up in bed and rubbed the sleep from his eyes before he flung the blankets off his lap and stepped down onto the carpet. It was plush and comfy beneath his bare feet.

The room he was staying in was the first at the top of the stairs. It had a private bathroom, which Darius used to splash cold water against his tired face, and large, glass doors that led to the balcony. He unlocked them and walked out. The brisk, autumn air was more refreshing than the water had been, and Darius closed his eyes and took in a long, deep breath.

The sounds of rural mornings greeted Darius as he looked out at the front of Teresa's estate. Birds chirped from the distant trees at the base of her driveway. Wind rustled through yellowing leaves. A kind, quiet voice floated up from the side of the house…

"C'mere, you little monster! We've got to trim that beak!"

Darius frowned and walked along the length of the balcony, which stretched all the way from one end of the home to the other, and peered down at the side yard below.

There was a small chicken coop and covered run about one hundred yards from the house, beside a lean-to structure and horse paddock. Teresa was inside the run, quietly and persistently following a bright yellow hen as it flapped around in the enclosure and tried to avoid capture. In the paddock, an old horse stretched its neck out and watched Teresa, his ears perked and alert.

Darius watched her, too. For several minutes, she quietly followed the chicken around until the animal finally caved in and allowed itself to be snatched up. Then Teresa gently flipped it over, pinned it between her side and her arm, and pulled a pair of shears out of her pocket. Darius's mouth fell open as she brought the tool to the chicken's face and—*snip!*—cut at its beak.

Then she plopped the bird back into the soil, where it ruffled its feathers, let out a little "bawk," and began to peck at the ground between its feet.

Teresa stood up and brushed her hands against the sides of her long, flowing skirt. Then she looked right up to Darius, like she could feel his eyes on her. She waved, and she smiled.

And that smile made Darius's heart give an uncomfortable, guilty flip. He waved back, sighed, and headed into the house. He threw on his clothes and shoes and went down the second set of steps two at a time. This staircase led to Teresa's kitchen, and from there, Darius exited into the sunroom, then the back deck, and walked around to the side of the house.

Teresa was still working with her chickens. Darius could hear her talking to them as he approached. She looked up at him as he crossed the yard, and her smile widened.

"Good morning," she said. Her voice was peaceful and alert—the opposite of how Darius himself felt. "How did you sleep?"

"Fine," he said, and he was surprised to realize it was true. Last night had been the most restful night of sleep Darius had gotten since the massacre. Maybe it was Teresa's Virtue—or maybe all the stress and restlessness had finally caught up to him. Teresa seemed to sense that—she was watching him with a knowing, maternal expression. It made Darius feel uneasy. He cleared his throat and gestured to the yellow chicken pecking at the ground behind her. "Did I just watch you *cut* that one's mouth?"

Teresa glanced back at the hen and let out a quick, melodic chuckle. "Oh, yes. That's Scissor Beak."

"Scissor Beak?"

"Yeah," Teresa said, and she turned to Darius and shrugged. "She was born with a genetic defect where her beak doesn't close right—the top and bottom jaw cross like scissors—so I have to come down and trim it every so often so she can eat, or she'll starve."

Darius raised his eyebrows. "Why not put her down?"

"That's what her original owners wanted to do," Teresa said with a nod, and she looked back at her chicken fondly again. "But I think she's worth the effort. Then there's Precious—see the one over there without feathers on her neck? She's too old to lay, so they were going to slaughter her, too. I offered to take both of them."

Darius looked at the haphazard collection of chickens over Teresa's shoulder and realized they were all a little off. Most of them seemed to be like Precious—old, well past their prime. They slowly toddled around the chicken run and scratched at the dirt. Now that he was closer, he could see the stallion was the same. His back bent oddly down, and he wasn't putting weight onto one of his back legs. Teresa watched as Darius considered the animals, and she answered the question before he thought to ask it.

"They're all rescues," she said, and she led the way out of the run and walked along the paddock. Darius followed behind her. "Most of them are just old, and their owners were looking to put them down, but I couldn't stand by and let that happen." She paused. The stallion had been walking along the side of the paddock fence beside her, and he reached his head over the bar and sniffed at Teresa's gray hair with massive, snorting nostrils. She laughed and stroked the horse's long face with gentle fingers. "It's a lot of work, but their company is reward enough for me."

Then she glanced back at Darius and offered him another of her bright smiles that seemed to melt his negativity away. "Anyway, I have a few more things to take care of out here," she went on. "Wanna help?"

For the next few hours, Darius followed Teresa around and helped with her morning errands, and all the while, Teresa talked.

She told him about everything—from her childhood, living in an abusive household with a violent father and an emotionally absent mother, to the moment she'd finally left. One of her high school friends had realized what was happening at home, and he'd taken it upon himself to get her out of it.

That friend happened to be a Martyr.

When she'd come to the Underground, it didn't take long for the leadership of the time to realize what she was and what power she had.

"But like I said last night," Teresa was saying as she and Darius shoveled horse manure out of the paddock and back toward Teresa's compost pile. She paused and wiped sweat from her brow. "Virtues are born with the power, but that power won't fully manifest until you've chosen to accept it."

"So they're not really Virtues until then?" Darius asked.

He was breathless—much more so than Teresa was. He had to give the old woman credit—she was stronger than she looked.

"Oh, no. They are," Teresa said. "They still have a positive Influence on the environment around them, and I've even heard of Uninitiated Virtues using some of their other powers unintentionally—that's what we call them when they haven't accepted their Virtue yet. Uninitiated. Those who have accepted it are 'Initiated Virtues.' Once the Virtue has been Initiated, their powers come in with full force."

"And if they never accept the Virtue?" Darius asked.

Teresa responded with a shrug and went back to shoveling. "Then many of the abilities remain dormant until the body dies, and they can be reborn again. Of course, the Sins don't care about that. If they find a Virtue, Initiated or not, they want them dead."

"That's got to be frustrating," Darius said, digging into the manure again, too. "Virtues not accepting their powers."

Teresa shook her head. "No. I get it. It took me years to accept mine."

Darius glanced up at her and frowned. "Why?"

Then Teresa paused, but for the first time, she didn't really look up to him. There was pain in the way her lips came together just before she said, "Because I didn't feel like I deserved it. The Sins found out about me, and even though I hadn't Initiated my Virtue, they were desperate to kill me. A lot of people died."

She left it at that. Darius waited a little bit. He didn't want to push her or force her to reopen seventy-year-old wounds, but he had to know.

"What changed?" he asked at last.

"My friend was killed," Teresa responded. "The one who saved me and brought me to the Martyrs. He was captured. Tortured for months. Then they used him as bait to try to get me to leave the Underground. It didn't work—but he didn't make it out alive."

Darius didn't realize his mouth had fallen open until he

had to close it to clear his throat. Teresa glanced at him, and at last, she smiled again.

"Maybe I thought I could avenge him," she said with a small laugh. They were finished cleaning the paddock, and she headed back to the shed to put her shovel away. Darius followed after her—eager to hear more. "But I couldn't. He was killed by Wrath, and I am meant for Pride."

"You didn't know which Virtue you were until you Initiated it?" Darius asked.

Teresa shook her head. "No. I thought I would be devastated to learn I wasn't Patience, but instead, it felt… natural."

"And then what happened?"

"Then I left. The Sins were desperate. Hungry to catch and kill me. I decided it wasn't worth endangering the Martyrs. We made a big show of my leaving—planted false trails for the Sins to follow—but there weren't many of them left. By 2025, all the Sins except Wrath had lost their hosts in the battles, so it was easy for me to get away undetected."

Then Teresa shifted focus. Darius sensed the pain the violence caused her, so he sat back and listened to her quietly as she went on to tell stories of her life beyond the Martyrs. She'd gone to school to study history and went so far as to get a doctorate in the field. Then she'd gotten married, had a couple of kids, and spent a long, forty-year career as an adjunct professor. She moved herself and her family from university to university all around the United States, hiding from the Sins, hunting down new Virtues, and doing more research to discover the secret to destroying the Sins for good.

For all her work, she never managed to find it. When she retired, she moved back east and continued to search.

But her research wasn't wasted. Teresa uncovered more about the Virtues than anyone had had the chance to do in centuries. It was Teresa who had learned the Virtues tended to be reincarnated close to the Sin they were destined to destroy, so there was a good chance the remaining Virtues would be in the North East. On top of that, she had spent a lot of time documenting evidence of the Virtues' superhuman instincts. Apparently, the Virtues' ability to read people and sense danger was unprecedented, and evidence for it was abundant in ancient texts featuring human heroes. She also discovered the Virtues were capable of many of the same tricks as the Sins. Influence, for example. The Virtues' Indirect Influence was well documented, but Teresa found evidence implying Virtues could also use Direct Influence. She'd even tested it herself and found that she was right.

"Using Direct Influence as a Virtue is trickier, though," Teresa said. She and Darius were leaning against the paddock's fence, watching the horizon as the sun slowly ascended higher over the line of trees in the distance. She turned to him and grabbed onto his shoulder for emphasis. "We have to touch the person we want to Influence."

"Why?" Darius asked.

"I don't know," Teresa said with an honest shrug. "It's a more intimate connection, I think. It's very similar to when we heal. When we're healing, we're giving our energy to the other person. With Direct Influence, we're giving them our thoughts."

"Giving?"

"Yes. I like to think of it that way because that's how it feels. To be effective as a healer, or as an Influencer, I can't be thinking about forcing my power onto someone else. I need to be thinking about how I am giving them something they didn't have before." She gave Darius a wink, and her bright, kind eyes lit up.

"I like the sound of that," Darius said, and he was smiling, too.

"Speaking of healing," Teresa said, and she glanced at the old horse. "There's one last thing we need to do before we go in and make breakfast."

She pushed herself away from the fence and walked around to the gate. The stallion had been hovering around the two of them, and his head slowly turned and followed Teresa's movements as she walked through the gate and approached him. She murmured a few words, and he gently lifted his left rear leg up and placed it into Teresa's hands.

Though Darius couldn't *see* the healing powers, it was evident in the animal's behavior. His ears and eyes relaxed, and when Teresa released his leg, he let out a contented whinny and stomped on the ground with a newfound fervor. Teresa straightened up and smiled. Darius shook his head, awed.

"Is there anything you *can't* heal?"

"Well," Teresa said with a slight frown. "No. Unless you count the Sins. We can't heal them, not that they need our help." She smiled, and Darius chuckled.

"And no injury is too bad?"

Teresa just gave him a small laugh. It was as intoxicating as ever, and Darius was drawn to her. Her presence felt almost as warm as the sunshine beating down against his back. "There are some limits. Genetic diseases, for example, but we can heal diseases that deal with damage to cellular structure. I cured my husband's cancer once, though he didn't know it. That being said, healing takes a great deal of our energy, so it can be difficult to repair severe injuries or handle a lot of casualties at once."

"What about scars?" Darius asked, and Eva's face came roaring into his mind. "I have a friend who has some pretty bad scars. Alan said you might be able to get rid of them."

Teresa bit her lip. "I can't heal old wounds," she said regretfully. "Once the body's healed itself, I can't make the damage disappear."

Darius's heart flipped a little sadly in his chest. "So you can't help Eva?"

They hadn't really talked about Eva in detail yet, but based on the way Teresa watched him, he knew she and Alan must have discussed the situation. Teresa took a deep breath and said, "I'm honestly not sure. I don't think I can prevent the scars entirely, but I do believe I can soften them.

Her skin is still creating new cells to replace the injured ones. I know Alan wants to bring Eva here. He's hoping it can help her have faith in the Martyrs."

She said it almost like a question, and Darius thought about it. He wasn't sure if it would help Eva believe...

But it certainly couldn't hurt. He looked down at his own healed hand.

"Mr. Jones." Alan's voice broke Darius's train of thought, and both he and Teresa jumped a little at the suddenness of his arrival. He was walking out across the yard toward them. His stark, hard-lined black coat was coarsely out of sync with the bright yellow grasses and blue sky around them. When he reached the paddock, he turned and looked at Darius. The horse snorted and trotted away.

"I just got off the phone with Thorn," he said.

Darius frowned. "What's the plan?"

"We leave tomorrow morning," Alan said. "We will take a modified route. It is longer but takes us quite a deal further north than the original road we came in on, so if the Sins are monitoring it, we should be able to avoid them. Thorn and a Tactical team will rendezvous with us an hour outside of the Underground to escort us back and provide backup, should we need it. I am hopeful we will not."

"Be careful," Teresa said. There was a stern, protective tone to her voice. Alan turned to face her, and if Darius wasn't mistaken, he saw the same kind of energy in his expression, too.

"Of course, my dear."

CHAPTER ELEVEN

When it was finally time for them to head back to the Underground, Darius found he was sad to go. If he didn't have Eva waiting for him and Saul, Juniper, and Lindsay somewhere out on the streets, maybe he would have wanted to stay here. It was quiet. Calm. Peaceful.

And he didn't seem to be the only one who felt that way. Darius was waiting by the car as Alan and Teresa said their goodbyes on the front porch. Alan held Teresa's hands in front of his chest and was speaking to her quietly. Then he brought her knuckles to his lips and gently kissed them before he finally released her and came back to the car. Teresa wiped tears from the corners of her eyes as she watched them drive off.

"You two seem pretty close," Darius said when Teresa and her house were out of view.

Alan's eyes betrayed just a tiny part of his sorrow at leaving, and he turned to consider Darius. He took a deep breath and said, "We are. Teresa is a remarkable woman and an important part of my life. Knowing her has made me a better man."

"When did you meet her?" Darius asked.

"Sixteen years ago," Alan said. "When her husband died

and she finally retired, she contacted me to meet in person. We had lunch at a restaurant in West Bronx to discuss the concerns of having her back so close to the Sins. Ultimately, we decided it would be acceptable if she lived somewhere remote. That way, her Indirect Influence wouldn't cause too much of a ripple effect in her community and attract unwanted attention. I would say we were correct. There has not been so much of a whisper about her presence here, not even from our own Research and Discovery department. Since then, we've kept in touch."

West Bronx. Sixteen years ago, Darius had been in West Bronx, too. He and his father had just lost their apartment and started living on the streets. It hadn't even been a year since his mother had died. Darius was harrowed to think of just how close he had always been to the Martyrs—so close, without even realizing it.

After that, the two of them traveled in silence. Their route was long and winding, and it took them through tiny towns on the outskirts of larger metropolitan cities. The only people Darius saw through his windows were the occasional beggars and hitchhikers sitting on the side of the highway. They watched the car speed by, peering at them through the glass, and it made Darius uneasy.

Two hours in, dark storm clouds drifted in overhead, and by three in the afternoon, rain pounded down hard on the hood of the car, almost loudly enough to drown out any conversation the two men could have had. By the time they were just about an hour away from the Underground, almost to the checkpoint where they were meant to meet up with Thorn, the sky was so dark it was as though night had already fallen.

And suddenly—something wasn't right.

The hairs on the back of Darius's neck stood up on end. A knot in the pit of his stomach twisted and churned. His throat ran dry, and it stuck together when he looked over to Alan. He abruptly sat up in his chair. "Where is the checkpoint?"

Alan must have sensed the tension in his voice, or else there was something Darius did not understand. His expression darkened, and his hands tightened on the steering wheel. "Why—"

He didn't finish asking the question. A man suddenly sprinted out onto the street, dragging something behind him.

Alan swore and violently turned the wheel, but he didn't have enough time. The car veered to the left. Darius was thrown against his window—his seat belt tightened against his collar and kept him from smashing into the dashboard. The man was still in the street—still attached to whatever he was dragging—when their vehicle slammed right into him. Darius's heart stopped as the guy's head crashed into the windshield. Bouncing off it. Spraying it with blood.

And a deafening *pop!* echoed through the cabin, and the car began to jerk in a totally different way. The world spun as wheels rumbled and lost traction on the wet road. The vehicle careened out of control, circling down the asphalt until—

It ran into a berm on the side of the highway and slammed to a stop. Darius flew forward into the belt. His face snapped back just inches from the dash again. Warning lights inside the car flickered to life. Alan turned them off. He shut down the engine. Locked the doors. He drew his phone out of his pocket, opened it, and slammed his thumb down on a red icon. The screen flashed, and he put it face down on the dashboard. Darius's heart pounded hard against his ribs. All he could see was the vague outline of Alan's profile against the gray, rain-pocked window as he turned to take Darius in.

"They have found us."

A seat belt clicked open. Alan reached around the back of Darius's chair and popped open a secret compartment. Then he thrust a cold, metal object into Darius's palms.

"Take this."

Darius felt around it, from the butt to the barrel— "Oh,

hell no."

He tried to give the gun back to Alan, but Alan pushed it further into Darius's hands. They were shaking. Alan's were completely still.

"Mr. Jones." Alan's voice was quiet, low, and controlled. "You will take this weapon, or you will die."

Darius swallowed hard—his throat was sticky. "What are we going to do?"

"We are *not* going to panic," Alan said. He leaned back to the rear compartment again. "We are *not* going to lose our heads."

"Where are we going to go?"

"We have nowhere *to* go."

Alan turned to look out the window. He held a pistol now, too, and Darius leaned over to see what Alan was talking about.

His breath caught in his throat.

People. A dozen people. Running at them through the rain. Darius could hardly make them out in the darkness. He saw nothing but the vague shape of them. Men and women, sprinting toward the vehicle with a mechanical, inhuman synchronization. Their faces seemed plastic and disconnected, like they were nothing more than store mannequins come to life…

They slammed into the car.

Darius watched in stunned, horrified silence as hands grabbed at the door handles—as fingernails pulled at the seams between the window and the frame with automated urgency.

"Who are they?"

"Puppets," Alan said quietly. Though the Puppets were quiet, the sounds of their hands against the car berated Darius's ears with a cacophony of thumps and scratches, punctuating the percussion of rainfall with violent noise.

"That means there's a Sin here?"

Alan nodded. "There are *two*."

Darius's mouth ran dry, and his hands shook so badly he

was afraid he was going to accidentally discharge the weapon sitting between them. Alan turned to take him in, a grave look on his face.

"Whatever we do, Mr. Jones," Alan said. "It is imperative we remain in this car."

Then Alan glanced over Darius's shoulder. The hairs on the back of Darius's neck stood up on end, and he turned around. The Puppets stopped moving in an eerie, synchronized motion. They drew back, opened a gap in the attack, and Darius spotted two figures coming at him through the pouring rain.

The one in the lead was a woman. Darius had seen her before. Once. In the file on Alan's desk. Which Sin was she? He couldn't remember. Her brown, rain-soaked hair dangled down around her head in dark, sinister tendrils, and her t-shirt was so saturated Darius could see the lines of her muscles beneath the fabric. Her steely gray eyes searched the car, and when they landed on him, her face broke open in a horrifying cackle.

Her voice was so loud it pierced through the sound of the rain.

"Dane!" she called out, and she looked behind her. At the mention of the name, Darius's heart leapt furiously into his throat. "Dane, look at this. Blaine brought us a *gift!*"

The second figure moved toward the car, and Darius's whole body surged with heat as Derek Dane walked into view. The Sin sneered down his handsome nose through the glass. Even sopping wet, he stood with his shoulders strong and proud. His cold eyes looked Darius over, and then glanced to Alan. He smiled as he turned back to Darius.

"Well, *well,*" he said, shaking his head. "I was wondering when I'd see *you* again."

Hearing that voice, silky and strong, filled Darius with a hot, loathing contempt. Dane reached down, the whole time keeping his eyes locked with Darius's, and grabbed the door handle. Pulled it. It didn't budge. He frowned, then took a few steps back as he turned to talk to the other Sin.

"What do you think, Hunt?" he asked, almost casually, as he threw Alan and Darius a smug look. "Should we shoot our way in?"

Darius glanced down at their waists and realized they both had a pistol clipped to their belts.

Hunt shook her head and walked up to the car. She dragged her finger against the window, just inches from Darius's nose. She locked eyes with him and smiled. Just before she drew back her hand, she tapped on the glass with her long fingernails.

"It's fortified," she said.

Dane frowned, and then, as though to challenge her, he drew his gun and pointed it right at Darius's face. Darius hardly had the time to scream and duck as the Sin pulled the trigger. With a dull *thunk,* the bullet lodged in the glass. The other Sin turned to Dane with a contemptuous look. Darius glanced at Alan. He was just watching the woman with a dark, cautious expression.

"I fucking told you," the other Sin said. "It'll take too long."

She leaned down, reached one hand out to grab the handle of the locked door, and pulled her lower lip between her teeth as she watched Darius with those wild, carnal eyes.

"Come on out." She barely spoke the words, but Darius caught them as clearly as though they were inside his head. His temples throbbed and ached, and his shaking hands tightened around the cold, metal gun in his hands. The woman glanced down at it and laughed.

"You'd like to use that, wouldn't you?" she said. He *thought* she said it, at least. Her lips barely moved. Did they move? "Or better yet, you just want to punch Dane in his *pretty, little face*, don't you? After what he did to your family? Go ahead. I won't stop you."

"Darius, *don't listen to her.*"

Alan's voice, now. Darius was vaguely aware of the other man's hand gripping around his shoulder. Alan's fingers around his arm were almost painful, but the pain in Darius's temples was worse. It clouded his brain as the anger in his gut swelled. He looked at Derek Dane, and all the rage and sadness and *hatred* overpowered him.

"C'mon," the woman said.

"Stay in the car."

"Come out here and *hit the fucker.*"

Darius snapped.

He unlocked the door, and as soon as he did, Hunt pulled it open. Darius tore out of Alan's grip and vaulted out of the vehicle. He barely registered Alan's voice calling to him as he leapt right onto Derek Dane. The Sin wasn't prepared for him. Darius's sudden movement and *weight* sent Pride stumbling backward, and Darius was on top of him. His gun forgotten, dropped somewhere on the wet asphalt, Darius threw a punch into the Sin's jaw that snapped his head back and sent pain shooting up through Darius's fingers.

But he didn't stop.

While Alan leapt from the car, *shooting* at the woman, and she ducked behind the door and *laughed*, Darius attacked Dane relentlessly. He heard gunshots—saw bodies drop as Puppets got caught in the crossfire between Alan and the other Sin. The rest of them swarmed around Darius, grabbing him by the legs, the shoulders—anywhere they could. Every time Darius punched at Dane, they all paused, like they were feeling the strikes, too, and occasionally, one would collapse, unconscious.

Darius kept punching.

He hit Dane again. And again. He hit him until his knuckles hurt, until they split and bled against Dane's teeth and skull, until they were so numb from pain Darius couldn't feel them anymore.

It wasn't enough.

Finally, one of the Puppets managed to get his fingers wound up in Darius's hair, and he was pulled backward—just far enough away for Derek Dane to reach between them and wrap his hand around Darius's throat. He roared as he twisted Darius around, and suddenly his back crashed against the road. His head knocked so hard to the asphalt his vision went gray. Dane had him pinned.

The chaos around him blared to life. Only three of the Puppets were left standing. They crowded in around Darius, flanking Pride on either side. Somewhere outside of his frame of view, he could hear Alan's voice as he screamed Darius's name, the furious snarling of some animal, and the other woman *roaring* in fury.

Darius could hardly focus on any of that. His attention caught on something far more terrifying: Dane's face was *changing*. A cut across the bridge of his nose stitched itself up as Darius watched. The swelling started to shrink back down. He looked straight into Darius's eyes, and Darius saw the same malice and evil he'd seen the night of the massacre. Dane's grip around Darius's throat tightened. Air came more slowly, and then not at all. The blood left his face, and he felt cold. No matter how much Darius kicked, Dane didn't move. Pride picked him up off the ground like a bag of garbage and held him out above the street.

Darius was going to die at the hands of the same Sin who killed his family. Eva would be alone. Forever.

Then a tiny, blue and red creature fell from the sky. It came, hissing and spitting, onto Derek Dane's face, tearing at him with sharp claws. The Sin roared, batted the animal away with his free hand, and then—

A shot rang out. Then another, and another. Darius's airway cleared. The remaining three Puppets collapsed, unconscious, to the ground as Dane cried out in pain and fell to his knees. Blood pulsed from his elbow, his shoulder, his stomach—squirting out between his fingers as he grabbed the wounds. Darius turned to his side and coughed as air surged into his lungs. He looked up to see someone sprinting toward him.

Thorn.

Soaking wet, full of a fury so palpable it may as well have been lightning, Thorn leveled her gun up and shot at Dane again. He anticipated the attack this time—leapt to the side, then to his feet—and he sprinted away from the scene. Thorn's dark eyes tracked him as he moved around the car, toward the trees on the side of the road.

"Williams, get Dane!" she screamed over her shoulder. "Chris, you're with me!"

Darius spun around to watch her run past him—and as he did, a firm hand grabbed him around the bicep and pulled him to his feet.

It was Alan.

"Come on," he said. He looked shaken but unhurt. His black hair was wild around his head, and the side of his face was smudged with dirt and blood, but he didn't have any cuts on him. Darius looked over his shoulder. Thorn and Chris Silver were closing in on the other Sin. She was retreating, furiously spitting insults and manic threats. Alan's pure black, wolf-like dog followed after her, snarling and biting and leaping at her throat as she tried to shoot it—but it was no use. She was about to disappear into the tree line—

The trees.

Darius turned and looked back into the trees, where Derek Dane had disappeared.

And William Michaels with him.

"We've got to get Dane," Darius yelled, and he tried to turn to fight, but Alan pulled him back.

"We've got to get you *to safety*," Alan insisted.

"But he's hurt," Darius argued. "This could be our only chance—"

"Darius!" Alan's fingers tightened desperately around Darius's arm. "You will *die!*"

A numb weight fell into Darius's chest. At first, it fanned his rage, but then the fire withered and died.

Alan was right.

Darius allowed himself to be led away—from the screaming Sins, the firing guns, the bodies littering the shoulder of the highway like roadkill. Less than fifty feet down the road, they found two Martyrs' vehicles. Alan opened one up and ushered Darius inside. Then, wet, cold, and shaken, they peeled out and sped away.

When the fight was well behind them, Darius turned to Alan and said, "Do you think they'll be okay?"

Alan paused before he said, "Thorn will be."

"What the *fuck* were you thinking?"

Thorn burst through the door to the hospital like a hurricane. Her eyes were wild. Her hair dripped wet from rainwater. Heavy blood dribbled from her scalp and onto her face from a gash so high up on her hairline it was hard to see. Her jacket was soaked through and clung to her rigid, shaking body. For a moment, she looked so strikingly like the Sin, Hunt, Darius's heart began to race.

"*Thorn!*" Elijah Harris stepped away from Darius's side, where he'd been attending to a cut lip and bruised eye. Raquel immediately stepped up to take the doctor's place and pressed a cold compress against the lump behind Darius's head. She squeezed his shoulder once, reassuringly. "I will *not* have you barging in on my—"

"Shut the *fuck* up, Harris." Thorn flew past the doctor and straight up to her uncle, angrily throwing a cot out of her way to get there. Raquel quietly retreated to the safety of the nurses' station.

"Thorn, stop—" Alan stepped forward, but Thorn slammed her fist down on a medical trolly by Darius's bed. Supplies went flying. She left a deep dent in the metal surface.

"Don't you *dare* tell me to stop."

She stepped up right in front of him. Despite being at least eight inches shorter than he was, Thorn's fury made her terrifying. Every muscle in her body was wound so tightly she shook. Alan didn't back down, but Darius could see in his eyes this was the kind of situation he had been trying to avoid. Dr. Harris grumbled as he made his way back around to Darius to apply butterfly bandages to his cuts.

Thorn went on as though neither of them were there. "I *knew* this was a huge mistake. This whole damned thing could have happened at the Underground, but you'll take any excuse you can find to see her again, won't you?"

"You know why we chose to," Alan began, but Thorn cut him off again.

"You almost died—you *both* did," Thorn said. Alan closed his mouth, his lips set into a thin line behind his goatee. Dr. Harris finished applying the bandages and whispered to Darius he was free to go and that he may well want to do just that. Thorn kept going. "And you didn't just put yourself and Jones in danger—we could have lost Chris and Michaels, too! It's a fucking miracle nobody died tonight! And for what? The Sins escaped, and the car is gone—"

"Thorn, please—"

Darius slowly got off the bed.

"God *damn it*, Alan!" Thorn was screaming now. The words echoed around the large, tile room. "We almost *lost you!* We almost lost *a Virtue!*"

And a hand gestured to Darius. Alan dropped his face into his palm. Darius's mouth fell open.

"What?"

Thorn's atmosphere shifted as she turned to him. The rage faded and was replaced with shock. She spun on Alan, and the rage roared back to life.

"Oh my GOD! And you didn't even TELL HIM!"

"We should discuss this in private—"

"That's the whole damned reason you even *took* this stupid trip—"

"STOP!" Darius leapt to his feet. He hadn't meant to yell, but it felt like the only option he had. The room around him went silent. Alan gave the doctor a look, and Harris quickly and quietly ushered the nurses out of the hospital ward. Thorn was breathing heavily, and she slowly turned her head to look at Darius. "What the hell is going on?"

"Please," Alan said, and he stepped toward Darius. "Let me explain."

"Why don't you?" Darius's chest felt tight, and he glowered at Alan. "What the hell is this?"

"Jones—" Thorn went to say, a tone of biting condescension hot upon her lips, but Darius stopped her.

"Don't," he snapped. "Just *don't.*" Thorn seemed taken aback. Her dark, half-empty eyes narrowed, but she didn't say another word. Darius looked between the two and shook his head. "Did you say that I'm a…?"

He couldn't even bring himself to say it.

Alan quietly nodded. Darius's stomach boiled. He felt the anger, the indignation, bubble up his gut and into his chest, where it spun and made him sick. He rubbed his temples.

It was all starting to make sense. The attack on his home. The deaths of his friends. Why the Sins cared so much that *he,* Darius, had survived.

"You're wrong," Darius said. They had to be. This couldn't be real. "I can't be."

"You are," Alan said. "That's why I wanted you to meet Teresa. She just confirmed it…" He glanced at Thorn. She simply glared at him in silent fury.

Darius's mouth gaped open in disbelief. "You knew?"

"We suspected," Alan said.

"Why the hell haven't you said anything before now?"

"To what end?" Alan asked. "What if we were incorrect, and you were not a Virtue? There was no use in worrying you over nothing."

"Is that why the Martyrs were looking for me?" Darius asked coldly. "You were looking for a Virtue? This whole time?"

"Yes," Alan said. He was as calm as ever, but now there was a hint of desperation in his voice. "We've known one was in the city for a long time. When Teresa moved back to the area and met with me, she sensed it."

West Bronx. Of course. Darius felt sick.

"She found me?"

"She *felt* you," Alan said. "We followed thousands of leads for *years.* All of them led to nothing. Then, three months ago, when we learned of the way you sacrificed so much to take in and raise abandoned children, we knew we needed to find you. There was only a marginal chance you were a Virtue, but we had to try. We are… stunned it is true."

Darius's heart skipped a beat. "And the Sins, too? Were they looking for a Virtue when they slaughtered my family?"

Alan said nothing.

"They died because of me? Because the Sins were looking for *me?*"

"That's not—"

"Answer the question."

Alan didn't speak right away. He watched Darius through those dark, cold eyes for a long moment before he simply said, "Yes."

Darius went quiet. He didn't know what to say. All this time, he thought he'd come in by mistake—an unfortunate casualty of a war he never belonged in—only now he knew the truth. He didn't just belong in this war. He was a key part of it. "You *lied* to me," he said at last.

Alan shook his head and raised his hands. His voice raised with them. "I did not want to upset you—"

"Upset me? I'm the *reason* my family is *dead!*"

The room went quiet. Thorn briefly threw Darius a look that could have been compassion, but it was quickly replaced as she turned back to Alan again with a furious, vindicated snarl. "I fucking *told you* this would happen," she hissed at him. Then she moved to leave the room.

Alan called her back. His voice was sharp, and the words boomed through the desolate hospital ward with tremendous strength. "*You,*" he said, and his tone was deadly, "will go straight to my office."

That was it. That was all he said. And yet, somehow, it

was the scariest thing Darius had ever heard him say. The furor in his voice was palpable. Even Thorn seemed to sense it. She glared at him but said nothing as she silently turned on her heels and walked away.

When she closed the door behind her, it was as though the anger in the room left with her. The air felt less charged and dangerous. Alan watched after Thorn, his brows furrowed heavily and his jaw tight. Then he turned toward Darius and sighed.

"I am sorry you had to find out this way."

"How was I *supposed* to find out?" Darius asked.

Alan walked back toward Darius a few paces and quietly clasped his hands behind his back. "To tell you the truth," he said slowly. "I had intended on telling you as soon as we found you, but that was when we still believed we had a chance to save your entire family."

Darius felt the blood drain from his face. His mouth dropped open. "What?"

Alan nodded. "Yes. Cyrus Murphy would not disclose information about your whereabouts. Our plan was to follow him home, but when we returned him to the city, the Sins were waiting for him."

It was as though the world had stopped spinning. Darius felt sick.

"At that point, it was us against them. Each of us was trying to locate you as quickly as we could. We were too late. By the time my people got to the scene, you had already lost *everything*. You were not in a place where you would be receptive to this information, so I made the decision to wait until I was confident you truly understood the war we are here to fight and the place you might have within it."

"You told me everything *else*," Darius said, and at last, color came back to his cheeks in an angry flush.

Alan's eyes glinted strangely. "How well do you think you would have handled that information with your family and everything you'd fought for so freshly murdered?" He asked. The muscles along his throat went tight, but he kept his dark voice level. "Mr. Jones, this is not my first foray into bringing people into this world. The Martyrs are an old and complex organization, and revealing too much, too early, can be catastrophic. Information must be carefully provided when it is critical and no longer a liability. I can assure you, had I thrust this weight onto your shoulders so quickly, it would not have ended well. You would have rejected the idea outright. Perhaps, you would have wanted to leave. That was not an option."

"It would have been better than *this!*" Darius gestured widely around the now-empty hospital ward.

Alan's frown deepened. "Would it?" he asked, some frustration slipping into his tone. It was sharp, like the cracking of a whip. "This situation has been far from ideal, and I was certainly looking forward to a calmer conversation, but had I known this is how things would play out, I would have changed nothing. You might not like it, and whether you like it or not is irrelevant. This is not about you. This is about *saving lives*. Had I told you too early and you decided to leave the Underground, the Sins would have killed you. They would have killed Miss Torres. They would have killed the Martyrs we would send to find you. More people would have died."

Darius's stomach dropped, and he slammed his teeth together. "You keep saying I'd have left," he said, but his strength was fading. God, he was so tired. "Maybe I wouldn't have."

"Perhaps not," Alan said. "But it was not a risk I was willing to take."

Silence fell between them. Darius's body felt simultaneously wound tight and worn thin. He didn't take his eyes off Alan's face. The Martyr leader watched him with a cold, unapologetic expression. At last, Alan spoke again.

"Do not misunderstand me." His voice was low and strong. "I would like nothing more than for you to willingly and enthusiastically join the Martyrs, not because of your Virtue, but because you are a man of conviction, strength, and determination." Alan paused and looked him over quietly. He seemed to be feeling weary, too, and the edge to his words felt duller now. "But my job is not to persuade you to stay. It is to keep you *alive*, and the Martyrs alive with you. Sometimes that entails making difficult decisions, not because they are *popular* or *fair* or even *honest,* but because they will prevent the most bloodshed."

Something jerked in Darius's chest. For a moment, he remembered Max Douglas and felt the phantom weight of unused antibiotics in his pocket.

At last, Alan brought his hands out from behind his back.

"Now," he said, and he cleared his throat. "You may be driven to prove me wrong and *not* make any attempts to leave the Underground, but I want to assure you that you are by no means a prisoner here. If you would like to leave, I can relocate you somewhere the Sins will not find you. My people will ensure that. They need you and the inspiration that comes from knowing you are safe. For the rest of your life, whether in the Underground or not, the Martyrs will protect you."

Darius's throat tightened, and he looked down at his feet.

"Think about what you would like to do," Alan said. He bowed his head and strode out of the room, leaving Darius alone.

The only Virtue in the Underground.

That night, Darius's mind raced with strange, uncomfortable illusions. The in-betweens of dreams and conscious thought bit into his brain and made him startle awake, soaked in cold sweat. He saw faces of the dead, heard Thorn's voice screaming in his ears. The guilt and anger crowded in around him like a dense, suffocating fog.

Darius dropped his face into his palms and shook his

head. His cheeks were damp, his shaggy hair matted with sweat and tears. Frustrated and tired, he hauled himself out of bed.

It wasn't worth it. The nightmares could wait.

Darius threw on some clothes and made his way to the kitchen.

The courtyard was empty at four in the morning. His footsteps echoed against the concrete floor as he walked across it. The place felt even more dead this late—this early. The lights above him had been dimmed so low it was like the cavern was lit by only moonlight. Darius headed to the front alcove in the kitchen to make himself some coffee, but he found the pot was already full and hot. A voice in the dark made him jump.

"You're up early."

Thorn was sitting at the counter behind him. Darius couldn't believe he hadn't noticed her there. He must have walked right past her. With her dark hair and clothes, she all but disappeared in the blackness of the room around them.

"So are you." He said it more angrily than he'd meant to—something about Thorn seemed to just *make* him angry.

Thorn either didn't notice or didn't care. She simply shrugged and said, "I'm always up this early."

It was a challenge. She watched Darius with sharp eyes, waiting for him to give his excuse. He didn't want to talk about any of this, especially not with her.

She seemed to sense that. As Darius brushed her off and began to walk away, she called after him.

"Wait."

Darius paused and turned. She had gotten to her feet and was walking around the counter toward him. Her silhouette moved smoothly, silently, like a shadow. The dim light from the kitchen fell across her face.

He expected her to speak, but she didn't. Instead, she held something out for him, and a steaming porcelain mug was pushed gently into his palms. The hot, humid scent of dark coffee wafted up from the surface. It awakened his senses and warmed his face.

"It's not your fault," Thorn said, and Darius was caught off guard. He frowned and looked up at her.

"What?"

"The Sins are vicious," she went on. "They would have killed your family—Virtue or not. It's *not* your fault." Her voice was barely louder than a whisper, and her empathy was half-formed. The words were a little too hard. Her body wound a little too tight.

A surge of something he didn't expect to feel for Thorn hit him. His chest ached at her emptiness, and it occurred to him he wasn't the only one who needed healing.

"It feels like it is," Darius muttered, and he looked back down into the mug.

Thorn continued to watch him for a few more quiet moments. He could feel her attention on him. This time, when she spoke, it was more natural.

"No. It's *mine*."

Darius looked up at her again.

"I'm the one who brought Cyrus into the Underground," she said. A twinge of *something* caught up in Darius's throat. Anger? Sadness? He wasn't sure. Thorn kept talking. "When he left, it was one of *my* agents who took him back to the city, and *I* was the one watching him to make sure he was safe. He wasn't."

Darius swallowed. He hadn't realized his throat had gone dry. Thorn still didn't look away from him.

"So, if you need to blame someone for what happened to you, blame me," she said.

Because she did. It was evident in the tone of her voice that Thorn had added this to the list of sins she had to atone for a long time ago.

But Darius couldn't put it all on her shoulders. He took a deep breath and shook his head.

"It wasn't—"

"It was my *responsibility*," Thorn cut in. "It was *never*

yours."

There was something in the way she said it that unraveled a thread in Darius's tension. He felt his bitterness ebb a bit, and the muscles along his jaw relaxed.

Then Thorn turned back to the coffee pot and poured herself another cup. Darius followed behind her. For the first time, he noticed the small, winged animal hanging onto her back. He was mostly obscured by her dark hair, but his leathery wings and long tail poked out at the bottom and sides. He peered out at Darius as Thorn raised her fresh cup of coffee to her lips.

"So." The tone had shifted—any openness shuttered itself up again. She faced him and leaned a hip against the counter. "Why *are* you up this early?"

"I just couldn't sleep," he said.

Thorn nodded. "You encountered the two most dangerous Sins yesterday," she said. "It's enough to keep anyone awake."

"Who was the other one? Wrath?"

"Yes. Pride—Derek Dane—may think he runs the Sins, but Autumn Hunt is the real threat," Thorn said. "She's kept the same host for ninety years, which means she's had plenty of time to build her Influence and her power. She's stronger than the rest of them combined. Even the other Sins are terrified of her. None of them will do anything to piss her off. Anyone who does—human *or* Sin—usually ends up dead. You're lucky."

Darius scoffed. He didn't *feel* lucky.

"*You* didn't die," he said. He had the feeling she had survived a lot. Darius raised his eyebrows—a challenge for her to explain how she pulled it off.

But Thorn didn't take the bait. "I'm good."

He couldn't deny that. She'd come back to the Underground with nothing more than superficial injuries.

One superficial injury.

"How's your head?" Darius asked. Thorn looked over the rim of her coffee cup and frowned.

"What?"

"Your head," Darius said again. He pointed to his scalp to indicate where she'd been cut. "It looked pretty bad."

"Oh," Thorn reached up and touched her hair. "It's fine. I've seen worse."

"I never thanked you," Darius said, and he realized in the drama following the attack, he hadn't stopped to do that. "You saved my life."

Thorn just shrugged.

"I suppose you had to, though." This came out a little more bitterly than Darius intended.

That triggered something. Thorn's shoulders went rigid, and her back straightened. "If I can save my people," she said, and a hint of her anger began to flash behind the words, "then I save my people. Whether or not *you* have decided to stay, I've decided to protect you, and I will."

Darius was a little humbled by that. He looked down at the coffee in his hands.

"But you could make my job easier," Thorn went on. Darius glanced at her. "You need to work on your defenses. You let Wrath in yesterday. She Influenced you out of the car."

"What?" He was almost offended. "No, I didn't."

She raised a brow. "Yes, you did."

"How do you know?"

"Why else would you unlock the door?"

Darius fought to remember it, and he realized he didn't have a good answer for her. Alan had explicitly instructed him not to leave the car, but he hadn't listened. Instead, he'd let his own drive for vengeance cloud his judgment…

Or so he thought.

He felt his face turn red. He hoped it was too dark for Thorn to see.

"Don't worry about it," she said after a tense silence. She didn't sound angry—she sounded like she'd had to have this conversation more times than she could count. "You were totally unprepared, and Wrath has the strongest Direct

Influence of any of the Sins. The fact she couldn't take over your mind entirely means you've got an amazing natural resistance. With a little practice, you'll be impenetrable."

But Darius *was* worried about it. It made him feel disgusted and terrified that a Sin had been in his mind—that a *Sin* had Influenced his decision and made him do something to put himself and Alan in more danger. He couldn't let it happen again.

"What can I do?"

"Train," Thorn said. "I'll talk with Alan. We'll set you up with someone to teach you."

Darius just nodded, and then the room went quiet. Darius was caught in his own mind, trying to remember more about the moment Wrath had fucked with him. He couldn't place it. That was the scariest part of all.

How was he supposed to learn to fight against it if he couldn't identify it in the first place?

A quiet, faint chirp disturbed the silence, and Darius glanced up as the small, blue-bodied reptile climbed up onto Thorn's shoulder. It broke Darius's thoughts, ripped him out of his head, and brought him back to reality.

A really weird reality.

Grateful for a change of subject, Darius gestured toward the animal. "Sparkie, right?" Darius asked. Thorn raised her eyebrows, almost impressed. "Alan told me."

"Alan talked to you about *Sparkie* before he told you about your Virtue." It wasn't a question. She sighed and shook her head. "What a fucking mess."

Darius just nodded. He didn't want to get dragged into whatever power struggle Thorn and her uncle were having, and he had to admit, he agreed with Thorn. There were a lot of things Alan had talked to him about before mentioning the Virtue.

"Yeah." Darius cleared his throat. "Well, thanks for the coffee." He lifted the mug between the two of them and nodded toward her. Then he turned away again, but Thorn called him back a second time.

And she paused when he faced her. Her mouth opened, then closed, and she considered him for a moment. At last, and like the words were hard for her to admit, Thorn said, "I know Alan offered you an out, but I think you should stay with the Martyrs."

Darius raised his brow. "Of course you do," he said. He remembered what Alan had told him. "You need me."

She didn't like that. Her eyes darkened, and she crossed her arms. "Yes," she said coolly. "But you need us, too. The Sins want you dead. They have people around the city Programmed to hunt you down. The Martyrs can protect you, help you unlock your potential… maybe even give you a place to call home and people to call family."

Darius was caught off guard. He just stared at her while she placed her coffee mug back on the counter. "Think about it."

Darius paused for a moment. He couldn't tell if Thorn was being disingenuous, but something about the look in her eyes, eyes that were somehow both tragic and honest, told him she meant every word. He gave a short, soft nod. "I will."

Thorn nodded, and then she left. She walked around him, leaving him alone in the dark, dismal loneliness of the kitchen. He looked down at the mug in his hands and saw the faint impression of her lips on the rim of the glass, opposite of his own.

He sighed, came around the counter, and sat where Thorn had been sitting just moments before. There, he spent the next several minutes nursing his coffee and his troubled mind.

He was a *Virtue*, at the center of an insurmountable war.

After a while, he lost track of the time he spent sitting alone. He finished his coffee and made another pot, and he was halfway through that one when he heard footsteps walking across the vast, concrete cavern. He turned and looked to see who was coming. A figure was barely halfway across the courtyard. If it had been anyone else, Darius probably wouldn't have recognized them, but this silhouette was familiar.

"Eva?"

Darius got to his feet, and before he knew it, Eva had run across the space between them and thrown herself into his arms. He wasn't ready for it—he barely caught her and held her as she wrapped her arms around his neck and nestled her face against his throat. He ran his hand over the back of her head and held her close. Her small, malnourished body almost disappeared beside his.

"I thought you were gone," she sobbed. Tears soaked his shoulder. "Abraham came and told me about an attack and said you were in the hospital, but I went by, and you weren't there! God, Darius, I'm so sorry."

"No," he said into her hair, and he closed his eyes and sank into their embrace. "No, it's fine. I'm okay."

"This place is dangerous," she whispered. "We have to go. We're not safe here."

Darius's heart clenched, and his whole body stiffened. Eva noticed. She gently pulled herself away. With her face just inches away from his, she whispered:

"You're not leaving, are you?"

There was absolutely nothing Darius could say to fix this, and it took Eva saying those words for him to realize she was right. Damn it. He'd been such an idiot to promise Eva anything before he knew the whole situation. He stepped back and grabbed her hands up in his own.

"No."

A new wave of tears filled Eva's deep, brown eyes. Her face twisted up as she tried not to cry.

"Why not?"

"It's complicated," he said. "I need to help. I've seen the Sins. I know what they can do."

"Darius, listen to yourself," she pleaded with him.

"I know what I'm talking about, Eva."

"Even if these 'Sins' *are* real, we don't belong here!" She pulled her hands out of Darius's grip. "This isn't our fight!"

And, though it terrified every fiber of his being to admit what he was about to say, though it implicated more than Darius was comfortable to accept, he shook his head and said, "This *is* my fight, Eva. I'm… I'm a Virtue."

It felt foreign on his tongue, like the white lies he told at the market to barter for goods. The air around them stung with Eva's pain and Darius's uncertainty.

And then she slapped him.

Eva's hand flew through the air so quickly and so suddenly Darius had no time to react. Her open palm struck him right beneath the eye Dr. Harris had bandaged just hours ago. The wound reopened, and warm, sticky blood dripped down his cheek in a thin line. The sound deafened him for a moment, and he gingerly touched his face as Eva reared back to strike again. She refrained.

"I can't *believe* you're doing this to me!"

"I'm sorry," Darius said through a wince. He glanced down at his hand—the pads of his fingers were dabbed in red.

New tears were streaming down Eva's face. Her hands clenched into fists at her side, her muscles so taut her arms shook with the tension. "These people have *brainwashed you!*"

He wanted to be angry with her, to bite back at her the way she was biting at him, but he couldn't bring himself to do it. It wasn't Eva's fault. "I'm sorry," he said again, "I know it's hard, but I belong here. I need to—"

"No, you don't!" Eva's voice was twice as loud now. "You *chose* to be a part of this. You chose this—this—whatever *this* is over us. After all we've been through, after all these years, you put *these people* ahead of Saul, Juniper, Lindsay… ahead of *me*." And then she turned on her heel and took off at a run across the courtyard.

Darius watched her go, watched the last person he had left disappear down the hallway. All because he was born with a Virtue inside him. How many people would it drive away? How many people would it kill?

Anger bubbled up in his chest until he couldn't hold it in anymore. Darius yelled and threw his coffee cup to the ground. It smashed against the tile floor into a thousand little pieces.

It couldn't get any worse than this.

But it could. And it did. Later that day, Abraham came knocking on Darius's door to tell him Eva had vanished from the Underground.

CHAPTER TWELVE

Thorn threw the glass doors to the Underground open and strode in from the parking garage.

It was just eight in the morning, but she was already exhausted. When she'd woken up at 4:00 a.m. the previous day and found Darius Jones wandering into the kitchen, Thorn hadn't known she was about to spend the next twenty-four hours wide awake and wired.

But here she was—and it wasn't over yet.

She rushed through the waiting room outside the hospital and down the hall. Alan and the other Martyr elite were already gathered in the first conference room, discussing what the fuck they were going to do now that they'd lost Eva Torres and the Underground was in jeopardy.

A fire lit up in Thorn's chest as she reached for the door, and she paused. She took a moment—closed her eyes and breathed deep, urging the beast down.

Things were already bad. The last thing she needed to do was make them *worse*.

From the minute Torres was dragged out of that bar, broken and bleeding, Thorn had hoped she wouldn't make it. It wasn't personal. It never was. But family—*attachments*—complicated things. She'd known it was only a matter of time before Torres became a *complication.*

And the time had come. The girl managed something even Thorn hadn't seen coming. She'd stolen out in the middle of the night, when the cameras in the Underground were automated and unwatched, and hidden in Caleb Claytor's car for *eight hours* before he set off back for New York City. If Thorn wasn't so angry, she might have been impressed.

By the time the security attachment assigned to watch Torres had noticed she was gone, she had been in the city for twelve hours—and twelve hours was more than enough time to disappear into the underbelly of New York. There were too many people—too many secret places someone like Eva Torres would know where to hide.

This never would have happened if Alan had let Thorn lock things down like she'd wanted, but "Darius and his guest weren't prisoners," he'd insisted.

The flame roared again. So much for stamping it out. Thorn swore under her breath and turned the handle.

"He can't stay here, Alan," Jeremiah Montgomery was saying.

The five people gathered around the large, oval table glanced up as Thorn stepped into the room and closed the door. She took her spot by Alan's side in silence.

Jeremiah waited until she was seated before he continued. Then he crossed his massive arms and leaned back in his chair. His thick biceps bulged through the standard-issue Tactical Unit black turtleneck, and he watched Alan with conviction. "Until we know the Underground is safe, Darius will need to be better protected."

"I agree," Alan said. He looked around the conference room, from Abraham, past Jeremiah, to Lina, Mackenzie, and finally Thorn. Then he went on. "This isn't a matter of *what* must be done as much as it is *how* it should be handled."

"What's so special about how it should be handled?" Mackenzie McKay shook her head. Her voice was colored with a light Irish accent and garnished with irritation. She leaned forward in her chair, and her vibrant, violet hair caught the light. "Just send him away. We have plenty of places to store him 'til we need him."

Alan took a deep breath through his nose. "He is not a *tool* we can just put into storage," he said. "As far as I am concerned, Mr. Jones is a valuable member of our team, and he needs to be treated with dignity and respect. If we want him to decide to join us and accept his Virtue, we cannot alienate him."

"Right, well, none of that will matter if we're all slaughtered, now, will it?" Mackenzie said. She leaned back in her chair and crossed her arms. She was tiny—no more than one hundred and ten pounds sopping wet—but she'd never let her size stop her from being the biggest person in the room.

"That's not funny," Lina said uncomfortably. A wisp of her caramel hair had escaped the tight braid down the back of her head, and she whipped it behind her ear.

Mackenzie impatiently clicked her tongue piercing against her teeth. "Do I look like I'm laughing?" she asked. "Look, I'm not trying to say I don't understand why we need him, but we have to remember what we're *doing* here. This isn't about Jones. This is about the Sins. The war is our first priority. We can't worry about hurting his feelings if it means forgetting what we're fighting for. If they catch Torres and find the Underground, we'll be in a lot more trouble than if Jones decides to leave."

Jeremiah nodded on the other side of the table, slowly and carefully, as he clasped his dark fingers in front of his lips and listened. Abraham sighed and shook his head.

"But Darius is an essential part of this war," Abraham argued. He was rolling the sleeves of his patterned button-up to his elbows—something Thorn noticed he did when he was nervous. "He's a Virtue."

"I'm not a fucking idiot," Mackenzie said. "I know that. But Virtue or not, he isn't Initiated so he isn't useful. Instead of arguing about how to make him most 'comfortable,' we just need to get him the fuck out of here so we can do our damn jobs and protect the people who *do* want to fight without worrying about him."

"I agree," Jeremiah said. "We need to find the girl before the Sins do. Sending Darius away will allow us to do that with clearer heads."

"*And* if he's not here, he can't get in the way trying to 'help,'" Mackenzie added.

"But finding Eva could take months," Lina said. Her fingers absently played with a silver pendant around her neck as she threw a skeptical look around the room. "Isolating him for that long could give him second thoughts about staying here."

"That's better than getting him killed," Jeremiah said. "If we put him somewhere safe and keep him alive, we can always win him over later. If we don't react now and the Sins find the Underground, we're going to lose a lot of people."

"We also need to consider the Martyrs' morale," Abraham said. "He's the only Virtue we have—and the only one any of us have ever met. The way the team is talking about our situation has totally changed. There's *hope* now. If we send him away, we could lose that."

Alan and Thorn shared a look. Alan cleared his throat. "These are all fine points," he said. Thorn crossed her arms and kicked back in her chair. "But I agree with Mackenzie and Jeremiah. We must move Darius to a secure location at once, but perhaps we can find someplace to send him that keeps him at least somewhat abreast of what the Martyrs are doing. That way, he will feel less alone."

"Well," Abraham said. "I could always talk to Jacob—"

"No," Thorn said. It was the first word she'd spoken since she sat down, and all eyes in the room shifted to her. Abraham's cheeks flushed red. "Jacob is a good agent, but he's too erratic. We can't leave Darius with him."

"I wasn't going to suggest he stay with him," Abraham defended, but his tone had weakened. He looked away from

Thorn and instead turned to Lina for support. She didn't meet his eyes, so he looked back. "Jacob has gone *weeks* without any of us being able to find him. Even Holly can't keep track of where he's going. He might know somewhere we could send Darius that's off the radar."

"So far off the radar that we'll never find him, either," Thorn snapped. "No."

"What about your contacts in the city?" Jeremiah asked. Thorn turned to him. "You must know people."

"My contacts aren't Martyrs, so they're not secure," she said. "I can't guarantee Jones's safety. If the Sins learn Jones isn't in the Underground, they will hunt down anyone they think is associated with us, even loosely."

"Then we don't tell them he's not in the Underground," Abraham said. There was sarcasm there. Thorn cast him a dark glare.

"Really? You want to take that chance?" she snapped. Abraham didn't say anything, and Thorn went on. "I *don't.* Jones will *not* be kept in the city."

"Then where do you suggest we put him?" Jeremiah asked. "Cain's?"

"No," Alan said, and he got to his feet. He began to pace along the side of the table with his hands clasped behind his back. "No. Cain has been soured on the Martyrs for years. I'm afraid he may just drive Mr. Jones away. I think our best option is Teresa Solomon."

Thorn's body went cold, and her muscles tensed. She knew this was coming. That didn't mean she liked it.

But the rest of the room didn't share her feelings on the matter. Confused looks crossed between the Martyr leadership until Lina said, "I'm sorry, who?"

Alan paused for a moment before turning to the table. "It goes without saying this information must be kept in the strictest confidence and does not leave this room," he said to a general consensus. "Teresa Solomon is Humility."

"A Virtue?" Jeremiah asked. "Why haven't we heard about this before?"

Alan gave a brief overview of Teresa's history. Very brief. Thorn noticed he kept certain, *key* details out—details the others had no business knowing. Thorn felt the muscles in her jaw set hard, and she watched the side of Alan's face with a cold stare.

"Ultimately," he finished, "sending Teresa away very likely saved her life."

Jeremiah raised his eyebrows and nodded, impressed, but Mackenzie furrowed her brows and leaned across the table again.

"You mean to tell me," she said slowly, pointing one brightly painted nail onto the table to accent her words. "That you've been hiding a secret Virtue—literally for *decades*? Oh man, John totally owes me ten bucks!" Mackenzie barked a laugh, turned to Lina, and elbowed her in the arm. "I knew about this, didn't I? I did. I said, 'I bet you Thorn and Alan've got a secret Virtue hidden away somewhere,' didn't I? 'That's how we keep getting tips from Alan on where to look!'"

Lina closed her eyes and sighed before she looked up to Alan. "So, what happens if the Sins find Mrs. Solomon's house?" she asked. "You and Darius *just* ran into them on the return trip. We should assume they know *something* is going on in that direction. If they track her down, we could lose *two* Virtues."

Mackenzie settled back into her chair, and her small, smug smile faded. Alan quietly nodded in Lina's direction.

"I have considered that," he said. "And I have instructed Holly to set up additional monitoring on the roads in and out of Pennsylvania to check for Sin activity."

"That system's not foolproof," Jeremiah said with a dark frown. "We've missed them before."

"Yes." Alan took in a deep breath. "We have. However, I think it is important to note the other major benefit to Teresa's house—a benefit which may outweigh the risks. Darius will be in the presence of a fully Initiated Virtue."

"Ah," Lina said. "You think she can help him Initiate

his?"

"Precisely," Alan said. "Teresa will understand Mr. Jones better than anyone here ever could."

"Great," Mackenzie said, with the distinct air of someone who was done with this conversation and wanted to get to work. She clapped her hands and rubbed them together. "Jones stays with Solomon and gets all Virtue-fied, and we find the girl. Let's get started."

She got to her feet. Thorn did the same. The less she had to think about Teresa Solomon, the better. Getting back out there to look for Torres would be the perfect distraction.

"Wait," Jeremiah said. "Lina brings up a great point about security. I think we should send a detail to provide extra protection."

"I agree," Alan said. "Miss Silver would be a good choice. She can be trusted with information about Teresa and her Virtue."

"I can brief her when we're done here," Jeremiah said.

"Uh." Mackenzie frowned and raised her pierced eyebrow as she looked around the room, pausing a little longer on Thorn before she said, "I think that's a garbage idea." Alan took a deep breath, then gave a curt gesture with one hand to implore her to go on. Mackenzie leaned over the table again. "You said this old lady Virtue lives, what, five hours away? Four, if we haul ass? They'll be shit outta luck if the Sins *do* show up. Chris won't be able to hold them off until backup can get there. She's good, but she's not *that* good."

"What are you suggesting?" Jeremiah asked. "You want us to send more people? We're shorthanded. We need as many people looking for Torres as possible." He turned toward Mackenzie and looked down at her. She was dwarfed next to him, but it didn't bug her. Not much bugged Mackenzie.

"*No*," she said, the word drawn out in a taunt. "What we *need* to do is send someone who can hold her own against the Sins, and there's only one person in the Underground who can do that."

She didn't even say her name—Mackenzie just cast Thorn a sidelong glance.

That tiny flame reignited in Thorn's chest. Her eyebrows twitched downward, dark and angry over darker and angrier eyes. She shook her head. "No way."

"Think about it," Mackenzie said, and she turned to face Thorn full-on. Thorn's stony expression didn't falter. Neither did Mackenzie's conviction. "You're the only one who's—"

"I said *no*."

"Now, hold on," Jeremiah said. He was nodding slowly, thoughtfully, as he leaned in over the table. "She's got a point. You *do* make the most sense from a purely tactical standpoint. If there's an incident, you may be the only one who can get Jones out alive."

If they were trying to win her over with flattery, it wasn't working. Thorn gritted her teeth and took a deep breath. "If you send me, I may compromise the mission."

Jeremiah frowned. "What do you mean?"

"Let's just say there's some personal history there," Thorn said bitterly.

"Is your 'personal history' more important than keeping Darius and the Underground safe?" Jeremiah challenged. His full lips were turned down in a small frown. Thorn's curled into a snarl, and she watched the Tactical Unit director venomously.

"Don't test me, Montgomery."

"Thorn," Alan said quietly, warningly, as he held up a hand. "Please."

It hadn't gone without notice that Alan hadn't said anything until then, and Thorn was furious about it. She turned and looked at her uncle, and he didn't make eye contact as he steepled his fingers and pressed them to his lips.

"Miss McKay is right," he concluded at last. Thorn's stomach twisted into angry knots. "Thorn does provide the best security from a distance without having to dedicate more people to the job. I think she should go."

"It's not happening," Thorn snapped.

"This is not a conversation," Alan said sharply. His words bit like a knife. "It is an order. You are our best operative for this sort of assignment. You will have to put personal feelings aside. Ms. Brooks." Alan turned away from Thorn then, leaving her open-mouthed and fuming behind him. Lina perked up and focused on Alan. "We will need Miss Claytor to run the Gray Unit while Thorn is away. Please prepare her. Mackenzie, organize the recon and research units to work on finding Miss Torres. Mr. Locke, please pack a bag for Darius. Assume it will be an extended trip. Jeremiah, we need someone to take Thorn and Mr. Jones to Teresa's estate. I think Miss Silver is the best option. You may brief her on what was discussed here. They will leave the day after tomorrow."

"And the rest of my men?" Jeremiah asked as he got to his feet.

While Alan explained the game plan for using the Tactical and R&D Units to help track down Eva, Thorn hardly heard him. She turned on her heel and stormed from the room, slamming the door behind her so hard it rattled against its hinges. She had half a mind to go back into the city, to find a Sin—any Sin—and pick a fight. She just wanted to punch *something.*

Thorn had thought her biggest problem was Eva Torres. She'd been so fucking wrong.

"So, you're headed off, huh?"

Darius was sitting across from William at one of the cast iron tables in the courtyard. William had made them lunch—chicken salad sandwiches that tasted as plain as they looked—and spoke through a mouthful of food as he watched Darius consider his plate with a frown. Darius glanced up at him. There was no mistaking the eager, almost child-like look in his eyes as he waited for an answer.

Darius cleared his throat and looked down again. "That's the plan. Tomorrow morning."

It was all he said—because it was all he *could* say.

News of the incident had spread like disease through the Underground, rife with rumors and half-formed theories. No one knew all the details. That was intentional. When Abraham had come to let Darius know the plan, he was sure to tell him not to discuss it with anyone.

But while the Martyrs might not have known where Darius and Alan had been, or why they'd left the Underground, everyone seemed to know the two of them had almost been killed by the Sins. They knew Darius had found out about his Virtue.

And they certainly knew Eva had disappeared.

The energy in the Underground had changed in the last two days. Where it had previously been quiet and distant, it was now buzzing and anxious. Recon Units were being called back. The Tactical Teams were getting ready to go on double shifts. Alan, Thorn, and all other Martyr leadership had all but disappeared—stuck in meetings, planning sessions, and god knew what else as the Martyrs gathered every resource they could and dedicated them to one single mission:

Finding Eva Torres.

William had been in one of the overnight search parties. He'd just gotten back to the Underground when he found Darius and asked him to join him for lunch. He didn't seem put off by Darius's lackluster response. He simply nodded as he brought a glass of water to his lips.

"For your safety?" he asked.

Darius didn't even confirm that. He took a deep breath and said, "I should be here, helping find Eva."

"I get it," William said. "But it's probably better for you to get out and get some fresh air. The last month has been a shit show. You deserve a break."

A break? Darius let out a short laugh. "How can I get a

break when Eva's out there being hunted by the Sins?"

"We'll find her," William said. He sounded a lot more confident than Abraham had been when he'd explained the situation to Darius earlier that morning. Darius looked up to him—desperate for some kind of hope. William went on. "We have tons of people looking for her. Holly is taking her photo and inputting it into some facial recognition software. She's tapped into cameras around the city. Don't worry. We got this."

Just like they'd "got it" when they were trying to find Darius before the Sins got to him. His chest clenched, and he felt an angry flush rise to his cheeks.

"I know her better than anyone else," he said. "I would be more useful here than locked away out in—"

He caught himself just in time. William was watching him with wide, anticipating eyes. Darius shook his head and cleared his throat.

"I just want to help," he finished.

"You are helping," William said. The tone of his voice shifted as he leaned back in his chair and looked at Darius. For the first time, Darius recognized something behind William's eyes that made his stomach flip uncomfortably: awe. "By just *being* here, you're helping. You're a fuckin' *Virtue*, man!"

Darius looked down at his plate. A heavy weight collapsed down onto his shoulders and made him feel like he couldn't breathe. "That's what they tell me."

"I'm sorry," William continued, and he tried to reign his excitement back in, but now that it was out, it was hard to do. "This has to be super overwhelming, but we've been fighting so hard for so long, and a lot of us were starting to think we were never going to win. You've given us something new to fight for."

But Darius didn't want people fighting for him. Being the Martyr's messiah was starting to feel suffocating. He shook his head.

"Maybe it feels like that for you," he said, and he felt a

bubble of anger start to inflate inside his chest, "but that '*something*' has gotten a lot of people I loved killed."

William's enthusiasm finally deflated. He nodded and looked away from Darius—down at his plate. "I know," he said. "I'm sorry."

"Well," Darius said as he finally admitted he wasn't going to eat and pushed his food away. "I'm not going. They can't force me to leave."

William laughed and shook his head. "Sorry, I don't mean to be a dick," he said when he caught Darius's frustrated look, "but you really think that's gonna work?"

"What are they going to do?" Darius asked. "Knock me over the head and drag me out anyway?"

William shrugged and took a sip of his water. "I mean… yeah. I bet Thorn would."

Darius spent the rest of the day trying to get a hold of Alan Blaine, but the man had disappeared. The conference rooms were locked down. Even Darius's most obnoxious, non-stop knocking did nothing but get Abraham to finally pop his head out and tell him Mr. Blaine would reach out to him as soon as he could before shutting the door in his face again.

So Darius resigned himself to sitting outside Alan's office. He was determined to talk to the man, even if it meant ambushing him in the hallway between meetings.

But it never happened. Darius paced the small waiting room for hours, but by eight that night, it was clear Alan wasn't coming back. Darius half thought about hunting for Alan's room in the living quarters, but there were hundreds of doors there. He'd never find it in time.

Frustrated, he decided if he couldn't talk to Alan, he'd have to settle for the next best thing. Darius left the waiting room outside Alan's and Thorn's offices and headed back down to the courtyard. There, he saw William again, this time sitting down and having drinks with Conrad and a few other Tactical Unit members. William waved at him as he walked over.

"Hey," Darius said, nodding once in Conrad's direction before turning back to William. He didn't look at the others at the table. They watched him with a tempered reverence, and it made him feel uncomfortable. "Do you know where Thorn is?"

"Oh. Yeah," William said. "She and Chris are training." He gestured across the courtyard to the wide, double doors leading to the gym.

Finally. Darius thanked William and made his way across the plaza. He was acutely aware of the Tactical Unit members watching his back. Their whispers chased after him like ghosts until he finally reached the gym. From there, muffled voices came through the doors. Darius opened them, peeked his head into the room, and froze.

Thorn and Chris were sparring on the mats to his left, but it wasn't anything like the rough street fights Darius had seen on the market. This wasn't clawing clumsily, desperately, over a loaf of bread. This was cold, calculated, and tactical. The women stood in proper form—shoulders squared, knees bent, closed fists held up in front of their faces—and they moved with a lethal grace. There was no inhibition, no resistance. Just pure power.

Power and blood.

Every strike from one body to the other sounded out through the room. Dull, bone-bruising thunks. The two of them parried. Ducked. Blocked and dodged. They were both dressed down, wearing form-fitting leggings, fabric wrist guards, and athletic bras that enabled quick movement and little resistance. That's where the similarities ended. It was like watching a battle between light and dark.

On one side was Chris. She was several inches shorter than Thorn, and though well-toned, her body was marred and damaged. Spotty, red bruises dotted up her arms; her pink skin was littered with fine, white scars and flecks of blood from a cut in her lip. Sweat drizzled down the divot of her spine—a long, deep scar dragged across her back from shoulder to hip. The elastic wrapped around her hair fell loose as she ducked beneath one of Thorn's strikes. Long, yellow strands clung to the dampness around her neck and throat. Through every hit she threw—and those she took—Chris vocalized with sharp, breathy *hah!'s*.

And while Chris was powerful, Thorn was a machine. She was taller, leaner, with a physique that looked like it had been carved from marble. Her complexion was equally flawless—no bruises, no scrapes, no evidence of past battles where she'd come out on the losing side. Even her dark hair somehow looked totally unaffected by the fight—pulled smooth and tight against the base of her skull. Thorn fought in total silence, with a sense of precision that was almost inhuman. Her expression was balanced and calm. Where Chris was red and tired, Thorn looked fresh and new. If it weren't for a small dribble of blood under her nose, Darius never would have known Chris had hit her at all.

Suddenly, Thorn twisted around. Her foot swept Chris's legs out from under her, and the blonde woman stumbled backward. When Chris fell, Thorn followed. Darius almost covered his face as Thorn's fist stopped just inches from Chris's nose. Thorn's bare stomach and shoulders glistened in sweat and trembled with power as she crouched there, poised. Focused. Darius gawked.

Then her eyes moved up—and found him.

"Jones."

Thorn's voice was crisp in the chamber. It echoed off the mirrored, concrete walls and padded floors. She straightened up. There was a peculiar expression on her face—her dark eyes were a little wide. Her chest rocked with full, heavy breaths, and she grabbed a towel off a nearby weight rack and dried her hands. The fabric wrapped around her knuckles and wrists was stained pink.

Chris stood and wiped the blood from her lip.

"How long have you been here?" Thorn asked. There

was an edge to her voice—annoyance, with maybe a hint of nerves.

Suddenly, Darius felt like he'd been caught snooping, and he quickly shook his head. "I just got here," he said as he stepped into the room. Thorn was watching like she was trying to open him up and peer at his soul. "Can we talk? In private."

Thorn considered him for a moment longer before she nodded. "Give me a few minutes," she said, and she and Chris turned away from him and walked back into the women's locker room. Something on Thorn's left arm caught his attention.

The wrist supports covered her palms to halfway between her hand and elbow. From the base of the fabric, thick, deep scars snaked their way up her inner arm. They dripped down her skin like someone had poured scalding oil onto her flesh. The tight, upraised marks extended almost to her elbow, where they came to sharp points.

A chill ran up Darius's spine. It occurred to him he'd never seen Thorn without long sleeves or gloves. Was she trying to hide these scars?

She cleaned up quickly. Thorn walked out of the locker room freshly washed, with dripping hair and a gym bag flung over her shoulder. Almost to confirm his suspicions, she wore a deep red, long-sleeved shirt. Where her wet hair fell on her back, the fabric was the shade of blood.

Darius glanced to her left arm again. The sleeves were so tight they prevented Darius from seeing the inside of her arm, but the scars wrapped around to the back of her hand. Tiny tendrils of raised, white skin twisted around her thumb joint and into sight.

"What happened there?" Darius asked, and he gestured to her left hand.

Thorn grabbed her wrist almost defensively. She paused for a moment, as though trying to decide how much of the story to tell him. Ultimately, she decided on not much. "Wrath happened," she said. "Call it a parting gift."

"You were captured?" Darius was shocked. He didn't think the Sins left survivors—especially not *Wrath*. "How did you get away?"

"I fought," Thorn said. "Hard."

His mind replayed the battle he'd just seen. What would it look like if Thorn had been fighting the Sins—if *Derek Dane* had been on the other end of those punches?

The door to the locker room opened again, and Chris stepped out. Even freshly showered, she still looked like hell. A bruise was rising up on her lip. Thorn reached out, gingerly grabbed Chris's chin, and turned her face to look at the injury. She was gentle. Darius saw a glimpse of compassion in the soft way her brows sloped down.

"I'm sorry," she said to Chris, and she sounded sincere. "I lost control."

Chris gave a short, curt nod. "You need to work on that."

Thorn sighed. "Too bad Jones hasn't Initiated his Virtue yet," she said as she opened the doors and led the way out into the courtyard. She was trying to be funny, but the attempted humor in her voice didn't translate well. The small smile on her lips didn't extend to her eyes. "He could heal you right up."

Darius cast Chris an almost guilty look, but the blonde woman just raised her hand and shook her head.

"Healing the old-fashioned way builds character," she said. She gave Thorn a pointed look and a smirk. "Anyway, I'll see you in the morning. I need to go talk with Alan about our plan for tomorrow." Then she nodded toward them both before taking off across the courtyard and toward the elevators. Thorn watched after her, and though her face was hard to read, Darius thought he saw a tiny bit of guilt in her dark, empty eyes.

When Chris was far enough away not to hear them, Thorn turned back to Darius. "So. What did you want to talk about?"

Thorn's focus on him was intense. She looked him

straight in the eye, unblinkingly. Now that he was actually talking with her, he wished he'd just gone searching, door to door, for Alan in the residential quarters.

"Well," Darius said, and he tried to hold himself as confidently as Thorn was. "I just wanted to tell you I'm not going."

One thin brow arched high on her forehead. "Excuse me?"

"I'm not going," Darius said again. "I want to stay here and look for Eva. I know her better than anyone and—"

Thorn didn't let him finish his argument. She held up a hand to silence him. "No," she said. "Absolutely not."

Darius, shaken a bit by the interruption, scoffed. "You can't force me to go."

Thorn's eyes darkened and narrowed. She didn't say anything, but she didn't need to. Darius remembered what William had said, about how she would probably be willing to knock him over the head and drag him along anyway. An angry flush raised up over his cheeks.

"Look," Darius went on through an exasperated sigh, "I'm not weak, I don't need protecting, and I won't just sit back and let other people do the dirty work for me."

"We're not doing this 'for you,'" Thorn growled. "We need to protect the Underground. If the Sins catch Torres, if she tells them where we are, you aren't the only one they'll try to kill. They will *slaughter* us. All of us."

"Then let me help," Darius exclaimed. William and the other Tactical Unit members were still sitting across the courtyard, and now Darius and Thorn's raised voices were starting to draw attention. "It's my fault that Eva took off. Let me find her!"

"No," Thorn said again. It seemed like her control was faltering. Her fists tightened around the strings to her bag. The poise and calm she'd had in the gym evaporated. "You're not trained to deal with the Sins. You can't even block Direct Influence!"

"Then teach me!"

"We don't have the time!"

"If I wasn't a Virtue, you'd have no problem letting me stay, and you know it!"

Thorn paused, and her lips pressed into a thin, white line. She took a half step toward Darius and got right up in his face. His first impulse was to step back, but he stood his ground. She was shorter than he was by a couple of inches, but somehow, she made him feel small.

"You're right," she whispered. He could feel her breath hot against his chin. Goosebumps raised up on his arms. "If you weren't a Virtue, I wouldn't give a damn if you were out there with a death wish, thirsty for revenge. But you *are* a Virtue, which means my people will *die* trying to keep you safe. If you're out there, dozens of good men and women will sacrifice themselves to protect you because they *believe* in you. I'm not going to give them the chance to make that sacrifice."

Darius opened his mouth to argue but found he had nothing else to say. He just stared, glaring, at Thorn. She glowered back.

"We leave in the morning."

Then Thorn took off across the courtyard, and Darius watched her until she got into the elevator and disappeared. If she'd been able to, he was sure she would have slammed the door behind her. He swore and made his way back to his room, avoiding the curious looks William was sending his way.

CHAPTER THIRTEEN

Darius took over the Martyr SUV's back seat on the long, quiet drive back to Teresa's estate. He stared out the window. Fall was beginning to fade. Leaves littered the side of the road, fluttering in the drafts as cars passed by. Trees stood like skeletons—naked and lifeless.

It had been hours since they'd left the Underground and met Alan on the edge of New York City. They pulled up at a gas station, and while Chris had filled the tank, Alan, Thorn, and Darius talked outside. It was the first time Darius had seen Alan since their conversation in the hospital ward just a few nights ago. He claimed he'd been out of the Underground, and he wanted to say goodbye and wish Darius well, but Darius wasn't sure he believed the whole story. Not only had Alan pulled up from the same direction they'd come from, but he seemed less concerned with saying *goodbye* than he did with lecturing Thorn.

As Chris and Darius had gotten back into the car, Darius overheard the two of them talking at the back of the vehicle. Alan stressed to her how important it was for her to keep a cool head. There was a strange note to how he said it, and Darius tried to pay attention, but he didn't have the chance to hear more. When Chris finished up and closed the car,

Alan's voice became muffled and unintelligible. Shortly later, Thorn climbed back into the passenger's seat and slammed the door behind her. Darius was already starting to develop a headache from too much worrying and too little sleep, and the tension just added to it. He'd rubbed his temples as Chris pulled them out and back onto the road.

Chris and Thorn said very little. Occasionally, their silences broke to talk, in minimal detail, about Martyr-related business Darius didn't really understand, such as TAC schedules and training routines. At one point, Thorn asked about Chris's lip, which was still swollen from their match the day before. Chris simply waved off her concern. Otherwise, they were quiet, and the quiet felt natural. Neither woman seemed pressed to fill in empty spaces with empty words.

But the silence still gave into tension. The closer they came to Teresa's house, the more Thorn's mood darkened. She had drawn a red pack of cigarettes from her satchel, and while she didn't light one, she tapped the box on the armrest. Sparkie, her small, flying lizard, was wrapped around her like a scarf. His crimson wings were flattened against her skin, as though he was trying to comfort her. Every time Darius adjusted, he lifted his head and gazed back at him with beady little eyes.

After a while, growing weary of staring out the window at the flashing landscape, Darius stretched himself out across the back seat. He felt heavy. He felt thin. He felt *bitter.* He hated being pulled away from New York, from Eva, and from everything he'd ever known just because of who he was. He hated feeling so useless and alone. He closed his eyes and took a deep breath.

Darius wasn't used to feeling this way. He'd never been this *powerless* before.

Maybe it was the gentle rocking of the car, or the quiet hum of the engine, or the *month* of long, restless nights plagued by nightmares and insomnia, but before he knew it, he was fast asleep.

He came back to consciousness slowly, lazily, with a hazy awareness of what was going on around him. The steady motion of the SUV. The unpredictable flickering sunlight flashing against his closed eyelids as they drove through dense trees. Thorn's and Chris's hushed voices from the front of the car…

"You need to be careful," Chris was saying. Her tone was quiet and reserved. That woke Darius up. He kept his eyes shut, but his ears strained to hear what she was saying. "And you need to stay in control—"

"I will stay in control," Thorn snarled. "I'll just stay the fuck away from her."

Chris didn't reply right away. Almost tentatively, as though she was afraid of the reaction it was going to trigger, she said, "Or you could talk to her."

"No."

Thorn's response was swift and merciless.

"Thorn, it's been years—"

"I don't care," Thorn hissed, and her voice grew increasingly agitated and angry. "I lost everything because of her. *Everything.* If it wasn't for Teresa—"

Something squirmed on Darius's stomach. He yelped and shot upright. Sparkie leapt off him and frantically scurried back onto Thorn's shoulder. She seemed just as shocked as he was as she turned around to look at Darius. He had the sense to pretend he'd just woken up and rubbed his eyes. "Sorry," he groaned. "I must've dozed off. Is he okay?"

Sparkie paced nervously on Thorn's shoulder, his wings flared around him. She quickly scooped him up and tucked him away in a satchel at her feet. A touch of pink had risen to her cheeks, and she said, "He's fine."

"I didn't hurt him?"

"No," Thorn said impatiently. She was much more flustered than Darius would have expected, and she quickly changed the subject. "Sleep well?"

"Yeah," Darius said. He cleared his throat and looked at

the clock, shocked to find he'd been asleep for almost half the drive. "Wow, I was out for a while."

"Good," Chris said. "Makes the trip pass more quickly."

Darius noticed she made a point to avoid looking at him or at Thorn. He wondered if they suspected he'd overheard them. He'd been led to believe Alan was the only one to officially meet Teresa, but it seemed there was more to the story.

When they finally arrived at Teresa's estate, Darius paid special attention to the way Teresa and Thorn interacted. Or, he wanted to, but they didn't. As Teresa stood on the front porch, Thorn gathered all her things. She picked up her suitcase, a duffle bag Darius assumed was full of weapons, and threw her satchel over her shoulder before she quickly walked around the garage to the back of the house. Teresa waited until she was out of sight before she stepped down off the porch and approached Chris and Darius at the car.

"Welcome back," she said to Darius as he opened the door and stepped out onto the gravel drive. She smiled, but if Darius wasn't mistaken, the light in her eyes was a little dimmer than it had been on his last visit. Teresa reached out and grabbed his shoulder in a light, tender grip before she turned to Chris and held out her hand. "You must be Christine?"

"It's Chris. Alan is the only person who calls me Christine anymore."

Teresa laughed. The magic came back. Her light flickered to life, and Darius felt drawn to her. This time, it made him feel uncomfortable. Was he only drawn to her because of his Virtue?

"Alan has always been *so* formal," Teresa said with a small smile and a nod. Then she gestured up toward Chris's lip. "What happened here?"

Chris seemed to have forgotten about the bruise. She gently touched the swollen spot with the tips of her fingers. "Oh, it's nothing. Just a training injury."

She didn't say anything about Thorn.

"Mind if I take care of it for you?" Teresa asked.

Chris just stared at her. Her bright green eyes opened a little wider, and she quickly glanced to Darius and then back to Teresa. "You mean—like, heal it?"

Teresa's smile deepened. "Yes."

This time, Chris didn't say anything. She just gave a quick, shrugging nod. Then Teresa stepped up a little closer and reached out. Her fingers brushed against Chris's lips, and within seconds, the swelling subsided and disappeared. Chris's eyes went wide. As soon as Teresa pulled away, her hands went right to her mouth and gently touched the fresh, healthy skin.

"There, that's better," Teresa said. "Now, would you care to stay for dinner? You've had a long day."

"Thank you," Chris said with an airy, distracted tone, but the nature of Teresa's question finally sank in, and she cleared her throat and dropped her hands back to her sides. She shook her head more professionally this time. "But no. I need to get going, unless you want me to…"

Then she paused and glanced up at the house. Darius turned and looked up, too. He noticed the blinds were closed on the windows to the room he had stayed in last time.

"Ah." Teresa gently folded her arms around her chest. "No, I can handle her."

Chris's eyebrows twitched downward, just barely—so subtly Darius wasn't sure he caught it—before she nodded. "Of course. It was a pleasure meeting you, Mrs. Solomon, and thank you." She reached out and shook Teresa's hand again, then she turned to Darius. They shared a brief, tense moment, and Chris just gave him a single nod.

"I'll see you soon. I hope."

Then she turned, got back into the car, and pulled away.

The tires crunched along the gravel until she made it down to the main road. Darius watched the car disappear around the corner.

Now he was alone with Teresa Solomon and Thorn Rose.

"Well," Teresa said quietly. "Let's get you to your room, huh?"

She led him inside and up to the second story. The door to the room Darius had used on his last trip was closed. Thorn had no doubt claimed it. It was the only room with both a private bathroom and balcony access. That meant she could spend as much time there as she wanted to without ever seeing anyone else in the house.

Darius got the one just down the hall. It was smaller, with light green wallpaper and a large sliding glass door, which also led to the balcony. Darius walked through the door and tossed his duffle bag onto the bed. It landed with a soft, unenthusiastic *thump!*

"I'm sorry you don't get the larger room," Teresa said, but Darius shook his head.

"It's fine."

He'd once shared a pile of blankets with a swarm of wiggling children on the floor. A painful flutter made his heart clench. The size of his accommodations was hardly important now.

"I'll let you get settled," Teresa said quietly. She stepped out the door and left him alone.

Darius walked toward the far end of the room, toward the sliding glass doors on the opposite wall. From here, he could see the front of Teresa's property. The driveway. The quiet road leading back to Wellsboro. For several minutes, Darius stared out at the horizon and watched the sun fade behind the trees.

He should have been happy here. He should have been relieved to be so far away from danger and to be in the presence of an old, experienced Virtue who could help him navigate his, but he wasn't. He was tired. He was sad. He was angry.

A muffled voice called up the stairs: "Dinner's ready!"

It broke Darius from his thoughts. He'd lost track of how long he'd been standing there; the sky was dusky and dark now. Darius quickly unpacked the standard Martyr clothing Abraham had collected for him and put them in the empty, dusty drawers of the dresser. Everything was slightly too much of something—too big, too light, too gray. He was briefly reminded of the children. They were always dressed in oversized clothes. It had made them seem so small. After slamming the drawers shut, he picked up the toiletries bag Abraham had packed for him and walked down the hallway to the other bathroom.

The savory smell of seasoned chicken and roasted vegetables made its way up the stairs. It ignited the familiar pang of hunger in Darius's gut. He plopped his bathroom bag onto the counter and headed further down the hallway, past the third bedroom, and into the second-story family room. Another set of steps led straight into the kitchen, where Teresa was already plating up food for the three of them.

"Could you help me set the table?" she asked when he hit the foot of the stairs. She grabbed two of the plates, he took the final one, and they made their way to the dining room.

Dinner was uncomfortable. Teresa and Darius said very little to one another. The third place setting was left untouched, which didn't sit well with Darius. How many kids could he have fed with this? What a waste. Teresa would probably give it to the *chickens*, when there were thousands of starving children struggling on the streets of New York City.

After a few long minutes, where the silence was broken only by the sounds of cutlery against ceramic and the chewing of food, Teresa cleared her throat.

"So, you know about your Virtue?"

Just the words were enough to make Darius's stomach knot up again. He slowly nodded and popped another bite into his mouth. It gave him an excuse to not say anything more about it.

"I'm sorry it all happened the way it did," Teresa went on. Darius gave her a puzzled look, and she said, "Alan told me everything. That must've been hard."

Again, Darius just nodded.

"Well," Teresa went on. There was a restless note to her voice, like she had spent so much time isolated that now, with the opportunity to share, she just needed to get it all out. "I know it's rough right now, but give it time. It's also going to be so amazing. You'll be able to help so many people!"

But the problem was, Darius's Virtue *hadn't* helped people. How was he supposed to answer for the awe-inspiring power of knowing he was a Virtue when all it left behind was a trail of broken bodies and shattered dreams? He didn't know how to reconcile the beauty with the horror, and he couldn't forget about the life he'd built, the changes he'd made, that this Virtue had taken away.

"Your life is about to absolutely *transform.*"

Darius stopped eating. His stomach was too twisted up to have any more. He put his fork down, wiped his mouth, and sighed.

"I never wanted my life to *transform,*" Darius said, and though he was trying to reign it in, knowing none of this was Teresa's fault, his anger at all that had happened to him was starting to spill out, and he couldn't stop it. "We didn't have much, but we had each other. We were a family. You know what I have now? My kids are dead. My friends are being hunted like animals. Everything I know has been ripped away from me because of this… this *thing* I was born with, that I didn't even know I *had* until it had already ruined everything that had ever mattered to me. And it's going to change me even *more*? I don't even know who I *am* now!"

By the end, he was yelling, and Teresa just watched him with wide, sad eyes. "Oh, Darius," she said quietly, and she reached across the table to grab his hand, but he pulled away and pushed his chair back from the table.

"No," he said. "I don't need anyone else to tell me they're *sorry*. I just need to be able to… to *do* something, but what can I do? How can I possibly help the world when I can't even protect myself or save the people I love?"

"Darius," Teresa tried again, but this time she brought her old, weathered hand back and folded it with the other on her lap. "I know you're suffering. God, I know. I've been there. But you don't have to. You can choose—"

"Choose?" Darius was yelling again. Even though he knew Teresa meant well, he just couldn't stomach it. "I haven't chosen *any* of the shit that's happened to me!"

Teresa clenched her mouth shut, but the pain in her eyes made Darius feel guilty. He quickly excused himself and headed back up the stairs. When he passed Thorn's room, he was angry all over again, but he couldn't even place why.

He slammed his door behind him, and then he felt guilty about that, too.

Darius heard Thorn coming before she walked into his room. Her door opened with a creak. Boots clicked the hardwood floor eight times as she walked down the hallway. She didn't bother knocking. She just opened his door—slowly, carefully.

"Jones?"

Darius was lying in bed, lights off, staring at the ceiling. His stomach was twisted up, his face set in a firm, frustrated expression. He didn't even look up to her as he grunted, "Leave me alone."

She didn't listen to him. Thorn peeked through the gap in the door, her pale face and throat a stark contrast against the darkness around them. Then she let herself in, walked to the other side of Darius's bed, and turned on the table lamp. He sat up and glared at her.

"I said I want to be left alone."

She just raised an eyebrow at him as she came around to sit on the foot of the bed. She was close enough to talk to him comfortably but far enough away to make sure she was respecting at least *one* boundary. For a few long seconds, she just watched him through those dark, empty eyes.

Finally, she said, "So. Did screaming help?"

Darius's rage flared. He got to his feet and pointed at the door. "If you just came in here to lecture me, you can get the hell out."

"You're angry," Thorn said, and she stood up, too. "Good." Darius was caught off guard. He'd opened his mouth to continue arguing but found he had lost the words behind his teeth. "You *should* be angry. What happened to you wasn't fair. It's not fair that your family was killed. It's not fair that you're a Virtue. None of it is fucking fair."

The volume in her voice was growing with each and every syllable until she was almost shouting, but she never quite went there. Her brows were furrowed deep, and her nostrils flared, like she was feeling just as furious as she was telling Darius he should feel.

"And being angry about it? Jones, anger is *normal.* You should be mad as hell this… this *disaster* fell on your lap, and now you have to be the one to clean up the mess. Get angry. *Let yourself get angry.*"

He just stared at her, and when she didn't shy away, when she didn't move those dark, knowing eyes away from his, he looked down—down at her left arm, where he could barely see the tips of her scars winding themselves out at the edge of her black, fingerless glove. He thought about everything Thorn must have gone through. This war had devastated her so thoroughly she'd rebuilt herself with a sharp, dangerous name. He wondered who Thorn had been before and what the hell it took to turn an innocent child into the cold, hardened woman Darius knew today.

"And then take that anger," Thorn continued, and her voice got quiet again. Darius looked back up to her face and realized she'd taken a step closer to him. He caught the light scents of cigarette smoke and sandalwood upon her hair and clothing. "And turn it into something you can use."

Darius frowned. "What do you mean?"

"Your anger can be an anchor," she said, "or it can be an engine. It can either hold you back, keep you trapped, force you to drown in your own misery and hate, or it can give you the push you need to move forward. You have a choice to make here—you can stew and pout and throw a tantrum, or you can pull your shit together and work hard to fix this. What do you want to do?"

He hadn't expected her to ask him anything, and he floundered for a moment. "What do I want to do?" he repeated. "I want to get the hell back to New York City! I want to help find Eva! I want to get back at the people who destroyed my family!"

Thorn nodded. "Right. And do you think you can get *any* of it accomplished by *screaming* about it?"

A new wave of shame washed over Darius. He furiously looked down at his feet.

"Don't feel bad," Thorn added, and Darius glanced back up at her. Her tone was sympathetic. "You *needed* it. You needed to vent, to release that energy. And now that it's out of your system, it's time to do something productive with your anger."

"Like what?" Darius scoffed.

"Train," Thorn said. Her tone was firm and unyielding, but her body language was the most relaxed he'd ever seen. Her shoulders weren't tense. Her fists unclenched. Even the muscles along her jawline seemed softer, somehow. Her eyes, though, were just as intense as always. "Learn how to block out Direct Influence so the Sins can't get into your head ever again. Learn how to fight and defend yourself. Learn how to drive a damn car. I don't care. Just work on gaining tools to help you get what you want. You have a goal in mind. Take steps toward it. Nothing is stopping you but your own damned hurt pride."

"My pride isn't—"

"You feel useless, like everyone else is doing something to correct mistakes *you* made. Stop feeling sorry for yourself. You're better than that. Instead, take action, or I swear to god, I'm going to have to punch you in the mouth."

And for the first time, the corners of her lips curled up into a small smile, and despite himself, Darius gave a soft chuckle.

"You could learn a lot here," Thorn went on, and now even her voice began to soften. "I can teach you the mindfulness exercises to hold off Direct Influence. I can teach you how to fight. We can go running. Whatever you need. And Solomon—"

At Teresa's name, Thorn's voice got hard and unforgiving again. Her spine went rigid, and Darius saw tension return all across her body.

"—Solomon has been studying Virtues for a long, long time. You have a lot you could learn from her, too."

Just the mention of the Virtues made a small flame of anger ignite in Darius's stomach again, but also quite a bit of sadness. He heaved a sigh. "I suppose that's what everyone's hoping for," Darius said. Thorn frowned and gave him an inquisitive look, so he added, "That I'll accept it."

She didn't respond right away, and Darius turned and sat back down on the bed. Being angry was exhausting, and he put his face into his hands and groaned. The mattress beside him shifted as Thorn took her spot at the foot of his bed again. After a few long moments, she said, "My people *are* hoping for that, but it's important for you to understand something." He uncovered his face and turned toward her. She had leaned in to emphasize how serious she was. He could see his reflection staring back at him from her dark irises. Then she reached out and grabbed his hand. Her fingers were cold, but her grip was strong. "You are worth so much more than your Virtue."

Darius didn't know what to say, and to his surprise, he found his throat had gotten tight, and it would have been hard to say anything, anyway. So he just nodded. Thorn watched him for a moment longer, frowning, before she nodded, too. She squeezed his fingers once before she let go of his hand and got to her feet.

"You're not as alone as you think," she said quietly. "If you need anything, you know where to find me." Then she let herself out of the room. He heard her boots click all the way back down the hallway until she disappeared into her own quarters and shut the door behind her.

When Darius laid down again, he found the swirling mix of guilt and frustration had begun to die down. It settled in his chest, and he took a deep breath to quell it further.

Thorn was right. If he was stuck in this situation, he might as well make the most of it...

Darius was *done* being a victim.

CHAPTER FOURTEEN

Darius's lungs burned. With every breath, they expanded and ached against the sides of his ribs. His dry mouth was coated with the metallic taste of iron as he pushed himself to keep up. Thorn was yards ahead of him—too many yards for him to even dream of catching up. He watched as she tirelessly kept the pace—never stumbling, never slowing, never stopping for a break.

The edge of the driveway was within sight now. He took a breath and cleared his throat, spitting mucous onto the side of the road. It was almost over. He was so close…

At last, Thorn slowed to a jog, then a power walk, until finally, she threw her arms up over her head and breathed deep. Her black, long-sleeve shirt pulled up a little at her hips, showing a sliver of white skin between it and the waistband of her leggings. Darius fumbled to a stop beside her and leaned over to clutch a stitch in his side. He was so drenched in sweat his t-shirt clung to him. Thorn looked him over. He almost felt like she was judging him but decided he was too damned tired to care.

"The Sins are stronger and faster than you," Thorn said. Even after sprinting the last hundred yards, her breathing was still even and relaxed. The only sign she'd been exercising at all was a slight pink tint at the apples of her cheeks. "You have to work *hard* to stay ahead of them."

"Right," Darius breathed, and he nodded. "Great. Perfect."

Thorn gave a cold chuckle and slapped him on the shoulder. It almost knocked him to the side. "Physical health is important. The Sins don't have to try—*you* do."

They started the walk back up to Teresa's house. Dawn was breaking over the horizon. The beautiful pink and pale-yellow clouds cast the property in stunning, pastel light. For the last several days, Thorn had woken Darius up to run with her. He hadn't expected it to be as hard as it was. Living out on the streets had kept him relatively fit, but it wasn't anything compared to Thorn. Darius was still struggling to catch his breath by the time they reached the front of the house. Thorn hadn't even broken a sweat.

"What's on your agenda for today?" Thorn asked as they paused at the base of the steps.

Darius inhaled a couple more deep breaths, cleared his throat, and said, "Well, I'm helping clean out Rover's paddock first. Then I think Teresa's teaching me to drive…"

Thorn raised one eyebrow high on her head. "Sounds exciting."

Darius laughed. "Is it weird that driving makes me more nervous than the idea of facing the Sins does?"

Thorn's lips curled into a tiny smile, but she didn't have the chance to say anything. The front door opened, and Teresa stepped out onto the porch. Darius glanced up to the Virtue, and by the time he looked back at Thorn, she had already walked halfway across the length of the garage. Teresa cast her a quick look before she cleared her throat with a little "ahem" and stepped down the stairs.

"Ready?" she asked Darius. When he nodded, she led the way around the house, toward where the coop and paddock sat.

Over the next few weeks, Darius found Thorn was right: channeling his frustration with the situation into other tasks may not *solve* his problems, but it certainly distracted him from them.

Every morning, after his run with Thorn, Darius helped Teresa care for Rover, the old bay stallion, and her flock of misfit chickens. After that, he took a quick shower and set out on whatever tasks and training Thorn and Teresa could throw at him. Teresa was introducing him to a whole host of "domestic" skills. He helped her in the kitchen whenever she prepared their meals, and after she'd caught him washing his clothes in the bathroom sink, she took him aside and showed him how the washer and dryer worked. She even taught Darius how to trim his own hair using an electric razor—and how to fix it when he messed up. Looking in a mirror with his old shaggy hair cut short and clean was foreign. He hardly recognized himself.

Thorn, meanwhile, focused on educating him in a different kind of skillset—one that would be more useful to a life battling the Sins.

Her first priority was his physical fitness. Besides their morning runs, Thorn was guiding him through daily resistance training routines. Using their own body weight or reusable grocery bags filled with canned goods, Thorn put Darius through rounds of squats, lunges, push-ups, crunches, and a range of other exercises he couldn't remember the names to.

Darius preferred this workout to the running. He was used to using his body this way. Between carrying merchandise home from the market and playing with the kids, he'd gotten a lot of practice. Even so, Thorn was shockingly more adept than he was in this arena, too. Darius marveled at how she was easily able to lift more weight and do more reps than Darius could without stopping for a break.

When he and Thorn weren't exercising their bodies, they were exerting their minds to better prepare Darius against Direct Influence.

"Direct Influence will feel like a tension headache," Thorn told him late one afternoon, a week into their stay, as they sat across from one another on the plush carpet in the upstairs living room. The sunset burst through the windows in vibrant reds and purples, throwing beautiful shadows across Thorn's face. Her eyes were closed, her legs crossed, and her hands folded gently in her lap. Darius watched her adjust her shirt mindlessly, pulling the long sleeves up higher over her palms to make sure her scars were completely hidden. She looked different somehow—more delicate than she ever had back at the Underground.

"Close your eyes," she snapped. Darius noticed she had peeked out and caught him staring. He obliged, and she continued. "It will start in the temples and sear in a band around your head. The more Direct Influence a Sin is impressing on you, the tighter the band will feel. If you start to get a headache around a Sin, they're trying to Influence you."

Darius nodded. "I think I remember that."

Thorn made a quiet noise of confirmation. "If it happens again, you need to clear your mind and sort out your thoughts."

"That's a lot easier said than done."

"Yes." Thorn's voice was dark. "It is. That's why it's important to practice this kind of meditation when you're alone and in control of your environment. It's easier for your brain to get back here in a tense situation when you're used to getting here already. Think of it like… how you worked in the market. You had to practice. Stay vigilant. Stay on your toes. After a while, it was as natural to you as breathing." Darius opened his eyes, surprised, but Thorn was still sitting with her eyelids shut and her face calm and neutral.

Darius frowned and closed his eyes again.

"Focus on your breath. In and out," Thorn said. Her tone shifted. It was level, almost hypnotic, and Darius followed her lead.

Combatting Direct Influence was about fortifying the mind by achieving a state of calmness and clarity. Thorn seemed to be the antithesis of these principles, but Darius was surprised at how easily she seemed to be able to slip into a place of peace—when she wanted to. Darius was not so good at it. He had a tough time clearing his head the way Thorn described. Thoughts kept creeping in, invading his silence. Sometimes they were mundane, like thinking about how he'd accidentally used the wrong soap and flooded the laundry room with bubbles. Other times, it was more serious, like worrying about Eva and whether the Sins or the Martyrs would find her first. Today, it was vivid. He thought back to the devastated orphanage. Blank eyes set in bloodied faces stared up at him.

He swore quietly, and to his surprise, Thorn offered a cold laugh. "Hard, right?"

"It's impossible," he grumbled, but Thorn ignored him and went on with the lesson.

"Sins are more likely to be able to Influence or Puppet you if you are in harmony with them," Thorn said. "That means the more driven you are by the things the Sin is driven by, the more likely they are to be able to get into your head and fuck it up. The more dissonant you are from the Sin, the harder it is for them. Sometimes, it's even impossible."

"How does meditation help with that?" Darius asked.

"Meditation and mindfulness keep you on neutral ground," Thorn said. "Neither harmonious nor dissonant. From here, you can more easily identify when a Sin is attempting to Influence you, and you can work against it. When you recognize it, and you've done what you can to clear your mind, it's time to figure out what thoughts are yours and what thoughts are the ones the Sin is implanting. Ask yourself the six basic questions: who, what, why, how, where, and when. Ground yourself. Who is around you? What are you trying to accomplish? How will the thoughts in your head affect the situation? You get the idea. When you take the time to critically consider them, you can quickly identify the ones that go against your real intentions."

Darius nodded, and then, realizing Thorn couldn't see

him with her eyes closed, he said, "Right."

"With enough practice, the Sins won't be able to get the footing they need to even try to Influence you. Most of the Martyrs are almost impervious by now. And," Thorn continued, this time a little more slowly, more cautiously, almost like she wasn't sure she should mention it. Darius peeked open one eye and found her watching him. "If you decide to embrace your Virtue, they wouldn't be able to get in at all."

He closed his eyes again and heaved a sigh. Maybe that would be better than this mindfulness practice…

Even though the meditation was a challenge for him, Darius took his new work seriously. It gave him something to do, something to distract him from the fact that he was stuck out here while the rest of the Underground was on a manhunt for Eva. In a way, he was working for Eva, too. She was his motivation. When he felt tired and beat up in the mornings and considered skipping out on his run, he'd imagine her face and lace up his shoes. In the middle of his meditations, whenever his mind wandered, he'd hear her voice in his head, prodding him back on track.

But Eva wasn't his *only* focus. Ever since he'd overheard Thorn and Chris talking in the car, the missing details of their conversation had been driving him crazy. If he wasn't worrying about Eva, he was obsessing over what the hell had happened between Teresa and Thorn.

"All right," Teresa said one afternoon as she and Darius wandered around in her old silver coupe. Darius was driving, and Teresa gave him directions as they drove through Wellsboro's quiet streets. "Don't forget to indicate your turn."

Darius used his left hand to tilt his turn signal on. It blinked on the dash, and little clicks sounded out through the car. They'd been practicing for a couple of weeks now, and he was surprisingly comfortable behind the wheel, though he suspected that wouldn't be nearly as true when he got back to New York. He slowed them to a stop outside the post office, put the car into park, and unlocked the doors.

"That was great!" Teresa grabbed a collection of letters up from her lap and opened the door. "Your stops are getting much smoother! I'll be right back."

He laughed as the old woman bustled out of the car and headed up to a blue mailbox outside the brick building. Darius watched as she slipped the envelopes into the slot. There was a familiar joviality to her attitude that reminded Darius of the first time he'd met her.

He hadn't seen as much of it since he'd been back here with Thorn.

"There we go," she said as she climbed back into the car beside him and buckled up her belt. "Now, do you want to head back, or should we drive around some more?"

"I'd *like* to drive," Darius said, and he glanced at the clock on the dashboard. "But Thorn has me scheduled for meditation in an hour."

The mood in the car shifted a little uncomfortably, and Teresa cast a look over her shoulder at Sparkie. The creature had taken to following Darius around whenever he was working with Teresa, and today was no different. He was curled up atop the back seat, soaking in the winter sun as it came in the window behind him. At the mention of Thorn's name, his beady little eyes opened. Teresa cleared her throat and looked back out toward the street.

"Meditation is important," she said, gesturing for Darius to move them back onto the road. "Working on combating Direct Influence?"

"Yep," Darius said. "Thorn's an expert in it."

The anxiety in the car only strengthened—the same way it *always* did when Darius tried to talk about Thorn in front of Teresa. For that reason, he did it often.

But Teresa quietly and gracefully shifted the subject in small, almost imperceptible ways to remove Thorn from the equation. "It's a vital skill. Direct Influence is one of the most dangerous things Sins can do. Have you worked on emotional awareness?"

Darius sighed but decided not to push too hard today. He glanced over his shoulder, out the back window, as he changed lanes to make a right-hand turn. He saw that Sparkie had closed his eyes again. "Mostly, I'm working on clearing my mind and staying neutral—which is *impossible.*"

Teresa laughed. "Not impossible. Just hard."

"So, what do you mean when you say, 'emotional awareness?'" Darius asked. "Not feeling them?"

"No," Teresa said. "It's about experiencing them, acknowledging them, and embracing them rather than being controlled *by* them. Ignoring them actually makes things worse. When we ignore our emotions, they tend to bubble up and grab us, which weakens your defenses and makes it easier for the Sins to get into your head."

Darius thought back to when he'd been Influenced—when Wrath had dug her filthy tendrils into his head and made him believe opening the car had been a good idea. His emotions had definitely been in control of him then. It sent a chill down his spine, remembering the look on the Sin's face when he'd hit the unlock mechanism.

God, he was so lucky he was alive—

"Darius, watch out!"

He snapped back. Realized he was about to drive through a red light. Darius slammed on the brakes as a truck laid on its horn. The sound was oddly reminiscent of old days back in New York City. Darius waved sheepishly as the other driver threw up his hands in the air and drove around the front of the coupe. As soon as he was gone, Darius groaned and covered his face in his hands. His fingers shook.

"God, that was *stupid.*"

To his surprise, though, Teresa laughed. He looked at her from over his shoulder, and she reached out to pat his leg. Movement behind them caught Darius's attention, and he turned to see Sparkie standing, alert and frazzled, his red, leathery wings raised much in the same way a cat's fur stood on end.

"It's okay," Teresa said. "Mistakes happen. No use getting worked up about things we can't change. Next time, just… pay attention to the road, okay? I didn't make it to eighty-eight to be taken out in a car crash. Let's go home, in *one piece*, if it's all the same to you."

The drive back was much less eventful. Teresa and Darius fell into a natural conversation about the values of meditation, which lasted up until they pulled into the long, gravel driveway. Sparkie never fully recovered from the shock of almost crashing. He sat, alert and on edge, on the center console. As they came upon the house, Darius saw Thorn staring down at them from the balcony, a cigarette smoldering between her fingers.

This was where she always was. Excluding when she was working with Darius, Thorn rarely left her quarters or the balcony outside them. He was confident she and Teresa hadn't set foot in the same room once in the last few weeks.

As soon as they parked and got out of the car, Teresa looked up at her. Their eyes met, then Thorn frowned, put her cigarette out, and walked back into the house. Teresa heaved a sigh.

"Better get to work," she said.

In the first month they were there, Darius learned nothing new about the conflict between Thorn and Teresa. Teresa was too good at diverting the conversation, and he was flat out too afraid to ask Thorn about it. The time they spent together was generally fine, if not grueling, thanks to how hard Thorn pushed him to work, and Darius didn't want to mess with the balance they'd found. He couldn't imagine how unbearable his training would be if Thorn were mad at him.

So he resigned to waiting for an opportune moment—either when Teresa finally gave way and answered one of his questions, or… well, any situation with Thorn that felt appropriate, if such a thing existed. Darius was beginning to feel like those moments wouldn't come, and he slowly started to forget about it.

It wasn't the only thing he'd started to forget about.

Thanks to all the hard work he and Thorn were doing to improve his endurance and strength, Darius was hungry in a way he'd never felt before. Instead of feeling pangs of hunger because he didn't have access to food, he was constantly craving food despite having more of it around than he knew what to do with. The calories he burned off during his exercises seemed to leave a vacuum behind, and no matter how much he ate, he was never satisfied—at least, not for long.

It was a weird feeling after more than a decade of scrounging for scraps on the streets.

One night, five weeks into their stay, Darius found himself standing in front of the open refrigerator at midnight, looking for something to eat. The last couple of days had been grueling. Thorn had added another half-mile onto their running route and a few new exercises to his resistance set. His muscles ached, his body was tired, but his stomach roared hungrily. Darius grabbed himself a couple of apples and sat down at the kitchen table in the dark.

As he raised the first one to his lips, he caught a glance at his own reflection in the window to his left. Something about it made him pause.

He looked like a stranger.

His hair was short and clean, and his cheeks were so smooth he looked like one of those clean-cut guys Saul liked to con out of their gas money. Darius's green eyes were brighter, wider. Even his body had changed. He could see his scrawny arms and legs getting bigger—and he could feel that they were stronger. The clothes the Martyrs had provided him with fit comfortably around him, instead of hanging off his body like rags on a starving child.

For the first time in years, he looked *healthy*.

And suddenly, he felt… guilty about it.

He couldn't place exactly when it had happened, but he realized he hadn't thought about his old life in weeks. Instead, his focus was on his work, the Sins, and what was happening at the Underground. He wasn't being tormented by dreams anymore, his sleep had fallen back into a regular schedule, and though Eva crossed his mind often, it felt less urgent. Maybe he was just too exhausted after working all day. Maybe all the meditation was paying off. Or maybe, Darius was afraid to consider, he was just… happy.

And the idea of being happy made him feel awful.

Light footsteps broke Darius's focus, and he looked across the kitchen to see Thorn in the stairway. Her feet were bare at the bottom of comfortable, crimson lounge pants, and her loose, long-sleeve top had a wide collar, which draped carelessly off one shoulder. Her milky skin seemed to almost glow in the moonlight coming in the window.

Darius could barely make out her expression, but he thought she looked sad.

"Couldn't sleep?" he asked.

Thorn jumped backward. Her left hand reached back for a weapon she didn't have in pockets she wasn't wearing. She turned at the bottom of the stairs to see Darius sitting at the table, and she exhaled a deep, long breath.

"Fuck, Jones."

He couldn't help it—he cracked a smile and chuckled. "Sorry," he said without really meaning it. "I wasn't trying to scare you."

Thorn didn't look sad anymore. Whatever emotions she'd been letting play on her face had been replaced by her standard, stoic look as she gazed down at him from the bottom step. Sparkie peeked his head out from behind the curtain of Thorn's black hair. "What are you doing down here?"

Darius held up the apple, took a bite, and said through a full mouth, "I'm hungry."

He tossed her the second apple. She deftly caught it and frowned at him.

"I figure that's why you're here, too?"

He knew he was right even before she shrugged, walked to the fridge, and opened the door. Brilliant, white light spilled out onto the floor. Thorn's slim body was cast in it; her shadow fell long across the room. Darius watched as she leaned down and shuffled around, grabbing a few things before straightening back up and closing the door. She completely ignored the plate of leftovers Teresa had made and set aside for her.

In the time they'd been here, Darius had never seen Thorn eat a meal. Between their training sessions, Thorn was either walking the property, smoking on the balcony, or sulking in her room. He had heard her, however, creeping past his room in the middle of the night, long after he and Teresa had gone to bed. Then she would sneak back, presumably with arms full of food, to hold her over for the next couple of days.

Instead of heading back up the stairs, Thorn joined him at the kitchen table. She put the food down in front of her as she sat across from him, gazed out the window, and took a bite of her apple. She was left-handed—Darius had noticed in their exercising she led with her left—and it was her left hand propped up with the apple tonight. Her sleeve cuffs held tight around the base of her hand so he couldn't see her scars except for the tiny tendrils wrapping around her thumb.

"Do you mind if I ask you a question?" Darius asked.

Thorn glanced at him. "Go for it."

"Why do you hide your scars?"

Darius had gestured toward her arm, but before the word "scars" had even escaped his mouth, she quickly pulled it under the table, as though the sleeves alone weren't enough of a cover. It was hard to tell how the question had made her feel. Not ashamed, particularly, but her brows furrowed heavily, and she pulled her lips in and gently bit them.

"I'm sorry," he added hastily. "I know it's personal, but I noticed you're really careful about it."

A few long moments passed in silence. Darius started to think she wasn't going to answer him. She was looking down at her lap, where she had laid her left forearm down against her thighs, with the scar-side facing her. Her frown deepened, but she didn't look upset—at least, she didn't look angry. If Darius wasn't mistaken, a little bit of the sadness returned to her expression. Sparkie shifted uncomfortably on her shoulder and disappeared down the back of her shirt.

"It just seems like a lot of work," Darius said. Thorn looked up to him.

"Well," she said at last, and she took a deep breath through her nose and exhaled it in a long, slow stream. "I don't like seeing them."

"Are you embarrassed?"

"No," she said quickly, almost snapping, and she closed her eyes and shook her head. "No. They just… they remind me of a time when I was a weaker person. Much weaker. And I don't like to think of myself as weak."

Darius nodded slowly. It wasn't for *others*. She kept them hidden for *herself*.

"Ever think maybe your scars helped turn you into this new, stronger person?"

Thorn scoffed and brought her apple back to her lips before deciding against it and placing it down on the table. "You sound just like Alan," she said. Then she got to her feet. "I need a smoke. Want to join me?" She seemed hungry for a change in subject.

"I don't smoke," he said.

Thorn raised an eyebrow. "I wasn't offering you one," she said. She didn't elaborate, but she didn't look away from Darius's face, either. For a moment, she just stood there and waited for him. Darius was hit with a sudden realization: she wanted *company*.

He felt foolish for not realizing it earlier. He wasn't the only one pulled out of his element, thrown across state lines without anyone familiar to talk to. It was lonely here—lonelier if you locked yourself in your room all day.

"Yeah," Darius said, and he got to his feet, too. "Okay."

Darius grabbed his sweatshirt off the back of the chair and followed Thorn through the sunroom and onto the back porch. The moon was full, and the bright light illuminated most of the field behind Teresa's house. The distant trees were draped in shadow.

It was chilly as they strolled along the back wall toward the side yard. Darius had almost forgotten they'd made the turn into December, and the winter solstice was only a week or two away. He pulled his sweatshirt tighter around his shoulders, wishing he'd thought to grab shoes, as Thorn took a pack of cigarettes out of the pocket of her lounge pants. She drew one out and lit the tip. The smoldering ash reflected in her deep, dark eyes. Her nightshirt was still draped down over one shoulder, but the cold didn't seem to bother her. The graceful curve of her collar bone lifted as she took a long draw on her cigarette and exhaled the smoke into the night. Darius watched it swirl around over their heads until it slowly disintegrated into nothing.

"I talked with Alan today," Thorn said after a few moments. Darius's heart skipped a beat, and he turned to watch her. She was looking down at the ground beneath her feet, carefully selecting each step in the dim light from the moon above and windows behind them. Her expression was as impassive as ever. "There hasn't been any progress on the search for your friend, but the Sins know something's up. They've noticed the increased Martyr activity in the city, so they're on high alert. I'm pretty sure they think *you* bailed, with how hard our people are searching."

Another surge of guilt moved through Darius's chest. "Has anyone gotten hurt?"

Thorn shrugged. "Nothing serious. Mostly they've run into Puppets, but the Martyrs have a lot of experience with them. They'll be fine. I can't say the same for Torres, though. I hope she was smart enough to get the fuck out of town."

Darius heaved a sigh. "She won't leave," he said as they came upon the paddock. The stallion raised his brown head and gazed over at them with rich, black eyes. "Her brother's still out there. She won't stop looking until she finds him."

"Ah, right," Thorn said, frowning. "Family always fucking complicates things…" Then she stopped by the fence and gazed out at the horse. He padded slowly toward them as Thorn went on. "I hope we find her soon. She's hardly going to recognize you when she gets back." Then she turned to Darius and looked him up and down with a small, sly smile. "You're a whole new person."

Darius glanced down at his own body and felt a flush rise to his cheeks. He gave an uncomfortable laugh. "Yeah. The haircut alone is gonna totally throw her off."

"It looks good," Thorn said, plainly, neutrally. "I think she'll get used to it."

"Maybe," Darius said, but the truth was, he wasn't sure. His new look may just remind her Darius wasn't who she'd thought he was—not anymore.

For a while, neither of them spoke. Darius was too caught up in worrying about Eva, and Thorn—well, Darius didn't know what she was thinking about, but she was quietly smoking her cigarette while gently stroking the top of Rover's long, coarse face. Darius reached out and touched the animal, too. He nickered contentedly. After several minutes, Thorn took another drag on her cigarette and broke the silence.

"So, how is your *other* training going?" she asked. Her voice was thick with smoke. She blew it out and sent heavy whorls spinning into the night. "With Solomon?"

"It's all right," Darius said.

"What are you working on?"

"Well." He took a deep breath and looked up at the starry sky as he thought about it. "Cooking. Cleaning. I'm getting better at driving. I also promised I'd help her organize some of her old things. Mostly housework and stuff kids usually learn from their parents—you know, when they have parents."

He gave a light chuckle, but Thorn just nodded. Darius went on. "Oh, and she also gave me another tip for fighting off Direct Influence."

Thorn frowned. "What did she suggest?"

"Emotional awareness," Darius said. "It'll be hard around the Sins, though."

He could only imagine being face-to-face with Derek Dane again. He wasn't sure he'd be able to keep his anger in check.

Thorn raised her eyebrows and shrugged. "Strong emotions do make it easier for the Sins to get in your head, but their strong emotions make it harder for them to maintain control. You're also a Virtue. You're more challenging for them to Influence anyway. If you Initiate it, they won't be able to at all."

Almost as soon as she'd said it, she looked down at her feet, bare against the loamy ground, and an awkward silence fell. Darius's heart squeezed deep in his chest. Thorn cleared her throat after a moment and went on. "So, she's not teaching you about the Virtues at all, huh?"

She took a long draw on her cigarette as Darius sighed. "No," he said. "But it's not her fault."

Teresa had offered to teach him more about the Virtues immediately, but he had told her he wasn't interested. Since then, she hadn't brought it up. She seemed to sense he wasn't ready for it. While she made it clear to him she was available and happy to help with any question he had about Virtues, she didn't force the subject.

"I didn't think it was," Thorn said coldly. "Why are you afraid of it?"

Darius frowned. "I'm not afraid," he defended, but even he could tell the words felt weak. "I just—I don't want the damn thing. I don't want anything to do with it."

Thorn's brows raised up on her head, almost like she didn't believe him. She took another drag and said, "Why?" The word billowed out of her mouth with a cloud of smoke.

He didn't really have an answer. On paper, being a Virtue sounded great: heightened instincts, the ability to heal people, being able to destroy a Sin. Everyone secretly hopes they're special, and here Darius was, with evidence proving he was one of only *seven* people in the world with the abilities he had.

But it made him uneasy.

"You're not the only Virtue who's felt this way," Thorn said almost casually. "The majority of them reject the idea outright at first. It never made sense to me. You've got this incredible power right at your fingertips. You've just got to *want* it. Why is that so hard to embrace?"

"There's more to it than power," Darius said. "For one, this Virtue is why my family died. It's what the Sins were looking for. But to tell you the truth, that's not really the biggest problem."

Thorn frowned. "No?"

"No," Darius said. "It's just… there's *so* much responsibility. Everyone is depending on me. You. Teresa. The Martyrs." Thorn quietly watched him. Her dark eyes were softer than he was used to as she slowly nodded. Darius was suddenly aware of how somber the mood had become. He shook his head and gave a lighthearted chuckle to break the tension. "I just know what I'm good at, and fighting isn't it. But I promise, if you run into a Sin with a weakness to piggyback rides and street market haggling, I'll be first in line to take it down."

Thorn laughed—a real, genuine laugh—and it caught Darius so off guard he just stared at her for a moment. Her rich, deep voice vibrated around them, out into the darkness, and Darius couldn't help but laugh, too. He'd never seen a real smile on Thorn's face before. It was radiant in the moonlight.

But as quickly as it had come, it disappeared. Thorn took a deep breath and shook her head. "Yeah," she said as she cleared her throat and raised her eyebrows. A small shadow of the smile still played upon her lips. "Yeah, I guess that's true. All the same, though, maybe you should let her teach you what she knows. Whether or not you ever decide to accept your Virtue, someone's got to pick up where she left off. She can't live forever."

The way Thorn said it was almost bitter. All traces of her rich laugh vanished, and Thorn's brows came together heavily as she raised her cigarette to her lips again. Darius decided this was as good of an opportunity as ever. He leaned against the fence and looked right into Thorn's face. "What's going on between you and Teresa? And—" he said quickly, because Thorn had just given him a look Darius knew all too well meant she was about to totally dismiss him "—don't tell me it's nothing. It's been a month, and you haven't said two words to her." Thorn watched him, evaluating him, and the muscles along her jaw tightened. "So… what happened?"

Thorn's tongue darted across her teeth as she turned back to look at the horse again, but the animal seemed suddenly unsettled. His ears flickered around, and he snorted before quietly walking back toward his shelter. Thorn's eyes narrowed and looked out in the distance. Finally, all she said was, "Solomon made certain decisions, and those decisions got people killed."

"Someone important to you?" Darius asked quietly. Thorn threw him a hot look out of the corner of her eye as a response. Darius figured that meant yes. He wondered who it had been. What had Thorn said in the car on the way here? She had lost everything thanks to Teresa?

"I'm sorry," he said after a few long, quiet moments. "Being here has to be really hard for you."

Thorn looked down at her hands. "It comes with the job." She flicked the butt of her cigarette, and a column of ash collapsed to the ground. Whatever softness, whatever vulnerability Thorn had begun to show evaporated. Her callous attitude came back up like a wall between her and the rest of the world, shutting Darius out and trapping Thorn behind it. She turned around, tossed the spent cigarette onto the dirt, and drove her bare heel into it to snuff out the flame.

"I'm going to bed," she said, and she led the way back into the house. Darius followed after her. "You should, too. I'm coming for you at six o'clock sharp. No excuses."

As they got into the back door and Thorn gathered the food she'd collected from the table, Darius glanced at the clock on the oven. He was shocked to see it read almost one in the morning. Their run was going to be *awful.*

Thorn turned to walk up the stairs. Darius called her back.

"Look, I know this has been hard for you," Darius said, and Thorn glowered down at him. "It's been hard for me, too, but what is it you said to me? You can either use your anger as fuel or an anchor? I think you're pretty anchored to your room right now."

That seemed to spark an interesting reaction in Thorn. He saw a bit of fury awaken behind her eyes as she furrowed her brow and stared down at him, but he thought he saw admiration, too, like she was impressed he'd been brave enough to use it against her.

"You can use it as an *engine,*" she corrected him sharply, but the anger didn't seep into her words. "Don't worry about me. I can take care of myself."

She moved to turn around again, but Darius had one last thing to say.

"How about this," he said. He walked up to the bottom of the stairs and looked up at Thorn. She was one step above him, and she stared down at him with a dark expression. She was difficult to read. Darius pressed on anyway. "Let's *both* do something that makes us a little uncomfortable. I'll start learning about the Virtues if *you* stop hiding out in your room all the time." All she did in response was narrow her eyes and turn her head. "Deal?"

For a moment, she was quiet, watching Darius with that half-empty, black stare. At last, she gave him one word:

"Fine."

Then she turned around and disappeared up the stairs. Darius saw Sparkie slither out from the back of her flowing shirt and gaze at him before he and Thorn faded into the dark.

CHAPTER FIFTEEN

The sunroom was Darius's favorite spot in Teresa's house. The tall, full-length windows let in so much light and warmth that Teresa could grow a multitude of green, leafy plants all year round. They sat in planters around the edges, hung from hooks on the walls, and curled around their pots, filling the room with bright color and a comforting, earthy smell. Outside, the scene shifted with the seasons. In the weeks since they'd arrived, the warm, rich colors of fall faded to the blues and browns of winter. Two days after Darius and Thorn's midnight talk, Pennsylvania's first snow began to fall.

Darius enjoyed his coffee, sitting in one of the wicker chairs as he stared out the windows. Large flakes came down gracefully from a gray sky and clung to the yellow grass. Teresa heaved a pleasant, contented sigh and leaned back in her chair to Darius's left.

"I wonder why Thorn's been hanging around lately," Teresa said—speaking Thorn's name for the first time since she and Darius had arrived over a month ago. Darius was so surprised by this that he turned his head too quickly and felt a vertebra crack in his neck. He rubbed it as she said, "Has there been an update from Alan?"

Darius looked back out the window, this time not at the sky but at the woman standing beneath it.

Thorn and Sparkie were out in the yard, enjoying the snow. Well, Sparkie was enjoying it. Thorn was bundled up almost comically against the cold, smoking a cigarette with a grumpy expression on her face while the lizard flew in massive, spiraling circles in the flurries overhead.

Say what you could about Thorn; when the woman made a deal, she committed to it.

In the last forty-eight hours, Thorn hadn't just started making occasional appearances around Teresa's house. She was a constant figure. While Darius and Teresa ate at the dining room table, Thorn would take her meals in the kitchen. If they were making lunch, she would do yoga in the sunroom. She even made a point to walk right through the great room while he and Teresa were in there working. On her way by, she'd throw him a pointed look that seemed to say, "Challenge accepted. Get to work, Jones."

"Darius?" Teresa's voice brought him out of his thoughts, and he turned to her.

"Sorry," he said, and he cleared his throat. "No, Thorn's actually out here because of *me*."

Teresa frowned. "What did you do?"

Darius couldn't help but give a soft chuckle as he looked back out the window. Swirls of smoke danced around Thorn's shivering shoulders as she watched Sparkie play in the snow. "We made a deal," Darius said. "I told her I'd talk to you about Virtue stuff if she stopped hiding out in her room. I didn't really think it would work."

He turned back to Teresa to find her watching him with a strange expression on her face. It was a weird mix of joy and apprehension. For a moment, she was quiet, and she turned to look through the wide windows. Against the white backdrop, Thorn was a dark, heavy shadow.

"I'm really surprised it did," Teresa said quietly. Disappointment crept into the words, but when she spoke again, she tried to hide it. "We don't have to study the Virtues.

Thorn doesn't get to decide when you're ready."

"Oh, no," Darius said, giving a playful frown and shaking his head. "Really. I'm fine. If I wasn't ready, I wouldn't have made the deal in the first place."

The eagerness on Teresa's face was bright and palpable. The wrinkles at the corners of her eyes pinched up as her grin extended from ear to ear. "Well," she said, and while she tried to hold back her excitement, it poured out like a fountain. "Only if you're sure!"

He chuckled and put his coffee down on the table beside him. "Bring it on."

The little cafe was busy. Holiday shoppers bustled in and out of the doors, checking out the merchandise and ordering food and drinks at the counter to Darius's left. He sat at a small wooden table, holding a warm, comforting cup of hot chocolate between his hands as the door flew open again and another burst of cold air came in. He glanced up as a few more people shuffled through, shaking the snow from their hats and removing their gloves, pink-nosed and rosy-cheeked.

When he'd agreed to learn more about the Virtues, he hadn't known what to expect, but it hadn't been *this.*

"Now." Teresa's voice drew Darius's attention, and he turned to see her sitting across from him again. She set a couple of paper-wrapped paninis on the table and adjusted her skirt. Sparkie had tagged along for the trip, and he was hiding in Darius's coat pocket. He felt the creature shift when Teresa spoke. "What were we saying?"

"Uh." Darius frowned and thought back to the question he'd asked before Teresa's name had been called, and she'd gotten up to grab their food. "Oh, I wanted to know which Virtues go against which Sin."

"Right." Teresa nodded and clasped her hands together. The room was busy with noise around them, and Darius had to lean in to hear. "I'm Humility, opposite of Pride. Then there's Kindness to Envy, Diligence to Sloth, Temperance to Gluttony, Chastity to Lust, Charity to Greed, and Patience to Wrath." Teresa counted them off on her fingers as she said them.

"And you've found evidence of the Virtues in history the same way the Sins show up?"

"And in mythology, fables, stories," Teresa said with a nod. "Basically, anything mankind has written down. If it was worth recording, chances are Virtues and Sins were involved. Some Virtues show up a lot, like Diligence and Charity, but others, like Patience, are less common."

"What's an example?"

Teresa thought about it for a bit, and she bit the side of her lower lip. "Are you familiar with any of the Arthurian legends?" Darius shook his head, and Teresa frowned. "Ah. Well, one of the characters, Galahad, was considered the 'perfect knight.' Stories vary, obviously, but his perfection included many things that imply a Virtuous presence—Kindness, I think. Apparently, he received 'full and holy sight' after finding the Holy Grail, and many of the legends say he was so 'pure of heart' his enemies couldn't defeat him. I always suspected that had to do more with his ability to sense others on the battlefield, which would give him an edge in combat."

Darius held up a hand. "Wait—sense them? He could *sense* them?"

"Yes," Teresa said, and her eyes glistened excitedly. "That's actually one of the reasons I wanted to come into town today." She adjusted in her chair and glanced around the room. Darius followed her lead and turned to take it in. The small shop was crowded. A dozen other customers sat at tables or walked around the displays set up against the walls.

"It's probably one of the most useful abilities we have," Teresa said, and Darius turned back to her. She was still looking around them, taking in not the scenery, but the *people* here, with a soft smile across her lips. "We *feel* people and their inner energy."

"What?"

Teresa nodded. "It's been documented everywhere throughout history. It's represented in the halos around angels and holy people in Christian Lore, as well as in Egyptian hieroglyphs. The Chinese called it 'chi,' and in India, it's 'prana.' I've always just called it an 'aura.'" She gave a silly little chuckle and waved her hand before turning back to Darius. "I know it sounds a bit strange, but it's the best word for it."

"What *is* it, though?" Darius asked.

"It's our energy field," Teresa said simply. "Our soul, if you prefer that term. This is the field the Virtues and Sins exist on outside of the human body. The Virtues and Sins themselves are static—either purely positive, for the Virtues, or negative, for the Sins. Human energy, on the other hand, exists on a spectrum, and it's fluid. Once we Initiate, we can sense the *positive* side of this spectrum. The more people are in harmony with the positive side, the warmer they feel."

"Good energy is warm?"

"Not 'good,'" Teresa corrected gently. *"Positive."*

Darius didn't see the difference, but he didn't press it. "Right, but it's warm?"

"Yes," Teresa said, and she gestured around the room again. "Each of these people feels warm to me, and they're all a little different. Their energy signature is as unique to them as a fingerprint."

"And you can feel all of them?" Darius asked. "What if they're *not* in harmony with the good—I mean, positive side?"

"I have honestly never experienced that," Teresa said. "The only way I *wouldn't* feel them is if they were so far to the negative side that they have no harmony at all, and the simple fact is, people can rarely exist at either extreme. The more harmonious they are, the stronger they feel, and the further away I can sense them. In general, though, I can feel most people's aura from several dozen yards. In here, since we're crammed so closely together, they kind of blur together, but I can still get a sense for each different one. If it's crowded enough, sometimes I can't differentiate at all."

"That's gotta be overwhelming," Darius said.

"It was at first. When I finally Initiated, I had what I'd call a 'burnout period.'" Teresa laughed and shook her head. "All that energy was so hot and uncomfortable, I felt like I was melting! But eventually, my body got used to it, and now I hardly notice it at all."

Darius looked around again. There was a strange familiarity to this place. In many ways, he was reminded of the market. The ritual of commerce, whether you were bartering for necessities in an underbelly economy or shopping in a quaint cafe on some small-town street, was the same. It built more than business; it built community. The room was full of "good afternoons" and handshakes, of smiles and jokes, with the shared custom of selecting and trading merchandise for currency.

But that's all it was to him. He didn't sense any energy.

"So, why did we need to talk about this here?" Darius asked. "I can't feel anything."

Teresa's smile just widened, and there was a mischievous glint in her eye. "Ah, but *can't* you? I said before, there is a lot of evidence that Virtues may display some subconscious abilities before they Initiate. This is one of the most common ones I've seen discussed pre-Initiation. You might not feel their energy as *warmth* the same way I do, but that doesn't mean you don't sense *anything*. Give it a try."

Darius frowned. "How?"

"Let's see..." Teresa smirked and looked around the room again. "Who do you think has the strongest energy here?" Then she sat back, clasped her hands in her lap, and waited.

Darius gave her an incredulous look. "Well, of course, it's *you*." He gestured to her across the table, and Teresa laughed.

"*Besides* me, then."

He turned around and faced the cafe again, but his frown only deepened. "I have no idea—"

"What did you do when you worked at the market?" Teresa asked suddenly, and Darius spun to face her. "How did you know who you could trust and who you couldn't?"

He thought about it a bit. "I don't know. I guess I just got this *vibe*—"

"You *felt* it," Teresa said, and her eyes glinted excitedly. "In your gut, right? Trust yourself. Trust what you *know*."

Darius's heart jumped a little bit. He'd never stopped to think if there were positive ways this Virtue had impacted his life before he'd come to the Underground. Taking a deep breath, he looked back out at the room again, and this time, he gave himself the time to *really* see it.

A dozen people. Three of them were employees—two behind the counter and one walking the floor, answering questions people had about merchandise and pricing. The other nine were split into four groups. A mother, exasperatedly trying to stop her two little kids from touching all the fragile things displayed way too close to the ground. A young couple, intimately whispering to one another over the rims of their ceramic coffee mugs. A group of friends, laughing and joking and throwing spent straw wrappers at each other. An old man, alone in the corner.

Darius took the time to consider them—slowly looking around the room, from one face to the next. If he were at the market, what criteria would he use to judge them? It dawned on him:

Who would he trust with his children?

"Him."

Darius pointed to one of the young men at the table with his friends. He was laughing, a full, genuine laugh, as he leaned down to pick up the straw wrappers and tossed them into the bin by their table. When he looked around the room, he met people's eyes and smiled. When others spoke, he turned, and he listened.

He couldn't place exactly why, but Darius knew he was right before Teresa's face broke into a grin.

"You see?" she said.

"But it's kind of a trick question, isn't it?" Darius said, and he glanced at the mother and her two young children. "I had a feeling you meant 'which adult' had the strongest energy, but I think those kids are stronger."

Teresa nodded again, and her eyebrows raised up on her head, impressed. "They *are*," she said. "Children generally haven't been corrupted by the world, so their energy is heavily weighted toward the positive end of the spectrum. In fact, it's so positive the Sins can't sense them at all."

"The *Sins* feel this energy, too?"

"Yes, but they feel the negative side instead," Teresa provided. "Where I feel people's positive energy as warmth, they feel people's negative energy as cold. Kids don't usually have enough negative for the Sins to feel it until they're ten or eleven. They can't feel *us*, either. Like I said, the Virtue is static, and that static positive energy masks the negative side of our souls. If the Sins get us alone, it's pretty easy for them to figure out what we are."

"Does that mean Virtues can't feel Sins, either?"

"Unfortunately," Teresa said solemnly, and she shook her head. "We can. The human body only has enough room for so much energy, so when a Sin takes over, they must rip the host's energy into pieces and attach to what remains. But that energy can't be *destroyed*, so the part that's been torn apart hovers around its old body, providing a sort of 'false aura' that we can sense. Sins feel just like a normal human being, which makes it hard to identify them until it's too late."

Darius breathed out a heavy sigh. "The deck is really stacked against us."

"Maybe," Teresa said with a shrug. "But the Sins don't have any way to destroy us permanently. That power is *ours*, and ours alone. It scares the hell out of them."

"A lot of good it does us," Darius said with a scoff, "since we don't know how to use it."

"Not *yet*," Teresa said, and she smiled. Then she cleared her throat and moved on. Her voice got a little deeper and a little more serious, and Darius leaned in to hear her. "I have done a lot of research over the years. My study probably has the most information on the Virtues collected in one place since the Spanish Inquisition wiped out the Order's records—and I have even *more* crammed in the attic. If you want, we can go over all of it, but I really want to make sure this is what *you* want. Once you start down this path, you might find that you can't turn back."

Darius didn't respond right away. Teresa's joy had faded a bit, and in its place sat a resolution and understanding Darius hadn't expected to see there. He looked down at the mug in his hands.

Studying the Virtues—and maybe Initiating his own—would make it so much easier for him to help the Martyrs. But it could also make it harder for him to find his friends. If he put this organization—this *war*—ahead of Eva and Saul, of Juniper and Lindsay, would he ever be able to track them down?

Would he even *want* to?

"I guess I'm most afraid of changing," Darius said after a long stretch of silence, where nothing but the white noise of the cafe filled the space between them.

Teresa nodded slowly, thoughtfully. Her eyebrows pinched together a little, and she said, "Change is inevitable. Change is *growth*. For me, though, Initiating my Virtue felt like… like finally waking up. It had always been a part of me. I'd just forgotten who I was for a little while."

"Did it cost you anything?" Darius pressed.

"It cost me dearly," Teresa said, and she was quiet. "My very *existence* as a Virtue led to so much loss. So much heartache. Hundreds of people were killed. I lost my best friend, his family—" Her voice cracked a little, and she cleared her throat. "In many ways, I think my Virtue led to all of it."

Darius frowned. "How?"

"Because I was too afraid of it, and in being afraid, I lost opportunities to save the people I cared about." Then she smiled, and she threw Darius a wink. "You know, no pressure."

He couldn't help but laugh, and he leaned back in his chair. "Yeah, no kidding." Then he sighed and looked across the room again. The woman and her children had filtered out, but the young man with the strong energy was still laughing and joking and filling the room with joy. Darius turned back to Teresa. "Right now, all I know is I want to help. I *hate* sitting back and doing nothing."

Teresa nodded. "Learning about the history of the Virtues can make it easier for you to understand them and track them down, whether or not you ever accept yours."

"Okay," Darius said, and he gave a firm, resolute nod. "I want to see everything you've got to show me. Where do I start?"

Teresa beamed. "You start with reading. A *lot* of reading."

A crackling fire filled the grand room with warmth and flickering orange light.

Darius sat in one of the plush armchairs, going over a binder filled with research. Every day for the last two weeks, Teresa had come out to the grand room with stacks of binders and notebooks for Darius to read through. Tonight, he was learning about Virtuous Influence on Ancient American cultures while Teresa flipped through a novel on the chair across from him. The room was quiet and dim. Warm light from the fireplace cast the walls in dancing shadows. A noise in the kitchen made Darius look up, and Thorn stepped through the door.

She was ready for bed. Her crimson lounge pants and swoop-necked black shirt made her look comfortable and relaxed, but the tight muscles along her throat betrayed the illusion. Darius watched as she made her way to the fire. He noticed Teresa was watching her, too, but as soon as Thorn sat down in front of the flames, Teresa's attention shifted back to her book, and the moment was gone.

Darius looked between the two women. Thorn—thrown half in bright, searing light and half in dark shadow, and Teresa—cuddled up in a chair so oversized that it made her seem like a child.

In the last fourteen days, Darius had been busier than ever. On top of maintaining all his scheduled training with Thorn, Teresa was burying him in research. The only times he wasn't busy cooking, cleaning, working out, meditating, or reading were meals and the precious few seconds right before he fell asleep at night.

But before that, every single night, the three of them would gather here, *together*.

It was a strange new normal in the house, but it was peaceful. These moments had quickly become Darius's favorite part of the day. While Thorn would stare deep into the flames, watching them flicker and dance in their brick dungeon, Teresa would observe her with a quiet kind of reverence, respect, and love. And, when she didn't think anyone was paying attention, Thorn would cast Teresa deep, hard looks, tinted with regret, sadness, and a little bit of rage, just under the surface. More than ever, Darius felt the hidden threads of their history pulling at them from beneath the surface.

He wanted to unravel them.

A few days later, Teresa and Darius were at the top of the stairs, opening the attic to get another box of Virtue-related paraphernalia down for Darius to study. Teresa reached over to a photograph of her younger self holding her doctorate degree and pulled it off its nail. Darius was surprised to see a small button on the wall behind the frame.

"The Martyrs paid to retrofit the house with a few secret places for me," Teresa said to Darius with a smile. "In case the Sins ever track me down, I have somewhere to hide out until help arrives."

She hit the button, and a quiet motor whirred to life above them. Darius looked up at the ceiling to see a trap door open. It was so well hidden in the ceiling panels that he would have never spotted it on his own.

As the trap door opened downward, a ladder folded out and landed at their feet. Teresa started up it, moving slowly in her old age, and Darius followed her. His head poked up into a vast room, as long as the house, with vaulted ceilings ten feet tall at the peak and two feet above the floor on the sides. There were two windows on either end of the attic, letting in the cold, winter light. Lines of dust highlighted in their beams and slowly settled back down to the floor.

The entire space was packed with keepsakes. Labeled boxes on shelves or littered across the floor told the story of Teresa's life. A disassembled bed frame rested behind the door, where it had become a home to spider webs and dust bunnies. There were rolled-up rugs, folded clothes, and piles upon piles of faded papers. Darius noticed there was also a bin of emergency food rations in a corner.

"It's back here," Teresa said as she moved toward the end of the attic. A couple of old boxes labeled "Virtue Fables" were stacked at the back of the room. "They're filled with books, so please be careful. I'd have moved them years ago, but age caught up with me. I can hardly lift them anymore. Thanks to all your hard work with Thorn, though, it should be easy for you!"

Darius was happy to oblige, and he squatted down to pick up the first box. They were totally isolated up here, well away from Thorn's keen ears, so he decided to go for it. "So, what's going on with you and Thorn?" he asked with a grunt as he lifted the box up from the ground. "I thought no one in the Underground had met you, but there seems to be some… I don't know, *history* here."

Teresa cast a quick, almost nervous glance around the room, like she was making sure they really were alone. Then, she gave a small sigh, a smaller smile, and said, "I'm sure you've asked Thorn. What did *she* say?"

"Just that—" Darius stopped, put the box down at the edge of the trapdoor, and cleared his throat. He didn't want to upset Teresa, but he didn't want to lie to her, either. "She told me you got someone killed."

He watched her carefully as he said it, and to his surprise, Teresa's smile didn't really falter. "Ah," she said with a slow, gentle nod. "So that's still how she sees things. That's how I saw them for a long time, too."

"What happened?"

"It's a long story," Teresa said elusively as Darius walked past her to pick up the second box. "And one I don't feel is entirely mine to share." She had one arm wrapped around her torso and the other propped up, with her fingers against her lips as she thought about it. Darius moved the second box across the room and set it down beside the first. Then Teresa took a breath and said, "Do you know anything about Thorn's life? Inside *or* outside the Martyrs?"

"Not much," Darius admitted. "Just that her family was killed by the Sins. All but Alan."

Teresa gave a soft, thoughtful nod. "In a way, she doesn't just blame the Sins. In at least one case, she blames me, too."

Darius frowned. "What did you do?"

"I abandoned him," Teresa said. "At least, that's what Thorn believes, and that by abandoning him, I opened the doors for the Sins to discover who he was and his connection to the Martyrs. She believes, if I had been there for him, maybe I could have saved him."

A tense silence fell between them. Teresa looked down at her feet, and if Darius wasn't mistaken, he saw tears glistening behind her long eyelashes. "Could you have?" he asked quietly.

The old woman looked back up to him and wiped a droplet from the corner of her eye. "Maybe," she said softly. "I can never know for sure, but I forgave myself a long time ago. I had to, or it would eat me alive. Thorn, though… Well, I think hating me was the only thing keeping her from hating herself."

Darius threw her a confused look.

"I may have been the *easiest* person to blame, but I was never the *only* one," Teresa simply said. Then she bustled past Darius and patted her hand on top of the boxes. "Now, let's get these down to the office."

Darius knew Teresa had dedicated a forty-year career to learning about the Virtues, but he didn't comprehend what that actually meant until he stepped foot in her study. It adjoined her bedroom on the first floor, and when Teresa opened the door, he was blown away.

It was a lot like Alan Blaine's office—clearly academic—but with a few key differences. It was messier, cluttered with newspapers, textbooks, and reports; it was bright, lit by a massive window looking out into the front yard; and it was homey, with walls covered by diplomas, awards, and photographs from Teresa's life. Bookshelves surrounded him, and the shelves were packed with volume upon volume of historical accounts, biographies, mythologies, and children's stories from everywhere in the world. There were translation dictionaries, fables, and old parchments that looked to be hundreds of years old.

Darius blanched and stood frozen in the doorway, clutching one of the boxes they'd pulled from the attic in his hands.

"*This* is where those binders have been coming from?"

Teresa laughed. "Welcome to my world." She bowed in a theatrical sort of way and walked into the mess. "You can put those over here." She gestured blindly to a small spot of open floor in front of the window. Darius put the first box down and then rushed out to get the second. He almost ran into Thorn in the foyer as he turned to head up the stairs.

"Jones," she said, a little surprised to see him. She was dressed for the cold, her black winter coat cinched up to her throat. Sparkie poked his head out from behind her hair.

"What are you doing?"

"Grabbing some stuff for Teresa," Darius said, and he pointed a thumb over his shoulder toward her office. "She's got *so much* Virtue research, it's insane."

Thorn just nodded, but there was an amused pull at the corner of her mouth. "I imagine."

"Where are you headed off to?" Darius asked as he looked down at her jacket and the satchel strung across her shoulders.

"I'm out of smokes," she said, and she held up the keys to Teresa's car. "I'll be back in an hour."

"Ah. Well, have fun," Darius said. He started up the stairs again. Thorn did nothing more than give a single-pump wave as she went through the door and disappeared. When Darius grabbed the second box and returned to the foyer, he found she'd left Sparkie behind. He was sitting on top of the coat rack, watching Darius with beady, little eyes.

"C'mon, then," Darius said with a grunt as he shifted the box in his arms, and the lizard leapt on top of it. Then he walked back into the office.

Teresa had shuffled a few things around on her desk, and she glanced up at Darius as he came into the room and plopped the second box down on top of the first. Sparkie gracefully maintained his balance, his wings flared up above him like a counterweight. Teresa gave the animal an almost nervous look, but when he curled up and closed his eyes, she turned back to Darius.

"Come here," she said. "I want to show you something."

She led Darius through the chaos to a sophisticated computer set up on the far side of the room. Three glowing screens blared down at them. Teresa sat down in the swiveling chair, and Darius leaned up against the desk with his hip. She clicked around on a few icons, opened a program, and typed in a couple of keywords before she turned to Darius.

"I developed this to track down Virtues."

The application she opened was flashing through dozens of different screens a second. Darius squinted as he watched.

"You use a *computer program*?"

"Mhmm. I sent it to the Martyrs years ago, but I'm not sure if they use it… Ah, here we go." The program stopped flickering and opened a new window with a list of results. Darius leaned in to see. They seemed like newspaper headlines. "It's a crawler," Teresa explained. "It goes through news and social sites to find information that may indicate a Virtue. Obviously," she added with a wry chuckle as she gestured to the list of over one hundred results, "it's not foolproof, but it gives us somewhere to start."

"What kind of stuff do you look for?" Darius asked.

Teresa gave a half shrug. "All kinds of things. I start with the big, obvious ones: protests, political or social movements, big, charitable events. I expect to see this kind of thing in communities where Virtues have been established for a while, where their Influence could be making systemic changes happen. Then I look for the easier to miss things, like random acts of kindness, or stories about individuals doing something extraordinary."

Darius was nodding absently as he looked over the list. There were over ten pages of results, with fifty results per page. "These can't all be real leads."

"Mostly, no," Teresa conceded. "Obviously, not all of the incredible things Virtues are up to ends up in the news—like you and your orphanage." She nodded graciously in Darius's direction. "And a lot of people do genuinely good deeds without the Influence of a Virtue, so I need to weed it out. The first step is to read through and cut out any that obviously don't fit." She scanned down the list and clicked on a bunch of articles right off the bat, reading the headlines out as she did it. "Most of these are easy—right time, right place kind of things. Man stops a shooting at a diner he was eating in? Probably just lucky." She deleted the results.

"Right," Darius said.

"I also try to pay a little more attention to things on the East Coast," Teresa went on, "since we know Virtues tend to be born near the Sin they're meant to destroy. Obviously, there are exceptions to that, or people move away, so I can't ignore the rest of the world. These settings here let me filter for location."

She did that, and the list shrunk by more than two-thirds.

"And then I just… follow my gut."

Darius frowned. "Like how you told me to read energy?"

"That's right," Teresa said. "Virtues have good instincts, remember? The energy thing, and this, are part of it. With most things in life, my gut feelings are usually pretty spot on. It's all about striking a balance between intuition and skepticism."

"And computers, apparently," Darius said, and he waved a hand, open-palm, at the screens.

Teresa laughed. "Yes, technology *is* amazing. Want to give it a try?"

"I haven't been on a computer since I was a kid."

"I guess it's time to learn!" Teresa said. Then she reached out, patted Darius on the knee, and heaved her old, fragile body out of the chair. Darius moved back to make space for her, but as he did, his elbow hit a stack of binders on her desk.

An avalanche of paper barreled to the ground.

Darius swore and tried to mitigate the damage, but it was too late. As he held one stack of binders up, another one collapsed, and soon the room was a mess of loose paper and Teresa's laughter. Darius was down on the ground, trying to pick things up, as Teresa nonchalantly waved her hand.

"Don't worry about it," she said. "This place needed a good organizing anyway."

But then Darius stopped. He was shifting through papers and books and various other things when something caught his eye. It was the corner of a picture frame, and if he wasn't mistaken, the woman in the photograph was…

"Is this *Thorn?*"

Darius lifted the frame from the debris and held it up. There was no mistaking it. The woman in the photograph *was* Thorn. She didn't look much younger than she was today, but something about her expression was full of youth and purpose. Her dark eyes were filled with love and joy. Her beautiful, happy smile extended wide across her face and wrinkled the bridge of her nose. The candid shot caught her mid-laugh, running one hand through her long, dark hair while the other arm was wrapped around a handsome young man who couldn't have been much younger than she was herself. He shared her dark hair and eyes, but where hers were cold and half-empty, his were warm and bright. His face was immortalized here in a full, hearty grin.

But before Darius could look at the picture in any more detail, Teresa swiped it out of his hands and quickly shoved it away in one of her desk drawers. She glanced up at Sparkie, who had raised his head at the commotion. The laughter was gone, and there was a look of real fear in Teresa's eyes.

"It's nobody," she said, and she cleared her throat. "I think it's almost time for lunch. Could you go get that started while I clean this up?"

Then she ushered Darius and Sparkie out of the room and shut the office door behind her. Darius heard it lock with a click. When he turned around, Sparkie had disappeared.

The next morning, Darius and Teresa were enjoying their coffee in the sunroom. Thorn was nowhere to be seen. In fact, Darius hadn't seen her since she'd left to grab more cigarettes. She hadn't made an appearance in the grand room the previous night, and that morning she'd missed their run. He was just starting to wonder if she was okay when suddenly the door flung open, and Thorn flew through it.

Sparkie was sitting on her shoulder, his wings flared up furiously behind him. In her hand, she clutched the photograph.

"What the *hell* is this?"

Thorn's voice was quiet and deadly as she slammed the frame down on the table in front of Teresa. The glass shattered, sending a spiderweb of cracks across Thorn and the man's smiling faces. The old Virtue's cheeks went white as Thorn glared down at her, but her mouth set into a firm, unyielding line.

"Let me explain—"

"How *dare you.*" Thorn hissed the words so venomously Darius got to his feet. She ignored him and pointed an accusatory finger right at Teresa's face. If there wasn't a coffee table between them, Darius would have jumped into the space. "He *worshiped* you. He *idealized* you."

"Thorn, wait—"

"Shut the fuck up, Jones."

Thorn was barely holding on. The muscles all along her throat were tight—the tendons rigid against her pale skin—and a vein bulged in her forehead. Thorn turned her attention back on Teresa. The old Virtue hadn't even moved. She sat as still as stone, her weathered hands clasped in her lap as she waited.

"You have *no right* to this," Thorn roared, grabbing the frame up from the table again. "He's dead because of *you.*"

"He's not."

Teresa's words were spoken barely over a whisper, but they silenced the whole room. Darius's mouth fell open as he watched her look up at Thorn with calm determination. Thorn didn't seem to know what to do about it. Her eyes got wider, wilder, and her chest heaved with furious breath as she stared down at Teresa. The old woman continued to speak.

"It's not my fault. I know you want to believe it is, but

it's not. The Sins found him long before he asked me to meet him at Central Park, and they found him because of Wrath."

What little color Thorn's face had left disappeared. Her eyes widened further, and her thin lips fell open as Teresa went on.

"He was exposed to Wrath for so long that he couldn't resist her Influence. He could block everyone else out, but not her. It made him a target… She knew who he was."

All the while, Teresa didn't move. She held herself with poise and grace. The only thing betraying her tension was a slight quaver to her voice.

And Thorn—Thorn's whole body just tightened like a rubber band, and she snapped.

"You're *lying!*" She screamed, so furiously, so fervently, spit flew from her mouth. Before Darius could move to stop her, Thorn picked the whole coffee table up and slammed it down onto the ground between them. It cracked and splintered on the tile with a deafening crunch. The glass shards of the frame still clutched in Thorn's left hand cut her thumb, but she didn't even seem to notice as she turned and lashed out at another piece of furniture. Droplets of blood sprayed across the floor.

As Thorn threw over a planter and sent shattered ceramic and soil across the room, Darius grabbed her by the shoulder.

"Jesus, Thorn—"

"Don't touch me," Thorn roared, and she ripped out of his grip so ferociously it almost knocked him over. Then she stormed from the sunroom and slammed the door behind her. The panes of glass rattled in their frames.

She disappeared into the house, and Darius turned to Teresa. The old Virtue heaved a deep sigh and reached out for her coffee cup on the side table. Her hands were shaking. "It was just a matter of time," she told him sadly.

Darius gaped at her.

CHAPTER SIXTEEN

The sunroom was a disaster. Cracked wood, fragments of ceramic, and dirt coated the tile floor. Pieces of the coffee table lay in ruins in front of the two wicker chairs. A small footstool was crumpled beside it, and a lemon tree lay across the threshold. It was sprawled out on its side like a dead body—an unfortunate casualty caught in the middle of a war Darius didn't understand.

He looked over the damage, broom in hand, stunned.

The whole incident did nothing but open more questions, and Darius wasn't getting any answers. Teresa refused to elaborate, again telling Darius she wasn't going to discuss Thorn's personal life with him more than she already had. Then she'd excused herself to calm her nerves. Thorn had immediately stomped into the front yard and made a call. For several minutes, she'd screamed into her phone so loudly her voice echoed across the meadow behind Teresa's house. Darius knew better than to get in her way, and now he stood alone in the wreckage.

Darius sighed. With nothing better to do, and needing something to distract his busy mind, he got to work cleaning it up.

First, he gathered up the large debris. Bit by bit, he

carried chunks of wood, shards of the broken planter, and other large items out the back door and around the house to the trash can by the garage. The animals in the side yard were agitated. The hens' feathers ruffled up around their throats, and Rover paced and whinnied in his paddock. Every time Darius walked past, the animal watched after him with wide, nervous eyes.

By his last trip around, Thorn was off the phone. She didn't look at him as he walked by. She just stood out in the snow, still as a statue, and smoked a cigarette as she watched the morning sun rise higher in the sky. She hadn't bothered to get a jacket, so she stood in nothing but her leggings and a loose, long sleeve top. Her shoulders were set in firm determination. After dropping off the last piece of the broken table at the trash can, Darius paused and watched her. Her lower jaw quivered, but he couldn't tell if it was from the cold, her fury, or something else entirely.

He was tempted to go talk to her, but what could he say? So he went back to the sunroom to start sweeping.

Teresa was there waiting for him. Her damp hair was braided down the back of her head, and she was wrapped in a warm, cotton robe. As he came in the back door, she smiled at him. "Thank you for doing this, but I can clean it up."

"Oh, no," Darius said, waving her concern away and picking up the broom. "It's fine, really. I don't mind."

Besides, it kept him distracted from all the things he wanted to ask—things he knew no one would give him the answers to. He began sweeping up the dirt and the pieces of Teresa's planter. The old woman quietly lowered herself into the chair and stared out at the snowy yard beyond the windows. It was silent for a while. Darius continued to clean up the wreckage left behind from Thorn's outburst, and Teresa sat lost in her own thoughts.

When he got the soil swept into a pile, he saw the droplets of Thorn's blood on the white tile under his feet. Finally, he sighed.

"What is wrong with her?"

It was more to himself. He couldn't understand getting upset enough to lash out like this—to slice his hand open and not even notice. Teresa gave a sad chuckle from behind him, and he turned around.

"Be kind," she said. "She was pushed past her limit."

"How could she hit her limit? Over a picture?" Darius couldn't see it. He'd spent the better part of two months with Thorn, and he felt like he knew her. Well, knew her as well as it was possible to with all the walls she hid behind. Despite her issues with Teresa, she'd always seemed to have a grip on herself.

"It's a lot more than that," Teresa said. She shook her head. "Don't let this ruin your opinion of Thorn. Your life with the Martyrs won't be any easier if you're on her bad side."

"What's she gonna do?" Darius scoffed, but he wasn't angry as much as he was sad. "Throw shit at me?"

Teresa could do nothing more than offer a sad smile, and she reached up to grab his hand in hers. Her fingers were warm against his palm; her skin was soft and comforting. Her calming presence helped him feel grounded again. He took a deep breath and came to sit on the chair beside her.

"It's easy to judge things you don't understand," Teresa said.

Darius could only nod. There wasn't really much else he could add to the conversation. He didn't know much about Thorn except that this war had stolen her name and left behind a web of scars. He groaned and dipped his face into his free hand. "I guess I should get ready for some extra painful runs in the next couple of weeks."

"I wouldn't be so sure about that," Teresa said gently, and Darius glanced up to her. She didn't look at him as she continued. "I just got off the phone with Alan. He's sending a replacement guard. Thorn's going back to the Underground."

To his surprise, Darius's stomach gave an upset little flip.

He frowned and sat up a little straighter in the chair. "Really?"

"Yes."

"Huh." He didn't know what else to say, and his shoulders slumped toward the ground.

"I'm going to miss her, too."

Darius raised a brow. *"You're* going to miss Thorn?"

Teresa shrugged. "I've missed her for a long time." She didn't elaborate. "Anyway, I'm sure you'll see her again soon enough. If Eva's not found in the next month, Alan's calling off the search."

"Oh." Darius's heart sank. He knew they couldn't search for Eva forever, but it was hard to think he may never see her again. He'd spent most of his time trying *not* to think about that. He heaved a sigh. "I can't imagine going back to the Underground without Eva there."

"You know," Teresa said slowly. "If you didn't want to go back, I'm sure Alan would accommodate you, the way the Martyrs did for me when I left." He looked at her, and she watched him back with love and wisdom.

"I don't think I could do that," he murmured.

Teresa smiled and gripped his fingers a little more tightly. "I didn't think you *would*."

Darius paused and drew his hand back. He folded it with the other in between his knees and looked down at the ground by his feet. She was right. He *was* going to go back to the Underground eventually—and it wasn't just because he wanted to help find Eva, Saul, and the others. It was because a part of him—probably the Virtue part—knew it was where he belonged. He knew he had some purpose to fulfill, and that was where he had to do it.

That's what his *gut* told him.

"It's weird," he said. He sat back in the chair, sighed, and ran his hands over his face. Teresa interlaced her fingers on her lap and watched him quietly. His head fell back onto the top of the chair, and he stared out the glass ceiling above him. The winter sky was a bright, icy blue. "Losing the orphanage felt like losing myself. I've felt… incomplete. Like I'm only *half here.* The Martyrs make me feel like I'm doing the right thing—like I'm on the right path to feeling whole again. I can't walk away from it."

He turned to look at Teresa, but everything about her changed. Whatever somber, sad air that had fallen over her since Thorn's outburst was gone. Something new dawned on Teresa's face. Her eyes were wide, her lips opened, and she watched Darius like she was just seeing him for the first time.

"What?" he asked, suddenly self-conscious.

"Oh!" Teresa blinked and shook her head a couple of times. "Nothing, it's just… Well, I think you're right. You need to find peace with the Martyrs, and with your Virtue." She winked at him but then quickly got to her feet. "I'm sorry, Darius, I just thought of something I need to do."

Then she quietly excused herself and disappeared back into the house.

Thorn wasn't outside anymore. Darius went out to say goodbye, but she must have come back into the house while he and Teresa were talking. He went up to her bedroom and knocked, but she didn't answer.

"Thorn?" he called. Still nothing.

He waited a moment before trying the knob. It was unlocked. He let himself in.

The room was empty, and, though it shouldn't have surprised him, it was also meticulously clean. It was more than clean. It was virtually untouched, like no one had been living here for the last two months. The bed was so neatly made it looked almost military. Dresser and nightstand surfaces were clear and uncluttered. There were no stray socks on the ground, no jackets hanging from the back of the door—nothing.

The only thing giving away anyone's presence here was

a single suitcase sitting open on the bench at the foot of the bed. Thorn's clothing—shades of black, gray, and red—were folded neatly and put away. Her winter jacket was rolled up beside it. Darius wondered if she'd packed this morning or if she'd never unpacked in the first place. He was going to turn and leave, but something sitting on top of the clothes caught his attention.

It was the picture.

His curiosity got the better of him. He *had* to know. Darius stepped into the room, gently closed the door behind him, and picked the image up. The broken frame was gone, and the photograph sat innocent and innocuous. Darius lifted it up. He had half a mind to take it back down to Teresa, but something stopped him. He had a feeling she'd want Thorn to have it. Darius looked down at the photo—at Thorn's smiling face and then at the man standing beside her.

Who was he, and what the hell had Wrath done to him?

One of his strong arms was wrapped around Thorn's shoulders, and in the other, he pinned a camera bag to his hip. His head was tilted in against hers lovingly, familiarly. There was something about him that was eerily like Thorn but somehow totally unlike her at the same time. Even in this photograph, where Thorn was happy and laughing and full of life, she seemed weary and cold, but him? He was bright and inviting.

Then Darius noticed something else. He almost didn't see it because Thorn's hand and wrist were buried deep in her long, rich hair—Thorn's left forearm was bare, and it showed no evidence of scarring.

He didn't have the chance to inspect the photo more closely. The door behind him suddenly opened, and Thorn's furious voice startled him so much his heart leapt into his throat.

"What the fuck are you doing?"

Darius quickly put the picture back down and turned around. Thorn's eyes were wild again, and as she glanced at her things, her lip curled. Darius took a step back as she strode across the room. She reached her suitcase in three steps and slammed it shut.

"I'm sorry," he said, and he was. He hated being caught invading her privacy. He held up his hands. "I was just coming to say goodbye. I heard you're going back to the Underground."

Thorn didn't respond right away. She was hunched over her belongings, her hands splayed out across them, and she took a deep breath. The dam had been broken, and Thorn's anger was closer to the surface than ever. Darius could almost feel it in the air around them.

Finally, she gave a short nod. "Yes. Thank *god*."

"When will they get here?"

"They're not coming all the way out here," Thorn said shortly. She straightened up and grabbed her jacket and bag. Sparkie slipped out from the back of Thorn's loose shirt and watched Darius with beady little eyes. "We're meeting halfway."

Darius frowned. "How?"

"I'm taking Teresa's car."

"*What*?" Darius raised his eyebrows and crossed his arms. "Have you asked?"

Thorn turned and shot him a venomous look. "Don't treat me like a child," she hissed. "I've used Teresa's car to run into town. This isn't any different."

"Yes, it is," Darius said. "This isn't a run into town. Halfway is a *two*-hour drive. *And* you just wrecked the sunroom." Thorn's nostrils flared again, and her lips pressed into a dangerous, thin line as she continued to glare at him, but Darius didn't back down. "I can't believe you think you can just take the car."

"Well, what do *you* suggest?" Thorn spat, and she slammed her suitcase back down on the bench so she could prop her hands on her hips.

"Why can't they come all the way out to get you?" Darius asked. Thorn's fury was infecting him. He felt his own chest swelling up with it, and he fought to keep it down.

"Because," she said more quietly, and Darius was shocked to see tears welling up behind her eyes as she forced out the words, "I can't *stand* to be here for another four hours. I can't do it, so if you won't let me take the *damn* car, I'll walk."

And almost to show her dedication to her threat, Thorn grabbed up her things again and stormed toward the door. Darius sighed, rubbed his eyes in exasperation, and followed.

"Fine," he yelled after her. "But I'm coming with you."

Thorn tried to call Alan and get him on her side of the argument, but to Darius's shock, Alan agreed with him. Darius was to stay with a Martyr at all times, whether Thorn liked it or not, and they established a checkpoint in a tiny town along the way to switch vehicles. Thorn was furious, but with Alan's explicit instructions, she couldn't fight it. Darius felt relieved. The truth was, he was concerned about her—and concerned she'd lash out again—and he wanted to make sure she got to the checkpoint point in one piece.

The drive was tense and quiet. Thorn was behind the wheel, and she gripped it with hands so tight her knuckles shone white against her skin. She'd put on her coat, and Sparkie was nestled in the inner pocket. Every so often, he'd peek his head out and watch Darius before disappearing inside the folds of black fabric again.

Thorn wasn't wasting any time. She flew down the highway with almost reckless abandon and weaved through traffic with expert precision. By some miracle, they never ran into any cops. Thank god. That was an experience Darius never wanted to have again.

But it went seamlessly. Darius spent his time locked in his own thoughts. He wondered how things would be at the Underground with Thorn back. Would she jump in on the hunt for Eva? Somehow, the idea of Thorn looking for Eva was comforting. The Martyrs were skilled, but Thorn's blind determination alone was a force to be reckoned with. He also found himself thinking about how life back at Teresa's would be so different without Thorn there.

Then he realized he didn't know who was replacing her.

"So," Darius said after a while. He figured they must be getting close to the meeting point now. They'd been on the road for more than an hour and a half. "Who are you swapping with?"

"The First Response Unit."

Darius sat up straighter and raised his eyebrows. It was about time for some good news. "Really? William's unit?"

Thorn gave a short nod. "And Chris's."

"So, you're being replaced by *two* people?"

"They're a unit," Thorn said, as though that answered anything. "They work together."

Whatever. Darius didn't really care. He was just happy it was someone he knew. William was the closest thing he had to a friend in the Underground.

They met up at a gas station in a little town called White Haven. Thorn pulled off the highway and up along the edge of the parking lot. Darius peeked out the window and saw a black Martyr vehicle slowly rolling toward them. William was smiling at him from the passenger's side, and Darius smiled back. He went to open his door, but Thorn called him out.

"You," she said, "stay in the car."

Darius raised an eyebrow. "What? I've just got to use the restroom."

He gave her a playful smirk and opened his door. Thorn glared after him incredulously, but she didn't try to stop him. She just got out of the car, too, and slammed the door behind her.

"Darius!"

William stepped down from the tall SUV, made his way around to clasp Darius's hand, and brought him in for a one-armed hug. His broad palm slapped down on Darius's shoulder as he laughed, then he pulled back and looked him over from head to toe. "Wow, you've been busy! Where'd all that hair go?" He roughly ruffled Darius's new haircut. Darius laughed.

"Chopped it all off," he said.

"And you've been working out! You look good, man! So." William put his hands on his hips excitedly, and he looked from Darius to Thorn to Chris, who was just coming around from the Martyr vehicle to join them. "There's a whole *other Virtue,* huh? Which one is she?"

"Humility," Darius said without thinking. Chris passed the two of them a stern look.

"William," she warned, but she was smiling all the same.

"Hey," he said, holding his hands up defensively. "You told me I couldn't tell anyone else in the *Underground*, but we're not at the Underground, are we? Besides, Thorn and Darius obviously know already."

"It's still good practice to keep your mouth shut," Thorn said. She looked around them carefully, but she didn't seem to see any immediate threat because she relaxed her shoulders a bit and took a deep breath. Then she turned to Chris and said, "I'm sorry to pull you into this."

Chris shrugged. Her yellow hair cascaded behind her shoulders. "It's part of the job."

"Get what you need switched into the other car," Thorn said. "I need a smoke, and Jones needs to *piss*." She rolled her eyes before she pulled a pack of cigarettes out of her jacket and walked across the parking lot. William watched after her and gave out a chuckle.

"Better get to *pissing*," he said, mocking Thorn's tone, and he grinned at Darius. "We'll have plenty of time to catch up on the way there. I want to hear *everything*."

"William," Chris called from the back of the SUV. Darius saw there was a ton of gear there—much more than Thorn had taken with her when she'd first come to Teresa's. "Come grab this for me."

"I'll help out when I get back," Darius said as he started off toward the station convenience store at a half-jog. It was a relief to be out in the open. The drive had been suffocating. Even though Thorn hadn't lit up the whole time, her foul mood hung worse in the air than cigarette smoke ever could.

While Chris and William started moving their gear into Teresa's car and Thorn smoked on the other edge of the lot, Darius quickly made his way to the bathroom and relieved himself. On the way back, he paused. He thought back to the last time he'd been in public, when he and Teresa had talked about energy in that little cafe. Something about the energy here caught his attention.

It reminded him of the market, but not in the way the cafe had. Instead, it reminded him of the way the *dark* side of the market had felt—of the vibe he got when he met people who didn't pass his criteria to take on one of his kids.

It made him uneasy—and then it made him scared.

He walked through an aisle, toward the door, and the little hairs on the back of his neck prickled up. His heart fluttered from his chest to his throat. He looked up in the mirror at the corner of the room and saw, to his horror, the cashier coming up behind him. Something in the woman's eyes was odd and unplugged.

He quickly turned down the next aisle and ran. Another store employee rounded the corner and tried to grab him. His expression was just as plastic and unreal as the woman's. Darius ducked beneath the man's hand. His fingernails scraped against the back of Darius's neck. He managed to get away and forced his way out into the parking lot.

Then there were six more.

People came in from all around—gas station attendants, the car wash supervisor, employees wearing navy blue vests came rushing at him from every direction. Darius froze in place. Chris and William didn't seem to realize what was happening. They were still busy with the car all the way at the other end of the lot. They didn't see him standing there, trapped.

But Thorn did.

A flash of black rushed up beside Darius as Thorn came in and pulled him behind her. Her cigarette was still clutched between her fingers as she threw a quick, snappy punch into the nearest attendant's face, leaving a circular burn on his cheek as he sprawled backward. He cried out in pain. Darius heard Chris shout something in the distance.

"Fuck," Thorn murmured as she grabbed Darius by the arm and thrust him away from the gas station, out toward the street. "There's more of them."

Darius threw a look over his shoulder and saw another four people surrounding Chris, William, and the vehicles. Chris jabbed the heel of her palm into a woman's throat. She dropped and clutched her neck.

Darius tried to turn around and head back, but Thorn's fingers tightened painfully around his bicep, and she pulled him further away. She elbowed one man right in the nose as he came for Darius. There was a sickening crack, and blood poured down his face. Another employee grabbed at Thorn and caught her long hair between her fingers. Thorn roared and turned, swiping the woman's feet out from under her and using her shoulder to slam her into the ground. The woman's head crashed into the asphalt with a disorienting crunching sound.

"Run!"

Darius stumbled backward and avoided another man's groping hands as he sprinted down the street. A fluttering sound behind him made him jump, and Sparkie swooped past, a blur of red and blue. Darius heard footsteps following quickly behind him. He looked over his shoulder to see a scrawny, pock-faced kid on his heels. He had the same mechanical, empty look in his eyes.

Sparkie was on him. The reptile arched high in the sky and dive-bombed the kid, scratching at his scarred face with tiny, sharp claws. The boy lost his footing and stumbled on the sidewalk. Darius took the opportunity to turn down an alley and out of sight.

And he just kept running.

He twisted and turned, going up different streets and down more alleys, past people walking along, bundled up in the snow. Darius didn't stop until the instinctual feeling of dread and imminent danger had subsided, and he was running on adrenaline alone. He had no idea how far he'd gone by the time he darted behind a dumpster and clutched a stitch in his chest. He felt his heartbeat in his ears, rapid and erratic. The taste of iron coated his tongue as he hacked phlegm and spat it onto the grimy alley ground.

Where the hell was he?

His mind immediately turned to Thorn, Chris, and William. The last he'd seen them, they'd been surrounded by people Darius could only assume were Influenced by the Sins. He groaned and leaned his head back against the brick building face. Though he knew he didn't have anywhere near the experience and expertise in fighting the three Martyrs had, Darius hated himself for running away—again. It seemed like all he did when the Sins were involved, and it made him feel worthless and pathetic.

Virtue or not, he needed to be better than this.

He decided to ask Thorn for combat training the next time he saw her… if he ever saw her again. For all he knew, she was dead, and he'd get caught by the Sins before ever making it back to the Underground.

Darius swore and kicked a metal trash can down the alleyway. It clanged and clamored as it bounced away and rolled, slowly, to a stop.

The short, winter day was coming to a close. Darius looked up at the dimming sky—the sun would be down soon, and then he would be in real trouble. He knew how to survive on the streets. He'd been doing it for most of his life. And one of the most important rules was not getting caught outside, at night, in the winter, without something to keep you warm.

The sweat he'd built up on his sprint away from the gas station was sticky and clung to him. His sweatshirt was damp and cold. It would only get colder. As his adrenaline levels dropped, the chill began to set in.

Who'd have thought he'd get dragged into this war with the Sins just to die from the elements anyway?

Darius pulled his hood up over his head and jammed his hands deep into his pockets as he started to walk down the alley and back onto the main road. There, he stopped. He didn't know where he was or even which direction he had to head to get back to the Underground. He couldn't ask anyone—what would he say? He didn't even have a number to call.

His best bet was to hitchhike back to New York City. At least he'd have familiar surroundings, and maybe the Martyrs would think to look for him there.

If they didn't just assume he was dead.

Darius looked up and down the road. It was empty. Most of the small businesses around him were either closed for the day or permanently shut down. No one was walking along the cold, icy streets. In the distance, he saw the telltale green sign indicating the direction to get back onto some freeway or another.

It was the best place to start.

He hadn't even taken two steps when something dropped down on him from above. Darius leapt in surprise as Sparkie landed with an awkward grip on his shoulder and tried to fly again. He chirped frantically as he grabbed onto Darius's sweatshirt and tugged him backward. His leathery wings flapped against Darius's face. They stung his cold, chapped skin.

"All right, all right!" he exclaimed as he batted the animal away and turned around. "I'm going. What's the—"

Footsteps rushed down from the other edge of the alley. Darius quickly jammed himself behind the dumpster and pinned his back to the wall. Sparkie trilled, jumped into the air, and disappeared. Then Thorn rounded the corner.

She was frazzled. Her black hair was pulled into a haphazard ponytail, her eyes wide and wild, as she looked down at Darius in disbelief. She reached out and grabbed his shoulders.

"Jones," she breathed, and her relief seeped from her voice and into her body. Her hands were shaking as they held onto him, her fingers digging in desperately. For a moment, Darius thought she was going to hug him, but then she just dipped her head down and heaved a thick, heavy sigh before pulling back and leaning into the dumpster for support. Sparkie was agitated. He flew in a few circles above her head and dove down to disappear inside her jacket. Thorn's dark eyes closed, and she took a deep breath.

"God," she said after a moment. "I thought I'd lost you."

"Where are Chris and William?" Darius asked. "Are they okay?" He leaned in close to Thorn. His breath left heavy fog between them. She opened her eyes again.

"I don't know. The last time I saw them, they were grabbing the cars." She stood back up and straightened her jacket. "Chris had Solomon's—she's probably on her way back to the Underground to make sure it's not intercepted. Michaels may be looking for us, and I'm sure they called backup. But the Sins are on their way."

"How do you know?"

"I don't *know*," Thorn grumbled, and she looked up at the sky above them. "But we have to assume. Most of the time they Program people, part of the Programming is to let the Sins know what's up. At least one of them is coming."

She grabbed Darius by the arm again and led him out of the alley—the opposite way he'd been going before. She looked up and down the street before turning to him again.

"We need to find a place to stay. It's going to get dark soon."

"Stay?" Darius asked incredulously. "If William is looking for us, we need to call him!"

"How?" Thorn shot back. "My bag was in Solomon's

car. I don't have a phone to call him *with*. Anyone in this city could be Programmed to look for us, so asking for help is out of the question. He'll find us—and if not him, the backup will, but we need to get somewhere safe, and we need to do it carefully… *Damnit*, they know we have some interest out in this direction. I should have known to be more careful."

She shook her head—didn't look at him. A shiver of sympathy jolted down Darius's spine. Or maybe it was from the cold. He crossed his arms and took a deep breath. "We shouldn't worry about things we can't change," he said. "What do you need me to do?"

Thorn turned to take him in. She seemed surprised, but it was fleeting. Her hard, determined look rose up again. "Just follow close to me," she said. Sparkie climbed out of her jacket and disappeared into the sky. "And if those Virtue senses of your start tingling, let me know *immediately*."

When Thorn said careful, she *meant* careful. The two of them walked through the town using nothing but back roads and alleyways. Thorn was somehow able to select streets that were totally abandoned. They didn't even see passing cars. After searching in silence for almost an hour, Thorn paused at a corner and held up her hand to stop Darius. They were standing across the street from a run-down, grimy strip motel. The lot was empty except for a half-dozen cars. Thorn watched it for a moment with dark, narrowed eyes before she said, "This will have to do."

Thank god. Darius was freezing. The sun was starting to set, and the thin sweatshirt he was wearing did almost nothing to keep him warm. His face and hands were so numb he could hardly feel them anymore. He was looking forward to getting inside, maybe taking a hot shower, when something suddenly occurred to him.

"Wait," he said thickly. His lips were so cold the words came out clumsy and awkward. "You don't have your bag?"

He assumed she didn't have any money, either, but she didn't seem worried. "I'll handle it. Stay here."

Then she disappeared around the corner, and Darius waited back and wrapped his arms around himself. Now that he wasn't moving, he was starting to shiver. He'd reached the point of cold where his joints ached. For several minutes, he didn't see anyone—not even Thorn—but then an old, haggard woman made her way into the motel's main office. Darius frowned. She was holding a red pack of cigarettes.

A short while later, the woman came out of the office and headed back the way she'd come. Darius peeked around the building to see Thorn waiting for her on the other side of the motel parking lot. She handed Thorn something and then continued to walk down the street. A block later, she pulled out a cigarette and lit it. By that point, Thorn had made her way back to Darius.

"How the hell—" he started to ask when she came back to collect him, but she just shook her head.

"We traded," Thorn said simply, but Darius could tell there was something not so simple about it. "Come on. Our room is on the second floor."

They quietly made their way across the street and to the motel. Thorn took them the long way around, avoiding the front office as well as she could. When they finally reached room 205 and shut themselves inside, Thorn let out a relieved sigh.

The room was musky. It smelled stale and damp. A single bed sat in the center. The closet on the far wall was empty except for a couple of hangers dangling from a white bar. There was an old, bulky entertainment center set up with an even older and bulkier television set. Darius moved to turn the lights on, but Thorn stopped him.

"Don't," she said. "No lights."

Darius stared at her like she was out of her mind. "Why not?"

"I don't want to draw any attention," she said. "As far as anyone out on the streets is concerned, no one's home."

Darius looked around. It was getting dark fast. The sun

had set, and the twilight sky outside was hardly bright enough to illuminate the room, especially since Thorn adamantly refused to open the strip blinds more than a narrow slit, just wide enough for her to look through. Darius shook his head. "What do you expect us to do?"

"Sit. Wait." She turned and cast him a dark look. "Be quiet."

Darius groaned, snatched a blanket, and wrapped himself up. He flung back onto the bed and stared at the ceiling above him. He was freezing. Thorn also insisted they keep the heater turned off, and while it was warmer than it was outside, it wasn't pleasant. His fingers started to come to life with an uncomfortable, painful tingling, and he flexed them to try to get the blood pumping faster.

Thorn stood by the door. She leaned against the wall by the window, staring out into the street. Soon, the only light coming into the room was from the streetlights around the edge of the motel parking lot. Darius laid back on the bed and watched her.

She was stoic, still as a statue, as she waited for something—anything. Darius wasn't sure. Soft bars of light fell across her face, leaving many of her features hidden in the shadows.

He may have been annoyed at having to sit here, cold, in the dark, but he had to admit, he was impressed with Thorn. He had no doubt she planned to stand guard all night if she had to.

He didn't have the chance to find out. After a while, despite himself, Darius was lulled to sleep. His body ached. His mind was tired. It was dark and quiet. His brain toyed with consciousness until he was out entirely.

It didn't last long. Darius was jolted awake by a sudden, guttural fear. He sat up straight in bed, the blanket falling off his shoulders, and looked to Thorn. She glanced up to him and slowly held one finger to her lips. Then, she gestured out the window.

Darius carefully got up and made his way next to her.

She was holding the bar from the closet in her hands like a weapon, her fingers tight against the painted wood, while she watched a woman slink around the parking lot. It was hard to see her in the dim light, but for some reason, she filled Darius's stomach with a cold, queasy panic. Finally, she turned, and the light caught her plain, ordinary face. Darius gasped.

"Envy," Thorn whispered.

Envy. Darius couldn't remember her human name. Cassandra? It didn't matter. Whatever she went by, Darius would always know her as the woman who had helped Derek Dane murder his family—the one who had carved the word "bitch" into Eva's stomach.

His fear mixed with anger in his gut; it made him feel sick. Darius grabbed the wall to steady himself, and he watched the Sin through the blinds as she looked around at the motel. "She Influenced all those people at the gas station?"

"She did a hell of a lot more than that."

Then Darius saw what Thorn was talking about. Envy wasn't alone. She'd been joined by three other people—three people with blank, placid expressions on their faces.

"Puppets?"

Thorn just nodded.

"What are we going to do?" Darius asked. An edge of panic tightened his throat.

"We're getting the fuck out of here," Thorn murmured, and Darius turned to her. "Montgomery is close. I just need to buy us a few more minutes…"

Darius frowned. "How do you know—"

"Shh!" Thorn hissed, and she gestured out the window.

Darius looked back. Envy and the Puppets split up. Two started to walk along all the rooms on the bottom floor, using master keys to open the doors and check inside. Two of them headed up to the second story to do the same. Envy was one of those. She started up the stairs.

Darius broke out in a cold sweat. Dread shivered all the

way down his spine and into his soul. Thorn's grip tightened on the rod in her hand.

"They always underestimated her," Thorn growled.

"Who?" Darius whispered. Thorn shoved him back against the wall. Envy was three doors down. They heard the door open, pause, then click shut.

"The other Sins."

Thorn situated herself directly in front of the door, just barely outside the arc it followed when it opened. Her feet were planted wide apart, and the rod balanced like a spear in her palms. The room was silent. Light, careful footsteps approached the door. Darius heard the click of a card in the lock and the soft squeak of Thorn's fingers tightening around her weapon.

The door swung open.

Thorn jabbed the closet pole directly into Envy's throat. The Sin let out a choking yell. Thorn jabbed again, and again, and the Sin stumbled backward. Thorn followed after her. The knife fell out of Envy's hand and clattered onto the concrete walkway. Before she had the chance to retaliate, Thorn held the rod out parallel to the ground and thrust it up and into her chin. Her head snapped back, and she stumbled over the railing. Darius heard her body crunch on the concrete below.

He flew out as Thorn was rushing back in and looked down at the ground. The Sin's wide, angry eyes caught him, and her lip twisted into a snarl. She started to get to her feet…

"She's getting up!"

"*I know*," Thorn roared, and before Darius knew what was happening, the TV from their room came crashing down. It landed on the Sin with a heavy thud. Thorn didn't wait to see how effective it had been—she just grabbed Darius's hand, and she ran.

They sprinted to the far end of the motel and rushed down the stairs so quickly Darius almost fell down headfirst. One of Envy's Puppets was crumpled at the bottom, and they had to leap over it. Did her control disappear when she'd been crushed? Darius didn't have the time to worry about it. He heard a sound behind him—broken glass and plastic scraping along the sidewalk—as headlights blared around the corner and a black SUV screeched to a stop. The driver's window rolled down. Sparkie leapt from it and flew high into the sky.

"Get in!" a man yelled.

Thorn pulled open the side door and practically threw Darius inside before she dove on top of him and slammed it shut behind her. The vehicle took off so quickly its tires squealed on the asphalt. The smell of burned rubber assaulted Darius's senses. He turned and watched the motel disappear behind him. Envy chased after them on foot, bloodied and screaming. Sparkie dove down—swiped at her face—then they turned a corner, and she was gone.

"Jesus, Jeremiah," Thorn snapped. "Cutting it kind of close, don't you think?"

"You're welcome." Jeremiah's deep, booming voice was tense and heavy. Darius didn't know him, but William had said the director of the Tactical Unit was named Jeremiah. Based on the black turtleneck and cargo pants, this had to be the guy. He was massive—his broad shoulders dwarfed the driver's chair and made Darius feel small. He looked up in the rearview mirror, and his rich, brown eyes moved from Darius to Thorn. "Are you all right?"

"Yes," Thorn said. Conrad, who was sitting shotgun, moved a rifle down from his shoulder and growled. Jeremiah sped through White Haven, onto the freeway, and back toward New York City. Suddenly, Sparkie flew back in through the open window and gripped onto Jeremiah's shoulder. He rolled the window up, and the lizard leapt back to Thorn and hid inside her jacket. Thorn zipped it up to her throat and looked back to the driver. "Where are Chris and Michaels?"

Jeremiah took a deep breath and shook his head. "Chris is fine. She should be back at the Underground by now.

William, though… His vehicle spun off the road and into a ravine."

The blood drained from Thorn's face. Darius shook his head. His heart was lodged in his throat. "Did he survive?" he asked.

"No. The vehicle caught fire. It's totally incinerated."

Thorn roared in frustration and punched the back of Conrad's chair. A strange yet familiar numbness settled over Darius. He turned away and looked out the window into the darkness of the night.

Darius never thought he'd be as glad to see the Underground as he was that night. The four of them were quiet and tense as they pulled into the car wash and started the subterranean descent into the Martyr's headquarters. Darius spotted Teresa's car by the main entrance. It looked like hell. The back glass was shattered, and bullet holes pierced the rear and side doors.

Thorn didn't even enter the complex. She got out of the SUV, immediately made her way to Teresa's vehicle, tore open the door, and grabbed her suitcase and satchel. Then she threw her things into one of the other Martyr cars in the lot. Jeremiah called after her. His brows furrowed heavily. "What the hell are you doing?" he asked. "Alan wants to talk to you."

"Fuck Alan," Thorn snarled as she got into the coupe, turned on the ignition, and pulled out of the lot. Darius watched her rear lights as they slowly spiraled up and out of sight. Jeremiah shook his head and pinched the bridge of his broad nose.

"This is unbelievable," he said.

The doors to the foyer opened, and Alan Blaine himself walked out. Darius stared at him, stunned. This wasn't the Alan he remembered. His clean, precise look was ragged. Stubble speckled his cheeks, and dark rings beneath his eyes betrayed his exhaustion. His red, button-up shirt was wrinkled and untucked. He turned to Jeremiah furiously. "You let her leave?"

"*Let* her? With all due respect, sir, I didn't *let* her do anything."

Alan swore and ran his hand down over his mouth and goatee. He took a deep breath and said, "Speak to the Gray Unit. Deploy TAC. *Find her.*"

The look on Jeremiah's tense, dark face said it all—he didn't think it would do a damn bit of good—but he agreed and disappeared into the Underground. Conrad followed after him. Then Alan turned to Darius at last.

"Darius," he said, and though he tried to maintain composure, the tight muscles along his throat made his voice sound strained. "I apologize for the hectic day you've had to endure."

Darius watched him for a moment. He knew there would probably be a better moment for this, but he didn't really care. His whole body ached. He was exhausted. His stomach growled, his head pounded, and he said, "That's it? You just apologize?"

Alan's brows pinched together, and the corner of his mouth began to twist upward. "Excuse me?"

"You had to know," Darius said. "You had to know about Teresa and Thorn. Why the hell did you think it was a good idea to send her with me? Something like this was bound to happen. Teresa said so herself."

A flash of anger passed over Alan's face, and his nostrils flared dangerously. "You do not understand the situation as well as you think you do," he said. The control Darius had always seen him have over himself started to crack. Darius didn't care about that, either.

"I understand enough," he said. Eva was gone. Now, Thorn was, too.

And William was dead.

Even exhausted, Darius felt his anger bubbling up his throat and pouring out as words. "You told me you made all your decisions to prevent the most bloodshed. Seems like you missed the mark on this one."

Alan stepped toward him, his long fingers balled up into fists by his sides. For a moment, Darius was sure he was going to hit him. There was a primal, terrifying fury behind Alan's half-empty black eyes. Darius made to take a step back, but Alan suddenly seemed to wake up. His eyes widened, and the fine line of his mouth opened in a small sliver. He stopped and took a deep breath to calm himself, staring down his sharp nose at Darius.

"Welcome back, Mr. Jones."

Then Alan turned around, walked through one of the glass doors, and slammed it shut. Darius just stared after him. In that moment, Alan was so much more like Thorn than Darius had ever seen.

CHAPTER SEVENTEEN

The streets were bleak and heartless. Slush, frozen in the gutters, was so brutally cold even the rats stayed home, huddled together for warmth in the sewers beneath the city. A neon crucifix hung in the stained-glass window of an old, brick building. The words "The Cross" blared bright, red light on the sidewalk outside. Inside, The Cross was half empty, holding service for the few disciples brave enough to walk to the bar in this kind of weather, this late at night.

Thorn sat at the counter and swirled her scotch in circles at the base of her glass. The amber liquid cast ovals of golden light onto the wood. The room hummed with the regular patrons. Divorced, middle-aged men fighting a losing battle against alcoholism. Washed up performance types living on government stipends that hardly covered their grocery bills. Recovered convicts drowning their anxieties in bottom shelf liquor after getting out of prison only to find the rest of the world had moved on without them.

And Thorn.

She'd become such a standard fixture here in the last three years that all the regulars knew her face. At first, she'd garnered a lot of attention—much of it inappropriate and unwanted—but all it had taken was a few sharp words and a well-placed punch to gain the respect and reputation she needed to sit at the bar without harassment.

Now it was the perfect spot for her to slink away when the stress of the Underground was too much. Company without the pressure. No hard conversations. No forced professionalism. No expectations.

At The Cross, Thorn could be *alone* without being truly alone.

God knew she'd been alone too much in the last couple months.

Seven days ago, the men and women of The Cross greeted her in the sincerest way they could. Waving at her from across the room. Slightly nodding their heads in her direction. Making jabs that a pretty, young thing like her must have finally realized she was too good for this place. All with small, awkward smiles and nervous laughs—a testament to how uncomfortable they were with getting close to other people.

Maybe that's why Thorn fit in so well here at this small, dingy dive bar on the edge of Mott Haven. It was easier to be distant.

Thorn slammed the rest of her scotch down and sucked air in between her teeth.

The last week had left a bitter taste in her mouth. Thanks to her fuck up in letting Darius come with her for the swap out, they'd been forced to abandon their plan to keep him safely away from the Underground. They couldn't risk going *anywhere* near Solomon's house now, but with the Torres girl still out here, they weren't safe. Not really. If the Sins found her, the Martyrs would be fucked.

On top of that, Michaels was dead. All because Thorn had been thinking with her heart and not her head.

Since she'd gotten back, Thorn had spent every waking moment trying to fix things, and she had absolutely fucking nothing to show for it. Her network was exhausted. No one Thorn knew had any idea who Eva was or where she could be hiding. The Martyrs had narrowed down the search area to Manhattan, for all the good it did them. Manhattan was a monster of a city, and Eva was always three steps ahead of them. Holly's facial recognition software would find her, but by the time the Martyrs got to the scene, she'd disappear again. In a few worst-case scenarios, the deployed units had run into a couple of Programmed Sentries who alerted the Sins to their work. The field was getting narrower. Both sides were getting closer.

The last time they'd been this neck-and-neck, a lot of innocent people had died, and Darius's life had been torn to shreds. Thorn wasn't about to let it happen again.

A bottle clinked against Thorn's glass as Jay refilled her scotch without having to be called over. He was always attentive to Thorn—regularly excusing himself from dealing with other customers to make sure her needs were met.

"Bad day, huh?" he asked.

She just downed the second shot.

Jay was a nice guy. He was in his late twenties, maybe early thirties. Thorn had never bothered to find out. His auburn hair stuck up at odd angles, an intentionally unkempt fashion statement for his generation. Thorn didn't really get it, but it looked good on him. So did the thin layer of stubble he kept on his chin. Jay's handsome features and sexual appetite were two reasons Thorn liked to stay at his apartment when she was spending the night in town. Another was his genuinely good heart. He wasn't as cold as the rest of the people here. That was hard to find, especially in this godforsaken city.

Jay filled up her glass again and leaned down against the bar. "What's up, Teagan? You seem distracted."

Of course, none of Thorn's city-side connections knew her name or what she really did for a living. As far as they were concerned, Thorn was Teagan Love, a journalist for some tiny paper based out of Brooklyn. Mackenzie had chosen the name years ago, after her previous alias had been uncovered by the Sins. When Thorn had complained, Mackenzie pointed out the name she had chosen for *herself* wasn't much better.

"Shit just hit the fan at work," she said.

It wasn't a lie, technically.

Jay reached out to touch her hand. He held on a little too long for Thorn's liking. "That sucks. Anything I can do to help?"

Thorn pulled her fingers out of his grip and wrapped them around her scotch. As she brought it back to her lips, she cast a smooth look above the rim of the glass. "Just the usual."

Jay stood up a little straighter and gave her a small, sexy smile. "I'm off in an hour. Maybe I'll catch you after."

He winked at her as he walked away to help another customer. When his back was turned, Thorn took a deep breath and tilted the rest of her scotch down the back of her throat.

She wasn't going to find Eva tonight. There wasn't any sense in spending it alone.

Thorn deftly slipped her naked body out from beneath Jay's sheets without waking him. She hunted for her clothes in the dark around the small, studio apartment and showered. Jay didn't make a sound. He never did. By now, he was used to Thorn stealing out so early in the morning that by the time he finally opened his eyes, not even her scent remained behind on the pillow.

She got dressed quickly. As she pulled on a sweatshirt and her heavy winter coat, she turned to look at Jay. His face was soft and relaxed. Thorn couldn't remember the last time she'd slept like that.

At last, she pulled her hood over her head, reached for the door, and stepped out into the frigid, December air. Her damp hair began to freeze as soon as she started to walk down the steps onto the street. Sparkie descended from the sky. It was barely beginning to lighten as the winter sun raised over the horizon. He immediately dove down into her jacket and pressed his cold, tiny body against her bare skin, seeking warmth against the frost. Thorn shivered.

Coffee. She needed coffee.

Grind House Coffee, her favorite shop, was on the corner three blocks down from Jay's apartment. When she stepped through the door, she was the only person in the room besides the barista behind the counter.

"Ah, my favorite customer," he said. He was an older man, probably in his late forties. It was one of those tragic cases of "I have a Ph.D. and nowhere to use it," which left him serving coffee to people less intelligent than he was and shoveling money into student debts he'd never live to see paid off. Thorn couldn't ever remember his name, but it was okay because he never remembered hers, either. "The usual, eh?"

"Yes, *please.*"

He'd already poured it—black with no cream or sugar—and handed it to her across the counter. She paid in cash, gave him a generous tip, and took in a sip. It warmed her all the way down, through her empty chest, until it settled in her stomach.

"So." The barista leaned against the counter and watched Thorn lift her cup back to her lips. Sparkie relaxed against her ribs. "Crazy what happened in White Haven, huh?"

Whatever warmth the coffee had provided was drenched in a rush of cold dread. Thorn frowned and shook her head. "What do you mean? What happened in White Haven?"

"You haven't heard?" he said, shocked. Thorn shook her head. He widened his eyes and released a mouthful of air in a quick, exasperated huff. "A bunch of people killed themselves. It was all over the news. *The Times* said it was over three hundred people—all hanged themselves in the parks around the town."

Thorn's shoulders went rigid. A dark, guilty flame lit up her chest. "Oh, *fuck.*"

"I know," the barista said. "The cops are totally stumped. They thought it might have been some kind of suicide pact, but there weren't any notes. Now they're wondering if there was some contaminant in the water that made everyone go crazy. Seems sketchy, though. I think there's something more going on they don't want us to know."

"Mmm," Thorn said, but she wasn't really listening anymore. Her mind went back to White Haven—to the civilians she'd had to fight there. How many of them were dead now because Thorn had stood in the way of Envy getting what it wanted?

She may have saved Darius Jones, but the victory felt hollow and ugly. Three hundred lives for one Virtue.

God, it better be worth it.

The bell by the door dinged, and another early bird came into the shop. Thorn took that as her cue to leave. She adjusted her satchel while the barista stood up straight and gave her a kind smile. "Anyway, duty calls. You have a good day, eh? I'll see you later." As he turned to help the other customer, Thorn waved and quietly slipped out of the building. The air was cold and unforgiving, but Thorn's gut was alight with hot, angry fire.

She wanted to scream.

But screaming wouldn't bring those people back, and it wouldn't find Eva Torres.

So instead, Thorn pushed that to the back of her mind, along with hundreds of other atrocities she hadn't been able to stop, and she got to work.

The first thing she did was check in on her team and assign the day's tasks. She took out her phone and made a few calls. The Claytors were on morgue duty—part of Thorn hoped Torres was dead in a drawer somewhere and they could put this all behind them. Cortez would check the hospitals. Mulligan worked in Pride's domain, so he would alert Thorn to any strange activity. Pride and Envy were the only two Sins who had seen Eva's face, so if anyone was going to find her, it would be one of them.

Locke didn't answer her call. Thorn hadn't expected him to. Jacob Locke was so well integrated into his undercover that life he regularly disappeared for weeks on end. While it made him one of her best men, it also made him hard to get ahold of. It had been almost three months since Thorn had last spoken to him. He better have some good fucking intel to make up for the lack of communication.

Thorn sighed and put her phone back in her satchel. With her team ready and working, all Thorn had left to do was search for Eva herself—alone and on foot. She tossed her empty coffee cup into a trashcan, pulled her jacket tighter to her body, and made her way westward. Once she hit Willis Avenue, she turned and walked until she crossed the Harlem River. It put her out right at 1st Ave.

And she started her search.

Thorn spent her entire morning walking up and down every street in East Harlem and the Upper East Side. Even early in the morning, with the sun just starting to peek out through the buildings around them, the streets were busy. Cars zoomed by. A belligerent man catcalled her and then screamed foul names when she ignored him. People huddled up in heavy winter gear as they braved the chilly weather. The garbage trucks were out, rattling down the road, grabbing up bags of trash from the gutter, and throwing them into the back.

Thorn locked onto everyone, bundled up behind jackets and scarves that obscured their faces, to see if she could recognize any part of Eva Torres there. She wished she'd spent even a little more time with the girl. Maybe then she'd have more to go off of.

By eleven, she hadn't made much progress. Just more of the same—cold people, living in a cold fucking world. She stood at the corner of 5th Avenue, at the edge of Central Park, and she paused.

Thorn had been avoiding coming here—after the picture she'd found at Solomon's house, the memories of this place felt too fresh—but she knew she needed to go. The park was huge, with plenty of secret places for transients like Torres to lurk. Thorn didn't have much of a choice…

She couldn't hide forever.

Central Park had once been a beautiful testament to New York's prosperity. In many ways, it still was. The city kept it more or less maintained, even though newer sights and attractions constructed in the last fifty years were drawing more of the tourism to other parts of New York. Most of the neglect fell upon the northern edges, where the park met Harlem. Large swaths of the area were overgrown and ignored. The "upstanding" people preferred to stay south, while the poor and sick huddled under gross shrubbery and old, forgotten monuments.

Thorn came into the park on the northern end and walked down the winding footpaths. People hurried past her. Around her. Early morning joggers huffed by—followed by a trail of their own hot breath in the cold air. Even in the dead of winter, this place swarmed like flies on a corpse. Thorn quietly deviated from the main path, moved down through a lesser-traveled part of the park, and found herself at the Huddlestone Arch.

This is where it had happened. Around this time of the year. Fresh snow had coated the ground. The trees had shined with frost and ice.

He'd died in her arms. Right here.

Thorn remembered it as vividly as if she'd just woken up from an awful dream. Blood, coating the snow, melting deep, red canyons into the pure white drifts…

She stopped briefly to pay a silent tribute before she moved on. This was all her life was about anymore. Moving on. Moving faster. Getting further and further away.

She made her way through the park, but she walked away with nothing. Thorn only ran into four unsheltered people willing to speak with her, and none of them had seen or heard of Eva Torres. Thorn thanked them for their time and handed each of them a hundred-dollar bill. The desperate gratefulness, the tearful eyes, made Thorn's chest constrict.

Her mother had always made a point to help others whenever she had the means to do so. When Thorn was younger, she'd thought her mother was being stupid—falling for easy scams—but now, it was one of the few things that made Thorn feel at peace with herself and the horrors of the world her life in the Martyrs opened her up to.

By the time she finished her walk through Central Park, the noon sun blared down on her with harsh, cold light. Gray and brown slush built up in the street gutters, and a chilly wind whipped by Thorn's legs and tore her hair out of her hood. As Thorn stepped onto the Grand Army Plaza, her phone rang. She pulled it out of her pocket and looked down at the name. Jay Coons. She answered.

"What's up?"

"Lunch?"

"Where?"

"Michelangelo's?"

Thorn thought about it. Sparkie squirmed around against her gut at the mention of food. "Okay. Give me thirty minutes."

"Awesome," Jay said. She heard a smile in his voice. "I'll get us a table."

She took the subway then the bus further south, on the very fringe of the Lower East Side. She lit a cigarette and walked the last four blocks to the restaurant. Michelangelo's sat near the pier. It was a relatively new establishment, especially for New York, with a new-age and artsy feel. Thorn didn't get the point, but their food was good, their service decent, and their clientele the typical low-income, I-suffer-for-my-art types. Jay suggested this place a lot. He probably felt connected—something about a dreamed-up music career. Thorn had never asked for the whole story.

The irony that she spent so much time here wasn't lost on her. While she would sit at this restaurant, getting a break from the pressures of the Underground, Darius had been living out on the streets less than two miles to the north. Alphabet City was the last place in the world Thorn would have ever thought she'd find a Virtue, but he'd been there the whole time, just under her nose.

Struggling to survive, while Thorn took for granted all the things that *kept* her alive.

Her bitterness returned—a sense of failure and undeserved reward—as she made it to the restaurant. She sucked the cigarette down, held the smoke deep into her lungs until it hurt, and breathed it out in a slow, quiet stream.

Then she threw the spent butt onto the ground and walked into the building.

Jay was already seated. He waved at her from a window-side table. She strode across the room and sat opposite of him.

"I ordered already," he said as she sat down. "I hope you don't mind."

She did mind. She always did when Jay did this boyfriend-type shit for her, but it wasn't worth the fight. The Martyrs had several apartments around the city, so Thorn didn't *need* to stay with Jay when she came into town, but she did need the release sex provided her. There wasn't a point in jeopardizing it. So Thorn shook her head and draped her jacket off onto the back of her chair. Sparkie slipped unnoticed into its sleeve. Jay watched her move with an almost carnal appreciation.

"Do you work tonight?" Thorn asked.

"No," Jay said. "I figured we'd stream a movie or two and spend the evening in bed." He smiled at her. "How's that sound?"

Thorn scoffed and took a drink of her water. "Sounds like a waste of a good night off."

"Oh, come on, Teagan," he said. "I hardly got to see you in the last couple of months. You didn't even tell me you were leaving!"

She and Jay weren't together—Thorn had made the terms of their relationship clear from the moment she pursued him—but she could tell he wanted to be exclusive. He probably expected it to fall into place eventually. Thorn always shut him down when he started down this road. Sex was one thing, but romance complicated matters.

Her life was complicated enough as it was.

"What, do you expect me to give you an itinerary?" she asked.

"No, that's not what I mean—"

"Then what *do* you mean?"

"I just missed you," Jay said, throwing his hands up. "Is that so wrong?"

Poor Jay. He had no idea what kind of monster he'd gotten himself wrapped up in. Thorn hadn't thought about him at all when she'd been gone. She'd been so busy he'd never once crossed her mind. And, now that she *was* back, he still didn't take up much of her cognitive real estate. She was much more concerned with fixing her mistakes—making sure the Underground was safe and that Darius Jones was safe with it.

"You didn't miss *me*," Thorn said. "You missed *fucking* me."

It came out harsh—and part of Thorn hated that she had to say it—but it was important. She'd set up boundaries, and she needed him to see them. Jay seemed taken aback by her candor. His eyes widened, and his mouth gaped open.

Finally, he managed to say, "That's not fair."

Thorn's eyes darkened and narrowed. "Isn't it?"

They both knew she was right. Jay knew very little about even Thorn's fake life, and Thorn had consciously avoided learning more than she needed to about Jay's. Neither of them knew any real, intimate details about one another. Jay looked away from her face. He could never stand up to her temper, so he just tried to avoid it.

"Look," he said. "I'm just worried about you. Since you got back from your work trip, you've been acting… weird."

"I'm fine," she said.

"Bullshit." Jay leaned across the table again. "What happened, Tea?"

"Is that why you wanted to go out to lunch?" Thorn

snapped. A boiling, venomous rage was building up in her chest again, and she fought to keep it in check. "To interrogate me?"

Jay sighed and rubbed his temples. "No. Forget it. Let's just eat."

The waitress showed up almost as soon as Jay had stopped talking and placed their sandwiches on the table. She did it quietly, like she could sense the tension. Thorn didn't doubt it. She had a way of infecting the room with her bad moods. She sighed and looked out the window and onto the street. She was annoyed—annoyed at Jay, annoyed at Torres, and annoyed at herself for getting stuck in this bullshit situation in the first place.

But all those worries disappeared as a young woman rushed down the street, frantically pushing her way through the pedestrians crowding the sidewalk. She looked remarkably like…

"No way."

The words came out in a whisper, and Thorn's heart started pounding hard against her ribcage. Jay's brows pinched at the center as he looked up to her. "What?"

Thorn sat up straighter in her chair.

The woman was being followed by two men. Two men and—

Derek Dane.

"Fuck!"

"What's wrong?"

Thorn didn't answer. She jumped to her feet, grabbed her jacket and her satchel, and sprinted from the restaurant. When she threw the doors open, Sparkie leapt from her sleeve and into the air. Thorn grabbed out her phone, opened her Martyr emergency app, and slammed the red alert button. Then she kept fucking running.

There was no time to wait for the backup to arrive. They'd just have to find her.

Thorn darted down the street, but Eva had disappeared. She pushed through the crowds, glancing up side streets and alleyways until something caught her attention. First, it was a tickle—the sensation of Influence touching at her temples—

Then someone was screaming.

Thorn turned down a dead-end alley—a narrow wedge between two brick buildings. There was Eva, pinned to the wall halfway between the exit out onto the street and a tall chain-link fence. Her wavy hair was wild, and a bruise was beginning to rise up on her left cheek. Derek Dane came down on her. While his two Puppets grabbed her and held her between them, Dane adjusted his jacket sleeves. The *Peccostium* peeked out at his right wrist.

"Let me go!" Eva screamed.

Dane ignored her. He examined his hands before he pulled back and punched her in the stomach. Eva lurched forward and let out a horrible, animalistic grunt. The Sin came down on her. "Where is the Virtue?"

"I don't know!" Eva gasped. "I don't want to be part of this. I just want to find my brother."

Dane punched her again—as hard as he could. Eva cried out, fell forward, and dry heaved. The Puppets held on and kept her upright as Dane reached out and grabbed her by the chin, forcing her to look at him. His steely eyes were vicious. "I'll ask you again: where is the—"

He never finished the question—because Thorn came sprinting at him from the other end of the alleyway.

Dane noticed her just in time to duck underneath her attack. His eyes were wide and violent, full of primal fear and hatred, as he twisted to the side. Thorn barreled past him—heard him say two words:

"Kill her."

And the Puppetted men grabbed knives from their pockets. Thorn spun and tried to run back, but Pride got in her way. He threw a punch at her. She leaned backward—under his arm—and jabbed an elbow at his ribcage. He swore and twisted to the side.

A blood-curdling scream echoed off the brick walls.

Thorn looked over her shoulder to see the Puppets with their knives buried hilt-deep in Eva's stomach. They tore them out, and she crumpled to the ground.

"NO!"

Thorn rushed toward Eva. One of the Puppets pulled back—kicked Eva so hard she sprawled sideways. The other lifted his knife again—

Thorn was upon them. One turned just in time for Thorn's fist to barrel into his jaw. She felt it dislocate beneath her knuckles. He staggered and collapsed. The weapon flew from his hand and skipped further down the pavement. A light flickered in his eyes as Pride's control disappeared, and the man passed out.

The other Puppet leapt at her. His hands clawed at her face and throat. He slashed out with his blade, swinging it wildly in Thorn's direction. She dipped beneath his arm and threw her knee up, catching him in the groin.

Pride's control disintegrated immediately. The Puppet let out a high-pitched scream and went down as the Direct Influence disappeared.

Thorn spun on her heels and ran to Eva. Her brown eyes flickered opened and closed. Thorn knelt beside her as Sparkie dove down from the sky and landed on Eva's chest. Thorn felt her pulse, touched her bruised and swollen face. Sparkie pulled the folds of her old, ratty clothes away. Two deep gashes opened her stomach, like gaping mouths, and ripped the word "BITCH" into pieces.

Eva groaned. Her lips were turning blue.

Fuck.

Pride walked back into the scene. Thorn felt his evil before he spoke. People strolled past the alley—ignoring it entirely—as Pride's Influence kept him and Thorn in a bubble of isolation. No one saw them. No one heard them. No one had any idea that just around the corner, a woman was dying, and Thorn was trapped with a monster.

And he was trapped with her.

"I *heard* you were back in town," Dane said.

Thorn slowly got to her feet and turned toward him. He adjusted his sleeves again, the *Peccostium* teasing from beneath the fabric by his right wrist. Then he reached behind his back and pulled a pistol from a holster hidden beneath his suit jacket. He aimed the weapon right at Thorn's stomach. Her left hand grabbed the knife in her back pocket and flipped it open.

"Now, Rose," Dane said, *tsk*ing his tongue as he looked at the weapon in her hand. "Bringing a knife to a gunfight? How *amateur*."

He was right, but it would have to do. She hadn't taken the time to grab a better weapon at the Underground. Another *stupid* fucking mistake. The knife was all she had.

Well… almost.

Sparkie hid inside Eva's jacket, pressing his tiny body against her erratic heartbeat. Thorn edged closer to her. Dane was approaching slowly, with a cocky swagger and the gun pointed right above Thorn's belly button.

"Back the fuck off," she whispered.

Dane chuckled, and he took another step toward her. "I want the girl."

Thorn moved closer to where Eva was lying. Bleeding. It was pooling on the ground beneath her now. "She won't make it," Thorn said. "You can't torture a dead woman."

"No," Dane said lightly. "But I think your little Virtue friend would want to get her back either way, don't you? She may still make good *bait*…"

Thank god it was Pride. He kept walking toward her—just five feet away now. Thorn shook her head and let a small, vicious smirk turn up the corners of her mouth. "Jesus, Dane, you are so fucking stupid."

He paused, and his smile disappeared. *"What?"*

"You should have shot me."

Sparkie bolted from Eva's jacket and scurried up Dane's leg. He furiously kicked out and swore. Thorn rushed on him, using her left arm to thrust his gun hand away while the other threw a powerful punch into his sharp jaw.

A shot rang out—the bullet clattered off the brick wall behind her. Someone screamed in the distance. Dane swung around, but Thorn dove beneath his arm and quickly rolled back onto her feet. She turned and slashed. Her knife cut through the shoulder of the Sin's suit jacket.

Dane spun and pointed the gun right at her again. His eyes were wide and wild, his upper lip curled up into a hideous snarl. Thorn arched back and kicked the weapon away. It landed by Eva with a loud clunk against the icy pavement. Dane roared and grabbed for Thorn's left wrist. She twisted out of his reach and, on the way around, plunged her blade into Dane's back.

He roared and yanked sideways. The knife slipped from Thorn's fingers—lodged between Dane's ribs as he pulled away. The momentum threw her off balance, and the Sin lunged for her. Thorn tried to dodge, but she wasn't fast enough. Dane's fist crashed into her chin, sending her head snapping backward and her legs sprawling from beneath her. Her teeth caught the edge of her tongue. Blood filled her mouth. Dane tried to drive his elbow into her ribcage—she twisted away just in time to avoid being crushed.

A new sound entered the fight. Tires squealing to a stop. Dane turned to see the Martyr vehicle pull up, and Thorn flipped back onto her hands and stood again. As the Sin started back toward Eva—back toward his gun—Thorn leapt on him. She grabbed him by the back of the head and slammed his face into the brick building beside them.

A sickening crack echoed through the alley. Thorn felt the bones around Dane's eye socket crumple. He cried out and tore Thorn off his back—flung her onto the ground by Eva's cold, shaking body. Blood poured from his ear and his eye, and he turned and sprinted toward the far end of the alley.

Conrad Carter and Maria Gonzalez hopped out of the Martyr vehicle. Thorn screamed to them.

"Shoot him!"

Carter and Gonzalez pulled pistols from their belts and

fired rounds after Dane. He was already halfway up the chain-link fence. He flipped over the top. A bullet hit his thigh, and he cried out.

But he still hit the ground running—and he ran until he was around the corner and out of sight.

"Fuck!" Thorn screamed. But she couldn't stay angry for long—she had another problem on her hands.

Eva Torres.

She was curled around herself on the ground. Gonzalez rushed up beside her while Thorn pressed her hands against Eva's injuries. Her fingerless gloves soaked up Eva's blood as Thorn worked to stop the bleeding, but it wasn't enough. Thorn could tell it wouldn't be enough. She swore again and brushed her own hair out of her face. Warm blood smeared across her forehead and temple.

"We need to get her out of here," she said. Conrad was already at the vehicle—he'd opened the back and moved tactical gear around to make room for the girl. Thorn hoisted Eva's broken body into her arms. She cried out in pain, but Thorn cradled her to her chest and turned toward Gonzalez. Warm, sticky blood poured out onto Thorn's stomach, saturating her sweatshirt to the skin. She rushed to the car—climbed into the back with Eva still clutched in her arms. Sparkie leapt in beside her. With Pride's Influence gone, people were starting to gather. Faces lined the opening to the alley. Sirens blared to life, somewhere in the distance.

As Gonzalez closed the back of the SUV, Thorn's eyes caught someone familiar in the crowd.

Jay stood, gawking at Thorn. At the woman dying in her arms. At the blood coating her throat and face.

Then the doors closed. Gonzalez jumped into the passenger seat, and Conrad got them out of there. Thorn adjusted herself beside Eva—laid the dying woman across the back of the car so she could more easily apply pressure to the wounds in her stomach. Eva's head flopped to the side. Dark eyes slowly opened and looked Thorn over. If there was recognition there, Thorn didn't see it.

"Stay with me," Thorn said, then she looked up to the front of the car. "Carter, hurry *up*."

"She's dying," Gonzalez said. She glanced over her shoulder at Thorn. Her mouth was set in a somber, familiar frown.

Of course she was. But Thorn didn't want her to die alone in the back of the car with people she hardly knew. Eva deserved to die in the arms of her loved ones. Loved *one*.

They needed to get her back to the Underground.

Thorn pressed her hands harder against the wounds. It didn't matter. The wounds were too large. Blood seeped between her fingers.

"At least it's finally *fucking over*," Carter grumbled. Thorn's stomach churned furiously.

Yes. It was over. The Underground was safe, but Thorn had lost. The Sins had beaten her, again, and someone else was going to die.

CHAPTER EIGHTEEN

The Underground was chaotic.

Since Darius had come back, the place was reeling. Units were being readjusted. More safety precautions were being prepared. The hallways of the Underground were a hive of activity he'd never seen.

With so many more people around, rumors spread through the place like a plague—rumors about him, about Thorn, and about what had happened. He didn't say much. He didn't know what *to* say. It seemed, for the most part, no one else knew about Teresa or where Darius and Thorn had disappeared for two months. All they knew was something big had happened, and now William was dead.

Darius was grateful no one seemed brave enough to ask him about it directly. He wasn't really in the mood to have to lie his way through that conversation.

What he really wanted to do was get out of the Underground to search for Eva and distract himself from the fact William had died because *he'd* been stupid enough to get out of the damn car.

Instead, he was trapped here—again. Without William and Eva around, Darius spent most of his time by himself. It was a strange contrast. At Teresa's house, there had been fewer people, but somehow, he'd had more company. He wasn't entirely alone, though. Chris had been pulled from duty for a few days, and whenever she saw him sitting in the courtyard, she joined him. Today, the two of them were drinking coffee at a table by the kitchen. Darius appreciated it. After all, Chris had lost someone, too.

"It's *not* your fault," she told him. He had just opened up to her about how responsible he felt about William's death, and she shook her head. "Hundreds of people around that town were Programmed to look for you. For all we know, they spotted you before you even reached the station. You can't put this all on yourself. And trust me," she said as Darius opened his mouth to interject, "I've been where you are—more than I'd like to think about, honestly. Obsessing over what could've happened will kill you. You can't let the guilt eat you up."

"You sound like a counselor," Darius said with a wry laugh.

Chris's face played with a smile. "Oh, Abraham will *love* to hear that," she said. "Maybe he'll let me off the hook for my next session."

Darius frowned. "What do you mean?"

"All TAC members are required to meet with Abraham after they've had any major conflict with the Sins," Chris said. "To help keep us sane, I guess. I've talked to him *three* times since William died." She looked down at the mug in her hands.

"Are you doing okay?" Darius asked.

Chris sighed and shook her head. Her long, yellow hair was loose around her face, and for once, she wasn't wearing her Tactical Unit uniform. It was weird for Darius to see her in jeans and a t-shirt. Most of the time, she was all work. The casual look suited her.

"As okay as I can be," she said. "The hardest thing right now is picking a new partner. As assistant director, personnel changes are my responsibility, so I get to choose who I want to work with."

"Why is that hard?"

"Because I lead the First Response Unit," Chris said, and she brought her coffee to her lips and took a sip. She didn't look up as she went on. "We're the first people on the line and the first ones to get shot at. William is the third partner I've lost in the last four years. It's starting to feel like I'm handing out death certificates instead of promotions."

A pause lingered between them. Darius offered a comforting, slightly ironic smile as he said, "You know, obsessing over what could happen will kill you…" She rolled her eyes, but all the same, she did give him a smile, so he considered it a win. He couldn't imagine the impossibility of her position, so he wouldn't even try.

But her position may have other benefits to it. Darius cleared his throat.

"So," he said, changing the subject as he looked down at the coffee in his hands. "Assistant director of the Tactical Unit, huh?"

Chris furrowed her brows and shrugged. "Yes. Why?"

"I was wondering if you could pull some strings and get me on one of the units searching for Eva."

Chris's eyebrows pinched even closer together. "I don't have *that* kind of pull. Why don't you talk to Alan?"

Alan. Darius hadn't seen Alan since their first night back. He'd thought about going to apologize, just to clear the air between them, but he decided against it. He wasn't sorry, and he wasn't going to pretend he was.

"Yeah… I'm pretty sure Alan doesn't want to talk to me," Darius said at last.

"Oh yeah?" Chris asked, but she had a sly smile as she took a sip of her coffee. She watched Darius with a keen, knowing look over the rim of her cup before she set it down. "Not a lot of people challenge Alan."

"You heard about that, huh?"

"Everyone heard about it," Chris said. "Conrad was waiting by the elevators and overheard everything. At least, that's what he says. I'm pretty sure he was snooping."

"Waiting to see if Alan kicked me out of the Underground?" Darius asked with a scoff.

"No," Chris said, shaking her head. "It's not like that. The only people I know who are willing to challenge Alan are the ones he wants in charge. He values the input. If he didn't, he'd never let Thorn have as much power as she has. No one challenges Alan more than Thorn does."

Darius nodded, but that brought up another thing—Thorn. He'd been back in the Underground for a week now, and as far as he knew, Thorn still hadn't come back. Of all the rumors circulating through the halls, what surprised Darius most was the peculiar *lack* of rumor around Thorn's disappearance. He'd asked Chris about it once, and she'd just said, "Thorn does this a lot."

Apparently, it was common for the Martyrs' second-in-command to go off on her own for several days. No one knew what she did or where she went, but she always came back.

"Speaking of Thorn, have you heard from her yet?"

"No. She'll show up sooner or later."

"It seems pretty risky," Darius said, "her spending so much time above ground. Isn't she a huge target for the Sins?"

Chris didn't respond right away. Her bright green eyes looked away from Darius's and down at the table beneath her hands. That piqued his interest. He leaned forward on the table.

But Chris just shrugged and said, "Thorn's killed more Sin hosts than anyone I know. I think they're afraid of her."

Darius's eyebrows drew together. There was something here, and he wanted to know what, but just as he opened his mouth to ask another question, a commotion near the elevators distracted him. He and Chris turned to see a few Martyrs gasp and back away from the doors. When Darius saw why, he gasped, too.

It was Thorn. A thick layer of blood coated her chest and dripped down her arms. It matted her dark hair and smeared her forehead and cheeks. She looked out around the courtyard, but before she spotted him—before she even called his name—Darius knew this had to do with him.

"Jones!"

He quickly got to his feet and made his way to her. His legs felt like jelly beneath him. She had to be hurt, really hurt, to have lost that much blood.

But as he got closer, he realized she didn't have a cut on her. It wasn't her blood at all.

His heart sank into his stomach. Thorn's half-empty eyes were dark and unreadable.

"Come with me."

The words were quiet and soft. His gut twisted.

Darius followed quickly on Thorn's heels, his heart beating so rapidly he could feel it in his fists. She didn't say anything else as she led him from the kitchen and to the elevators. Sparkie watched Darius from beneath Thorn's hair the entire ride up. Her black locks were clumped together in dried, crimson swatches.

When they got to the waiting room outside the hospital, Thorn stopped and turned toward Darius.

"This will not be easy," she said quietly.

Every sound but Thorn's voice faded away. It was just them—just them and the news Thorn was about to break. As much as he tried to deny it, Darius knew what it was about.

"We found Eva," Thorn said.

"Oh, no," Darius moaned. His knees felt weak. Thorn gently grabbed him by the shoulders and lowered him into a chair. She knelt in front of him and gripped his knee with one hand. The other held strong, supportive, to the crook of his neck.

"She's not doing well," Thorn said. Darius looked at her. His eyes were wide and scared—he could see them reflected in her dark irises. "She's going to die."

"No," Darius said again. Tears welled up behind his eyelids. His lungs rejected his breath and constricted so he couldn't draw another one. He furiously blinked and shook his head. "She can't."

Thorn's lips tightened, and she took a deep breath. "You should be there for her. She needs you."

Darius swallowed hard and forced his lungs open again. His throat was dry, and his voice shook when he spoke. "How long does she have?"

"Not long," Thorn said. "She's got a lot of damage. Her back is fractured. There's internal bleeding—"

"Jesus."

"—Elijah wants to give her a drug that will let her sleep, so she doesn't have to be in pain."

Darius's mouth fell open. He didn't even realize it. Just as he didn't notice the tears beginning to fall down his face.

"I can't do this." Darius furiously shook his head. "I can't—she's going to *die?*"

Thorn nodded.

"Oh my *god.*"

"Jones, listen to me." Thorn reached up and grabbed Darius's face. Her fingers felt cold against his cheeks. He looked straight into her eyes. What he saw there was understanding and a callous truth that Eva would *not* be the last person Darius watched die here. "Eva is alone in that room. She's scared. She knows what's happening. She *knows* she's dying. You are the only person in the world she has left. *She needs you.*"

And Darius thought back to the orphanage, to Juniper and Lindsay. But mostly, he thought about Saul. Saul, his best friend, whose little sister was lying on her deathbed because the Sins wanted to see Darius ripped to shreds.

What could he do?

"Come on," Thorn said. Her voice was a whisper. "I'll be there right beside you."

She got to her feet and held out her hand. Darius stared at it. He could see tiny spikes of her scar sneaking up onto her palm from the cuff of her sleeve. The skin was speckled with dried flakes of Eva's blood.

For a long moment, she simply waited. Darius had the feeling she would wait forever.

He reached out and grabbed her fingers.

She eased him up. His body felt like air.

"You can do this."

He wasn't sure he could.

He was even less sure when Thorn led him through the hospital ward. It was quiet and desolate, like all the nurses knew what was happening and made a point to keep their distance. And it was worse when she opened the door to the emergency room. There, he saw four people. Alan spoke quietly in the corner with Dr. Harris while Raquel cleaned up rags from a small medical tray and tossed them in a bin. Her gloved hands were smeared with bright scarlet blood.

And on the table, pale and cold, was Eva.

Her shirt had been cut open. Her body was covered waist down in a blanket, and a towel reached across her torso. Darius's stomach twisted. He had to turn away. He was vaguely aware of a body moving up closer behind him. Thorn reached out and grabbed his hand again. Her grip was firm and reassuring.

"Mr. Jones?"

Alan came around and stood in front of him. Darius had to arch his head back to look into his eyes. Like Thorn's, Alan's were dark and sad but all too familiar with death and dying. He put a hand on Darius's shoulder and squeezed.

Darius glanced behind him. Dr. Harris and Raquel were both attending to Eva now. "How is she?" His throat tightened at the question.

"Not well," Alan said quietly. "But conscious. Aware. You may speak to her. Elijah has given her painkillers, so she may be a little confused."

"Can she feel anything?"

"Yes. The medication has dulled much of the pain, but not all," Alan said.

"So this is it," Darius said. His voice cracked.

Alan nodded. Thorn's fingers squeezed around Darius's

hand.

"Go talk to her," Thorn said quietly. "She needs you."

Darius knew that. He knew the very least he could do for Eva now, after abandoning her for the Martyrs and the war against the Sins, was hold her hand when Elijah put the needle in her vein and help her drift off to sleep. Maybe, just maybe, that small piece of comfort would help her forgive him—and help him forgive himself.

Jesus Christ, Eva was dying.

After what felt like ages, Darius finally found the strength to put one foot forward, and then the other. Thorn released his fingers, Alan let go of his shoulder, and suddenly, he was alone, walking across the room to the single operating table in the center of the emergency hall. Raquel moved to the side. She gently grabbed Darius's forearm as he neared, but he hardly felt her, just as he hardly felt his own legs as they pulled him nearer and nearer to Eva's bedside.

From here, he could see just how ashen her skin was and how heavily her blood saturated the towel covering her injuries. The left side of her face was swollen—a purple bruise raised up beneath the sallow flesh. Her eyes fluttered open as he approached her. Those brown irises were so dull. In the morphine delirium, she managed to put a small smile on her dusky lips.

"Darius." Her voice was weak and quiet. "I didn't think you'd come."

"Oh, Eva," he whispered. He leaned down to her, put his face right beside hers, and pressed his forehead to her cold cheek. A shaking hand ran through her hair. It was caked in sweat and blood. "Of course I'd come."

Eva tried to laugh, but the sound came out harsh and pained. "I'm so sorry," she whispered. "I never should have left. I was so stupid."

Darius's chest felt hollowed out, like someone had taken everything that made him human and torn it from his soul. He came back and shook his head as he fought away the tears. They swelled painfully behind his eyelids and began to fall anyway. "You're not stupid."

"If I hadn't left, I wouldn't be… I wish I stayed with you, Darius. I want to stay with you."

Darius wrapped his hand firmly around her stiff fingers and cried. Tears streamed down Eva's face, into her hair, and onto Darius's knuckles.

"Are you ready, Miss Torres?" Dr. Harris came up beside them. In his hand was a syringe filled with a blue liquid. He held it gingerly just above Eva's left arm.

"No," she cried. They all knew she didn't have a choice.

"This won't hurt," the doctor told her. His voice was quiet, but his reserve was breaking. He cleared his throat. Shook his head. "It will be like falling asleep."

Eva's head nodded backward, and her eyes closed. Rivers of tears flowed freely from the corners.

And as Dr. Harris prepped her arm for the injection, as he neared the needle to her skin, Darius collapsed onto her and hid his face beneath her chin. He was scared, and he was angry. He wasn't ready for this. He wanted Eva to stay. Darius wanted her to stay so badly he was willing to give up everything he had just to keep her alive—to give her a second chance.

This all happened because he was a Virtue—

A *Virtue*.

And then it clicked. As Dr. Harris began to pierce the needle into the vein in Eva's arm, Darius's world was set on fire. The room around him burned, filled with sweltering heat so intense he jumped backward. The doctor stopped and looked up to him.

"Mr. Jones?"

But Darius didn't hear him. Something miraculous was happening.

His hands pulsed with something more than blood. They pulsed with *power*—power aching at the tips of his fingers, seeking a release.

Darius knew what to do.

He neared Eva again, fighting through the wave of heat emanating from her very being, and he pulled the towel off her stomach. The scarred writing, "BITCH" in crude, capital letters, had been ripped into pieces by two deep, gaping slashes. He put his hands right against the wounds. Her flesh burned like fire, and Darius cried out in pain, but he did not let go. He could not afford to let go.

"Darius!"

Thorn's voice behind him was an echo. The power from his body surged forward and into Eva. Every second, Darius grew weaker, his brain hazier, but Eva grew stronger. He watched, awed, as the wound on her stomach began to stitch itself together. Raw, pink flesh circled the edges and pressed them into fine white lines before they disappeared altogether, leaving behind nothing but smooth skin and old scars.

And then Darius's legs collapsed beneath him. The world spun in his vision as he clattered backward onto a medical tray. He was vaguely aware of Eva shooting up on the cot or Thorn's voice from the other end of the room calling his name again. Only one thing was clear to him. One simple word repeated itself in his consciousness without ever speaking itself at all:

Kindness.

A warm, hazy fog hung heavy in the room. It pressed in around Darius's face… his chest… every part of him. The heat moved and shifted like it was alive. Sometimes it was closer, more suffocating, and then it would wander away and become a little more bearable. It bubbled and boiled in pockets. It was like he was in a sauna, and *damn it*, he was hot.

There was one warm spot that didn't move with the rest. It sat static, like a heat lamp pointed right at him.

Darius rubbed his eyes. His arms felt heavy, thick, and

uncoordinated. His face was coated in sweat, and his knuckles slipped and slid against his cheekbones. Slowly, his other senses started to work. He became aware of a rhythmic beeping. The quiet patter of feet against a tile floor. The smell of antiseptic.

Wait. He knew this place.

Darius opened his eyes to the hospital ward. The lights were dim. It must have been late. The nurses had pulled the curtain around his bed to give him privacy. He heard them—and *felt* them—moving past, hot beacons of warmth in the room.

But the hottest beacon of all was sitting next to him. He turned his head, and his heart skipped a beat.

It was *Eva*, and she was burning like a fireplace.

But she wasn't actually burning. Eva was fast asleep, wrapped up in a thin hospital blanket with her chin tucked into her chest. She looked freshly showered. Her hair was clean, her clothes neat and new. For a few minutes, Darius just watched, dumbfounded, as her chest slowly raised and fell with her quiet breathing.

And while she sat there, Eva's warm, good energy sent a thick, oppressive wave of heat around him.

This could only mean one thing: Darius had Initiated his Virtue.

It was all hazy as he tried to remember what had happened… Thorn, and the blood. Eva, dying on the table. The syringe with the bright blue liquid inside of it. The way the needle neared Eva's arm. And then Darius's fingers had surged with power, and he'd healed her.

And now… now, he was here, and it felt like the world was on fire. Teresa had talked a little about this. She'd called it the "burnout period," where good—no, *positive*—energy would be hot and uncomfortable, but this went a little bit beyond "uncomfortable." Not only did Eva feel like a furnace, but Darius was acutely aware of all the other people in the hospital room. Even though he couldn't see them, he could *feel* them—through the curtains, hell, through the *walls*. He felt the warm energies move around, but they were blob-like and indistinct. It was hard to differentiate one from the others.

Darius tried to sit up, and a pounding pain shot through the back of his head. He reached around and felt a big lump at the base of his skull. How many times was he going to fall and slam his head on something? He groaned and laid back down.

Eva jolted awake. She sat straight up in her chair, her hands gripping the arms, as she looked at Darius. "You're awake," she breathed. Then, more loudly, "He's awake!"

And she jumped to her feet and embraced Darius in a tight squeeze.

Darius cried out.

Her flesh was scalding hot against his. Everywhere they touched, Darius felt like his skin was melting. The warmth of her aura overtook and overwhelmed him, and for a second, all he knew was searing pain.

Eva pulled herself back as quickly as she'd come in and covered her mouth with her hands. "Sorry!" Tears welled up behind her eyes, but she didn't look sorry. Her mouth had broken into a smile so wide it crinkled the corners of her eyes and the bridge of her nose. "They told me that would happen. Darius, thank god you're okay!"

Darius wasn't sure that was the word he'd use. He felt them coming before they arrived—more warm energies swarming toward him from the other end of the ward. The closer they came, the hotter they felt, until they were just as overwhelming as Eva. The curtain pulled back to show an older nurse and Elijah Harris. The doctor was wearing a sweatshirt over his green scrubs, and he yawned as he looked down at Darius's bed.

"Well, Mr. Jones, it seems you're here to put me out of a job. Colette, darling." He turned to the head nurse and gestured toward Darius vaguely. She came up and began to take his vitals. She was careful to avoid skin-to-skin contact, for which Darius was grateful. The doctor crossed his arms over his chest and focused on him. "How are you feeling?"

"Hot as hell," Darius said through a wince as Colette's fingers grazed his forearm while she took his blood pressure.

Dr. Harris nodded. "Yes, I read that this Initiation Phase can come with some pretty severe hot flashes." Colette finished her work, took the cuff off Darius's bicep, and handed the doctor a tablet before she quietly slipped away. As she left, the inferno around Darius subsided a bit. Dr. Harris looked down at the screen and frowned. "You're also running a fever, and your heart rate and blood pressure are both elevated. I'll just assume this all has to do with the Initiation Phase, too, but seeing as you're the first Virtue I've tended to…" All he could do was give a noncommittal shrug.

"How long does it last?" Darius asked.

"I have no idea. Could be hours, days." Dr. Harris shook his head and tucked the device under his arm. "All I have to go off of are records from over fifty years ago, and it was a sample size of *one*, so I'm afraid I don't have a lot of answers for you. Except, it seems, you've accepted your Virtue." He gave a half-smile. "Congratulations."

His Virtue… Darius rubbed his eyes again as that single word bounced around his brain. "Kindness," he whispered. Dr. Harris frowned.

"Excuse me?"

"I'm Kindness," Darius said, more sure of himself now. The word stuck in his head like an identity, as much a part of him as his body and soul. It felt weird to imagine it hadn't been there just hours before, because now, he couldn't really imagine himself without this piece attached.

He was surprised to see Dr. Harris's frown deepen. "Kindness?" he asked, then he looked over his shoulder and thought briefly before sighing again and shaking his head. "Well, if it's all the same to you, Mr. Jones, I'll still refer to you by your given name."

"God, please do," Darius said with a single, hard laugh. Dr. Harris smiled down at him.

"I'll leave you two alone," he said. "I have to go give this report to Alan." He slapped the backs of his fingers against the tablet. "I want you to remain in the ward for observation, at least until the Initiation Phase has worn off."

"Is there something wrong?" Eva asked. Her voice cracked a little with emotion as she wiped a fresh wave of tears from her eyes with the pads of her ring fingers.

Dr. Harris shook his head. "No, no. I just have no idea what to expect. The last thing I would want to do is send you to your room only to have you pass out from dehydration. We'll wait out the next few days, see how things go. In the meantime, get some rest. You've earned it."

He passed them a smile and walked away, shutting the curtain behind him. Darius felt his energy move across the ward until it left the room and slowly faded away. He shook his head in astonishment.

Eva just sat there, at the edge of her seat, and she watched him. When he turned to look at her, he found silent tears falling down her cheeks. She shook her head. "Jesus, Darius, I was so scared," she whispered.

He reached out for her hand but touching it hurt too badly for him to hold on long. He settled for patting it. "Me, too."

Eva nodded, choking on emotion, but she managed to force a smile. "You are a *Virtue*," she breathed.

He smiled.

"I am *so* sorry."

"Don't be," Darius said. "You're here. That's all I care about." And it was true. Darius was so relieved Eva was okay that he didn't care much about anything else. He didn't care about leaving Teresa's safe, peaceful estate. He didn't care that he'd taken on an immeasurable responsibility and the power that came with it. He didn't even care that he could hardly breathe in the room with Eva's heat making the place muggy and uncomfortable. All he cared about was Eva, here and alive. "Where were you?" Darius asked. "How'd you stay hidden for so long?"

Eva raised her eyebrows. "Stay hidden? I was just surviving."

"The Martyrs had search parties looking for you," Darius said. "And the Sins, too. The whole city was trying to track you down."

Eva shrugged. "I'm good at keeping my head down." She sniffed and dabbed at the corners of her eyes with the blanket.

"Did you have any luck finding Saul?"

Eva shook her head. "No. I asked around, checked the street market, and a few days ago, I even managed to visit the old orphanage again."

The orphanage. Darius's stomach did an uncomfortable flip. He wasn't sure he'd be able to muster up the courage to go back to that place, even if he'd wanted to. His last memories there were filled with blood, bodies, and Derek Dane's smug smile.

"Do you think he's still alive?"

Eva thought for a moment. She looked down at her hands, slender and malnourished in a way Darius's weren't anymore. "I have to. It keeps me going."

A pang of sympathy twisted inside Darius's chest. He reached out for her hand again. This time, he forced himself to hold on despite the pain. "I'll find him," Darius said. Eva looked up at him. "I promise."

And, even knowing full well Darius could make no such promise, Eva smiled and gripped his fingers tightly within her own. The burning intensified. "You mean the Martyrs will find him."

He was surprised to hear her say it without any hint of the bitterness she'd had the last time they'd talked. He nodded, wincing at the heat surging where their hands touched. "I am a Martyr."

Eva smiled, then released his palm. "Okay," she said. "Then so am I. We're in this together."

Darius's heart swelled with love and relief. He wanted nothing more than to reach out and hold Eva to him, but the threat of pain kept him from doing it. Virtue or not, she was all he had left of who he used to be, of the Darius before Kindness set in, and he wanted to keep that. To hold it close. To hold onto it forever.

CHAPTER NINETEEN

Thorn knocked on the door to Jeremiah's office twice before she opened it. It wasn't Jeremiah, but Chris, who was sitting at the desk. The bright light from the computer screen highlighted her face, accentuating the dark, solemn look across her pretty features. She glanced up as Thorn came into the room before focusing back on the screen.

"Hey."

Thorn closed the door and walked to one of the chairs in front of the desk. Jeremiah was a man of few words and even fewer belongings. He kept his office so clean it looked like it had been taken right out of a furniture catalog. Single desk. Simple chairs. One tall bookcase full of training materials and firearm manuals. There was just one personal item: a photograph of Jeremiah's son, dusty and forgotten, on the top shelf. Thorn glanced at it before she sat down and centered on Chris. Finally, Chris turned toward her.

"Have you chosen a new partner?" Thorn asked.

Chris sighed and shook her head. "No."

"You need to."

"I know," Chris said. Her voice tightened. "I'll do it after I'm done setting these patrol schedules."

She took a deep breath and looked back at the screen,

but her eyes had stopped moving. She just stared at a single point, and the muscles along her jaw tightened. Thorn watched her for a few seconds. A glimmer of sympathy passed between her lungs.

"If you want, I can select the assignment for you," she said, and Chris turned to her again. Thorn knew how much this job could suck—how awful it was losing someone and replacing them, like you were just ticking boxes off a list until you ran out of items to cross off. Thorn had watched a lot of people die here—had led a lot of missions that *resulted* in death.

But those deaths couldn't stop the operation from running. They had to look forward to move forward.

"I have no problem being the bad guy," Thorn said.

"No." Chris let out a little groan and leaned back in the chair, at last exposing a little of the anxiety she was feeling. She raised her hands and ran them down her face. "No. It's fine. I should do it." Then she glanced up to Thorn, and a smile teased at her lips. "Thanks, though."

Thorn nodded. She had never been good at accepting gratitude. So often, it felt undeserved. "If you need me, I'm here for you."

Chris's eyes softened. "I know."

Then Thorn got to her feet. She turned toward the door, but Chris shifted behind her and made her pause. Chris cleared her throat, and Thorn turned back around.

"Since we're on the topic of things we *should* do," Chris said. "Have you gone to see Darius yet?"

Thorn's shoulders tightened, and her stomach clenched. She crossed her arms and watched Chris for a moment. "No."

"It's been four days since—"

"I know how long it's been," Thorn said. Everyone in the whole damned Underground knew how long it had been since Darius Jones had accepted his Virtue and brought Kindness into their walls. It was all anyone could talk about. They were elated—and rightfully so. Thorn wanted to be elated, too.

But right now, it just complicated matters, and Thorn *hated* complications.

After a brief silence, where Chris considered Thorn from the other side of the desk, she said, "He asked about you. It felt wrong lying to him."

A guilty surge made Thorn's stomach twist up angrily. "If we had done things *my* way," Thorn said, and she felt her chest swelling as she came back and slammed down into the chair across from Chris again, "you wouldn't have to lie to him at all, and I'd have seen him days ago."

Fucking Alan—digging them into this hole, trapping Thorn behind protocols. He'd made it *very* clear she wasn't allowed to see Darius right now—not until the two of them had the chance to sit down and meet with him together.

Chris nodded with a small, understanding furrow to her brow. "When does Alan want to talk to him?"

"As soon as he's out of the hospital," Thorn said. "Should be any day now."

"What are you going to say?"

Thorn took a deep breath—felt the monster swirling in her chest. "I have no fucking idea. How do you *gently* break the news to someone that you're—"

Chris's phone suddenly blared to life. The ringtone cut through the room and stopped Thorn's words in her throat. Chris glanced down at the screen, and her frown deepened.

"Who is it?"

"Unknown number," Chris muttered, and she answered. "Hello?"

Thorn's eyebrows fell dark over her eyes. The system the Martyrs phones worked on was so secure that no one could get through unless they knew how to sort through the protocols. Unknown callers weren't a thing, unless—

"William?"

Thorn's whole body went cold.

"William, wait—wait, hold on."

"Put it on speaker," Thorn demanded.

Chris hit the button. Her hands were so shaky it took her three tries to get it right. Then William Michaels's voice rang out in the room.

"—want to. I'm so sorry."

"Where are you?" Chris asked. Thorn got to her feet.

"The Sins." Michael's voice was strained. Exhausted. "They know about the old Virtue. I'm so fucking sorry. I held out for as long as I could, but they—"

His voice cracked. He let out a throaty sob. Chris's eyes filled with tears, and she threw Thorn a desperate look.

"Michaels, *where are you?*" Thorn said as she started walking toward the door. "I'm coming for you."

"I-I don't know."

Thorn turned to Chris. "Get me his coordinates," she said. Chris nodded, and Thorn opened the door. "Text them to my—"

"Fuck!" Michaels cried into the phone. The speaker was suddenly a cacophony of frantic movement. Footsteps. Haggard breath. "They found me. Chris, I—"

Then Micheals swore. The blood drained from Thorn's face as she slammed the door and rushed back to the desk.

"William?" Chris cried. He didn't respond. They heard more swearing, more struggling, and then a horrifying, guttural scream. "William!"

The phone went quiet. Soft, familiar voices in the background crackled through the speaker.

"That was too fucking close." Derek Dane said.

A woman laughed. The sound filled Thorn's empty heart with so much rage it felt like it was going to explode.

"It's *fine*," Wrath said. She sounded joyous. "We got him. Now, let's go get that old bitch—"

Then the phone scrunched and went dead. Chris looked up to Thorn. Her eyes were wide, terrified, and angry. A few silent tears escaped their corners and trailed damp paths down her pale cheeks. Thorn's stomach broiled.

"Get TAC together," she growled. "*Now.*"

For three long, grueling days, Darius melted in the hospital ward.

He spent all his time laid out on the bed in nothing but boxers as he obsessively drank ice water. He was starting to think he'd been lied to—that the powerful, sweltering sensations would last forever. It was suffocating. Overwhelming. He was almost ready to jump into one of the Martyr vehicles and drive into the middle of nowhere just to get some *relief*…

Then he woke up the morning of the fourth day, and finally, he could breathe. As soon as Darius opened his eyes, he sat up in bed, frowned, and focused.

The heat was gone. The overwhelming, intense sensation of fire had been replaced by something more subtle—so subtle it was *captivating.*

Tiny spots of warmth—of *energy*—moved within his awareness. It was surreal. These spots existed in a strange, separate space from the rest of his senses—and they existed *despite* what his eyes could perceive. He felt them shift about—near and far, above and below—in tiny, precise movements. Some would wander distant enough to slowly fade away, while others approached and suddenly came to life.

"This is *insane*," he whispered to himself.

One of the closer energy spots stopped what it was doing and came in his direction. He heard the soft *pat-pat* of tennis shoes on the tile. The aura got stronger and more distinct the closer it came. Raquel pulled back his curtain and smiled at him.

"Good morning," she said. "How are you feeling today?"

Darius's face tightened up in a wide smile. "*Much* better," he said, and he threw his legs out over the edge of the bed. He'd stopped being self-conscious about being in his underwear almost seventy-two hours ago, and he heaved a sigh of relief as the cool air of the room swept across his body. Then he reached out for Raquel. “Let’s test something,” he said. “Touch me.”

She gently grabbed his fingers in her own. It didn’t sear his skin anymore. He let out a loud, sharp “ah-hah!” and she laughed.

“Well, I’m glad,” Raquel said as she typed up a few notes on her tablet. “Dr. Harris will be by in a half-hour, but I’m sure he’ll clear you to go. Is there anything I can get you in the meantime?”

“The only thing I need at this point is a *shower*.”

He’d tried to take a cold shower in one of the hospital ward’s bathrooms on the second day, but he’d somehow managed to sweat through the icy water anyway. Since then, all he’d done was sweat. A *lot*.

“Help yourself,” Raquel said, and she gestured to the bathroom across the hall. “I set aside some spare clothes for you on the counter.”

Then she excused herself. Darius made his way into the bathroom, turned the water to warm, and stepped in. For several minutes, he just stood in the hot stream and soaked it in. He felt the sticky sweat melting off his skin like wax.

Three and a half months ago, he’d been in this same shower—sick, skinny, and scared. It felt like a lifetime.

By the time he cleaned up and made his way back out to the main ward, Eva was sitting by the head of his bed, and Dr. Harris was waiting with her. Their energies blended together in one big, hot ball, and he couldn’t tell one from the other. As he approached, they both got to their feet.

“Raquel tells me you’re feeling better?” the doctor asked.

“Much better,” Darius said, lifting his arms by his sides and flashing a wide smile. “Still need me for observation?”

“No,” Dr. Harris said, typing something onto his pad and stuffing it back under his arm. “I was just telling Miss Torres that you need to keep an eye out for more hot flashes, that sort of thing, but I don’t think it will be an issue.

You're free to go." He held out his hand and smiled. Darius gave it a firm shake.

Then the doctor left, and as soon as he turned his back, Eva rushed up to Darius and wrapped him up in a long, proper hug.

"I've been waiting *four days* to be able to do this," she murmured against his throat. Her breath sent hot goose-bumps up the back of Darius's neck, and he held her tighter. Her warmth encompassed them and brought them together.

"Me, too," he said, and after one last, loving squeeze, he pulled back and put his hands on her shoulders. Eva smiled up at him, and he took her in. She looked different than she had when they'd first come to the Underground. Older. Stronger. More vibrant.

"Are you hungry?" she asked him. "We should go grab some food and head back to your room. I want to hear more about this other Virtue."

"Yeah, okay," Darius said, and he took a deep breath as he wrapped his arms around his chest. "But we've got to be careful. I haven't made sure it's okay for you to know yet."

Eva frowned. "They *still* haven't come to see you, huh?"

Darius's heart skipped a beat. A flicker of resentment twisted up his stomach. "No."

Throughout his burnout period, Darius had seen a lot of people. Eva was his most consistent visitor. He was still technically under strict orders not to tell anyone about Teresa, so for the first two days, he just listened as she recounted her search for Saul. His plan had been to ask Thorn or Alan if he could talk to Eva about all he'd been through before he did it.

But they hadn't come by. Not *once*.

It seemed everyone in the Underground was eager to talk to him. The very first day after Darius had Initiated his Virtue, Chris had been by bright and early, and she made sure to visit at least once a day. Lina and Abraham had stopped in on the second evening. Even Conrad Carter made an appearance to ask how he was doing—and, Darius suspected, to confirm to other Tactical Unit teams that Darius was alive and well. He saw Martyrs he'd only met in passing, and he was introduced to others he'd never officially met before.

But the two people Darius had expected to see the most—the people in charge of the whole damned organization—were markedly absent. He'd asked Chris about it the previous morning, and she'd just said something vague about Thorn's schedule. It had felt like a lie, and after that, Darius told Eva about Teresa Solomon. He didn't see the point in hiding it anymore.

"That's *so weird*," Eva murmured as she and Darius headed toward the exit. "Isn't this what they've wanted?"

Darius just shrugged. He'd certainly thought so.

Eva seemed to sense it was a sensitive subject, so she didn't press it anymore. Instead, she just wrapped her hand in his as they walked out of the hospital and into the waiting room outside it. Darius squeezed her fingers. He was grateful for the space and understanding.

So they walked down the hall in silence. His Virtue senses gave him a whole new appreciation for the Underground. Steel and concrete didn't change Darius's sensitivity to the energy signatures of the Martyrs around him. He could feel people everywhere. Behind, in the hospital. Below, in the courtyard. Beside him, a huge lump of energy gathered in the tactical and conference rooms—

Darius paused and turned around with a frown.

"What?" Eva asked.

Darius just shook his head. "I'm not sure," he said quietly. "Wait here." He let go of her hand, doubled back, and walked down the hallway. He reached out and touched the wall that separated him from the tactical room. There were a lot of people here. Too many people.

He quickened his pace and turned up the other hallway leading to the conference rooms and offices. He could tell the offices were empty—there was no warm energy in that direction—but the first conference room was not. It was bustling with activity. He couldn't easily differentiate between the people there—their energies blended together. He knocked on the door, and the energy beyond it froze and waited. After a pause, part of the ball pulled away and moved toward him. The door opened, and there stood Abraham.

"Can I help you?" he asked. His voice was tight and uncomfortable. Behind him, Darius saw five others: Lina and Chris, as well as Jeremiah, the large, muscular Black man wearing the standard Tactical Unit gear who had rescued Darius and Thorn when they'd been trapped in White Haven, and the petite Irishwoman with bright purple hair and an eyebrow ring. The last person was Thorn. She stood on the far end of the room, and she glared at Darius from across the conference table.

"What's going on?" Darius asked. He didn't even look at Abraham. His eyes cut past everyone else and landed directly on the Martyr second-in-command. "I can sense all the units getting ready in Tactical, so don't lie to me."

A tense silence fell around them. Darius felt Eva approach the hallway, but she waited back in the foyer and watched him quietly. Thorn's attention bored into Darius like a drill. Her lips pressed together, and her white hands were laid out on a map on top of the table. She narrowed her eyes, but at last, she answered him.

"The Sins found Solomon," she said.

Darius's heart dropped, and his mouth followed. "W-what? How do you know?"

"That's not important," Thorn snarled. "We need to—"

"You're going to send help, right?"

"Yes, we—"

"I'm coming."

Thorn slammed her palm onto the table and pointed a finger at him from across the room. He moved to take a step in, but Abraham blocked the door.

"No. You're not," Thorn said. "Locke, get him out of

here."

Abraham went to grab Darius by the shoulders, but Darius ducked under his arm and into the room. Lina, Chris, and the other woman stepped closer to Thorn while Jeremiah walked around the table toward Darius. He stood his ground.

"I need to help," he said, but Jeremiah put his broad hand on Darius's shoulder. His grip was so firm Darius couldn't pull away.

"You'd get *slaughtered*," Thorn growled. For the briefest moment, Darius saw a glint of concern in her eyes, but it was gone as soon as it had come. Her hardened, stoic facade raised up. "Montgomery, see him out."

Jeremiah nodded, but Darius took a step back and ripped out of his fingers. Then Abraham shut the door in his face. The energies in the room all congregated together again and became one mass of warmth. Darius swore and rushed back toward the waiting room. Eva was watching him with a hard frown, and she grabbed his hand.

"It's really important to you to help her?" she asked. Darius looked down at her, and his mind went back to Teresa's estate.

He'd never even had the chance to say goodbye.

"Yes," he said.

Eva nodded.

"Okay. I have an idea."

As Abraham closed the door and Darius disappeared behind it, Thorn heaved a sigh of relief.

She didn't have time for this shit.

"So," Jeremiah said as he turned back toward her and crossed his arms. "What is it you were saying about a trap?"

"Right." Thorn cleared her throat and looked out at the Martyr leadership. "It's a trap. The Sins captured Michaels and let him go so he could warn us about Solomon."

"Why do you think that?" Jeremiah pressed.

"I can count on one hand the number of Martyrs who have successfully escaped the Sins," Thorn said. "For him to not only escape but also contact us just before getting caught again? It's too convenient." Thorn shook her head and propped her hands on her hips. "The Sins let him go, let him *think* he got away. They want us to know they've found her."

"Then call her," Abraham said. "Tell her to leave."

"We tried," Lina said. Her voice was quiet and tense. "The phones have been cut off."

"They've probably known about her for hours," Thorn said. "They're waiting for us there."

"But why?" Jeremiah asked. "What's the motive? Why wouldn't they just kill her and not risk a confrontation with us?"

"It's Jones," Mackenzie said. Thorn turned to her. The Irishwoman's arms were crossed over her chest, and she clicked her tongue piercing against her teeth as she thought about it. "If Michaels told them about Solomon, he probably told them Jones stayed with her. They'll know he'll want to help. It's what Virtues do. They're hoping Jones is going to come along so they can kill *two* Virtues and weaken us even further."

"Well, they're not wrong," Abraham said with a sigh, and he gestured to the door where, minutes ago, Darius had been trying to do that *exact* thing.

"So, if it's a trap," Mackenzie went on slowly, and she cast her bright eyes around the room as though she knew she was about to voice an unpopular opinion. "We just shouldn't go. Is it worth risking dozens of lives for *one* Virtue?"

A tense silence fell as they all considered that. Part of Thorn agreed with her, but it wasn't an option. Whatever issues she had with Teresa Solomon, whatever memories the old woman forced Thorn to relive, she couldn't let her die at the hands of the Sins. She'd once promised Teresa she'd never let anything happen to her. She wasn't about to break that promise now.

"We have to," Thorn said, shaking her head. "It's not just about rescuing Solomon. She has a massive library of research, all about the Virtues. The Sins can't get their hands on it. It would give them an advantage we can't afford to let them have."

Mackenzie gave a conceding grimace. "Yeah, all right," she said. "But I don't like it."

"It fucking sucks," Thorn agreed. "So, here's the plan." She turned to the big table, where a map of Pennsylvania was already unfurled, and circled Wellsboro. "Teresa's house is in the hills just outside here. I have a feeling the Sins have set up a block somewhere between Wellsboro and Morris—probably Wellsboro itself. They're going to let the first Martyr response unit through because they'll assume that's where Jones is, but they'll stop everyone else. We need to let them think they've got him, play into their hand a bit. Chris," Thorn turned to the other woman. "You, Carter, Hess, Gonzalez, and I will be in that car."

"Conrad's already getting it packed," Chris said.

"Good. Our plan is to go in, destroy the research, get Solomon to safety, and that's *it.* If a couple Sins die while we do it, fine, but no heroics. We need to get in and barricade her as quickly as possible. Here's the blueprint of her house." Thorn unrolled another document. "There are a handful of hideouts built into the plan. She'll be in one of those. It's just a matter of finding which one. Now, Montgomery." Thorn turned back to the map. "I want three follow-up units to come in here, here, and here." She pointed out three different rural roads leading into Teresa's house from other directions. "My team will aim to neutralize the Sins and secure the situation so that when you arrive, we can get Solomon out safely."

Jeremiah nodded. "Where will Alan be in all of this?"

"I'll be in one of the following vehicles."

The door to the conference room swung open, and Alan

walked in. His sharp face was set, stern and angry, but much more controlled than Thorn herself ever felt. She envied that about him. He came up and looked over the map. Rae padded in behind him. Her ears were high and alert, but her tail dipped between her legs. "How many cars are we preparing?"

"All twenty TAC Units are ready to go, sir," Jeremiah said. Alan nodded.

"The Sins will be expecting us," he said. "Everyone must be fully armored and ready."

"The rest of the Tactical Units are to go through Wellsboro," Thorn continued, glancing to her uncle for confirmation as she said it. He nodded quietly. "If I'm right, and the blockade is set up there, we'll need to distract the Sins for as long as possible so that my unit and the backup units can get Solomon out and destroy her office without them sending more people after us. They'll be using an army of Puppets, and I want to limit civilian casualties as much as we can. You know what that means—try to avoid lethal shots. It'll knock the Sin's Influence right out of them, and they'll pass out."

"Yes, ma'am," Jeremiah said.

"I want Rae with those units," Alan said.

"Sparkie, too," Thorn agreed.

"And what about the rest of us?" Lina asked. Thorn turned to her. "What do we do?"

"Hold down the fort," Thorn said. "Lock it down. Wait to hear from us."

Mackenzie groaned. "Well, don't keep us waiting for long, then. And be careful."

Thorn threw her a somber look before she turned her attention onto Chris. "Let's get going," she said as she heaved a sigh and made her way for the door. Chris followed quietly on her heels. "We've got a long drive ahead of us."

As they made to leave the room, though, Thorn paused and turned to Alan. She reached out to him and grabbed his shoulder. "I'll get her," she murmured, and Alan cast her a look out of the corner of his eye. The others may not have been able to see the fear there, but Thorn could. After all these years, there wasn't much Alan could hide from her anymore. "I promise."

Thorn and Chris went into the tactical room to get Hess and Gonzalez and then made their way out to the garage. Their vehicle was sitting there, ready and packed, but Conrad Carter was nowhere to be seen.

"Where the fuck is he?"

"I'm here, I'm here," Conrad said as he made his way through the foyer. "Sorry. That new girl—Torres? She was up here panicking and crying 'cause she couldn't find Jones."

Thorn's stomach flipped, and she narrowed her eyes. "She *couldn't find him?"*

"Yeah," Conrad waved her suspicions away with one broad, thick hand. "He just got released from the hospital, but she didn't know it. She was freaking out, so I walked her down. We found him in his room."

Thorn took a deep breath and pinched the bridge of her nose. "Okay, good. Got the checklist?"

Conrad handed her a notebook as Chris closed the back of the SUV. Thorn read items off the list: tarps, large weaponry, helmets, bulletproof vests, food rations, water, and a medical kit. "Good. Let's get going." The five of them piled into the car. Thorn put it into drive and pulled away. She didn't ask if they were ready. They were Martyrs. They were always ready.

The trip was painfully long. Thorn drove because she had the highest threshold for risk and the quickest reflexes. Both of these traits came in handy more than once as she avoided deer, medians, and other drivers who were being far less reckless than she was. The Tactical Unit team sat in tense, stoic calm throughout the journey.

Thorn, meanwhile, was caught in her own thoughts. She'd sent Sparkie out as soon as the news of William Michael's murder had made it back to the Underground. The Sins would have made it to Teresa's long before now, and Thorn needed to gather as much information on their status as she could. She hated walking into a situation she didn't immediately and completely control.

So Thorn spent the three and a half hours it took them to make the drive figuring out how to turn the tables. She was running dry on ideas. They made it to Wellsboro in record time. The town was eerily quiet. As the Martyr vehicle moved through the streets, townspeople suddenly stopped. Mid-walk, on the sidewalk. In their cars. Peering out from windows. They watched the Martyrs drive by with plastic, blank expressions. The Sins were here, all right. Thorn could feel their power.

"Chris," Thorn said, turning to the woman sitting in the passenger's seat as they drove past another group of zombie-like people on a street corner. "Text Jeremiah and verify Sin activity in Wellsboro. It's swarming with Puppets." Chris nodded and took out her phone. Thorn drew in a deep breath. At least they'd been right about one thing. Their backup would arrive without an issue. Hopefully.

They pulled up in front of Teresa's house thirty minutes later. Thorn still had nothing new. No new angles. No new tricks. She parked on the road down the drive from Teresa's house—the same road she and Darius had jogged, every day, for two months. They'd run this route less than two weeks ago. That was hard to believe.

A couple of unfamiliar vehicles sat in front of the estate, and the place was filled with more Puppets. Thorn could sense they were being watched.

Sparkie had been circling the house from above, and he dove onto Thorn's shoulder. He was somber. Dane was nowhere to be seen. Thorn had a feeling he'd show up when it was least convenient. God, she hated this fucking game.

With a sigh, she shut off the engine and got out of the car. Her team followed suit. "This is bad."

"No shit," Conrad grumbled.

Thorn rounded on him. She grabbed him by the collar, pulled him off the ground, and slammed him into the car. "This is not the time for your shitty attitude, Carter. If you can't leave it behind at the car, you can start walking back to the Underground. What's it going to be?"

Conrad choked a little against her grip, but he managed to agree. Thorn dropped him back onto the ground, and as he got to his feet and brushed himself off, she turned to Chris. "Did we pack binoculars? I didn't see them on the checklist."

"I'll look."

Chris moved toward the back of the SUV with Conrad and the others to get their gear on. Thorn stared up the snowy slope to Teresa's house. There were probably twenty people up there, and at least one of them was a Sin. It would be hard to get through, especially if they were going to try to avoid killing innocent civilians who had been dragged into this mess. Thorn frowned.

"Maybe we should—"

Thorn never got to finish the thought. Chris suddenly stopped rummaging through things in the back of the SUV, and Gonzalez swore.

"Oh, *shit.*"

"What?" Thorn spun around and walked toward her. She and Chris were simply staring into the back of the vehicle. Their eyes were wide, and they shared a tense look. Hess barked a cynical laugh. "Did we forget the binocu—"

Thorn stopped dead. Her mouth dropped open.

No fucking way.

There, hiding beneath their weapons and armor, was Darius Jones.

CHAPTER TWENTY

For most of the long, aching ride, Darius had been trying to figure out what he was going to say when they found him at Teresa's estate. He hadn't really expected this to work. After Eva had run into the garage, sobbing, and convinced Conrad to help her, Darius climbed into the back of the SUV and buried himself under as much gear as he could. He'd been sure Thorn was going to double-check everything before they took off and find him there.

But she hadn't, and now, she was *pissed.*

"I can't *believe* this!" Thorn screamed. She rounded on Conrad. "I thought you saw him in his room!"

Conrad scratched the back of his head. "Well, *no*, the girl just opened the door and said—"

"Damnit, Carter, she *lied* to you! And you fell for it!" Her voice echoed off the surrounding hills. Darius fumbled from the vehicle and landed on his hands and knees on the gravel road. His left leg was numb.

Thorn turned on him next. Sparkie had taken to the sky and was flying in agitated circles above their heads. "What is *wrong* with you? *Fuck,* Jones. *FUCK.*"

He got to his feet awkwardly, stomping his left one on the ground to regain some sensation as he stared up at

Teresa's estate. Thorn's words bounced around him, but they didn't sink in. He was distracted by the big house on the hill. While Thorn continued to scream and Chris and the others started to get into their armor, he stared at it.

There was something… different. It wasn't the strange cars in the driveway. It wasn't the instinctual sense of dread that had overcome him as soon as they'd hit Wellsboro. It wasn't the distinct, eerie *silence* where even nature seemed to be holding its breath. It was a *pull.* A quiet, compelling draw toward the house. It was like something was there, a giant magnet when Darius was a steel rod, just far enough not to drag him into it but close enough to tug.

"Get in the goddamned car," Thorn said. "Are you even fucking listening to me, Jones? *Get in the car.*"

His eyes widened. He knew what it was.

"Teresa," he breathed.

"Jones, I swear to god, I will—"

"It's Teresa," he said. Thorn lifted her arms into the air as though she meant to strike him. She turned on her heels instead, roared frustration into the cold air, and punched one of her fists into the side of the SUV. The metal dented, just barely. Darius went on. "Teresa's alive!"

Chris and Conrad looked to one another and the other two Tactical Unit members Darius didn't know. Conrad frowned and turned back to Darius. "How d'you know?"

"He's a Virtue," Thorn said.

She turned around and took him in again. Darius just nodded. She looked back up at the estate and said, "Can you sense how many people are up there?"

Darius focused on the house. It was hard to tell. His gift was still so new that the energies of the Martyrs around him blended together, and those in the distance were nearly drowned out by the magnetic essence that had to be Teresa. But they *were* there, and as Darius concentrated, they became clearer.

His stomach dropped.

"Yes. There's a lot. I can't tell how many."

Thorn nodded, though she didn't seem surprised. "Okay. Jones, get in the car."

"No." Darius shook his head. "I'm coming."

"Get in the car."

"No. I came all this way to help, and I'm going to help."

"You can *help* by getting back in the car and staying out of trouble."

"What makes you think I'll be safe here?" Darius asked. "Wellsboro was swarming with Puppets—isn't that what you said?" Thorn's eyes narrowed, and her nostrils flared, but she didn't argue. "If they figure out I'm here, they'll send for help. I'd be as good as dead."

"They already know you're here," Thorn snarled. "This is a *trap*. A trap for YOU, and you walked right into it!"

Darius opened his mouth but then closed it again. "Well, nobody told *me* that."

"I shouldn't have to," Thorn said. "You shouldn't be sneaking around!"

Chris cleared her throat. Both Darius and Thorn turned toward her. By now, she was all geared up. All Darius could see to tell her apart from the others was the lower half of her face and the blonde ponytail sticking out at the base of her helmet. Her eyes were hard to make out through the tinted visor. "Darius is right," she said. "If they come back this way and he's alone at the car, they'll kill him."

"If they even *check* the car," Thorn roared. "The Sins can't sense him, so if he stays hidden, maybe—"

"Look," Darius said. He was getting impatient now, and he pointed up at the house. "They've already seen us—they know I'm here. They'll tell the others where to find me. If you try to leave me behind, I'll just follow you."

Thorn's pale face went even whiter as she thought about what he'd said. He could tell the moment she realized he was right; she swore violently and kicked the snow at her feet. It fanned out in a wide arc of soil and ice chips. Then she turned on him and glared. He didn't falter. All that mattered was getting Teresa out of the house and back to the Underground where she could be safe. The how was irrelevant.

And Thorn knew it. She just stared at him for a moment longer. Three months ago, Darius would have melted under her glare, but not today.

"You can't wait forever," he said.

Her eyes flared with rage. She took a step toward Darius but was careful to keep her distance. She probably wanted to make sure she didn't actually lash out and strike him, no matter how much she may have wanted to. She pointed one finger, half-covered by her dark gloves, directly at Darius's nose. "If you get out of this mess alive, god help me, I will *kill* you."

"Fine. Let's get going."

Then Thorn was all business again. She turned to Conrad. "Get him geared up."

The two men walked back to the rear of the car, and Conrad helped get Darius into full-body armor and a helmet. Then he pushed a pistol into his hand. Darius shifted the weapon awkwardly from one palm to the other.

"D'you know how to shoot, kid?"

"Point and pull the trigger?"

Conrad laughed. It was a quick, gruff sound. "Close enough. Hopefully, you won't even have to use it, but I doubt it."

Darius's stomach tightened.

They came back around to the side of the car. Thorn was cinching clip belts around her waist. A pistol was strapped against the small of her back. Sparkie spiraled around overhead one last time before he flapped his leathery wings and flew off toward Wellsboro. Thorn turned to the Martyrs. "All right. Let's get this over with."

"Don't you need armor?" Darius asked, aghast.

"You're wearing it," Thorn growled, and Darius felt blood rush to his cheeks. He hadn't considered this side effect. Thorn grabbed her gun from its holster. "Carter, Gonzalez, go around the back. Silver, Hess, you're with us.

Jones," she turned to him and looked him straight in the eye. There was a hint of concern there. "I'll follow your lead. Let's go get her. Now…" Thorn spun around and started up the driveway. "If anything moves… shoot it."

The six of them made their way toward the house. Darius had no idea what he was doing, so he just mimicked everyone else—crouching low to the ground, his weapon pointed down. Conrad and another armored Martyr broke off and moved around toward the back while Thorn led the rest of them up to the front door. The Martyrs were moving with the grace and diligence of seasoned professionals. Darius followed awkwardly behind them, hunched like a child playing a game he didn't really understand. Now that they were moving, his beating heart lodged itself in his throat. They reached the porch, and he jumped as Conrad's voice rang out from a speaker in his ear. His helmet must have had a radio attached.

"Nothin' out here but a dead horse and a bunch'a slaughtered chickens," he said. Darius's heart clenched.

"The Sins are already inside," Thorn said. Her voice was both right beside Darius and in his ear. Chris gave her a look, and Thorn reached out for the handle. Darius's nerves got the better of him. He grabbed her hand. He could feel them waiting, just on the other side of the door. People were hidden around the corner in Teresa's foyer.

"Thorn, they're—"

"I know," she growled. "Just let me do my damn job."

Thorn pulled her cold fingers out of Darius's grip. He took a step back, and she jiggled the knob. It was locked.

Darius's guts churned. Every cell in his body screamed at him. *Danger! Get out!*

Thorn raised her gun and shot the handle off. Darius jumped backward and almost tumbled off the stairs.

Then there was a flurry of gunfire. Darius heard it in his helmet. Conrad must have broken down the back door and entered the house. Chris and Hess slipped into the foyer ahead of Thorn and Darius, their weapons drawn. A bullet zoomed past and blew out part of Teresa's front door trim. Thorn entered the house, and Darius followed behind her.

An older man stepped out from the closet, a hunting rifle in his hands. Chris shot him in the thigh, and he collapsed. Thorn shot at another man who was pointing a gun at them from down the hall. He ducked around the corner. She turned to Darius. She somehow looked both fragile and unbreakable in nothing but plainclothes. Her shining black eyes were driven and fearless. "Where is she?"

Darius couldn't focus. His heart pounded wildly in his throat. Sensory overload clouded his brain. Human essence, everywhere. People crouched in the hallways. In the kitchen. The foyer was clear. Chris and Hess rushed down the hallway. Another blast of gunfire. Shouting. One of the human essences blinked out of existence.

"Gonzalez is down," Conrad's voice said in his ear, then he let out a painful growl, and Darius's head filled with static. He ripped the helmet off and threw it to the side.

"Jones." Thorn's voice broke through the chaos. "Where's Teresa?"

Then he remembered—the magnetic force was coming from above them. Directly above them.

"In the attic," he breathed. Thorn grabbed him by the arm and dragged him up the stairs. They hit the landing, and a bullet blew sheetrock off the wall. Thorn raised her weapon and shot a young woman in the throat. Her energy disappeared in an instant. Darius stared at her dead body, eyes wide, mouth gaping. Thorn grabbed his vest and pulled him forward.

"Move!"

More gunfire from somewhere below them. The energies were converging. Chris shouted something Darius didn't understand. More people. How were there *more* people? They were in the rooms on either side, moving closer. Teresa's Virtue pulled at him from above.

Darius's grabbed the photograph off the wall with shaky hands and hit the button behind it. The attic door dropped down, and the ladder rolled out. Thorn raised her eyebrows as Darius started to climb up. Teresa appeared in the opening above. Her face was white, her eyes wide and scared, but she smiled when she saw him.

"Darius!"

"Teresa!" His voice felt harsh. "C'mon, we've gotta get you out of here."

"Get out of the way."

Thorn pulled Darius down from the ladder and vaulted up the rungs with lithe grace. She grabbed Teresa under the arms, lifted her as effortlessly as though she were a child, and clutched the old woman close to her chest, almost desperately. Darius felt the energy of someone move in the room beside him.

"Shoot them!" Thorn screamed.

The door opened. A man turned the corner. Another Puppet? His face was passive and blank. He pulled out a gun, but before he had the chance to fire, Darius raised his weapon and pulled the trigger. The bullet tore through the man's knee. He collapsed, and just before he lost consciousness, Darius saw his eyes clear and become his own again.

His hands were shaky when Thorn came up beside him. She didn't put Teresa back on the ground. The old Virtue looked frail and vulnerable. Thorn must have felt the same way.

"We need to get out of here," Thorn said. Another gunshot beneath them. Another light blinked out. Thorn closed her eyes and groaned, like she felt the loss, too. Darius prayed it wasn't a Martyr. "Take her."

Darius shoved the gun in the holster at his side and lifted Teresa from Thorn's arms. Thorn grabbed her weapon out again and started back down the hall. Most of the energies were gathered in the room right below them, but Darius felt them separate out as they moved. Thorn's eyes got wild and frantic as she stopped by the room Darius had used during their stay. It was empty.

She turned and opened the door.

"Move, move, move!"

Darius quickly ducked under her arm and into the room. The energies were drawing closer to him now. People came up the stairs on either side of the house, but they all blurred together so much it was hard to tell how many were coming. Thorn closed the door, pushed the dresser up against it, and then made her way to the balcony.

"What are we going to do?" Darius asked breathlessly. Thorn shook her head.

"Jump, if we have to."

"We can't," Darius said. "We can't get away if we break our legs."

Thorn swore. Teresa climbed down from Darius's arms and said, "Which Sins are here?" She wasn't talking to Darius. She looked Thorn straight in the face, and for the first time, Darius saw Thorn look back at her without a trace of fury or hatred in her eyes.

"Pride," Thorn said. "And Envy."

"Pride," Teresa said. The word fell out of her mouth in a whisper, and she shook her head. "Leave me behind. Get Darius out of here."

"No." Thorn pointed a finger at Teresa's chest and said, "I won't let you die here. I *can't*." Teresa's mouth opened in surprise. Thorn took a deep breath and shook her head, but she never looked away from Teresa's face.

To Darius's astonishment, Teresa reached out and took Thorn's hand in a light, loving grip. Thorn held back fiercely. Tears glistened in the corners of the old Virtue's eyes.

But the moment was interrupted by the sound of scraping—and of screaming. Darius spun around as a mass of warm energy forced its way into the bedroom then stepped onto the balcony.

"Well, isn't this *touching*."

Derek Dane came through the glass doors. Thorn spun and leveled her weapon at him, but she didn't pull the trigger—because Dane wasn't alone. One of his hands was wrapped up in Chris's long, blonde hair, and he held her in front of his own body like a shield. Her helmet was gone, her head tilted back roughly, and Dane held the barrel of a gun to her throat, just under the edge of her jawline. Blood dribbled down from a cut on her cheek and painted her lips red. She winced as Dane gripped her more tightly. Darius's lungs contracted.

Thorn seethed beside him. Her face was white, her eyes wide and angry. Dane looked the three of them over with a smug, victorious smile.

"Throw your weapons over the edge here," he said, gesturing his chin over the railing and to the front yard below. "Or I put a bullet through her head."

Thorn's hands were shaking on her weapon. Her anger almost energized the air around them like static. Darius felt it lapping at the edge of his awareness.

Dane raised an eyebrow. "No? Well, if you insist…"

His finger tightened on the trigger. Chris closed her eyes.

"Wait!"

Thorn raised her hands and took a step back. She tossed her gun off the balcony. She didn't look away from Dane's face. Her lips were such a thin line they almost disappeared. Darius didn't know what else to do. He took his gun from the holster at his side and tossed it over the edge, too.

"Smart move," Dane said.

"Let her go," Thorn hissed.

Dane laughed. "*That* wasn't part of the agreement. Cassandra, it's safe to come out now."

Another hot beacon was waiting just inside the bedroom, and at Dane's words, it moved to the door. A woman slinked her way out onto the balcony beside him. She was tall and slender, with undefined muscles and a drab, gray complexion. Her face was long, her eyes narrow. They passed over all of them before settling on Darius. He knew who she was, and she seemed to recognize him, too. She gave a small smile as she took him in, and he swallowed.

Envy.

The first time they'd met, she'd thrown him from a window. He could still feel her fingers tight around his throat.

She was still that dangerous. There was a wild and untapped look in her eyes. When she tore them off Darius at last, she glanced up to Pride, like she depended on him. Maybe even desired him. Her heavy eyelids made her look bored, but her pupils were pin-tight, crazy, and sharp with hunger.

"Two Virtues," she said sweetly. Darius's stomach twisted up at the sound of her voice. It was higher pitched than he'd imagined it, and softer, but laced with a horrifying joy. "You were right. He did come."

"Of course I was right," Dane said, and he waved his gun-hand dismissively. Chris winced as he moved. Cassandra curled her lip up at him from behind his back, but she didn't say anything else. Dane locked onto Thorn and smiled at her. "What *I* can't believe is they *let* him. Hunt was sure you'd recognize the trap. In fact, I think she was *hoping* for it. She loves to watch you flounder."

Thorn's fists tightened into hard, white balls, but she held herself high and dignified. "I'm surprised she's not here to watch me flounder herself," she said bitterly.

Dane laughed. "She has other business to attend to. I'm sure you felt her in Wellsboro. Is that when you realized this was a trap and you'd made a mistake bringing your new toy out to play?"

Thorn didn't respond. She pursed her lips and watched Dane venomously. His smile didn't falter. He just waited a few moments to let the enormity of what was happening really sink in before he sighed and said, "Well, this has been fun, but I was hoping for more of a fight from you, Rose. I'm a little disappointed. Now, give me Jones and the old woman, and I'll let this one go." He shook Chris again, and she let out a small, pained gasp.

"You're not getting them," Thorn said. She stepped forward a little and stood between the Sins and the Virtues, like a desperate last line of defense. Even outgunned, outmanned, and outmaneuvered, Darius was shocked at how much power Thorn still commanded.

Dane seemed to feel the same way. His smug smile faded as he pointed the gun right at Thorn's stomach. She stopped, her arms held tight against her side, and glanced from his weapon to his face. His confidence quaked, and he worked hard to erect it again. The Sin shook his head. "I was hoping you'd make this easy. I hate getting dirty…"

Then he gestured his head toward Cassandra. She pulled a pocket knife from her jeans. Darius's eyes widened as she walked around to Chris. With one hand, she grabbed Chris's face. Chris slammed her jaw shut and tried to shake her head, but the Sin's nails dug in deep and pinched at her cheeks until she had pried her teeth apart. Then she shoved the blade into her mouth. Chris stopped struggling as the cool metal touched the corner of her lips. She sucked in a gasp—her eyes widened with carnal, wild fear.

Darius's body felt numb. He watched in horror as Dane focused on Thorn. His gun was still centered on her gut. Her shoulders were rigid.

"One last time," Dane said. Chris's body shuddered. Tears welled behind her eyes. "Give us the Virtues, Rose."

Thorn's fists quavered in fury. *"Fuck you,"* she whispered.

Dane shrugged.

Cassandra tore the blade through Chris's face.

She screamed and thrashed. Dane tightened his hold on Chris's hair as she writhed—as she kicked at the air and cried gut-wrenching cries that were eaten up in the silence across the snowy meadow. He held firm until she finally succumbed to shock and went limp. Blood dripped from the tear in her cheek. It flowed down the curve of her lips, the gentle slope of her jawline, and dribbled down onto the wooden deck beneath her feet.

Teresa let out a quiet sob. Darius wanted to turn away, but he couldn't. He stared, his stomach sick, as Dane lifted

Chris up like she was a wounded animal.

"Your Virtues," Dane said again. Thorn hadn't moved. Every muscle in her body was wound dangerously tight. Dane took her silence as another no. He shook his head with a sigh. "Have it your way."

He glanced at Cassandra. She examined the blade in her hand again before approaching Chris a second time. Dane pulled Chris's hair back, and her face tilted upward, toward the bright, blue sky above. Her eyelids fluttered as she looked at the knife. The cut in her cheek opened with her mouth, exposing bloody flesh and pearly white teeth as she said, "God, no. Please."

Cassandra slipped the blade into her mouth again, pressing it against the other cheek. Chris sobbed. Tears fell down her face and mingled with the blood on her throat.

Darius looked away. He couldn't watch this again—

Thorn lost it.

She flew across the deck so quickly that by the time Darius looked back up, she had barreled into Dane and sent them sprawling backward. His gun discharged—shot high into the sky—and flew out of his hand, landing on the far side of the deck. Chris fell to the ground. Her whole body shook as she gingerly touched the wound across her face. Her eyes were wide and distant.

Thorn was on top of Dane. She had him pinned—

Then she punched him. Thorn roared as she punched him again and again. His head slammed backward, and she threw another one, and another. With every strike, she let out a guttural, animal scream. Over and over. His nose broke. Blood sprayed the white painted wood beside him.

Cassandra rushed in. She moved in behind Thorn, reaching around to grab her throat. Thorn ducked beneath her outstretched hands like she could feel them coming. Dane twisted beneath Thorn's body as she turned around and swiped Cassandra's legs out from under her. Then Thorn bounded backward. Dane lashed out and tried to grab her by the hair. He missed. She kicked out and caught him in the knee. He hit the deck again.

"You little *bitch!*" he roared. His eyes were wide and wild. Blood streamed down his face.

Thorn kept attacking. Now Envy was on one side and Pride on the other. They both came for her, trying to land hits on her—*anywhere*—but Thorn ducked and dodged and retaliated with mechanical precision and furious fervor. Her face was contorted in effort and rage as she moved back and forth between them. Striking. Twisting. Lashing out.

But she couldn't keep her edge forever. Finally, Dane managed to hit her—at the small of her back, above her kidney. She cried out—turned and thrust her elbow at him. He arched back. She missed.

Darius watched. Shocked. Silent. His heart beat painfully in his chest, threatening to burst from behind his ribs, as Cassandra came in and grabbed the hem of Thorn's jacket. She yanked her backward, raised the knife up above Thorn's head—

He panicked—and ran forward.

Cassandra didn't sense him coming. Darius leapt on her back, wrapping his arms around her neck as his legs cinched at her slender waist. She snarled and released Thorn. The knife fell from her hands as she stumbled backward. Then she slammed Darius into the side of the house.

The force knocked the air from Darius's lungs and made his vision go gray. Thorn called out his name as his grip on the Sin loosened. He slid to the ground—

And Thorn screamed.

Teresa rushed up to Darius's side and helped him sit up as he fought to breathe. Cassandra darted across the deck. She lunged for the gun and snatched it up. Darius's chest finally opened, and he sucked in air. He looked up—just to see Thorn on her knees. Her left wrist was clasped in Pride's vicious grip.

Dane wiped the blood away from his face. His swollen nose was starting to mold and shrink as it healed. With one hand, he held Thorn up. He dug his fingers deep into her arm, just beneath her joint. Thorn cried out again. It was like all the muscles in her body had gone limp and weak. She clutched at Dane's hand with meek, groping gestures.

Darius's chest constricted around his lungs. He clambered to his feet as Teresa grabbed his hand. Cassandra came around and pointed the gun at the back of Thorn's head.

"God fucking *damn it*," Dane screamed as he yanked Thorn's arm upward. She winced and held onto her forearm just below his hand. "I can't *wait* until Hunt gets sick of keeping you around so I can finally *tear your fucking throat out.* I'm going to *enjoy it.*"

"Fuck you," Thorn managed to spit. Her voice was strained. She tried to get to her feet, but Dane backhanded her. Her head flew to the side. A line of blood dripped from her mouth, over her bottom lip.

"Learn *your place!*" Dane's voice boomed out around the clear, winter air, and he shook Thorn. She cried out. "And *fucking stay there.*"

He backhanded her again. Thorn dipped her head. A column of dark hair fell between herself and Pride. Then she threw her chin back and glared at him through knotted strands of black. She said nothing, but her expression was filled with pain, loathing, and a hot, pure flash of fear. She spat a slurry of blood and saliva into the Sin's face. Dane roared and pulled his hand back to strike her.

"Please, stop!"

Teresa's voice silenced them all. The old Virtue squeezed Darius's fingers one more time and stepped around in front of him. Her small, tender hands shook against her chest as she took a step forward.

"Please. Let her go. I'll go with you. Just let her go," Teresa said gently. She took another step. Dane watched her as he slowly lowered Thorn closer to the ground. She sucked air in through her teeth and grabbed at her wrist, but he didn't let go. Teresa's eyes glistened with tears, but they didn't fall. "Don't hurt her anymore."

"What the *fuck* are you doing?" Thorn hissed through gritted teeth. "Get back!"

"I can't watch him hurt you," Teresa said. Dane stared as she approached, but he did nothing to stop her as she grabbed Thorn's shoulder and gave it a firm squeeze. The old woman knelt beside her and whispered, "I'm so sorry, but this is how it has to be. You protected me for so long. Now it's my turn to protect you. If that means letting them have me, then that's what it means. We can't stop this."

"To *hell* we can't."

Teresa didn't respond to Thorn. She got to her feet. Dane towered over her by almost a foot, but she held herself tall anyway, and she said, "It's over now."

"Teresa," Darius took a step toward her, but he stopped when Cassandra cast a paranoid look his way. "What are you doing?"

She looked over her shoulder and said, "It's time for me to pass in the light." Then, almost imperceptibly, while neither Sin could see her face, Teresa winked at him.

Dane's mouth erupted into a wide, bloody grin. He roughly threw Thorn down and reached out to grab Teresa by the throat. The Virtue gasped and gagged as he lifted her up from the ground with one hand. His sleeve pulled back, revealing the *Peccostium*, black and evil, as he dangled Teresa in the air. Thorn groaned and grabbed her wrist. Chris was staring, bloodied, wide-eyed, and distant, as Dane's hand tightened around Teresa's windpipe. "I've been waiting for this for a *long time*," Dane growled.

Then Teresa's hands wrapped around Pride's arm, and she choked out two words: "Me, too."

Dane screamed. The balcony exploded with vicious, thunderous sound. A sharp wind rushed around the conjoined Sin and Virtue. It pulled at the sky—drawing a tumultuous cloud into a spiral above them, blotting out the sun and casting the house in shadow. Dane roared and collapsed to his knees. The place where Teresa's fingers latched around his wrist shone bright, almost blinding, and while he fought to pull away, he couldn't escape. Teresa's old, leathery hands held him tight and radiated with power. The whirlwind whipped her silver hair out of its bun and into a vortex around her head. The harder Dane tried to escape, the harder he screamed.

His voice didn't sound human anymore.

"What are you doing to me?" he cried. The words screeched around them. Haggard. A dying animal. *"Get off me! Get off!"*

Teresa said nothing. Her mouth was set, her eyes tired, but she held on.

And Dane burned. Thick clouds of heavy, gray smoke poured out of his open mouth, the dilated circles of his nostrils, and from his eyes like tears. It filled the air around them, floated down to the balcony floor, and seeped out through the railings and into the yard below—a thick, dark mist of death.

Then he crumbled into ash. One final, demonic cry warped Darius's senses. He covered his ears, closed his eyes. The ringing made every muscle in his body vibrate and ache.

When the screaming stopped, Darius's head flew up. Teresa collapsed. Dust puffed up around her and settled, leaving the old woman gray and quiet.

Her Virtuous pull blinked out.

"Teresa!"

He ran forward. Cassandra turned on him. Her gun pointed straight at his chest. He didn't have the time to move. Thorn jumped to her feet. Cassandra's eyes were wild and panicked as she pulled the trigger.

The shot rang out—then another. Thorn fell backward and collided with Darius, sending them both sprawling onto the wooden deck. Her back pressed up against his torso, and he shook his head. Hot, sticky liquid seeped through the seams of his armor and onto his chest.

Thorn swore. Darius's heart sank.

Cassandra stood before them. The weapon shook in her hands. Her face was tight, her eyes wide and horrified, as she looked back and forth between Darius and the pile of ash on the ground behind her. At last, she settled on him. Her lips tightened against her teeth.

"Which Virtue are you?" she asked shakily. Darius swallowed hard, quieted by fear and shock. Thorn's blood soaked through to his shirt. Then Cassandra screamed, her face contorted, spit flying from her mouth: *"Which Virtue are you?"*

Darius didn't say anything. He didn't know what *to* say, because he was Kindness—he was the Virtue destined to destroy Envy, and if she knew that, he knew she would kill him.

But it didn't seem to matter if he kept his mouth shut. She was going to kill him anyway. The wild look intensified. It warped her entire face, and Darius saw her terror. He wrapped his arm around Thorn's shoulders. She tried to prop herself up again, as if she were in any position to take another bullet for him.

Cassandra's finger tightened on the trigger. The gun was focused right between Darius's eyes.

The point of a blade slashed across her throat. It sliced fast and deep, from one jugular to the other. Sheets of red poured down Cassandra's neck and chest as she dropped the gun and spluttered, uselessly grabbing at her collar. Her eyes settled on Darius, furious and terrified for one last moment, before the life blinked out of them, and her energy disappeared.

Chris stood behind her. Envy's bloody knife dropped from her hand and clattered on the wood. Her green eyes were distant, empty, and numb.

Then she fell to her knees and dipped her mangled face into her hands.

Darius gaped at her, and at Envy, and at Teresa, lying motionless in the disintegrated remains of Derek Dane across the deck…

He roughly shoved his way out from underneath Thorn. She swore again, but Darius hardly heard her. He stumbled over to Teresa's body, but he knew before he got there, before he turned the old woman over and looked into her open, lifeless eyes, that she was dead. The energy of her life, of her spirit, was gone. He reached down and gently closed her eyelids with shaking fingers. Tears welled up behind his own, and he clenched his teeth.

Thorn groaned as she sat up and leaned against the balcony railing. Her left arm was limp against her side as she stared at Teresa, awed. "She did it," Thorn whispered. Her voice was tight, constricted with emotion. *"She fucking did it."*

There was the crunch of tires on gravel. Sparkie suddenly flew up and over the edge of the balcony and wound himself around Thorn's throat. Darius wiped a tear from his eyes and glanced over his shoulder. Three Martyr SUVs were coming up from the bottom of Teresa's long driveway. Thorn looked down at them, too. Chris… Chris didn't look at anything. Shock had set in. Her face was white, her pupils dilated and unseeing, as she stared out into the distance. She had one hand tenderly pressed up against the gash in her cheek.

Darius came around and knelt beside her. He grabbed her face in his hands. Power surged into his palms. It collected in his fingers and flowed into Chris's skin. Her face filled with color as her flesh stitched itself up. Her eyelids fluttered and pooled with tears as she gingerly touched her cheek with trembling fingers. She started to sob. Darius gripped her shoulder firmly and squeezed it once before he turned to Thorn.

She was getting to her feet. Blood poured from holes in her chest and shoulder, soaking her jacket. There was a wheezing sound, like air was escaping her lung, and Darius's breath caught in his throat. He rushed up to her, but Thorn tried to push him away. Her breathing was harsh and forced.

"I'm fine," she said, but he shook his head.

"You've been *shot!*"

"It's really not that bad," Thorn said. Her eyes were full of panic. Sparkie frantically pressed himself up against her wounds. His blue scales were coated in slick, dark blood.

"Just shut up and let me help you," Darius said. "Here." He grabbed her by her good arm and forced her to sit back down against the balcony railings. People below were shouting and slamming doors as they left the Martyr vehicles and made their way up to Teresa's house. Thorn tried to push his hands away, and Sparkie nipped at his fingers, but Darius unzipped the front of her jacket anyway and pulled the neckline of her shirt to the side. One of the bullets had shattered the joint in her shoulder, and the other was down below her collarbone, far enough to have hit the lung. It gurgled blood with every breath she took.

"Stop," Thorn said. She tried to fight him off, but Darius held her back while he pressed his palm against the wounds. Energy surged to his fingertips. She grabbed his hand and gripped it tightly.

"Please, Darius," she said. He looked at her face. She was terrified. "Just leave it alone."

"It will only take a few minutes," he said gently.

He pushed his fingers against her cool, bloodied flesh. Thorn took a deep breath and held it. Sparkie froze on her shoulder. Darius pressed on. The power settled in his hand, waiting, eager for a release. Darius willed it forward and…

It stopped.

Where his skin met Thorn's, the power came to a halt. He tried again, but it was like something was prohibiting his energy from entering her body. The injuries wouldn't heal. The power was trapped in Darius's hands. He frowned.

That didn't make sense. The only people he couldn't heal were—

Darius's stomach dropped.

"Darius," Thorn said. Her fingers tightened around his hand. He pulled away as he realized something terrifying.

Thorn didn't have an aura.

Thorn's energy didn't exist.

He'd been too distracted to notice before, but here Thorn sat, staring at him, without a soul.

"Oh my god."

"Darius, listen to me."

But Darius didn't listen. He shoved her right arm away and lifted her limp left one from the ground. She didn't bother trying to push him away this time.

This couldn't be happening. There was no way this was happening.

Darius pushed Thorn's sleeve up, pulled her elbow-length glove from her hand.

Beneath her left wrist, surrounded by a tangled mess of deep, white scars, was the *Peccostium.*

CHAPTER TWENTY-ONE

"What the fuck."

"I can explain."

Thorn grabbed his hand again, but Darius ripped his fingers out of her grasp and jumped to his feet. He backed up slowly, staring at that terrifying, gruesome mark on Thorn's arm. She pulled the sleeve of her jacket back down, but Darius had seen it already. He knew it was there.

The mark of the Sins.

He shook his head.

"What the fuck."

"Darius, wait."

She got up after him, but her breathing was heavy and labored. She turned and coughed. Specks of blood sprayed the white-painted banister beside her. Sparkie took off into the sky and flew in anxious circles above them.

It didn't make sense. Even the Sins had an aura—he'd felt it himself—felt them move, felt them *die*. So why didn't Thorn? And why did she have the mark of the Sins on her arm?

The voices from the Martyrs inside seemed dull and distant—their energies a haze of warmth from somewhere below him. Darius took a step back, then another, and he turned and ran into the bedroom. Then he froze.

Alan was pushing his way through the door, forcing the dresser that had been half obstructing it further into the room. Darius gawked as he watched the Martyr leader. He hardly noticed his wolf-dog dart past him and onto the balcony.

Because Alan Blaine didn't have an aura, either.

As soon as their eyes met, Alan paused. The two men watched each other in stark, heavy silence. Alan took a deep breath and said, "I will explain everything. I promise—but now is not the time. Where is Teresa?"

Darius said nothing. He just weakly pointed out onto the balcony behind him. The look on his face must have given it away; for a brief moment, a haunted, painful look warped Alan's expression. He rushed past, but just before he reached the door, he turned back to Darius and said, "Mr. Carter is wounded. He could use your help."

Then he was gone, and Darius was left staring after him.

How could Alan *possibly* expect him to help the Martyrs now?

Darius thought about going back out onto the balcony—about confronting Alan and Thorn right here and now—but something stopped him. The movement of energy beneath him. Most of it was busy. Frantic.

But not all of it. A few points laid, as motionless and still as corpses.

Conrad.

Wounded. Maybe dying. Darius shook his head, turned away from the balcony, and walked into the hallway.

On the way through the house, Darius pushed through more armored Tactical Unit members. They moved between the rooms, carrying cases of books and papers or dragging lifeless and unconscious bodies. The world around him felt like it was made of fog and light—like he was moving through a dream. He felt distant from everyone and everything—including his own body. Jeremiah's booming commands to his team sounded dull and muffled as he ushered people out through the doorway and back to the fleet of Martyr vehicles parked in the driveway.

Casualties had been gathered in the grand room. Blood pooled on the hardwood floor and streaked across it where bodies had been hauled in from other parts of the house. There were fifteen people Darius didn't recognize—people who, he could only assume, had been Puppetted by the Sins in Wellsboro before the Martyrs ever got here. Five of them were dead, and the other ten were unconscious with superficial wounds.

Three Tactical Unit members were among the injured. Two of them—Gonzalez and Hess—were gone. Their bodies were lifeless and gray. The bright, vibrant energy they'd had coming into this house had been extinguished. Beside them, Conrad Carter moaned. His eyes fluttered and focused on Darius. Blood was pooling from a puncture in his armor, near his right kidney.

"Jones," he whispered with a gruff laugh. His face was red and swollen, and he reached up a hand. "Boy, am I glad to see you…"

Darius didn't know what to say, so he said nothing as he grabbed Conrad's fingers in one hand and pressed his other to the wound at his side. The energy surged to his fingertips and into Conrad's body. He groaned as his injuries reversed themselves. Darius's stomach gave a queasy flip. Teresa had warned him about this, too.

"Healing takes a lot out of a Virtue," she'd said.

Within minutes, Conrad was good as new. He heaved a sigh and sat up, throwing Darius a smile. "God, I wish we had you eight years ago. Would'a saved me a lot of scars…"

Darius's teeth gnashed together. A bubble of indignation broiled between his lungs, and he needed to get away. Without saying a word, he moved past Conrad, toward the line of injured Puppets—innocent civilians the Sins had dragged into this mess…

And he started to heal them, too.

He worked quietly, like a ghost, moving mechanically

from one person to the next as he fixed broken femurs and shattered shoulder blades. He tried not to pay attention to the bodies he couldn't heal. He tried not to think about how, upstairs, the Martyrs were gathering up Teresa's remains, sweeping Pride into a bucket, and trying to figure out what the hell to do with Darius now that he knew Thorn and Alan's horrifying secret.

By the time he'd finished mending wounds, Darius was exhausted. His head spun as he walked around the casualties, through the kitchen, and into the sunroom. The back door was kicked from its hinges and fell haphazardly onto the tile. Darius tore off his armor, sank into the familiar chair he'd used every morning for two months, and stared blankly at the empty spot beside him.

Teresa would never sit here again.

He was too numb to grieve—so worn from all the healing he'd done that he felt transparent and gray. He laid his head back and stared at the blue sky through the glass ceiling above, and he waited.

Thirty minutes went by. Or was it an hour? He had no idea. Then a figure appeared in the doorway.

A figure without a soul.

Darius turned to see Thorn standing there. Her left arm hung in a sling at her side, and her breathing was still heavy. She held something red in her right hand. Darius couldn't see what it was. He also didn't really care. He just stared at her, and she watched him back. Her half-empty, black eyes were somber. She was quiet for a long time. When she spoke at last, she only said three words.

"I'm so sorry."

Her voice was low. Compassionate. Emotional. Darius couldn't even frown. He just continued to gaze at her in silence and confusion.

If he had the energy for it, he'd have been livid.

But right now, he was just so tired.

"I've wanted to tell you," she said hoarsely. She stepped down into the room but stopped there, like she wanted to get closer to him but was afraid to. "For… a long time. But the longer we put it off, the deeper in we were. The harder it was to explain. I… I'm sorry."

Thorn was remarkably humbled now, and for a moment, Darius was reminded of that night in the kitchen when he'd asked her about her scars. He'd seen a different side of her then, and she felt the same way now.

"I understand if you don't want to have anything to do with the Martyrs," Thorn went on when Darius had still not said anything. "But please, let us explain."

She tucked the item she was holding under her arm, took a tentative step forward, and held out her good hand. Darius stared at it for a moment.

He'd trusted her—god, he *wanted* to trust her.

"This time, you'll explain *everything*," he said.

Thorn nodded. "Everything."

Darius heaved a sigh and took her hand. It was cold against his skin. She helped him to his feet, but before they left, she handed him the item she'd been carrying. It was a book, bound in glossy red leather, embossed with intricate, vine-like designs. He looked down at the cover: Bhagavad Gita, it read. Attached to it was a sticky note with the words "For Darius" scrawled in Teresa's neat handwriting.

"We've cleaned out Teresa's office," Thorn said quietly. "To take all her research to the Underground. This was in there. I wanted to make sure you got it."

Darius nodded, and his throat tightened up. Suddenly, he felt the ache of loss in his chest. Thorn gently touched his arm, and he cleared his throat and began to walk. Together, they went out through the front door and walked down the lawn. Chris was waiting for them by the car. Everyone else was already gone. Teresa's house was nothing but an empty shell.

Darius woke up when the movement of the car shifted.

He slowly opened his eyes to see them disappearing down the dark tunnel into the Underground.

Healing Chris, Conrad, and all those injured Puppets had worn him out more than he'd realized. He'd passed out almost as soon as he and Thorn got into the car and slept the entire drive. Waking up felt surreal—like everything that had happened in the last twenty-four hours was a dream.

But he looked up and saw Chris, still covered in her own blood even though the horrifying gash in her cheek was nothing but a faint memory now; and Thorn, while her left arm was no longer in a sling, still had two tight, clean bullet entry wounds in her body. They didn't look fresh anymore. Instead, they were aged, like the fight had happened days ago.

As soon as Chris parked, the vehicle was rushed by medical personnel. It felt a lot like the first time Darius had come into the Underground. He was tired, confused, and covered in blood, with a lot of big questions that needed answering.

This time, though, the nurses were calmer. Gentler. Raquel tearfully embraced Chris as she stepped out of the car. Colette, the older nurse, gently eased Darius out and onto his feet. She asked him if he needed a chair, but he declined. To his surprise, the doctor himself came out to greet them next—and Alan Blaine was with him. Darius cast Alan a quick, hard look, but the Martyr leader just gave him a curt nod.

Dr. Harris turned to Thorn with a smug smile as she got out of the SUV. Sparkie unwound himself from her neck and bounced off, disappearing into the Underground.

"Well," Dr. Harris said, putting a hand on Thorn's back. "Darius may be able to heal everyone else in this godforsaken place, but at least I'll still have *you*." Colette and Raquel quietly disappeared as Dr. Harris led Thorn and Alan into the hospital ward. Darius was about to follow them, but a light hand on his shoulder kept him back. He turned, and before he knew what was happening, Chris wrapped her arms around him in a tight, tender embrace.

He was so caught off guard at first that all he did was stand there as her warm, human energy surrounded them both. Then she whispered against his neck.

"Thank you."

Those two simple words melted something inside of Darius. He allowed himself a small smile and hugged Chris back. A few hot tears fell from her cheek and onto his collar.

"You're welcome."

She took a deep, shuddering breath before pulling herself away and disappearing into the foyer. Darius watched her go, and then he turned and walked into the hospital ward with a renewed sense of purpose.

No one spoke to him as he strode through the main hall. A handful of people laid in beds around the ward. They all watched Darius almost eagerly, but he kept his eyes straight ahead as he made his way to the operating room. When he opened the door, he saw Thorn sitting on a table. Dr. Harris set up a tray beside it, and on the tray was a scalpel and a strange instrument that looked like a pair of long, narrow pliers. Thorn removed her jacket so the doctor could see her injuries more clearly. She hadn't put the glove back on her left arm, and seeing the gnarled scars swarming around the *Peccostium* sent a chill up Darius's spine. She glanced up at him as the doors closed, and he walked up beside Alan.

"Hmm," the doctor murmured as he leaned in and examined her wounds. "Punctured a lung this time?"

"Yep."

Dr. Harris put his stethoscope in his ears and placed it against her back, listening to her breathe for a moment before he nodded. "It seems to have mostly resolved, but the bullet is still in there causing some problems. Here." He pushed her back on the bed—Darius noticed, without a lot of bedside manner—and picked up the scalpel. He cut the entry wound into her chest a little wider open, quickly grabbed the pliers, and poked them into the injury. Thorn winced as Dr. Harris carefully but rapidly pulled a bullet out of her body.

Darius could only stare as the wound began to close up again. Dr. Harris moved onto the bullet in her shoulder joint and removed it in the same way. After pulling the second slug out and dropping it into a plastic dish on his tray, Dr. Harris looked up at Darius for the first time.

"Standard protocol is to leave bullets in, providing they aren't in a dangerous location," he explained. "Thorn's body pushes them out all on its own anyway, but it speeds up the healing process to just get them out of the way. Part of that Sin business."

Then he cast Thorn and Alan a look before he said, "Now, I have other patients to attend to. I'd ask Darius to stay and help, but—" he gave a dramatic sigh and opened his arms up in defeat "—I have a feeling you'll all be busy for a while. You know the way out."

Then Elijah Harris made his exit. The door swung shut behind him. Alan looked to Darius and said, "To my office, then?"

"I don't care," Darius said shortly. He was rested now, and the shock of everything he'd been through since Teresa's estate was wearing off. Now, he wanted answers.

Alan gave a polite nod. "Please, follow me."

He didn't bring Darius to his office. Instead, he led him to the same conference room Darius had barged in on the other day—or earlier that day? It felt like such a long time ago. Darius figured this was to keep them on even ground instead of dropping him in the middle of Alan's domain. He took the head of the table. Thorn and Alan sat on either side of him.

It was weird to be here now. The room felt oddly empty—devoid of human essence, but not devoid of life.

But Darius had to wonder… Were Thorn and Alan really alive?

"So." Darius crossed his arms and sat back in his chair. He looked between Thorn and Alan. After everything he'd seen, part of him felt like he should be threatened by them, but he wasn't. His Virtue instincts were telling him he was in no danger here. In a way, that made it worse. "What the hell is going on? You're clearly not human," he said as he gestured to Thorn's arm, where her *Peccostium* was still visible. She didn't try to hide it, but she did tear off the right glove, which she'd still been wearing, in frustration and threw it to the table. Darius looked back up to Alan. "But you're not Sins, so what are you?"

"No, we're not Sins," Alan said calmly, but there was an edge behind his voice. It betrayed his worry. "Not anymore."

There was a long, tense silence. Darius's eyes widened, his eyebrows furrowed, and he said, "You *escaped?*"

"Yes." Alan paused, like he was trying to gauge how Darius took the information. "The old-world term for what we are is '*Oblitus Peccatum.*' That roughly translates to 'Forgotten Sins.' We're what's left behind when a Sin has abandoned its host before the body has died. When they leave, a little piece of them stays behind. We remain corrupted by them, connected to them, and possessing most of the power and abilities they themselves possess."

"Why would they abandon a host before it died?" Darius asked. "Especially if those hosts are left with Sin powers? That has to be a *huge* threat."

Alan gave a dark chuckle and nodded. "Oh, it is, but being inside the host when the body is killed is exceptionally traumatic for the Sin who survives. Whenever a Sin loses its host, they lose pieces of their memory—at random—and the more often it happens, the more fragmented that Sin's memory becomes. They can lose track of the things they're working on, the plans they've made, the plots they've been scheming for centuries. If they are still attached to the human energy when it blinks out, the damage is more severe, so most of them try to leave the host right before the moment of death to ensure they retain as much memory integrity as possible. Sometimes their judgment is wrong, and the host manages to survive.

"Other times," Alan went on, "the host becomes aware enough to fight the Sin for control. Those hosts can be dangerous for Sins to maintain. When you're aware of something else inside you, something evil, your first instinct is usually to kill it… using whatever means necessary." Alan's eyes went heavy. "If the host gains enough control to attempt suicide and succeeds, again, the Sin is heavily traumatized, so those hosts are often abandoned to be later hunted down and killed."

"And that's how you escaped," Darius said.

Alan nodded darkly.

"And you?" Darius looked to Thorn.

Thorn glanced down. Her arms were crossed defensively over her chest. It was Alan who answered.

"Thorn managed something more remarkable," he said, and Darius could hear a tone of awe in his voice. He turned back to Alan, and he was watching Thorn with paternal admiration. "She gained full control and forced the Sin out on her own accord. It's the only record we've seen of it happening, and she did a hell of a lot of damage in doing it. Wrath has *never* fully recovered."

But where Alan was clearly impressed by this feat, Thorn scoffed and shook her head. "Wrath has been unhinged ever since. All I did was make it more fucking dangerous. Maybe we'd all be better off if I had never pushed it out in the first place."

Alan was about to argue with her, but Darius was overwhelmed with a different piece of information. He cut him off, looked to Thorn, and said, "You were possessed by *Wrath?* And you forced it out?"

"Yes," Thorn said. Her voice was hard and cold. "And she hates me for it. She keeps me around for the sheer *joy* of watching me suffer. She even has standing orders for the other Sins not to kill me. Like a cat playing with its prey…"

"Why would she want you alive?" Darius asked with a frown. "You've got to be a huge threat to her!"

"Killing Thorn would be too easy," Alan provided.

"When Thorn escaped it in such a devastating way, it went mad with hatred. It wants Thorn to suffer, and as far as it is concerned, keeping her alive so she can watch it destroy everything she cares about is greater revenge than death could ever be."

"But she could kill its host and mess it up even more," Darius argued.

Alan nodded. "She could. And she has. Thorn is the only Martyr who has ever killed one of Wrath's hosts, decades ago. But Wrath is not *logical.* It is heavily driven by a need for vengeance. That's why it possessed both Thorn and myself in the first place."

"Wrath possessed *you*, too?"

Alan nodded. "Wrath took me first. I was a sniper during World War II—one of America's finest. I inadvertently killed Wrath's host during a mission, and it tracked me down to 'get even.' Eventually, I managed to gain enough control to attempt suicide, and Wrath fled. When it learned I survived, it targeted my sister and her family to further punish me by taking away the most important person in my life. It had no idea what it was dealing with." He looked up to his niece and gave her a small smile. She softened a bit, but Darius was distracted.

"World War II," he breathed, closing his eyes and counting in his head. "That would make you…"

"Almost one hundred and eighty years old, yes," Alan said.

Darius was astounded. He turned toward Thorn. She shook her head. "I'm not quite there—yet."

That was insane. This all was. Darius just looked between the two of them for a moment, and finally, he shook his head. "Don't take this the wrong way or anything," he said quietly, "but don't the Sins possess people who are, you know… evil?"

"A lot of them do," Alan conceded. "When someone is 'harmonious' with a Sin—already possessing the qualities the Sin itself values—the possession goes by much more quickly, and the host is easier to control. Naturally, many Sins prefer to find harmonious hosts. Sloth and Gluttony are particularly guilty of this. Others have different criteria. Lust seeks out young and beautiful hosts—primarily male. Pride selects hosts based on status. Greed, by wealth. Wrath, as I said, often possesses out of a thirst for revenge. These possessions may take longer, but the Sins seem to think it's worth the wait."

"What's Envy's pattern?" Darius asked.

Alan sighed. "Envy is hard to predict. It seems to choose new hosts based on the whims of whatever it desired most around the time its current host was destroyed. What that could be is anyone's guess. I have no idea where Envy might go next."

Darius nodded, frowning. "How long does possession take?"

"It depends. When a host is harmonious, it can be as short as just a few months, though that is rare. The average is a year or two. If I had to guess, my possession took between five or six years. Thorn's took seventeen."

Darius's mouth fell open. *"Seventeen years?"* he said, and he looked, again, to Thorn. She just watched Alan talk in stoic silence, content to let him tell the story. Darius suspected it wasn't one she liked to relive.

"Wrath started the possession when Thorn was ten and largely untainted by the corruption of the world," Alan said. "Because her soul was so pure, it took a long time for it to pick the pieces away and fully bond to her."

"Okay," Darius said. His head was starting to feel heavy as he took in all this new information, and yet there was still so much he didn't understand—so much he needed to understand. He pressed his fingertips to his temples and took a deep breath. "Let's look at that really quick—her soul. I don't feel a soul, from either of you." He looked from one of them to the other again. "What's that about? I understand the Sins have that… that 'false aura,' or whatever. So… why don't you?"

Alan paused and thought of how best to describe it. He furrowed his brow and leaned across the table. "What do you imagine happens to energy outside the host when the Sin has left?" he asked.

Darius frowned. "I have no idea. It goes back in the body, I guess?"

Alan nodded. "Yes, that's what it *wants* to do, but it can't. When the Sin leaves and that little bit of corruption stays behind, it makes the energy inside the body *incompatible* with the energy outside. The two can no longer join. This leaves behind a vacuum, and the force of it—the sheer *pull* of those two halves trying to reconnect—draws that external energy into a physical form and creates a manifestation of the host's energy." He paused and, at Darius's confused expression, gave a brief shrug. "At least, that's the theory. We may never really know for sure."

But Darius just shook his head. "What the hell does that even mean?"

"It's Sparkie," Thorn snapped, sending Alan a hot glare from across the table. "Sparkie is the rest of that energy."

Darius's eyes widened. *"Sparkie* is your *soul?"*

Alan nodded. "Rae and Sparkie are the ejected part of our human energy, the part of us Wrath tore off to attach itself to us. They are a truer representation of the people we were before the possession. You cannot feel our energy, or the energy within Rae and Sparkie, because there simply is not enough of it for your Virtue senses to pick up on. The Sins cannot feel it, either. We are too… vacant."

"They're your *souls*," Darius breathed again.

"Yes. We suspect Forgotten Sins played a big part in the development of witchcraft and sorcery mythology, particularly in the stories where magic wielders were joined by animal companions. Familiars, they were called, and we use the same term to define what they are to us, as well."

"Can they die?" Darius asked.

"If *we* die, they will die as well, but not on their own," Alan said. "However, they can experience pain. As for us, we feel what they feel. We know what they know. We are, essentially, one and the same."

That was maybe the strangest thing for Darius to wrap his mind around. He shook his head and rubbed his thumb and fingertips against his eyes.

"So, that's it?" Darius asked. "You're Sins, but not Sins?" Alan simply nodded. Thorn didn't move at all. She watched Darius with a cool, curious expression on her slender face. Darius shook his head again.

"I've got to say… I don't really get why you're fighting."

Alan frowned. "Why not?"

"It seems like you get all the benefits without any of the downsides," Darius said. "You live forever. You heal at like, two-hundred times the rate of normal people. You've got superhuman strength. What's stopping you from just going out and enjoying it?"

"Enjoying *what?*" Thorn said, and her voice was suddenly low and angry. She leaned forward and glared at Darius from across the table. "It's not a *blessing.* With our energy cut in half, we're left hollow. We feel a deep, aching loss all the time. That empty feeling you get when you lose someone you love more than you've ever loved anyone before—" Thorn's voice cracked, and she closed her eyes and turned her head away to beat down an onslaught of emotion. She cleared her throat and turned back to Darius. "Then, we have the *privilege* of getting to watch the people we care about grow old and die. It's a curse, and I want this curse to end."

Darius didn't know what to say. He just stared at Thorn for a moment, and Alan said, "That's one reason I started the Martyrs. When the Sins are destroyed—when *Wrath* is destroyed—the parts of it tainting us will be destroyed with it, and we can finally be human again."

A dense, heavy silence filled the room. Darius watched Alan for a moment before he turned again and took in Thorn.

"Why the hell didn't you just *tell* me?" he asked. Thorn's

dark eyes darted to Alan furiously, and Darius turned back to the Martyr leader—the Martyr *founder*—himself. Alan didn't answer right away. He looked at Darius for a long, hard moment.

"I could not afford to lose you," Alan said at last. "The Martyrs are my *life*. This generation has never seen a Virtue, and for the first time, they had hope that they could win this war. Losing you would have meant losing everything. The Martyrs could not have survived it. It was not an option, and I made the call to wait until I was sure you were ready to stay."

Darius frowned. "All this secrecy pushed me away."

Alan nodded. "But you *did* decide to accept your Virtue and join us."

Thorn threw Alan a hot, almost reproachful look, and Darius glanced between them. Then he sighed and focused on Alan again. "It ends today. No more secrets."

Alan gave a small smile. "No more secrets," he agreed.

"Well, there is one more," Thorn said, and her tone shifted away from anger and back toward what Darius had heard on the balcony at Teresa's house: awe. "Teresa figured out the secret to destroying the Sins… and she took it with her."

Darius frowned as a realization suddenly struck him. "Actually," he said, "I don't think she did."

He got to his feet and rushed from the conference room. Thorn and Alan followed quickly behind him. They made their way back through the waiting room and into the garage. The car they'd taken to Teresa's was still parked near the triage entrance. Darius pulled open the back door and looked around.

There it was. It had fallen onto the floor while he'd slept, and he had totally forgotten about it. Darius leaned into the car and picked up the leather-bound book.

Alan frowned. "The Bhagavad Gita?" he asked as Darius looked down at the red cover and the sticky note with his name on it.

"What is it?" Thorn asked. She rolled her left shoulder and massaged the bullet hole by her joint—or what remained of it. Her wounds were nothing more than red, irritated circles on her skin.

"It's part of an epic Hindu poem," Alan said. "May I?" He held out his hand, and Darius passed the book over. Alan opened the first page and looked down at it. "Much of the mythology here was probably influenced by the Sins and Virtues, like most of human history. Do you think Teresa gave this to you as a clue?"

Darius nodded. "Right before she destroyed Pride, she said something, and then she winked at me. It was weird—it didn't sound like her, more like she was quoting something. I bet this is what she was quoting." He gestured to the Bhagavad Gita, and Alan nodded quietly.

"It seems you may be right," he said. There were dozens of bookmarked pages, and on those pages, passages were highlighted in bright, yellow ink. Alan flipped between a handful of them before he stopped. In the middle of the book was a scrap of paper. Alan frowned, then read a highlighted passage from the text out loud. "There are two ways of passing from this world—one in light and one in darkness. When one passes in light, he does not come back; but when one passes in darkness, he returns."

"That's it!" Darius said. "That's what she said! It was time for her to 'pass in the light.'"

"Interesting," Alan said, but his face had gone dark as he looked between the page and the scrap of paper. Darius recognized Teresa's handwriting on it. "The 'light' may be referring to the Virtues themselves," Alan went on. "Teresa highlighted this passage as well: '*Those who know the Supreme Brahman pass away from the world during the influence of the fiery god, in the light… Those who pass away from this world during the smoke, the night, again come back…*'" Alan took a deep breath as he handed the note over to Darius.

Darius grabbed it from his fingers and read it out loud:

"Supreme Brahman is Universal Oneness. Sins and

Virtues are not individuals—they're two halves of the same whole. This is why they both return in death. They are *incomplete.* To end the cycle of possession and rebirth, we must come *together* and pass in the light—as One."

Thorn swore as Alan cast her a somber, defeated look, and Darius frowned. "What's that mean?" he asked, but in his gut, he already knew the answer.

"Teresa always suspected the secret to destroying the Sins lay in some kind of sacrifice," Alan said quietly. "It seems that sacrifice may be the Virtue itself."

Darius's chest tightened around his lungs. His throat went dry as he quietly said, "So that means…"

"You have to die to destroy Envy," Thorn said bitterly.

Winter had been kind to the Martyrs Memorial Garden. A thin, beautiful veil of frost clung to the trees and caught the sun as it shone through their branches, making the walking paths sparkle with magic and light. Darius stood back and admired a gorgeous, intricate gazebo surrounded by twelve naked maple trees.

He had to give credit where credit was due. Cain had done an incredible job.

Darius slowly walked up the footpath and paused. There were three steppingstones here, each one beautifully carved with names Darius didn't know. He paused to read them.

"The Martyrs who died trying to save the orphanage," a light, airy voice said behind him. Darius jumped in surprise.

It was Cain. Darius hadn't sensed him coming, but he should have been prepared for it. On the drive to the garden, Alan had warned Darius this might happen. It turned out he and Thorn weren't the only Forgotten Sins in the Martyrs.

Cain Guttuso had once been Envy.

"I thought it was fitting they stand guard here," Cain went on. He was standing uncomfortably close behind

Darius's shoulder, and he gave a broad, expectant smile. A glass of wine perched delicately in his fingers.

"It's beautiful," Darius said.

And while he was a little uncomfortable with Cain, he was grateful for all the hard work he'd done. Darius turned around and admired the gazebo again. He never could have imagined such a touching place to lay his family to rest.

Cain was almost giddy at the compliment. His smile widened, which Darius was surprised was even possible, and he briefly lifted onto the balls of his feet. "It's the least I can do," he said, but when Darius did nothing more than give him a tense smile, he bowed his head and cleared his throat. "But of course, you'd like to be left alone. If you need me, you know where to find me."

Then he dipped down and walked away. Darius noticed he was much less quiet when he was making his exit.

After Cain's figure disappeared around a bend in the trail, Darius walked up the path and into the gazebo. It was just as gorgeous inside as it was outside. A circular bench sat in the direct center of the structure, and fitted to the walls around him were small, stone disks engraved with names, dates, and delicate, intricate details. He reached out, touched his hand to Sophie's name, and sighed.

He hadn't had breakfast that morning. He'd hardly eaten anything in the three days since they'd gotten back. Eva was worried about him. She kept asking what was wrong, but he hadn't had the heart to tell her the truth—that when the time came for him to destroy his Sin, this was where he'd go. Not back to the Underground. Not back out into the world, to live some kind of life beyond the Martyrs. Here. He sat on the bench.

Darius wondered if Cain could make space for another tree around the gazebo… and another plaque with the name "Darius Jones" written with just as much love and attention as these ones had been.

Being part of the Martyrs felt different now. Death had already been one of the options on the table. In war, it always was. But now, the inevitability of it felt heavy, like a dark shadow, hovering over every thought, every motion. Darius hadn't ever had to really consider his own mortality before. Not with this kind of certainty.

"Mr. Jones?"

Alan made sure to announce his arrival, which Darius appreciated since he couldn't feel him approach like he could other people—people who hadn't been cut in two by the Sins. Darius looked up to see him standing on the other side of the grove. He looked out of place here. His long, dark hair and black trench coat made him a shadow in this bright, white place. He slowly walked to the entrance to the gazebo.

"May I join you?"

"Sure."

Alan climbed the two steps and sat beside Darius. For a moment, he just looked around them and admired the memorial. "Cain has truly outdone himself."

Darius nodded. "D'you think it's because he's obsessed with me?"

Alan gave a short laugh, and he nodded, too. "In part, I think so. Only two things in this world can make the void in Cain's chest feel full again: Envy's destruction and you. The Virtue in your spirit masks the emptiness in his, and Cain has felt that emptiness for a long, long time."

"How long?"

"Since the 1400s. He was a rising artist before Envy took him and ruined his career. If things had played out differently, it could have been Cain Guttuso, and not Leonardo da Vinci, in our history books."

"That's over *six hundred years*," Darius marveled.

"Yes," Alan said. "You can imagine his excitement at meeting Kindness."

Darius nodded absently. "So Cain knew which Virtue I was the moment he met me. I'm assuming you'd known the whole time, too?"

Alan sighed and shook his head. "Unfortunately, no. Of

course, I knew you were a Virtue, but Cain neglected to tell me you were Kindness. He and I have a complicated history. I'm sure he quite enjoyed getting to have something all to himself, even if only for a short while."

"Which Virtue makes you feel complete?" Darius asked. "Patience?"

Alan nodded.

"Have you ever felt it?"

"Yes," Alan said, and he took a deep breath. "Long ago. And I'll say, I understand why Cain behaves the way he does. It is... *intoxicating*."

Darius nodded, but he didn't really understand. How could he? His energy was intact. He had no idea what it was like to live with that kind of aching emptiness—forever. Thorn had said it felt like *loss*. He remembered back to when the orphanage had been destroyed, when Teresa had been killed, and the deep, intense pain he'd felt nestled between his lungs...

"Can I ask you something?" Darius asked then, mainly as a way to avoid the conversation he knew Alan had come here to have. Alan cast him a sidelong glance, and Darius continued. "Teresa... You knew her when she was young, didn't you? Before she accepted her Virtue?"

"Yes," Alan said. "We were very close."

"You were in love."

Alan didn't respond right away. He watched Darius for a few more quiet moments before he turned and looked back out at the shining, frozen garden again. He took a deep breath, and he nodded.

"What happened?" Darius asked.

"This happened," Alan said, gesturing all around them. At the garden. At the death. "This *war*, and what it has turned me into—it all stood in our way. Darius—" Alan said his name almost suddenly, emphatically, and turned back toward him. There was a dark seriousness in his expression. "I cannot ask you to do this for us. It is unfair. I can relocate you and Miss Torres. I can get you property and protection.

The Sins will not find you. I can make sure of it."

Darius frowned and looked back at Sophie's name—at Thad's and at Aren's and Alejandro's—as he thought about it. Alan was willing to give him what he had given Teresa. A home. A family. A life without worry, far away from the Sins' Influence.

"What about the Martyrs?"

"The Martyrs will endure," Alan said, and he got to his feet. "We always have. Please, take some time and consider what you would like to do." The Martyr leader clasped a firm hand to Darius's shoulder before he turned away and left him alone. Darius watched him walk off and disappear into the garden.

What did he want to do?

A few minutes later, Darius got up and made his way back to Cain's house, too. Alan and Cain were nowhere to be seen, but as he rounded the last corner and saw the house, he caught sight of Thorn. He'd been surprised she wanted to join them to say goodbye to Teresa, but when Cain laid her urn in the ground near the back of the property, Thorn stood arm-in-arm with Alan and paid her quiet respects. If Darius wasn't mistaken, he'd seen a few tears glisten behind her long, dark eyelashes.

Now, she was standing by the solitary gravestone to the side of Cain's back deck. Her hand rested across the name, and Darius had a sudden realization. It was him. The man from the photograph.

Donovan Rose.

Darius stepped up beside Thorn and shoved his hands into his pockets. She moved just slightly, enough for him to know she noticed him, but she didn't say anything. Her shoulders heaved up in a sigh, and she slowly brought her hand back to her side.

"Who was he?" Darius asked quietly.

"My son."

Thorn's voice broke over the last word. She didn't look at him. She didn't move at all. She just continued to stare down at the gravestone with quiet resolution. Darius's heart ached in his chest. He wanted to reach out and comfort her, but what could he do? He knew all too well words were hollow, and enough of Thorn's life was hollow now. Finally, he settled on, "I'm so sorry."

"Don't be." Thorn cleared her throat, as though shaking herself from the emotion. "It's not your fault. It's not even Teresa's fault. Donovan wanted to join this war. I tried to stop him, but he was a Martyr… and Martyrs die fighting the Sins."

She didn't elaborate. Darius didn't expect her to. She took a deep breath and turned to him. Her black, void-like eyes looked deep into his. Sparkie, her Familiar, her *soul*, popped his head out from the back of her sweatshirt.

"Alan talked to you," she said. It wasn't a question.

"Yeah."

Thorn nodded briefly, waited a moment, and said, "I want you to stay." He knew that. Of course Thorn would think giving his life to destroy the Sins was a worthwhile trade. After how long she'd been alive—after all the devastation she'd seen the Sins bring into the world—how could she think any differently?

But he was surprised by what she said next.

"But I don't think you should."

Darius frowned. "What?"

"Why would you want to? If I were you, I'd get as far away from here as I could. In the last three months, you've been through a lot, all because of us. We dragged you through hell. We almost got you killed. We lied to you, the whole time."

For the first time, Thorn broke eye contact with him. She quickly glanced down at her feet, as though she was ashamed. Then she looked right back up and into his eyes with conviction. "If I were in your position, I'd take Alan up on his offer to get the hell out of here as fast as possible."

"But—what about the Sins?" Darius asked.

"They're not going anywhere. Go. Live your life. In sixty years, I'll come find you."

"Thorn, a lot can happen in sixty years—"

"And you should experience every bit of it," Thorn said. Darius was taken aback. He just stared at her, mouth open. She shook her head and looked back up to the house. "It's easy for us to take life for granted. We've gotten more than our fair share of it. More than we deserve. You're just starting out. It's not fair for us to cut that short for you. You deserve more than this."

When she turned back to him, though, Darius knew what he had to do. If they gave up like this—if they waited for every single Virtue to experience a long, full life—then Thorn, Alan, and Cain would go on indefinitely. Forever. Trapped in this weird half-life—not quite Sins, but not really human, either.

He couldn't leave them this way.

Darius shook his head.

"No."

Thorn furrowed her brows. "What?"

"Look, I'm not abandoning you," Darius said.

"Don't be stupid—"

"I'm not being stupid," Darius said. "I'm a Martyr, and Martyrs die fighting the Sins."

Thorn just stared at him in disbelief, but Darius felt empowered. He may have to give up his life, but he had something no one else had: he knew his death would mean something.

Darius was taking Envy down with him. No matter the cost.

ABOUT THE AUTHOR

MC Hunton is a bright personality with a shockingly dark taste in the stories she writes. She has been obsessed with storytelling since she was a child and has been honing her craft for over two decades. MC graduated with a bachelor's degree in Creative Writing in 2010 and has been working on her debut series, *The Martyr Series*, since 2005. She has a penchant for fast-paced action, deeply-rooted sociopolitical and spiritual themes, and emotionally driven plot and character development.

Check out what she's up to by visiting her website:
www.MCHunton.com

CPSIA information can be obtained
at www.ICGtesting.com
Printed in the USA
LVHW080920010721
691360LV00029B/269/J

9 781955 479011